AN ETHEREAL END

Nick wasn't saying any of this to make me feel bad. At his core, he was a guy who said what needed to be said. It wasn't his fault the words cut deep.

He had hoped I would trust them enough, trust him enough, to stay. And it hurt him that I hadn't. But he was also telling me he understood. That it was okay.

"Sometime, Grimm, you're going to have to give us a *chance*," he said. "There's a scale out there I need to balance."

I didn't like myself right then.

"Jen is all I can take right now," I said, my voice low.

"I know," he said, and his voice broke a bit. "But we're all here, man. We all would do anything, rather than let you go at this alone."

"I don't know that I'm worth that," I said.

"We know," Nick replied, and said it again. "We *know*."

I waited a long moment. "Maybe I'm a bit broken," I finally said.

"We know that, too," he said again. "But it's what friends are for."

BOOKS BY CHRIS J. CRANFORD

AN ETHEREAL END

A Grimm Story

CHRISTOPHER CRANFORD

Forged Iron Press

First Paperback Edition Dec 2021

Cover Design by J Caleb Design

Published by Forged Iron Press
www.forgedironpress.com

www.chrisjcranford.com

Acknowledgements:

When you create something like this, this saga, part of you still can't believe it. It's incredible, because for me I've gone from reading stories like *The Hobbit* and *The Black Cauldron* and the *Foundation Series* as a kid, to actually writing one.

Even now, it's a little … I wish I could describe the feeling. I think it's like what people get, looking out in space. Wanting to visit the unknown stars. Knowing these other worlds exist. Knowing one day they'll get there. Just not sure of what will happen, when that day comes.

I guess I feel a little like that. Knowing that this is just the beginning. That though I've been a part of these worlds, there are more worlds out there. Of not knowing what will happen when I find them, but that one day I know I'll get to all of them.

This is the beginning for me. I couldn't be more excited about these characters, these people, this story of friends and family and what they mean to each other. What they face, and what they could be. It's a story of connections, of meaning something to one another. Of standing up when you need to stand up. Of becoming something greater, together.

So, saying all that, this book is dedicated to the most important person in my life. Who lives the kind of life that instills that kind of meaning in me. Who knew one day I would reach the stars.

She believed, long before I did.

Thanks mom. You are the storm.

CHAPTER ONE

I stood among clumps of grass, the uncut stalks waving slightly under a small breeze, the patches of turf spreading out into a large field and thickening into brush. The brush was mostly green in Louisiana, even this late in the fall. The pasture spread before me, growing and alive, the field heading west. At least, it was all alive until it hit an invisible line.

Everything after that line was dead. Brown. Lifeless. Patches of tan clay dotted the landscape there, the fields mottled, as if the earth carried a disease. Tall weeds poked out with brittle stems, some of which had already snapped under light gusts of wind. The soil was hard. A nip seemed to be in the air; it was going to be a cold November. Especially for this far south.

A pale blue sky curved above me. Thin wisps of braided clouds trailed each other, stretching out over the western horizon, strung like torn bits of cotton. The sun, a faded yellow, radiated no warmth to those standing underneath it.

I tugged my jacket tighter around me. Not my army jacket. That had been thrown away weeks ago. Something Nick got me, a black jean jacket with some kind of fur lining. It was too warm, but my body seemed like it couldn't make up the heat it lost, and I was weak enough as it was. I hadn't eaten or drunk anything in a while, and just this morning got out of bed. The first time in a week.

Tiny pops echoed from over the southern horizon. Like the constant rattling of firecrackers. Gunfire. Occasionally there was a large rumbling boom of larger guns, or the whistling of missiles tracking targets. The president had sent the army into New Orleans two days ago. They were struggling to pull out survivors now.

They were calling the area the Dead Zone.

A few feet from where I stood marked the division. Right beyond the line. The fields looked little different by my feet than beyond, except for the hard line of death. And when I looked at it with my ethereal sight, the vision I used to see the spiritual energies around us, I saw it more clearly.

A hard red line appeared in front of me, north to south. A crimson boundary. Everything inside the line took on a smoking shade of scarlet, as if glowing embers burned underneath the ground and colored every-thing above. Grass, soil, trees, all had a crimson hue, as if it rested under-neath a heat lamp.

The line was part of a pentagram that had been built around New Orleans, spanning thousands of acres. It had been carefully constructed using phone lines across most of Louisiana. Azazel had wanted his own kingdom, away from both heaven and hell. The demon had wanted his own piece of earth. And he had finally gotten his foothold.

I didn't know what Azazel's next steps would be. Creating his cities had been a plan thousands of years in the making. In addition to New Orleans, five more pentagrams had been created, all around major cities. Cairo. Mexico City. Paris. Hong Kong. Rome. All powered when Azazel had sacrificed another demon, Buné, during the desecration of St. Louis Cathedral.

And he had killed Jen.

My jaw flexed.

"You sure you want to do this?" Johnny asked. He and Nick stood by, wearing black flak vests under blue jean jackets.

"Yeah," I said. I was into one-word answers today. I didn't have the energy for much more.

Today was a day about finding a purpose, for me. To see if I could go on.

On the road next to us was a hastily constructed checkpoint. The army had erected barricades once they saw they couldn't take the city. To keep people out, or keep whatever was in the pentagram in. Sawhorses held orange-and-white-striped two-by-fours across the road. A big stop sign mounted in the middle of each long strip of wood. A couple of military army jeeps, painted dark green, one jeep parked behind each sawhorse.

Soldiers lay against a jeep, tied up with black cable ties. Four of them.

They hadn't wanted to let me by. And I had asked politely.

Sarah sat in one of the jeeps. She looked much like her sister, just a thinner version of Jen. Blond hair, fragile where Jen had been strong, narrow where her sister had been curved. She was dressed just like the rest of us. A flak vest, a nine-millimeter in one hand. None of us were taking any chances anymore.

"No one comes out, man," one of the soldiers said. A man needing a shave. Young for a sergeant. His name tag read Lutz.

"We did," I said. In the south multiple large booms resounded. The attack had stepped up. Dark clouds bloomed up, one after another, explosions tracing their way west. Toward New Orleans.

And I was just going in for the day.

"We need to get going, if we're going," Johnny said.

He was right. I wasn't sure why I had paused. Maybe I should have waited a day or two. Gathered my strength. I was weak and tired, but there was something I needed to see. His comment hit me the wrong way. "I can still go on my own."

"We've had that conversation," Johnny said. And we had. My friends weren't going to let me into the Dead Zone alone. They hadn't wanted to before, and they definitely weren't going to now.

We had gotten here. The soldiers weren't going to let us by. I had tapped a ghost and subdued them in an angry rage. And then I had collapsed.

Which was why we were standing around now. My friends were waiting for me. Ethereal energy wasn't a replacement for food or water. I was too thin. Emaciated from starving myself. From wanting to die, after Azazel had killed Jen.

I had gotten up this morning with thick black circles under my eyes and too-prominent cheekbones. I had rinsed my hair under the bathroom sink, and the dark curls had hung limp from my head, like a plant that had been without water for far too long.

I also had searched for Jen, using a kind of spiritual radar. Usually ghosts would pop up on it, like dots on a map. Spirits were hard to find in the daytime, though, and I hadn't found her again. It had made me doubt I had seen her at all.

Until last night I had thought my life was over. I had failed Jen like I had failed Danny. I had lost the one person I would have given anything for.

Nick had been the one to convince me to keep going. I had been ready to die, just lacked the energy to pull the trigger. I just lay in the motel bed we all were staying at, not eating or drinking anything they brought.

It was a slow death, but I *was* dying. My friends had known it. They had all tried to convince me to keep going, to get back up. They had held water to my mouth and it had just dribbled down my cheeks. I hadn't responded to anything they did, until last night.

Nick had come in last night for a final attempt. He had told me he had known what it was like, living with the slimmest of hopes, something so thin the idea was barely worth thinking about. And he wanted to give me that same hope. Something to live for, even if the thought was ludicrous.

He thought I could bring Jen back to life. I wanted to laugh. It was a ludicrous idea, the slimmest of hopes, but it also was something I couldn't just toss aside. My mother had brought me back. I was part angel. So before I gave up completely, I needed to at least see. To be sure, one way or the other.

"Grimm?" Johnny asked.

I held a hand up. I was weak, but I needed to move. If I stopped moving, if I lay down, I might never get back up. But I also knew what it felt like in the Dead Zone. I wouldn't be able to access the ethereal plane, to use its energy to keep me going. And I had to keep going.

I needed to see if Jen's body still lay where she had fallen.

I found a ghost nearby, and tapped it. There were plenty around. The memory of the spirit forced its way through my mind, making me live it. A woman, screaming at a man, stabbing him over and over in the chest before slitting her own wrists.

It was one of a thousand evil memories I had lived. All of them, I had pushed down, away, deep inside me. I didn't know what happened, but my hope was they disappeared, after a time. Sometimes I feared I stored them, like in some kind of vault, cramming more inside me. Sometimes I thought I felt that pressure build, of all the evil acts of all the ghosts, each building on the next, and I was just waiting for the day the vault door burst and all the memories I had lived would then live me instead.

The ghost fought me, like they all did now. But I subdued it and pulled the energy in. And I crammed the memories alongside a thousand others, deep inside me. Another price I might have to pay later. Another bill that would come due.

Ethereal energy flowed into me, and I fed it into my body. It didn't replace nutrition, but I hoped it would hold me for a bit. For long enough to get me in and get me out.

A light thrumming ran through my nerves, and I took a deep breath and let it out, standing a bit taller.

Nick arched an eyebrow at me. His wire-rim glasses had a piece of tape across the nose. Cuts and gashes crossed his face, from his fight with Oriax. He had held her off so Jen and I could take on Buné and Azazel.

I nodded. I was as ready as I could be.

Nick walked over to Sarah, talking to her for a bit. I tried not to focus on his hand on her arm, or the way she looked at him, worried.

"You shouldn't go in," Lutz said. One of the many times he had said it, like he had been handed it on a card, and he read it, over and over.

"Shut up," Nick said. The soldier did. Nick had an air about him that scared people. He was thin, wiry, and looked like a nerd. Until a person looked at him twice. That was the moment they understood he was dangerous.

I had good friends. Nick maybe the best of them. His idea had been crazy, but it also had gotten me thinking. If not quite believing.

I had woken up later that night, after he had left. And I had found Jen floating above me, as a ghost. Watching me sleep.

This morning, part of me hadn't believed it. I thought it had been a dream. But maybe what Nick thought was possible. The first step was going back to the beginning. I would find Jen's body, or I wouldn't, and I would go from there.

I needed a purpose. Right now it was going to be bringing Jen back. It was what I had, and I would do it, or I would die trying.

CHAPTER TWO

I headed to the second jeep, stepping over the invisible line and into the Dead Zone. Immediately my bond to the ghost cut off, like a pair of scissors had snipped through the ribbon between us. I got to the vehicle and leaned against it. My legs trembled underneath me.

Johnny followed me over. The Dead Zone didn't appear to affect him. "You good?"

"Yeah," I said. The Key thrummed, ever so slightly, against my chest. I put a hand over it. Not sure if I was imagining it.

"Eat something, man," he said, and pulled a bar out of his vest.

I took the bar and ate it. It was thick and hard to chew, and tasted like chocolate and peanut butter. It had been the second or third one this morning that Johnny had given me.

Nick talked with Sarah. He handed her his phone. We were going to use Johnny's, as long as the communication worked once we were inside the zone. Sarah was just staying here to keep the checkpoint clear for us.

"If we're late, just meet us at the motel. Don't follow us in," Nick said.

It was a useless warning. If we didn't make it back, Sarah would come in after us. But the appearances had to be kept, and someone did need to stay to keep a way out available for us.

Sarah quietly told him to be careful. Their hands touched for a moment. Nick leaned forward and kissed her forehead, quickly, then pulled back.

It was unexpected. I stopped breathing for a moment. It looked, and felt, something like something Jen and I would do. Had done.

Nick headed our way, stopping a moment to squat by the soldiers. All four were lined up by the rear of Sarah's jeep, wire-tied at their wrists and ankles. He waited until he got their attention.

"I'm only saying this for your sake," he said. "Don't give me a reason to come find you."

He waited and made sure they all understood, especially Lutz. Then he stood back up. Sarah watched us over his shoulder, her mouth frowning a little. She believed I blamed her for Jen's death. That we would never have had to come to New Orleans if we hadn't had to get Sarah her exorcism. But she was wrong, I only blamed myself.

Nick got behind the wheel of the jeep. Johnny helped me up before getting into the passenger's side. There was a cooler in the back, and a bottle of water found its way into my hand. Nick fired the jeep up, turned it around, and headed into New Orleans.

Johnny flicked the safety off his assault rifle, and laid the muzzle on the doorsill, pointing the gun out the window. The air felt the same in the Dead Zone as outside, cold as it brushed by me. I shivered and flicked on my sight.

The land lit up red around the jeep. We followed a red-tinged road west. In the distance homes and vehicles appeared. White sparks hid in some of the homes we passed, signs that humans still lived in them, but most of the places were empty. To the south of us was the ruby-colored Lake Pontchartrain.

As we got closer, other sparks took their place. The purple shades I associated with vampires. The darker red glimmers that usually meant something evil, something tainted with a demon. A lot of other colors and shades I couldn't put a creature to.

At first we passed just a few, but as we drove closer to the city the sparks thickened. Dozens of them became hundreds. No ghosts, though. Or at least, ghosts as I thought of them. Spirits abounded, but they flowed along the earth, not tied to a plane anywhere. They were free to roam, and walked the earth where they willed.

"No other cars," Johnny remarked. Nick didn't answer. Neither did I.

We had hopes that the battle in the east was occupying everyone's attention, but we had no real idea if that would be the case.

This seemed like a dead place. Thoughts of my mother circled my mind. She had brought me back from the dead, back in Grafton. I remembered bleeding out, after pulling her sword out of my chest. The hard stuttered choking of my heart. Dominic, leering above me and commanding my body to live, curious to see if the geas would still work after my death.

And I clearly remembered my death. It had been too painful to forget.

I had woken up the next day with a tiny white scar over my chest. My mother sat next to me.

"That one," she had said, staring at the scar, *"had been trouble."*

So Nick's slimmest hope burned through me now, fervently. The thought threatened to consume me. Before I could let that happen, I needed to see something. I needed to see if Jen's body was still where it had fallen. Where Bartholomew had found me, and carried me away.

"Hold up," Johnny said. Nick slowed the jeep down to a stop.

Johnny put the scope on the rifle to his eye. "There's something ahead."

Nick took the rifle and did the same thing. Then he swore.

"They've piled up some cars ahead," he said. "Up at a junction."

"We're not going to get around without a fight," Johnny said. Not adding that I would be pretty useless there.

"Is it by the bridge?" I asked. New Orleans had a causeway, crossing the lake north to south.

Nick gave me a thumbs-up.

"Let's go south from here, then," I said. "Find a boat."

Johnny and Nick looked at each other. One of many similar motions they had made since I told the group I was going back to the city that morning.

"You guys can keep doing that," I said, "but I'm still going. I didn't ask you all to come along."

One final look at each other. Then Nick turned the jeep off the road. The ground was still hard, and we bounced up and down until he doubled back southeast and turned onto a road, heading toward the lake. We followed it, passing by occasional shacks and homes, tall fields of grass, the fronds motionless in the air.

Then we came upon the lake. There houses stood on large stilts, at the edge of the water. Some were constructed on large piers. Boats dotted those piers, in places. I found a home without any sparks inside or out, and pointed it out to Nick.

He pulled the jeep beside the house and we all got out. I felt stronger, after a little food and water. I moved around more like my old self. More determined.

Johnny looked at his cell phone. Tried sending a text and waited a moment, before shaking his head. It looked like whatever had built the Dead Zone, whatever constructed the pentagrams, also cut out any kind of communication with the world outside each zone.

I wasn't too worried. It wasn't like there was a cavalry we could call. And if we didn't make it back in the next day, Sarah would know that we weren't ever going to make it back.

A small bay boat lay tied up to the pier, a silver-bottomed, twin-engine craft with a hard white top over the steering wheel. Like someone might take out for the day to fish. The keys to it hung by the door in the house, and the engines started up after a couple of tries, as smooth and quiet as motors could run.

Johnny untied us from the dock. Nick pulled the boat away. The lake's surface was flat, placid, and held very little chop. A wind of our own making blew past us as we headed south. The skyline of New Orleans beckoned us, towering over the farthest edge of the water.

Other boats drifted over the surface, unmanned. A few had flipped over, resting hull-up under the sun. We passed some kind of sailboat, half-sunken in the water.

To our right the causeway led into the city, miles of roads built across the middle of the lake. Nick paralleled our course to it, but kept us distant. Both Johnny and I took turns with the scope of his rifle. There was no traffic on the bridge, but buses had been stacked horizontally across the middle of the causeway, blocking anyone from driving in or out.

I sat on a bench seat behind the driver. The motors left two twin Vs in our wake, tiny waves that rippled the surface of the lake. Curious, I peered deep down into the water, using my sight.

And swallowed. Something large rested in the bottom of the lake, a greenish, brownish glimmer underneath the surface, dim under all the water. The only reason I had seen it was the sheer size of it, maybe bigger than a house, even a small store. Whatever creature could produce a spark like that would be larger than a whale, larger than one of the sky-rises we looked at in the south. It was maybe the size of a mountain.

"Let's be as quiet as possible," I said, my voice low.

"What do you see?" Johnny asked.

"I wish I knew," I said. Whatever it was, I didn't want to wake it. "Something big."

Azazel had told me once that hell had existed a long time before the demons began renting a space there. It made a kind of sense; I wouldn't go around building a house without having a place to put all the trash. I wondered what else had ended up in hell. Surely it hadn't been sitting there empty, before Lucifer moved in.

Could there be a Medusa in residence? A Grendel? A Vlad the Impaler? Was there enough room for a kraken, or any one of the creatures only known in old tales, by word of mouth, stories from parent to child, until they were finally written down in a book somewhere?

If any of those stories were real, would those monsters have gone to hell? Was that place the trash can for everything rejected from earth? While humans survived, and even thrived?

Humans did have an advantage. We were great at populating places. Whatever the supernatural world took from us, we always replenished. And so, over time, the earth had become ours.

Now it was a new world, though. Things had come back to reclaim what was once theirs. Azazel had opened up the gates of hell and invited everyone and everything back to the surface. Creatures long dead. Monsters better left to old stories and imaginations.

The news from the other cities had been too wild to believe. What Johnny had told me, at least. There had been even rumors of a dragon, but I hadn't believed them. At least I hadn't until the moment that large spark had appeared below us in the lake, the sign of an ancient, malevolent, evil creature.

Some things should stay dead.

"We're going into the cemetery, right?" Johnny asked.

"We are," I said.

"Want to tell us why?"

I didn't. I wasn't ready to tell them I had seen Jen. I still half feared it had been a dream. "Does it matter?"

"Man, we're here, right?" Johnny said. "We're with you. You could tell me we're going to get the best crawfish in New Orleans, and I'd load up and go."

I frowned. "It's not crawfish."

"Good," Johnny said. "I'm not a fan of eating giant bugs. I'd have had to get the gumbo."

Nick snorted.

The lakeshore came up, quietly. At first it was just an edge of land; then it grew quickly in size. Became a beach in places, a seawall in others. A long road paralleled the beach. Shops and restaurants were set up behind the beach and led into taller buildings behind them, sky-rises, offices, apartments. A lot of piers, quite a number of them with boats tied up on them, craft of all sizes.

People walked around there. Just a few, here and there. Normal white-sparked people. A few were on the boats, doing normal boat things, like working on engines, or tying up sails, though none looked our way as we pulled up.

Nick steered the boat to an empty section of dock and cut the motor. We drifted closer until we bumped up against the section of the pier. Johnny tied us up, and then we climbed the ladder onto the dock. The wood was thick and dark and weathered, as if it had been there for a hundred years.

A man met us up there, an older man. Thin, with dark gray hair and a darker beard. "You folks from the North?"

"North of the lake." I didn't want to give out anything more.

"Surprised you made it," he said. "Something in that lake don't like people traveling across it."

"I'm surprised there are people here," I said.

The man cursed. "We're what's left, I guess. A few of the things that came out are still around. But most of them went east a few days ago."

To the battle.

"Is it safe in the city, then?" Johnny asked.

The man laughed. It was a grim laugh, and short. "It ain't safe anywhere. But if you're headed in, best do it in daylight. At night, you find a good place to lock yourself in."

Gunfire sounded from the causeway then, small pops in the distance. Johnny looked through the scope, but shook his head, as if he couldn't see who was doing the shooting.

"The rest of us are making a run for it," the older man said.

"Across the lake?"

"Soon," he said. "No better time, with what the things are doing east of here."

Over all the piers, there were maybe a hundred people, working a quarter that many boats. I guessed they would head out en masse, and then strike out in all different directions. One of them might wake what slumbered on the bottom of the lake, but maybe the group hoped that the sacrifice would be worth it, if the others made it. Or maybe they just hoped they weren't the one.

Nick pointed to the causeway. "They keeping people from leaving?"

"I can't rightly tell you," the older man said. "Ain't no one come back from trying it, though."

"What about heading into the city?" I said. "Like the Garden District?"

The man frowned, scrunching up his nose.

"Wear a mask," he advised. "The stench gets pretty bad."

A few others had come up. They expressed the same surprise that we had traveled the lake without waking the creature, and that led to some optimism they might make it themselves.

"We should leave now," one of the women had said, a younger, dark-skinned lady.

"You leave now if you want to, Luce," the older man by us said. "Or you can leave when the group goes."

"If that thing is sleeping, we all can make it," she said.

"We ain't got no way of knowing what it's doing, or not doing," he returned. "Maybe it was busy eating something else the moment these boys pulled over it."

CHAPTER THREE

The group began to argue. The three of us left them to it and headed down the pier. Here and there patches of sand lay scattered across the wood, and made scratching sounds as we walked over it.

I unbuttoned my jacket. The air carried a salt scent to it, thick and wet, and it felt warmer in the city than it had been outside the pentagram, as if something slightly boiled underneath us all.

"If they wake the creature, that's going to make it difficult for us to get back out," Johnny said.

"One step at a time," I answered.

"Man, Grimm, I'm starting to worry this is a one-way trip," he said.

I didn't tell him it could be. If we found what I didn't want to find, it might be. For me, at least. And maybe for my friends as well. They didn't deserve that, but I hadn't asked them to come along, either.

"If we get back here," I finally said, "I can see where the creature is. We should be able to steer away from it."

Johnny frowned. We were only a few blocks from the pier. "Shouldn't we go back and tell those people that?"

His worry hadn't occurred to me. When the people at the pier had started arguing, I just left. There was one thing for me to do now, one focus, and if I found what I wanted, then there would be other steps for me to do. Other items on the list.

Right now I wasn't into helping others.

That had been burned out of me.

"We got a small window of time," I said. It wasn't noon yet, and we all wanted to get in and out before night fell. "Let's use it."

Johnny stared at me for a long moment. "Man."

I kept walking. The city streets had very little people on them. When we saw someone, they looked much like us. Armed. Nervous. And keeping wide berths from each other.

The stoplights still worked at every intersection, flicking from red to yellow to green, then back to red. But the roads were packed with cars, bumper to bumper, as if everyone had tried to leave at the same time and ended up in the same citywide traffic jam.

And the old man had been right, the smell was horrible. The sweet scent of decay mixed with mold and human waste. Corpses rotted behind the wheels of the cars, bodies lay on the streets. They looked picked on, though no crows, no vultures fluttered over the dead.

The fragrance got so thick we felt like we were choking on it. Nick broke into a store and we grabbed a few shirts, cutting those up and tying them around our faces. All those did was mask the faint smell of rotting eggs with a mothball-like scent. I had to breathe through my mouth.

"The good news is Azazel won't be able to smell us coming," Johnny said, with a waggle of his eyebrows.

Nick rolled his eyes.

The demon wasn't my goal. At least, not right now.

We headed south, down the streets. The Garden District was on the other side of the city, but we made good time, with no traffic or crowds to slow us down. I had expected more sounds of battle to the east, but it had grown quiet. For now.

As bad as the smell was, it grew worse as we neared the cemetery, Lafayette Cemetery No. 1. We tried wetting the shirts with water and holding them over our faces, but we still took turns gagging at a wrong breath.

In the streets outside the cemetery, corpses lay by the thousands, some of them so decayed they look like they had melted into a puddle of brownish liquid, holding a few gray bones. All of the bodies had dropped where they stood when Buné was killed.

"This is crazy," Johnny said, picking his way through. All of our shoes were soaked in a mix of fluids I didn't want to guess at.

We got inside the cemetery, though. The grass was still green, among the tombs, though the blades would take on a scarlet hue if I flicked over to my sight. We walked in from the north, so the first thing we came upon was the pit. It originally had been a mausoleum, before Jen had blown the top off the crypt.

The bier Sarah had lain on still remained in the bottom of the pit. Nick climbed down and worked his way through the rubble. He stopped for a moment and dug one of his knives out, from the fight a few days ago.

"This where you wanted to be?" Johnny asked.

"Yeah," I said.

Johnny waited for me to add anything, but suddenly I was afraid what I desperately wanted wouldn't be there. Or would be there. And I froze.

Nick looked over the bier, a few other places. Not finding much. A Templar body still lay under some rocks, in the pit. He had died when Azazel shot him with one of the demon's black bullets. Nick found the Templar's dog tags and pulled them off, then looked up at me, one eyebrow arched over his glasses.

The crypt, the pit, everything looked so different in the light of day. Most of the mausoleums had been broken, white stone walls shattered, rubble strewn throughout the grass. The pale yellow sun hung overhead, paused high in the blue sky. It seemed like everyone was waiting for me to move.

It might be a good sign that I didn't want to check. It meant a part of me wanted to keep living, even if I discovered the worst.

I recognized the tomb I had killed Buné in, and I circled that way. I found the place – exactly where I had stepped out of that crypt – where Azazel had been standing with his black gun pointed at Jen. I stood in the exact same spot again, staring at the crypt I had stepped from, living the memory, where Azazel had smiled and fired.

I followed the trail of that imagined bullet, to where Jen had fallen. To where I had ended up, pulling her into my arms. To where Jen had died.

And her body wasn't there.

I let out a deep breath.

I hadn't imagined her ghost. I hadn't dreamed it. After Nick had left my room last night, after I had woken and seen Jen and felt the Key thrumming against my chest, I thought maybe it had all been a crazy dream. A crazy last hope.

I had held her when she died. She had gotten smaller in my arms, until she was gone. Up until last night, I had attributed that feeling to someone who was half-mad and stricken with grief. I thought feeling her get smaller had been my body trying to get my mind to see the truth. To tell me she was gone. I didn't believe she had *actually* gotten smaller, until Jen had appeared to me last night.

"Is this the place?" Nick asked. He had climbed back out of the pit, and stood next to me. Johnny next to him.

"Yeah," I said. My hand touched the Key. Was the thrumming there real or imaginary? "Her body isn't here."

"We told you that," Johnny said. "Bartholomew said he only found you."

"I had to see it for myself," I said.

Johnny didn't say anything, but it looked like he wanted to.

"If she's not there," I asked, "where is she?"

Her body wasn't here. Hope burned in me, stronger now. It had told me Jen was where I believed she was, now. That some part of her was alive, *here*, on earth.

Somehow I had put Jen inside the Key.

If so, maybe it was possible to bring her back. After all, the Key had been a prison, designed to hold fallen angels for thousands of years. Why couldn't it hold a person for a few days?

The stone felt cool under my touch, like it had been bathed in a cool spring rain, though maybe it was just my imagination putting that particular image in my mind. The Key did feel *alive*, though, in some way. Different than when it imprisoned the demons. More open. More free.

"So you think it's possible," Nick said.

"Maybe," I said. I wiped my eyes with the back of my hand. The slimmest of hopes, but enough.

"Really?" Johnny said. "This is what we came in for? You guys think Grimm can bring Jen back?"

Apparently the whole group knew about Nick's idea. And there were various thoughts on whether it was possible. Nick cocked his head at Johnny, like they had had this conversation before.

"You don't think she's worth the effort?" I asked, quietly.

"Man, it's not that," he said, embarrassed. "I thought we were coming in so you could, you know, so you could say good-bye."

We all were quiet then. I swallowed my anger down. It was hard for me to be mad at Johnny, when he had been willing to come all this way because he thought I was looking for a way to let Jen go. I understood where he was coming from. I had trouble believing it myself. Even now I wavered.

It was my fault, for keeping it secret from them. For not telling them everything. I had learned this lesson already, back in Grafton.

For some reason it hadn't stuck. For some reason it kept coming back to haunt me. As soon as trouble hit, I went back to being a loner. I took everything on myself, and allowed no one in, no one to help carry the burden.

I couldn't afford to do that now. If I could bring Jen back, then she deserved every effort I could give, everything I had, and that meant withholding nothing from my friends. I had to trust them. I needed them more now than ever.

"I'm sorry," I said.

Johnny blinked a few times, then wiped his eyes. "Man, me, too. I'm with you. I didn't mean for it to sound like it did."

"It's hard for me," I said. "This is not something I'm good at." Though it had been something Jen was helping me with.

Nick just shook his head a little, as if telling me *no big deal*. Of course, he was the one person most like me.

Johnny went a step further. "None of us is good at something like this, Grimm. But even if I say something fucked up, we're all with you. No matter what."

It was a hard concept for me. I had no problem giving everything I had for my friends, even trading my life for theirs, but it was almost impossible for me to accept their help in return. To need them, to need their belief, their trust.

Something was broken in me, with that. Maybe for a little bit it had been fixed. Maybe Jen had fixed it for me. I had started to lean on her, to need her. We were a good team together.

And then she had been taken away.

Now I was scared. I couldn't handle much more doubt, especially by my friends. I carried enough of that particular fear on my own. I needed them to be strong. I needed *them*, and that concept by itself was hard for me to accept.

It was so much easier sometimes, doing things alone. But I couldn't with this. Not if there was a chance to bring Jen back.

"I saw her last night," I finally said.

They were both quiet. Nick spoke first. "As a ghost?"

"Yeah," I said. "After you left, she appeared, floating above me."

They looked at each other.

"I got to ask," Johnny said. "You don't think it was a dream?"

"Not until now," I said. I told them about how she had felt smaller to me as I had held her. Then Bartholomew had found me, and she was gone. "I think a part of me knew what had happened, and wanted me to see it. I think that's why I kept wanting to go back and get her."

"But don't the ghosts you see stay in one place?" Johnny said.

I tapped the Key. "I think she's here. I think somehow I put her in the Key. And if she's there, then maybe Nick's right, and maybe I can bring her back."

The Key had held demons for thousands of years. Who was to say it couldn't hold Jen for a little more?

"What's next?" Nick asked.

I had made sure Jen's body wasn't here. And the sun still shone overhead. We had plenty of time. So now I had a little more personal mission. "The bishop's mansion."

CHAPTER FOUR

We took off east. Again we had to pick our way through slushy bodies of corpses, sticky on the pavement. The sedan was where I had last seen it, flipped upside down about halfway down the cemetery. We were able to walk without squishing through the puddled remains of humans with every step.

After this, I was going to throw away my shoes.

We walked the streets. I set the pace. We weren't but a mile away, and I meant to get there quickly and then get out.

Johnny nudged me and pointed out a building. Shadows moved behind the windows. I flicked on my vision and saw the dark red glimmers I normally associated with something evil, and ugly.

Nick pulled the shotgun out of his shoulder holster and pumped it. Johnny grabbed his rifle and walked between me and the building. None of us had any idea if the silver knives or the bullets dipped in holy water would have any affect inside the Dead Zone. It was just what we had.

The building stayed quiet, though. Nothing came out to greet us as we passed, and though the sparks gathered at the windows, no faces appeared behind the glass. It was as if we were being watched by ghosts, ghosts I couldn't see, and it unnerved me enough to walk a lot faster.

A few blocks later we saw the cathedral, poking up over the street in the east. Steeples, once tall and bright white, were now slumped and twisted and black. Charred. There were holes all over the stone walls where crosses had burned off.

The entranceway was still open. The doors had been blown off, and inside it was dark, like a gaping mouth. But we didn't want or need to get into the church, and headed around back, to where the bishop's residence had been.

It hadn't changed much. It was a large manor, like any southern mansion. Big porches, tall columns. A window broken out on the second floor, where I had jumped out of it on my way to the cemetery.

That was the room I wanted. The bishop had been a Templar, and he had a large library. I hoped we could find something about the Key there. In my mind, the more I learned, the better chance I had of bringing Jen back.

The front door of the house lay open, as if someone had left and never come back. The place seemed empty inside. There was a quiet I attributed to a home no one lived in anymore. Our feet echoed across the tile as we entered.

The entire house had a thick scent, like cloves. All the holy symbols I had seen before looked like they had spontaneously lit on fire where they were placed. Chalices, crosses, candles, all melted and black on tables, shelves, or stands. The paintings on the wall, of the Virgin Mother, of the Saints, all now were frames of blackened canvas.

We headed up the stairs, not speaking. Nick and I had been there before and we knew where we were going. The second floor was as empty as the first.

I swore when we entered the library. We wouldn't find anything here. In a lot of ways it looked the same. There was a large oak desk in the center of the room, mostly well polished. A wall of windows behind the desk, one of them broken outward. And three large walls of floor-to-ceiling bookcases, tall oaken shelves, full of books.

The clove scent was strongest here. All the books here looked as if they had been consumed in bursts of flame. The shelves were dark with ash. Here and there a volume had fallen off the shelf. The floor was littered with the open flaps of covers and burned pages.

We walked through the room. The same three chairs were still in front of the desk, where Nick and Jen and I had sat when we first met the bishop. Lying on the desk was the pad of paper the man had written on, a thick blackened spot on the corner of the pad, where tiny gold crosses had been. Some of the drawers were stuck, and one was locked.

"Not going to find much here," Nick said, opening some of the drawers.

I agreed. But started going through the shelves anyway, hoping. It was odd, the fires had burned up just the books, so bad in places there was only ash left for me to sift my hand through. Piles of it drifted to the floor, leaving tiny clouds of gray dust hanging in the air, catching the sunlight.

Dammit.

Healing was something I had learned how to do. But freeing someone from the Key, bringing them back from the dead, that was something I didn't want to learn on the fly. I needed to understand that more, before trying it, before possibly hurting the one shot I had at bringing Jen back, and I was hoping we would find something, *anything*, here to help me with that.

Nick and Johnny were working on the locked drawer of the desk. It was a thick wood, and the edges were tight enough around the drawer that it was difficult to pry.

"I'm going downstairs," I said. I needed my duffel bag.

"Want company?" Johnny asked.

I shook my head. The house was empty. "I'll be back."

The desecration of the holy objects in the house looked greater, standing on the second floor. Blackened streaks lay everywhere. I walked back down the stairs, fingering the smooth banister as I walked, and the cracked pit on the top of the newel post at the bottom, where a cross had been.

Bartholomew had ducked off to the right with my bag when we first walked into the house, a week ago. I went that way. There was a large entertainment area there with white couches and divans, all facing each other. Burgundy and gold pillows in the corner of the seats. Some of the pillows had burned faces, and left black stains on the couches.

There was a closet there, in the back of the room. Next to a door leading deeper into the mansion. I opened it and found my duffel bag inside, on the floor. It was a black canvas bag, and I recognized it by the tiny baseball hanging from a strap. The ball had been something Nick bought to hang from the rearview mirror of the Camaro, a reminder of Danny.

I dragged the bag out. Inside was my shotgun. It had been with me for a while, and I had missed it. It felt good in my hands. The .38 was there, too, the small gun with the concealed hammer I always had in a jacket pocket.

And plenty of ammo. It had all been blessed, and some of it was silver, but none of it had exploded, or burned, during the desecration. I wondered what that meant.

And tucked into a pocket of the bag was the picture. The one Danny had taken of Jen and me, when we were sixteen. I pulled it out and stared at the photo. Jen was laughing, it had been windy, and her hair had blown across my face. Danny had snapped it right when I tried to blow her hair off. He had caught me with crossed eyes and pursed lips.

I had taken the photo from her room, the night before rescuing Jen at the factory, and I had kept it with me since. I raised the picture in the air so that it caught the light, watching it play across Jen's face.

If I was honest, I had come back for that photo more than anything else.

Which seemed like a silly thing to die for.

Symbols, for some reason, had become important to me, though. The shotgun. The baseball. The picture. Some things I felt comfortable with. Some things fit me. And some things I needed. The photo, in particular, reminded me of a happier time.

I took a breath and let it out. What the fuck did I know about happier times? Maybe I had known them back when we were all kids, before Danny had been killed, and even those days had had their ups and downs. I had lived in a halfway house, other kids had come and gone, and Parker had never been called cheerful.

Jen had been the first person I had relaxed around. I had felt comfortable with her, been myself. Even as a kid around her, I learned more about who I was, who I felt like I could be. This past week with her, I had been happier than at any moment on the run.

And now that was gone.

"That's a great pic," a voice said. A voice I recognized, and thought never to hear again.

I spun around. Raphael sat in the corner of one of the couches, facing me. He was wearing dark pants and a white button-up shirt. His hair looked a little messed up, especially where I had punched a bat through his skull, but that might have just been bed head, or bad product. Other than that, he looked like the vampire I had killed a week ago.

I didn't know what to say.

"Surprised?" he asked. A tiny grin on his face. His eyes burning with some inner interest.

"How are you alive?" I said.

"If I had to be honest, I'm not sure I am," Raphael said. "Or at least, not like I was."

"So how are you here?" I asked.

His grin grew wider. "Think about it, Grimm. I'm part vampire and part human." He made a motion with his hands, waving them over his body. "Want to guess where the human part ended up after you killed me?"

Hell. Down below. And Azazel had just opened up a new place for the souls there to move to. Maybe a higher class of place, for those who used to be stuck below.

I pulled the shotgun out of the bag. "Maybe we'll see if I can send you back."

"Not if I order you to stop," he said. "But I don't want to do that."

He meant the geas. The curse that held me and my parents subject to the commands of the vampires who held it. The curse had been handed down from vampire to vampire, parent to child, over the past few thousand years.

But if I had killed Raphael, had I also killed Raphael's ability to use it? What was he, in this place? A former ghost of himself?

No time like the preset to find out.

"Go ahead," I told him. "Order away."

The house was quiet for a moment. A corner of my lip turned up. I had guessed right.

Raphael shrugged. "It was worth a shot."

I pumped the shotgun. "So is this."

"Hold on, now." He held up both of his hands, the universal gesture of *I come in peace.* "Do you really want to bring anyone else around?"

It was going to be tough to get out as it was, this deep in the city. Shooting him would bring attention I didn't want. But if I didn't shoot him, I was leaving him free to do whatever he wanted. Maybe he had a bunch of friends waiting outside.

"Give me a minute," he said. "Shoot me if you want to, after that."

I had come here looking for answers. Hoping to find some information about Solomon, or the Key. And I had struck out.

But Raphael likely knew where his father was hiding. And Dominic would have my mother around. She had brought me back from the dead once. And I needed that information.

The ex-vampire held his hands out, waiting.

I let the shotgun fall to the side, the barrel pointing to the floor. "What do you want?"

"You know me," he said. "Same thing I always wanted."

"Killing your father?" I guessed. "What's that going to do for you here?"

He shook his head. "You mentioned something to me, right before you killed me."

"Yeah," I said. "I told you I was where these things ended."

"Was that why you were staring at that photo?" he asked. "Something happen to your girl?"

My jaw flexed. "This was a bad idea."

"Hey, I apologize," he said. Which was a new thing for Raphael. "You know me, I'm not that great with people."

"I tell you what," I said. "I'll listen to whatever you have to say, if you tell me where I can find your father."

"You going to kill him?" he asked.

"There's a chance."

He leaned back on the seat, and propped his legs up on the table in front of him, as if he had to think about it. "Deal."

Outside the windows, the sunlight lessened against the drapes. The white cloths darkened a shade, as if a cloud had passed in front of the yellow orb, or maybe it had begun its descent. Nick and Johnny would be coming down soon. We needed to get going.

"So talk," I said.

"After you killed me, and I got sent to hell, all I thought about was what you had told me," he said. "About substituting one father for another."

He meant Azazel. And that had my interest. Azazel had manipulated Raphael, back in Grafton. He had pulled events together so that Raphael would be under his thumb, so he could use the ex-vampire to order my mother to kill Buné.

Azazel had changed his plans for Raphael, once he had discovered I was my mother's son. And that I was an angel, too. The demon had said it had been more fun this way, but there was a lot about Azazel we didn't know.

The bishop had believed Satan blamed the demon for the fall. Azazel had been the scapegoat for what had happened to the fallen angels. And Azazel likely was responsible for the geas, for imprisoning seven angels in a lifetime of bonded service.

I was beginning to believe there was something in Azazel's past. Not only between Azazel and the rest of his demon brethren, but between Azazel and the angels before that. He just didn't play well with others.

Raphael had hated his father with a passion. I never understood why, except for maybe a quiet moment between us, when Raphael had told me he was who his father had *made*. Raphael hadn't been born in this world like a regular person, or even a regular vampire. Azazel had helped Dominic create Raphael, like an embryo in a lab, using demonic powers and dark magic. Raphael had wondered, once, if he had a soul.

I guess he had his answer now.

"It being hell, it was easy to find out about him," Raphael said. "Especially when he opened up the new digs."

"So, what, then?" I said. Raphael had always hated being told what to do. He had hated his father for it, and he would hate Azazel even more. The ex-vampire had something inside him that always chafed at being ordered around. It surprised me to realize we were the same, in that regard. "You were manipulated and you want revenge? Get in line."

"That's what I'm saying," he said. "I know it's a long line. I know you're in that line. So I was thinking, why not help each other get to the front?"

I paused. That was something to think about. Here I had a guy on the inside of the Dead Zone, someone who had come up from hell. Who had survived being killed, and had come back to some kind of life. And who hated Azazel maybe as much as I did.

It struck me then, I had *killed* Raphael. Irrevocably. I had punched a broken bat through his skull. But the ex-vampire stood again before me now, as alive as he had been before.

I took a deep breath and fought the urge to shoot him. Here was Raphael, and Jen was dead, a ghost. How was that fair? What kind of world did we live in, where people like him got multiple cracks at life, and good people disappeared from the face of the earth?

Maybe that was why I was still here. I had never thought I was good. I was maybe part angel, but I had never believed it. My past was filled with things I had done, less than angelic things. Inside myself I laughed, a furious, dark laugh. So the world wasn't fair—when the fuck had it ever been?

Raphael and I had a long history. He had always been a bully. A conceited jerk of a kid with a rich dad who had grown up into a narcissistic asshole of an adult. And those were his best qualities.

I wanted to find my mother. Raphael might be able to help me with that. But I couldn't fake liking him, or wanting to work with him. The ex-vampire had a lot of crazy in him. His sane days were far outweighed by his megalomaniac moments.

And he had killed Danny. That wasn't something I could ever forgive, or forget.

"You want me to trust you," I said. "It's just not something I can do."

"You know, I'd have to trust you as well," he said.

"That's not improving your argument," I said.

Raphael stood up, one of his hands balled up in a fist. "Let me ask you, who else here will help you? Who else inside these cities wants Azazel dead? Not many, from who I've been around."

"I don't need any help killing him," I said.

But that wasn't quite true. Before these pentagrams and cities of the dead, I could have used my ethereal sword to kill Azazel. After all, it had worked with Kimaris and Buné.

Now, though, my powers wouldn't work in the Dead Zone. Not as I understood them, at least. If I couldn't summon my sword here, and Azazel stayed in New Orleans, he could live without fear from me.

Maybe that had been the demon's goal the entire time. A place of his own, without fear. A place where he could rule in the manner he wanted, without fear.

The demon wouldn't just stop there, though. It was not in his nature to stop. He'd want more than just a place to live. I didn't think he'd be satisfied until he owned the world. Until he had taken what had been created for humans, what angels and demons fought over, and made it all his.

It was the revenge every scapegoat would want.

Would Raphael help me there? Tell me what he could, with Azazel? Get the demon to a place where I could kill him?

Maybe. Maybe not. But chances were not. He was Raphael, after all. A person I could never trust. Especially not with Jen in the balance.

"You think you don't need me," Raphael said. "But you haven't seen what I've seen."

He was wrong. I had a glimpse, with the creature in the lake. Or maybe Raphael was talking about other beings like that creature, monsters hidden in hell for so long the rest of the world had forgotten about them. What else might have risen from its purgatory, and want to take its anger out on the world?

I didn't know. And I wasn't worried about any of it now. Not today. All of that would take a backseat to what I needed to do now. Even killing Azazel was down on my list. The only priority I had was getting Jen back.

"I'll still pass," I said.

The ex-vampire stood there. His eyebrows lowered, his eyes narrowed, and his mouth moved like he wanted to say a million things, but he held them all in.

"I never fucking liked you, Grimm," he said. "But I was hoping we could help each other."

"Feeling's mutual," I said. He owed me his part now. I had refused, but I had listened to him. "Now tell me where I can find your father."

Johnny walked in through the door behind me, his assault rifle pointed at Raphael. He must have come down the stairs and looped around to the back of the house.

"Johnny, my man." Raphael grinned. "Talk some sense into Grimm, would you?"

A large boom split the air in the room. The boom of a shotgun. Not mine, Nick's. Raphael took the shot in the side. It spun him around and tossed him over the coffee table.

Nick walked in from the area by the front door, smoke drifting up from the barrel of his shotgun. He was as furious as I had ever seen him, pumping the shotgun with an angry ratcheting sound. "That enough talking sense, fuck?"

Raphael got to his knees. He shook his head. His hands checked his body. There was no blood spatter anywhere on the couch, but his shirt hung in tatters. After a moment the ex-vampire leaned back and brushed his side. Buckshot fell off the shirt and made little ticking sounds on the tile floor.

I focused on Raphael's side. His flesh had been ripped open in places, exposing bone and flesh. Red lightning traced its way through the wounds, stitching muscle together, pulling skin closed. It looked like it felt when I tapped a ghost and healed myself.

In a few moments, his body had fully regenerated. He looked as good as new, though his shirt wasn't.

"Well," Raphael said, "that's interesting."

Nick fired again. The blast flung Raphael against the far wall. This time I flicked on my ethereal sight. An electric red glimmer sat inside Raphael, and little bolts flew out from it to each of the holes in his body. There the bolts exploded in waves of crimson, the healing began, and the wounds closed up. Again.

Before his death, Raphael's spark had been the purple I associated with vampires. He had also swirled with tiny firefly-like white and red lights, and at the time I had assumed it was from drinking the demonic drug he had made.

But now his spark was full-on demon red. Had he been truly three things before? Part human, part vampire, and part demon? Was only the demon part left now? If so, that terrified me, here in the dead zone.

Nick's shotgun *clack-clacked*.

I held out a hand. "Hold on." Nick looked at me curiously.

"It's not going to hurt him," I said.

Raphael stood up, wincing. Buckshot fell off what was left of his shirt. "Well, I wouldn't say it doesn't hurt."

I amended my statement. "It's not going to *kill him*."

"We can't know that if we don't keep trying," Nick said.

I shook my head. "We can't. Things might already be headed this way."

"So we just leave him here?" Nick asked.

"What else can we do?" I said. "Unless we plan on holing up here until Azazel comes."

"The fuck should be dead," Nick said.

"Yeah," I agreed, but a lot of the rules had apparently been bent when I killed Buné. The place of the dead had changed. The finality of death, for things like Raphael, was no longer final. It felt like all the work we had done, everything we had accomplished in Grafton, had been for nothing.

Not just for nothing. For less than nothing, with Jen dead.

"It's on the list of things you can blame me for," I said.

Nick rolled his eyes. "You know that's not what I meant."

I did know. Nick didn't blame me. I blamed myself. And I had just taken it out on Nick, like I had with Johnny, earlier.

"Yeah, man," I said. I didn't know how to get around how I was feeling. A large part of me still wanted to give up. I had let Jen die. I had let Danny die. Who would be next?

The part of me that I was going on, the part that kept me moving, was a much smaller part. It held out the tiniest of hopes, that bringing back Jen was possible. That it was something I could do. Maybe even was made for.

"I'm still struggling," I admitted.

"You are," Nick agreed.

A corner of my lip lifted, the smallest of grins. Nick had called me out on my pity party. Being Nick, it was his way of trying to keep me going, and I was surprised to find it worked.

Nick mimicked my grin, lifting a tiny corner of his mouth back at me. Then he waved his shotgun at Raphael. "So, what does he want?"

"I can speak for myself," Raphael said.

Nick fired the shotgun again. Buckshot dotted the wall around the ex-vampire, and some of it smacked into him, but Raphael stayed standing.

"Didn't ask you," Nick said.

"You know, Nick," Raphael said, taking a deep breath. His chest swelled up, like what a boxer might do before stepping into the circle. "I'm starting to think you and I need to go a few rounds."

We couldn't afford that. Not if Raphael was what I thought he was.

"I'm fully loaded." Nick ratcheted the shotgun again. "Let's see who stands back up."

"Hold on." I said. I didn't think it would stop him this time, but Nick held off on pulling the trigger. Barely.

Raphael sneered. "Good boy."

"You can stop your shit, too," I told the ex-vampire. Or the new demon. Whatever the fuck he could be. "I'm sure you don't want Azazel coming around asking questions, right?"

We all waited a moment.

"So, we're all going to go on our way," I said. "After Raphael tells me where his father could be hiding."

"Why do we need to know that?" Johnny asked. I had told my friends about my mother, but not about her bringing me back from the dead. And I wasn't ready to share that part of my plan. It sounded crazy enough, just to me.

"He's got a hard-on for some reason," Raphael said. "I don't understand it, either. I'm all for you killing the bastard, but why in the world would you want to go after my father *now*?"

His eyes opened, as if he had put two plus two together and found out it equaled five. "Something *did* happen to Jen."

"What's it matter to you?" I said.

"You don't want my father," he said, his voice taking on the better-than-you tone I remembered from when we were kids. "You want your mommy."

"I asked you, what's it matter to you?"

"Ha." He grinned, figuring it out. "Is your Jen even alive?"

I jumped him. I couldn't help myself. I was fast enough that I even surprised Raphael.

I snapped his temple with the butt of the shotgun. Raphael fell back against the wall. I hit him multiple times until the flesh split on his temple, until the bones cracked underneath my swings.

Raphael held his hands up, protecting himself. He was trying to say something. He wasn't talking, though.

He was *laughing*.

I stopped midswing. The ex-vampire leaned against the wall, with a big shit-eating grin plastered on his face, laughing.

At the same time, the skin began to close, where I had opened it up.

Raphael laughed, tears streaming out of his eyes. He had trouble catching his breath.

I stood there, chest heaving, feeling like I had run a marathon. I was exhausted. My legs shook a little underneath me.

I was not ready for a fight of any kind. Not here. And not against Raph.

"What's so funny?" I asked.

It took a minute before the ex-vampire to speak. He wiped his eyes, but kept the large smile on his face. "It's that you just don't get it."

"I don't get what?"

"You're going to need me, Grimm," he said. "Maybe more than I need you."

My jaw tightened. "Enlighten me."

"You need to help your girl, right?"

"That's none of your business," I said.

"No matter." Raphael waved his hand, like he didn't care about my response. "I've seen how you get around her."

"Does he ever get to the point about something?" Johnny asked.

"No one appreciates a showman," Raphael said. It was an echo of something Azazel might say. That scared me.

"Just tell me," I said.

"Is Jen hurt? Bad?" Raphael asked. "Or dead? I've seen what your mother can do, Grimm. She damn near brought my father back from the dead, right in front of me."

"You're getting close to me letting Nick find out how many pieces we can divide you up in," I said.

"I'm starting to wonder if you will," he said. "Actually I'm starting to wonder if you *should*."

And there it was. He understood there was more about this than just his guess about Jen. He had figured out there was something more about himself.

We would be in trouble if he took it one step further. If Raphael was a demon, maybe he had been created from both Dominic and Azazel.

I shivered. That was a bad combination.

If he was a demon, in this world, inside the pentagram, Raphael would be able to kill all of us. Especially if the blessed bullets were just regular bullets here. If the silver knives were just regular knives. We had nothing else, no power to speak of.

"Fuck," I said.

Raphael just kept on grinning. He had said I would need him, more than he needed me. I feared he was right. I needed to know where his father was. I needed to find my mother. And I needed to know whatever Raphael knew about my mother.

"We don't need him," Nick said.

"You don't," Raphael agreed. "But *he* will."

The room was quiet.

"Let me tell you guys something," Raphael said. "Something about failure, something my father intimately instructed me in. About how it eats at you."

"Shut up," I said, but the words were hollow.

"Your boy Grimm here has failed a lot in his life," he said. "Dead friends. Dead girlfriends. Did you have something to do with what's happening here? Did you fail something in New Orleans, too?"

With each word, Raphael hammered another nail into my coffin. Everything he said, I felt was true.

"Maybe you all felt good, after Grimm killed me." Raphael grinned. "But here I am, standing again, too."

It had been my exact thought.

"It *eats* at you, doesn't it?" he whispered.

It did. It always had. Running, fighting, none of it had helped me deal with my failures. They were both just ways of continuing on.

The ex-vampire – no, I would call him demon – looked at me. "You've failed everywhere you've been in life," he almost whispered. "How many friends are you going to let die? How many times are you going to fail here, Grimm?"

"Man, don't let him get in your head," Johnny said.

Nick was next to me. I hadn't heard or felt him move. But he pulled me back from Raphael, and his face looked worried. His eyes, behind his glasses, kept searching out mine.

I let Nick keep pulling me back into the foyer. Johnny circled around, keeping his rifle between the vampire and us, grabbing my duffel bag along the way.

"Think of helping me this way," Raphael said. "If I somehow end up dead, you could actually count that as a victory, the way your life is going."

"Let it go, man," Johnny told me.

I didn't say anything. I feared Raphael was right. Something was broken in me, bad. I had great friends. Better than I deserved. And I had brought both of them here, where they could both be killed. Just because I hadn't wanted to go on living, and I was looking for a way to keep going.

And they had both come, without reservation.

I needed to learn how to accept help from my friends. I was bad at it. But there was a part of my brain, nagging me, always providing easy reasons for me to leave them. The easiest and largest being that my friends seemed to die whenever I hung around.

I knew my friends could die helping me. But another part, a smaller part, knew I still needed them.

Danny had tried to show me that. Jen and I had talked about it. I had told her how difficult this was for me. Caring about someone enough to let them stay with you. Understanding it was their choice. That my friends viewed my life worth their loss.

As hard as it had been then, it was far too great a responsibility now. Maybe I could have tried to handle it before, when Jen was alive. But not now. I was too fragile, and this burden too heavy.

Dominic still could control me, with the geas. If he was at all rational. My mother, far older than me, could kill any of us. How could I bring my friends into that?

I might be able to bring Jen back. But could I say it was worth her life, if I lost Nick, Johnny, or Sarah along the way? Would Jen want that?

She would not.

We got to the front door. Nick took a spot by the window and peered out the curtains. Over his shoulder was the rear of the St. Louis Cathedral, cracks spiderwebbing along the back wall, black streaks crisscrossing the white surface like dark wounds that would never heal.

"When you're ready to help me with my thing," Raphael called out, still leaning against the wall, "I'll be waiting."

"Wait all you want," Johnny said. "I hope this place has cable."

Nick opened the door and nodded at us. Johnny stepped out first. Nick went next. Raphael and I eyed each other as I walked out.

The demon winked at me.

"You change your mind," he said, "come find me at Tylertown."

Nick reached back through the door and dragged me out.

CHAPTER FIVE

It was midday, but it wasn't easy to tell. The usually bright light of noon outside, here in the South, was something lesser now. The sky was less of a pale blue. It had taken on a darker shade, like the inkiness of night had leaked from the edge of the night and into this day. It felt colder as well, but maybe that was just me.

I hugged my jacket tightly around me. It *was* colder. But suddenly I also was afraid.

We walked down the middle of the street, heading back toward the cemetery. We turned north after a few blocks, and passed a place called Haunted History Tours, an old mansion that promised to tell us everything we didn't know about spirits and ghosts.

I would have taken them up on it, had they been there.

There were a number of bars and clubs we passed. A brick building on the corner, mostly a shade of gray, with two levels. A railing and a walkway ran around the outside of the second level, and a sign hung over the front. Something called the World Famous Cats Meow. I had no idea what that was.

For the most part the buildings and homes lay quiet around us. As we walked, though, I kept feeling things staring at me, from behind windows, from deep inside alleys, from rooftops. Nothing and no one I could catch, just a feeling, a growing unease that increased with each block we walked, with every inch the sun descended in the west.

"You're not letting him get to you, are you?" Johnny asked, as we walked. He was still in front of us, Nick behind me, and Johnny had turned back a little to me.

"No," I lied.

"We're with you," he said.

"I know, man," I said, stepping around a corpse in the street. The body was small, and one little hand held a football out to the side, the brown leather a little deflated. "I know."

Johnny kept walking. My bag hung on his shoulder, the tiny baseball Nick had bought hanging from one of its straps. Something that reminded us all of Danny.

Danny had given his life for me. He had stood up to Raphael when I couldn't, and Raphael had killed him for it.

I had run from that for most of my life. I had always believed I had failed Danny. Then I had come back to Grafton. And Danny's ghost had appeared above me, he had given me his memories, his ethereal energy, and that had helped me kill Raphael.

Well, apparently kind of kill him.

What was important though is I had felt what Danny had felt right before he was killed. Worry for me. Concern for me. A great love for a friend. And deep in Danny's memories something I would have said was pride when Danny had thrown his baseball at Raphael's face.

When I had needed Danny, he had stepped up to the plate. He had been there.

And he had been killed.

Jen had tried to convince me, on the drive south to New Orleans. She had wanted me to know it was impossible for me to protect everyone, but also, that I needed to be protected sometimes, too. That my friends thought I was worth that sacrifice, if it came down to it. *"You have to get it, Gus. You have to understand we're all here with you. That we all understand what can happen to any of us. That we've made that choice."*

I had understood what she had told me then. But at the time I had also known it was something I would never allow. I might never *get* it. I just couldn't allow my friends to give their lives for me. It wasn't the way I was made. I would always put myself in danger first, before that danger came to my friends.

I wanted to be buried, long before any of those I cared about were.

I hadn't had that chance, with Jen.

It was so much harder, living on, with her gone.

We made good time back to the docks. Reports of gunfire picked up in the distance. Tiny crackles and pops, behind us a bit and to the east. Maybe the battle was beginning there again, now that the sun was setting.

The people on the docks were gone, but they hadn't made it far. Debris and flotsam littered the lake to the north. Hulled boats floated here and there, capsized, flipped over, bottoms torn open. They dotted the surface of the lake, far to both the east and west. It was hard to tell from the wreckage, but there were at least thirty or forty of the craft, all different sizes.

I wondered what kind of monster rested deep in the waters of the lake. Was it a many-tentacled Cthulhu beast? A titanic whale-shaped creature, with teeth the size of cars? Quite possibly it was neither, but something else entirely, something beyond what my short human existence could imagine.

Whatever it was, the surface of the lake was still again. Placid. No corpses hung suspended in the surface of the water. I didn't think any of the people trying to flee had made it out, and nothing good could come from guessing what might have happened to their bodies.

We stood on the pier, above the boat we had stolen. Nick began to climb down into the craft. Johnny and I looked over the water, and both of us were quiet.

Earlier, if we had taken just a few minutes out and come back, I might have been able to help all of these people. I could have at least told them where the creature in the lake had been sitting, or resting, and directed them in a safer direction.

They would have wanted more, though. People always wanted more. They would have asked or begged for me to lead them all the way across. And, if we had made it, I would have had to come back. Too much time and uncertainty, when I had but one goal here.

Maybe I should have still tried. Helping these people should have mattered to me. But I hadn't.

I was still hurting. That statement was true enough. I was still trying to find out if I could keep going on myself, after Jen's death. I needed to figure out if my life was still worth living, if I could be the person Jen had told me she believed me to be.

But now, looking at all the bodies on the water, the destroyed craft bobbing by, I couldn't help but feel that all these people had been killed just because I had been trying to figure that out about myself.

Maybe I wasn't the person Jen thought I was. At least, I hadn't been, in that moment. I certainly hadn't tried to protect them. I hadn't even *walked back* to give them a word of caution. I had been too wrapped up in my own grief and hope to care. To want to give more than what I had.

Nick and Johnny were quiet beside me. While these thoughts rolled around in my head. Not saying much, not laying any blame.

Just because I was ready to die didn't mean I had to take down the people around me. I hadn't thought much more than about myself. And these people had paid the price for that.

It was maybe how life worked, chance just hadn't been fair to them. I wondered how far into my future I would make it before the same thing happened to my friends.

CHAPTER SIX

Whether the creature at the bottom of the lake was full or sleeping, it didn't matter. We made it back across the lake without an issue. I had seen the glimmer of its spark, in much the same location it had been in before, and I had pointed out a path Nick could pilot our boat around to avoid it.

Such an easy thing to do.

It took us closer to the causeway than we had traveled coming in. Maybe the piles supporting the road, concrete wedges driven deep into the earth, were spaced close enough together the creature couldn't spread itself out. Maybe it couldn't feel comfortable around them, or it just preferred the flatter bottom of the lake.

I was just guessing.

It took a little bit of time to find the house where we had parked the jeep. The sun was low in the west. The sky had turned a deep blue, with a darker purple rising from the east. As we neared the pier by the house, the lake grew a bit choppy. Large waves pushed our boat toward the shore, and we rose up and down in tiny swells. I grabbed the side of the boat to stay balanced, and Johnny did the same.

The lake behind us bubbled, out in its deepest part, like a pot of boiling water. Something large and black and flat rose out of the center of the bubbles and slapped the surface of the lake. The sound was like a mountainous giant had clapped his hands, once.

Then the surface of the lake grew still. The bubbles got smaller, then disappeared. The waves rocking our boat lessened, and Nick worked to get the boat lined up to the pier. We bounced against the wooden posts a few times, and then got tied up.

The jeep ride back was uneventful as well. At least, through the Dead Zone. We drove into the darkness, the sky darkened ahead of us to the east, like a theater dimming its lights before the show began.

Nick drove a little faster than he had, coming in. Johnny tried his cell a few times, and just shook his head. Maybe it was the pentagram, built of phone lines, or maybe it was just the Dead Zone itself, but whatever it was, phones weren't going to work.

Finally Sarah's jeep appeared over the horizon. A bit farther down the road was the sedan we had "borrowed" to get us to the border, something silver and nondescript. Her slim form leaned up against the sedan and faced our direction, as if searching.

Johnny peered through the optics on his rifle.

"She's good," he said. Then Johnny looked again, as if double-checking something.

"One of the soldiers is gone, though," Johnny said. "At least, he's not sitting with the others."

A frown appeared on Nick's face. Something heavy and hinting at thunder. I wouldn't have liked to see what it would have been, had Sarah not been okay.

We pulled up. The other soldier hadn't made it far. He lay facedown, twenty or thirty feet past Sarah's jeep. The other soldiers remained where we had left them, backs to the vehicle, hands in their laps, black wire ties still tight around wrists and ankles.

Nick got out and went to Sarah. Her face was flush, as if she had cried a good bit. They talked to each other, voices low. Nick held himself in the way he did when he was angry, shoulders tight, chest out. Sarah pulled him to her and hugged him, weakly.

I walked over to the soldiers. Their leader was the one who was missing, the sergeant. Each of the three left was pale.

"What happened?" I asked.

"It was Lutz," one of the soldiers said. "We told him not to."

Nick came over then. The soldiers leaned back from him. "I told you guys what would happen," he said.

"We told him not to," the middle soldier said, his voice high-pitched and panicked.

"Nick," Sarah called out, "leave them alone."

"We won't say anything," the guy to his right said. "Man, I'm just in the reserve. I'm a programmer. I got a deadline this week. They just called us up for this."

"Lutz was the lifer," the third soldier said. His voice was low, as if he was resigned to his fate. "He felt like he had to try."

Nick's jaw tightened. "I still told you."

"We're tied up," the programmer screamed. "We couldn't stop him, man. We couldn't stop him."

"Nick," Sarah said, and took one step closer to our group. The three soldiers actually started scooting away from her. "They didn't do anything."

Nick reached a decision. Maybe a hard one, for him. But he stepped back to Sarah.

"You guys are lucky," I said.

The programmer's forehead was beaded with sweat, and his skin was pale. He kept blinking, way too much. The resigned soldier actually spoke to me.

"Man, tell them we won't say anything," he said. "But you got to know we're going to get asked about the body."

"I don't know that the decision is up to me," I said. A week ago it would have been. And I would have let them go. But it was a different world today. And though it had been my choice to go into the Dead Zone, it would be my friends that paid the price for going in.

The programmer swallowed. "None of us want to die, man."

If these soldiers lived, they would definitely tell what happened. They would probably give good descriptions about the rest of us. It would be linked to all the news articles about our group that had been put out in the past week.

As busy as the government was, with the Dead Zone, they would still likely find the time to hunt us down. At the very least, it looked like we had something to do with the appearance of the zone. Which was only the truth. So my friends would be in more danger now. We were hunted before, after Kimaris had attacked us at the Welcome Center, but now we would all be hunted to find out what we knew about these cities.

I walked over to where the sergeant lay. His body was facedown, his arms still wire-tied underneath him. He was missing a boot, and the strap that had been holding his ankles together was just around the leg that still had a boot.

I turned him over. His body was surprisingly light.

I was glad I was exhausted, mentally and physically. Or I might have screamed.

Lutz's skin was pockmarked and dimpled, as if something had sucked him out from the inside. It was also thin and cracked in places, more maybe torn, like an old piece of tissue paper. His body looked like he had been emptied, and lumps bulged where his skin had been pulled tight over bones, or organs. His eyelids had shrunk, and his eyes looked like white raisins, dotted black, where the irises had been.

Nick came up next to me. "Sarah doesn't like her power."

I could understand that, if this was what happened when she used it.

"She tried to stop Lutz, by just using a little of it," he said. "She can leech life force from a person. When she uses it in little amounts it'll sap their will. Make them suggestible. Or even lethargic."

Nick shrugged. "Something with the curse messed up her control. She pulled everything from this guy."

"I can't imagine how that feels," I said. Although I had lived many monstrous memories of ghosts, I had never sucked the life from a real person. It looked, and felt, horrifying.

Nick chuckled, dark and bitter. "She didn't want to shoot him. She's not great with guns. She thought she might kill him."

So she had tried to sap his will. And her power had reached out, uncontrolled. And in a moment faster than anyone had wanted, Lutz had been killed.

"They are going to know we were here," I said.

"Yeah," he said. "But that was always going to be the case. The difference is just in the degree."

"We killing the others?" I asked.

Nick looked at me, as if surprised I would ask that. Or maybe surprised I had asked at all. Before, I would have been the person to decide something like that.

Nick was leading our group, though. At least now. And this had to do with Sarah. I would leave it up to them.

The choices being made didn't feel like they were mine to make anymore. Like nothing I did or said could change anything that happened. That the only time I made a decision, the choice could drastically alter the lives of my friends. Or even end them.

It's a horrible feeling, knowing the only decision a person could make would be one that could hurt those closest to him.

"Nah," he said. "But at some point they are going to talk about this."

"Let's help them come up with a story, then," I said. "Maybe something came out of the Dead Zone."

"Yeah," he said. "Best we can do. We'll try to make them stick to it."

CHAPTER SEVEN

We were in the sedan, heading back to town. The jeep had crossed the roads like an all-terrain vehicle, engine angry, vehicle jostling as the tires bounced with every bump, the road noise a high-pitched whine. The sedan was quiet, steady and smooth. The road rolled by underneath us, and the engine hummed quietly underneath the sounds of the radio, playing a Top 40 song. It was relaxing, and tiring.

We had grabbed everything from our rooms that morning, so we didn't need to find a new hotel. Nick thought it would be good to get to another city, before stopping to eat and find a place to sleep. My friends were hungry, and though I wasn't, I needed to eat.

I had made my decision, sometime back at the checkpoint.

I was going to take Raphael up on his offer.

My friends couldn't suffer, or die, because of some fool's errand I was hell-bent on. And I wasn't going to allow them to be in that danger. Jen wouldn't want them to die for her, any more than I would.

In many ways, this would be my last journey. Either I would bring Jen back or I would die. Our friends could live on, if I left them now. I would take that outcome, no matter what happened to me.

So I pretended to be hungry. We stopped by a buffet, and I watched Sarah grab salad plate after salad plate. She wasn't hungry, either, but forced herself to eat, just like me. The place had sheets of lasagna in big pans, and I went back for seconds, and thirds.

Johnny gave Sarah the rundown of everything that had happened in the zone. With a glance at me, he glossed over the lake. He told her about Raphael, and Sarah's hand grabbed on to Nick's during that. And then Johnny told her we didn't find Jen's body.

"So, you think Jen is where," she said, "in the Key?"

"I think so," I said.

"And you can bring her back?" she asked, her voice carrying the hope I felt inside me. "You know how?"

"I don't know," I said. I didn't know how to heal someone who wasn't there. And if her body was in the Key, I didn't know how to bring her out of it. I would find a way to do both, though. "I'm going to figure it out, though."

Every now and then I fingered the cold stone of the Key, wondering if Jen was there, if she could see all this. It had stopped its strange thrumming when we left the Dead Zone, and now it just felt cool against my chest. Although the scent of honeysuckle would come over me, every now and then, almost randomly. Especially when I took a deep breath and was thinking about nothing in particular.

"You okay?" I asked Sarah. She picked at her plate, stabbing a random vegetable and then chewing it almost angrily.

"Yeah," she said. "I'm not happy about what happened today. But I don't know what I'd have done differently."

Her voice had always been a little lighter than Jen's. More fragile. But now when she talked it was somber. Reflective. And holding a little sorrow.

"I understand," I said. She hadn't wanted to kill the soldier, but it had happened anyway.

She gave me a tired smile.

"I do understand, you know," I said again. "Sometimes things happen so fast there's nothing you can do about it afterwards, except keep going."

And even then it was tough. Tough to move forward, when all that followed you was death. Sarah's eyes were sad. I began picking at my plate as well.

I pretended to smile when Nick and Johnny got into their ice-cream-bowl contest. I even poked fun at them. Sometime in between bowls five and six, Johnny stopped. His bowl was full of chocolate and vanilla goop, with threads of caramel and sprinkles in it. He took a large breath, as if trying to create more room inside his stomach. "We know what we're doing next?"

Nick looked up at me, as if waiting for me to answer.

I knew what I was going to do. Just a couple of things. I needed to learn if, and how, I could bring someone back from the dead. The other was keeping my friends safe.

My mother could teach me one of those things.

So I began the lie to my friends with the other.

"Is Bartholomew in Rome?" I asked.

"Yeah," Johnny answered. "Left a few days ago."

"Is there a way we can get a hold of him?"

Johnny shook his head. "It's not like he carried a cell phone."

"Hmmm." I pretended to think. "Maybe we backtrack through churches. Find a branch of the Templars, someone still here in the States."

"To figure out more about the Key?" Nick asked. His eyelids were a little lowered, as if he was trying to look through me.

"Exactly," I said. "If Jen is in there, we need to know how to open it."

Johnny had pulled out his phone. "The oldest Catholic church close to us would be …" He tapped his thumb across the screen, and we all waited. "The Cathedral of San Fernando, in San Antonio."

"Then that's our next spot," I said.

"There's a bishop there as well," Johnny said. He made a wincing face. "Hopefully he doesn't hold what happened here against us."

Sarah rolled her eyes, but didn't laugh.

Johnny tried harder, even doing his eyebrow waggle. "I mean, how many hell on earths can we possibly get blamed for in just one week?"

That just got a snort from Nick. Not much else.

"Tough crowd," Johnny and Nick said at the same time, which surprised me enough that I laughed, and which got all of us grinning.

I'd miss these guys tomorrow.

"Might be time to work on new material," I said.

"It just might be," Johnny said. "Right after I beat this man in ice-cream bowls eaten. It just got personal."

I was doing the right thing. There actually might be a chance the bishop there would know something. I wasn't necessarily abandoning my friends. I was just going to let them take the less dangerous task.

"I like the San Fernando church thing, though," I said. "If the bishop there doesn't know anything, maybe he'll help us get a hold of Bartholomew."

"If that guy is even alive," Nick said. "He was going into Rome."

Nick said that like Bartholomew was heading into World War III.

"We made it out of New Orleans okay," I said. If we could do that, a saint could make it into Rome, surely.

Nick waved his hand, as if to say we didn't make it because of anything special we did. We were just lucky. And he might have been right. But that still didn't mean Bartholomew couldn't get lucky, too.

"Interesting," Johnny said, still on his phone. "There are reports of something flying around in Paris."

Another one of the cities surrounded by the pentagram. The three of us looked at each other. We all were thinking about the boiling, back in the lake. The house-sized bubbles bursting from the water. All the broken boats. And the large flat limb that had slapped the surface, before sliding back into the depths.

None of that mattered now, though, to me. I had eaten as much now as I had in the past week, and I was going to try to get a few hours of sleep before I escaped my friends.

I stretched my arms like I was tired, though my yawn was real enough.

"Me, too, man," Johnny said. "Me, too."

So after that we found a small hotel on the outskirts of the town. Some place that had the light on for us. I went in and got three rooms. One for Nick and Sarah, one for Johnny, and one for me.

"Separate rooms?" Johnny asked. Maybe he thought we were going to bunk up in the same one.

"Just in case," I said, motioning to the Key.

If Jen appeared again, ethereally, I wanted it to be just her and me. Maybe I didn't want to share what I had with her. Maybe I just didn't want someone watching me with her, seeing how close I was to tears, to how open I was, even with her ghost.

I was full of this weird mixture of excitement and despair. Excitement, because in some way, in some form, she and I were still together. Despair, because I had no idea if we would ever be together again, in the way we had been.

I didn't want to imagine a life without her. Or her, as a ghost. Jen lying beside me. Me trying to gather her to me, my arms slipping through her ethereal form, holding nothing. Jen would be here, and at the same time she wouldn't be *here*. We couldn't talk, or hold each other, or sleep next to each other.

I pulled the bag from the bishop's place out of the sedan, checking to make sure my guns and cash were in there. Nick and Sarah had gone shopping while I lay in bed. They had bought all of us an overnight bag, with some clothes and bathroom stuff. Things like toothpaste and toothbrushes.

I walked into my room and set the bag down. A shower would be good. I turned on the water, hot, and vigorously rubbed myself down with the small bar of soap there. I tried not to think of the last shower I had taken in a motel room, with Jen.

I scrubbed and scrubbed. Every now and then I would catch the scent of the decaying corpses we had walked through, and each time I would pour more shampoo into my hand and lather up my hair. No matter how many times I washed myself, it seemed like that funk still stuck to me.

Toward the end I rinsed out my boots. Globs came out of them, reddish and gluey, chunks that hung around the drain. I rubbed them down and tried not to think about my lasagna dinner, and then scrubbed myself down again.

I let the tub run for a long time when I was done. I wanted whatever rinsed down the drain to stay down there. I used the hair dryer hanging on the wall to dry my boots. I wanted to throw them away, but they were custom, and I had had them awhile. Silver covered the toe plates, and that would be hard to replace.

Then I brushed my teeth and got into bed. I set the cheap alarm clock for two in the morning. I would sneak out then, when my friends were all asleep.

I woke up before two, though.

Jen floated ethereally above me. Again, in a transparent, ghostly blue light. Her face sad. The Key was cool against my chest. It did thrum, lightly. And I unmistakably smelled honeysuckle.

As soon as my eyes opened, she disappeared. Fading into the darkness. I had the feeling it wasn't something she controlled, as her eyes were the last thing to vanish. They were wide and frustrated and sad.

CHAPTER EIGHT

It wasn't two in the morning, but I was awake, so I left anyway. I got dressed and put on my boots. They were still a little wet, and a lot cold. I winced as I slid my feet into each, and the soles squished as I walked around in them.

I left the bag Nick and Sarah had bought for me, after transferring some of the clothes and other items they had bought into my own duffel bag. In their bag I put a few rolls of money, from what I still carried, and then dropped their bag on the bed. Then I left the hotel, making sure before I did to slide my key card under Johnny's door.

The parking lot was dark, and it was still cold. The road leading back toward town was a black strip in a blue-black night. A single light tossed a nimbus of yellow around the front of the hotel, and tiny white dots buzzed in a large cloud around the lamp.

I walked toward town. Crickets chirped from the woods on either side of the road, occasionally falling silent as I passed, then picking back up. The town lights lit an area over the trees, in the distance. A large eighteen-wheeler roared by me, the wind of its passage buffeting me, so that I started walking a bit farther off the shoulder.

One of the first places I came up to was a used car lot. I had seen it when we were looking for a motel. It was a small building with twenty or thirty cars and trucks in a gravel parking lot. I tapped a ghost and broke in through the building's roof, by pulling out one of the attic vents there. Not many alarm systems cover that area.

It didn't take long to find the box with all the keys. I picked a fob at random, and a small red coupe chirped outside when I pressed the button. The car only had a quarter tank, but I didn't need much to get where I was going. I was more worried about the *$9999* in big red and yellow bubbled letters drawn across the windshield.

Oh well. Beggars can't be choosers. I found some towels and tried to wipe off the colored numbers the best I could. I found a dealer's plate and slapped it in the back window, and then took off.

A few hours later I was back at a storage place, east of New Orleans. The one Jen and I had dropped the Camaro off in. The lights were on in the building by the gate, but no one looked at me from the window. I pulled up to the gate, punched the code in the little box, and drove the coupe to the storage unit, parking it just a bit past the roll-up door.

I grabbed my bag and walked over to the door. There I worked the numbers of the combination lock until it opened.

Nine-five-one-one.

"The day we met, silly."

I swallowed, and pulled the lock open. Then I rolled the doors up. The Camaro sat there, waiting. Other than a light layer of dust, it looked much the same as it had when we dropped it off.

Like the shotgun, and like the photo of Jen and me, the Camaro was something I didn't want to let go. It seemed like the more that got taken away from me, the harder I tried to hold on to what I had left.

I patted the trunk, then opened it. There were still some loose items there, some food from our trip down, a few more guns and some ammo, some of the last clothes we had bought at the superstore. I tossed the duffel bag into the back, then took the tiny baseball off the bag and hung it back on the rearview mirror.

The Camaro fired right up. The rumble of the engine reverberated along the floor and into my feet, through the wheel and into my hands. I had missed my car.

I threw the car in reverse and turned to look back. The sunflowers still lay there, in the backseat. The ones I had bought Jen. They were a faded yellow now, withered, stems brittle and brown.

I let out a deep breath and backed out, staring out the back window. I did a quick three-point turn and pulled the car past the door, feeling the Camaro chug its way across the pavement. Then I got out and drove the borrowed coupe into the unit and locked it up.

I got back on the road and stopped by the gas station. The one Jen and I had called Nick from. I got some food and drink for the road, and atlases of Louisiana and Mississippi. I searched for Tylertown. It was a small town, north of New Orleans, somewhere in Mississippi. Tracing it out with my finger, I saw Tylertown was in the tip of the Dead Zone, somewhere in the northern point of the pentagram. A state road would take me almost the whole way there.

I got on the road and drove, heading north. The gas stations and hotels and fast-food places quickly flew behind me, and I was into the country. The headlights picked out the blacktop, and the Camaro hummed along behind the twin beams.

I hoped Raphael would be easy to find. Part of me couldn't believe I was going to take him up on his offer. But at least my friends would be safe. It was best, if I was going to tilt at windmills, to tilt at them alone.

And if I went down, I would take Raphael down with me. That was the promise I made, in order for me to feel better about abandoning my friends. It made sense to me. I was doing something crazy, and dangerous. I was going somewhere that the geas could control me, where my mother could be ordered to kill me, looking for a way to bring Jen back.

In order to protect my friends, I had to do what I was doing alone. I was convinced that the only way to keep them safe was to keep them away. And if everything went to shit, I would make sure Raphael didn't crawl back out of hell a second time.

It occurred to me I was doing the same thing now that I had done ten years ago. Danny had died, and I had run away. Jen had died, and again I was running away.

My jaw tightened. I had believed I had changed, after Grafton. I had thought I was someone who my friends could count on, who would fight to protect them. But then Jen had been killed.

So maybe Parker had been right. Maybe a man is what he does, in the moment. Because in the moment, I was running. The hand had been dealt, the chips were down, and I was already leaving the table.

The facts were hard to argue with. Danny had died, and I had run. Jen had died, and now I *was* running. It seemed like I hadn't changed at all, from the kid who had fled Grafton ten years ago. If I wanted to be someone different, then I needed to do something different.

My friends deserved better from me, this time.

So I stopped at the next town. I went into one of the superstores, walked to the back of the store, to the electronics department. I bought a prepaid phone there, and asked the kid there to start up the phone and set it up for me. I was never any good at that kind of stuff.

He looked at me funny, but got the card entered and the phone working. He told me I needed to enter another card at the end of the month to keep using it, and I told him I wouldn't need the phone that long.

I took the cell out to the Camaro and plugged it into the cigarette lighter. I programmed Nick's number into the contacts from memory, then hit the call button.

He answered on the first ring, like he hadn't been asleep. "So you've left."

"You knew?" I was surprised.

"Of course, man," he said. "I knew right when Raphael made his pitch."

He had been quiet the whole way home. I had thought that had been typical Nick. Then I remembered the way he had looked at me, over dinner, when Johnny asked, "What's next?"

"Why didn't you try to talk me out if it?" I asked.

"Could I have?"

He knew. Nick had thought it through, then. My friends were all I had left of a life I had desperately wanted, and I couldn't afford to lose any more of them. "No."

"That's what I figured," he said. "If there's anyone who knows how you are feeling, it's probably me."

"What do you mean?"

"For years I was alone, man," he said. "Angry. I did a lot of stupid stuff. I blamed a lot of people. Every day became like every other day. I wondered when it would be over, for me. I even tried to make it over, picking fights, that kind of thing."

Johnny had called Nick a dark fucker, back in Grafton. I had agreed with him at the time. Now I was ashamed, because all Nick had been was devoted to the rest of us, when we all went our separate ways. Me most of all.

Nick had proven himself, over and over, since then. Once I had thought we were a lot alike. We both felt like the world was against us, and we both took everything on ourselves.

There the comparison ended, though. I had run away, after Danny died. Nick had stayed and fought what he could. I was running now, and Nick was still fighting to keep our group together. He was as committed as anyone could be to us.

"When you came back, I started to understand," he said. "You showed me what it was like, having friends again. People who cared about you. People who would do anything to make sure you were okay."

"Nick, I–"

He cut me off. "Listen to me. I didn't give you a chance when you first came back. I was angry, because you had left us. Because Raphael had Sarah, because a lot of things. But I gave you a chance, and look what happened."

I didn't understand what he was saying. I didn't think he had given me a chance. He had helped me break into the factory to rescue Jen. He had taken on a group of wights, distracting them, while I snuck into the building.

"You saved Sarah and me," he said. "You took on Raphael, and tried to give us time to get away."

I was quiet then. I had jumped Raphael, at the end. Nick had been taking a beating, and Sarah had been knocked silly from Raphael running his car into theirs. At the time I had done it almost without thinking.

"I never told you, man," Nick said, "but when I came back for you with the tire iron, and Raphael had that bat in his hand, your skull was cracked almost in half. I thought you were dead then. And all I could think about was that you had died for me, for me and Sarah."

"I didn't know," I said.

"Of course not," he said. "But I knew it then. I knew you'd give your life for us. And I understood then why you had run, back in the beginning. All in a flash.

"And how did I repay that kind of trust?" he said, bitter. "I gave Azazel the Key."

"Nick, that wasn't your fault," I said. "I told you I understood. I'd have done the same."

He laughed, a dark laugh that cut off abruptly. "See? I knew you'd say that. And it doesn't matter. What matters is *I* gave Azazel the Key. And that led to everything that's happened since.

"And you haven't blamed me once, since."

I shook my head, though he couldn't see it. "Nick, none of this is your fault. I don't even know if it's mine. All it is is I can't have any more of my friends die because of something I'm doing. I just can't."

"I understand, Grimm," he said. "But I wanted to be honest with you. Because you need to know all of us, any of us, would give our life for you."

"I *can't*," I screamed, then pounded the steering wheel of the Camaro until something in my hand broke with a loud snap.

For a while then there was quiet over the line. I closed my eyes and took a large, deep breath. Then took another. This wasn't going the way I wanted it to go. I just wanted them to understand why I had left. But they had known that already.

"I get it," Nick said. Then he waited. We both waited. I closed my eyes and took calming breath after calming breath. Nick had been a steady presence, these past few weeks. Someone I counted on. Someone who was committed to his friends, and always saw a thing through, no matter what it took.

Even now.

He broke the silence first.

"After Raphael today, I figured you would take off," he said. "It's how you would want to protect us. But I had hoped you would stay. So we all could help you, so *I* could help you, like you helped us."

Nick wasn't saying any of this to make me feel bad. At his core, he was a guy who said what needed to be said. It wasn't his fault the words cut deep.

He had hoped I would trust them enough, trust him enough, to stay. And it hurt him that I hadn't. But he was also telling me he understood. That it was okay.

"Sometime, Grimm, you're going to have to give us a *chance*," he said. "There's a scale out there I need to balance."

I didn't like myself right then.

"Jen is all I can take right now," I said, my voice low.

"I know," he said, and his voice broke a bit. "But we're all here, man. We all would do anything, rather than let you go at this alone."

"I don't know that I'm worth that," I said.

"We know," Nick replied, and said it again. "We *know*."

I waited a long moment. "Maybe I'm a bit broken," I finally said.

"We know that, too," he said again. "But it's what friends are for."

We were both quiet again. It struck me again, what Danny had shown me. How proud he had been, standing up to Raphael for me. Even though it had killed him. He had been the happiest, showing me that, hoping it would let me understand it was okay, that he was okay.

"I appreciate it all, Nick," I said. "Everything. You tell Sarah and Johnny, everything."

"I will," he said.

"Thanks."

"Now promise me something," he said.

"If I can," I said.

"You call us when you need help," he said. "And we'll be there."

I didn't deserve friends like this. "If I can, Nick, I will."

"That's all we ask," he said. "You don't have to do any of this alone. Never again."

There was another quiet moment.

"You know, I wouldn't even be here, if it wasn't for you," I said.

Nick had been the one to put the idea in my thoughts, that I could bring Jen back. He had given me place to start, giving me a path, even hope. I wanted to thank him for that, but maybe he understood I couldn't yet.

"It's what friends do," he said. "Help each other go on."

There was a last silence, between two people who didn't know how to end the conversation. There was a part of me that wanted to drive back, who needed my friends around me, holding me up. The foundation I had built myself on had cracked, and I remained standing, but just barely.

But ahead of me was a mad vampire, driven crazy by a demonic drug.

That vampire held a geas that could force me to do anything. And he also had my mother to protect him, as lethal a killer as there ever had been.

I didn't know what I had left. If I had the strength to face either of them. If I brought my friends into that, it could only end one way.

"Good luck, man," Nick said.

"Thanks," I answered. "For it all."

Then we both hung up.

And I kept driving on. Alone.

CHAPTER NINE

Nick slid his thumb over the screen of the phone, ending the call, then let out a deep breath.

"You okay?" Sarah asked from one of the cushioned chairs by a small round table, under the window of the hotel room. She had woken when Nick answered the call, and had gone to get Johnny.

He still looked half-asleep, lying back in the other chair, his feet out before him. The two of them had missed most of the conversation, until the end.

"Yeah," Nick said. He quickly went over everything with the two of them.

"He sounds bad," Sarah said, her eyebrows frowning. She missed her sister as much as Grimm, and felt like her sister's death was her fault. That Grimm blamed her. Nick thought all of his friends, himself included, sometimes took too much onto themselves. He recognized it in himself, and had made it his job to help the others see it, too.

He didn't know where Sarah and he were, in their relationship. Only that something had changed the other day, before he had shadow-walked to New Orleans. Sarah had been talking with Grimm, and had been crying, when he pulled up with a new car to the garage they had been hiding in.

Sarah had walked away from Grimm, and had immediately hugged

Nick. Hard. The action had surprised Nick, and he still didn't know what Grimm had said back then. Sarah and Nick were closer now. There was a relationship there between them, but it was undefined. Headed in an unknown direction. Sometimes it felt as if they were together, and other times it felt like they both were navigating something new.

Either way, Nick believed he owed Grimm.

"You know Grimm," he said. "It always sounds bad."

"Is he going to be okay?" she asked.

"He will be," Nick said. "We're going to make sure."

"I wish we didn't let him go," she said.

"He would never have stayed," Nick said. "It's the only way he feels he can protect us. It's why he ran before, when Danny was killed."

"So, what's the plan, then?" Johnny asked.

"We know where he's going," Nick said, looking at Johnny. "We just have to find out where that is."

It took a moment for Johnny to get it.

"You want me to ask Gabrielle," he said.

"I think we need to," Nick said. "Her family probably has tabs on all the places Raphael's father has over here."

"It's going to be tough," Johnny said. "Dominic has been here hundreds of years. He's going to have hiding places no one knows about."

"It won't matter how many there are, we'll check them all until we find him," Nick said.

Sarah smiled. "You sound like Grimm."

"I'm just not going to let what happened before happen this time," Nick said.

"What do you mean?" Johnny asked.

"The last time he ran. When Raphael killed Danny," Nick explained. "I was furious. I blamed Grimm, blamed him for Danny and everything that happened after that."

Nick remembered slipping out of the shadow, tire iron in both hands, swinging it at Raphael's head with everything he had.

There was a loud bonelike ring, andRaphael had fallen forward, taken a knee. Nick had glanced over at Grimm then, lying in the middle of the parking lot.

Nick would never forget that image. Grimm was on his side, his face lying in a thick, dark pool. His mouth had been moving, but no words came out. Part of his skull had broken away; a plate of bone hung off a bit of scalp.

One of Grimm's eyes stared forward, unmoving. The other wandered aimlessly, as if looking for something it couldn't find.

Nick's anger at his friend had burned away in that moment. He hadn't given Grimm the benefit of the doubt, and Grimm still had given everything he had for his friends, regardless of how they had felt about him.

Whatever Grimm thought of himself, Nick knew he was the most selfless person he had ever met. Nick had never wondered about what Grimm had to live with, after Danny. What Grimm had to carry around, all by himself. Nick wondered if he could have done the same thing, and how long he could have lasted, under that kind of burden.

He realized he hadn't spoken for a bit, lost in the memory. Sarah got up and sat next to him, on the bed, and placed one hand on his back. Lightly, her fingers like feathers.

"I always blamed Grimm for what happened," Nick said again. "But then I thought about what he had done, and why he did it. He had run to keep us safe. Everything he suffered through, he did because he thought he was protecting us. And he did it alone."

Johnny and Sarah were quiet, maybe thinking on what Nick was telling him.

"All the things he's done since," Nick said. "He's been hit by a car, shot, attacked by demons. Each time he has to heal himself, he has to live a ghost's memories, and it's always something evil. Jen told me about a ghost he had to pull from back in Lewiston."

Nick swallowed. "I don't know how he can do something like that, and still be the type of person he is."

"We're going to help him," Sarah said.

"We are," Nick said, and smiled at Sarah. A sad smile, with a tiny bit of hope. "I was an ass for a long time, Sarah. And you guys thought me hard." He looked at Johnny. "Dark."

"That was me just saying something," Johnny said.

"A lot of it wasn't me being hard," Nick said. "Some things I don't process well, and when I don't, I just stay silent. It's easier for me to focus then."

Nick likened it to how a light could flicker through a room and destroy one shadow, and at the same time create many more. That kind of mix was tough to work in with what he did. He just preferred things to be pure. Light or dark. On or off. Simple.

The heater in the room kicked on then, stirring the curtains on the front window. They all looked as the drapes waved, the ends kicking up around Johnny's chair. He leaned over and turned the fan down.

"So Grimm came back, and even though he had been gone for ten years, even though I treated him like I did, he still helped me when I needed it," Nick said. "When we needed it. It made me wonder how things could have been different for him, for all of us, if we had reached out when he first left. Maybe he wouldn't be broken now. Maybe none of us would be."

"You know," Johnny said, "that's the most I've ever heard you say. Ever. Maybe even if I added it all up."

Sarah patted Nick's back, her hand light and soft.

"I just want to do it right this time," Nick said. "We're not letting him go this alone. We're going to help him."

"You know, we never told him what we found," Johnny said. "In the bishop's desk."

When Grimm had gone down to get his bag, and when he had met Raphael, Nick and Johnny worked to break into a locked drawer in the bishop's desk. Inside had been a thin silver case, without any kind of decoration or symbols. It was flat on every edge except for a metal combination lock on the side, which was locked. It looked like it could hold letters or papers, or even a thin book.

Right now it lay in Nick's bag. "We'll find a time to tell him," Nick said. "We got to find a way to open it first."

"Sounds like a plan," Johnny said. "I'll call Gabrielle."

"Think she'll come back here?" Sarah asked, looking at Johnny. Nick felt like she was worried about Johnny. Maybe that he was alone now?

Nick had never thought about it. He had always had a thing for Sarah, and she had always been in the same town. They had never really been apart, even when she was with Raphael.

Nick had never liked Gabrielle. But maybe some of that was because she was a vampire. Raphael was a vampire, and he hadn't liked him. Nick believed it was more than that, though. He didn't like the whole vampire/thrall dynamic. It seemed parasitic to him.

He snorted. For years his relationship with Sarah had been similar.

She had only raced to him when she fought with Raphael, when she needed to feel better about herself. She had counted on his feelings for her to help her through some tough times, when it seemed like she had tried her worst to punish herself.

Nick had never understood that part of Sarah. And things had changed now. Their relationship had deepened. So maybe Johnny and Gabrielle could be the same.

"I always ask." Johnny gave them both a sad smile, and tilted his head left and right a few times, as if saying he didn't know. "Sometimes we all have to wait, right?"

CHAPTER TEN

It was late enough in the night to be early in the morning. For a while I sat in the car and listened to the little thumps of car doors opening and closing. Tall light poles stood guard across the parking lot. One of the lights flickered a bit, as if the bulb was close to going out.

Here and there a shopping cart rested, perched at an angle on an island, nestled against speed bumps, one alone on the sidewalk in front of the store. Everywhere but returned to where they should be.

I was a little drained, after the call with Nick. I had only wanted to let them know where I was going, but it evolved into something deeper. I felt different now than before the call. Better, maybe. But also tired.

As I watched, a couple of young men got out of a sports car and weaved their way up to the entrance, speaking way too loud to each other, like they had just come from a club.

I glanced over the map. I was a couple of hours away from Tylertown. I wondered why I had been in such a hurry to get there now. If I left now, it would still be dark when I got there, and that probably wasn't the safest spot to be at night. Not with a demon waiting for me.

I wasn't in a hurry to get there. I had just been in a rush to *get away*. The call had helped with that, some. The muffled silence in the Camaro was soothing. There was a stillness in the car I found peaceful.

I locked my door and leaned my seat back. The sunflowers still lay there on the backseat. The yellow petals were wilted, and had curled in on themselves. There was nothing left of their fragrance, maybe a faint dusty scent of pollen, if I took a deep enough breath.

I lay back and stared at them for a bit. At some point my eyes closed. For a while there were sounds outside, the thumps and snicks of the car doors, the beeps and boops of alarms turning on and off, the occasional loud muffler rattling loud when it passed. Then it was just quiet, and I slept.

Sleep came fast, and deep. There were no dreams, unless I counted floating in an inky darkness, swimming in a blackness that muffled everything around me. I bobbed up and down in slumber, until I finally neared the surface.

I woke.

It was the twilight before dawn. I had been asleep a few hours. The lights in the parking lot had all timed off. An orange glow lit the horizon on the east, the edge a dark reddish brown where the orange pushed against the dark blue of night.

I got out of the car and stretched. My hand throbbed where I had broken something the night before, and I quickly found a ghost and healed myself. The sharp injection of energy woke me like a deep breath of smelling salts. The stretch became a jerk. Joints cracked and popped as I moved around. Sleeping in a car wasn't as comfortable as it used to be, even if it had just been a couple of hours or so.

The air outside was cool and smelled clean, the brisk scent of morning. I went back into the store, used the bathroom, and picked up some breakfast pastries. Jen's favorite ones, the cinnamon rolls covered in icing.

I grabbed some cold coffees as well, the mocha-flavored drinks bottled in glass jars. Then I got back in the Camaro and drove along the road, heading west. I cracked the window a bit and let the air blow in, fresh and cold and invigorating.

The road was poorly paved and the tire noise was loud. I turned on the radio and found a sports station. Or what used to be a sports station. All it talked about now was the current news. Which, today, meant the cities surrounded by pentagrams.

The president had recalled the army from the Dead Zone. Whoever was left in New Orleans wasn't going to get out. Whatever was left of the army, they, too, had been left. The government had accepted defeat.

People were being told to avoid the zone at all costs. The anchor said the army was being told to restrain people from going in just as much as going out. Apparently more people had gathered in groups to head into the zone. Not just fanatics and devil worshippers, but also advertisers, politicians, lawyers. People who saw an opportunity and wanted to make a play for it.

I chuckled, something bitter and ugly. Whoever thought an opportunity existed in the Dead Zones, well, they could go in and try their luck. Take their shot. Azazel would sort them out, just like he had me. If anyone thought they could pull one over on him, they were in for a surprise.

I did smile briefly at the thought of Azazel having lines of lawyers, or politicians, wanting to talk to him. People looking to take advantage of every loophole, in every contract, every shake of the hand. Thousands of people, trying to one-up the demon and carve a piece of their dreams out of the Dead Zone.

Of course, Azazel lived in hell. Surely he had met most of these people's types, if not the exact persons, already.

My smile disappeared.

Mile after mile passed by. I became aware of the passenger seat next to me, the leather cold and stiff without the heat of a body pressed into it. Jen had only been with me a week, and the car felt empty without her. I kept seeing something out of the corner of my eye, like her hair whipping in the wind. Ghosts of memories.

I will get you back.

The thought burned strong in me. Sometime during my talk with Nick, a switch had flipped. I had begun thinking, I had actually begun *knowing* I could bring Jen back. All that was left was the doing. And I was as hardheaded a son of a bitch as there was. If it could be done, I would be the one to do it.

The Key thrummed against my chest, the stone cool on my skin.

Maybe it was just the vibrations of the car rolling on the road, echoing the force of my thoughts. A purpose.

I did feel different now, after speaking with Nick. After the call. I no longer felt like I was running, or fleeing. *That* was it. That was the difference, between running from my friends after Danny's death and running now.

Just calling them had shifted my perspective. Even though we had argued and fought. Even if it had gotten emotional. Being able to talk to them about it had helped, even if we hadn't agreed on what I was doing.

I had made a decision to go this alone. I had stuck to it, even if Nick wanted to help. This time, though, I had included my friends. Even though I wanted to keep them from me, keep them safe, I had found out they were still there for me, across the distance. They understood, and they were there for me to lean on them.

It was important to me to keep them safe. I had told Jen I would. Neither she nor I would want any of our friends in danger, for this.

My mother was as lethal a killer as there was in this world. Unstoppable. Who knew what she would do, what Dominic would order her to do, when I showed up?

All I knew was that it could only be bad. Mistakes would only mean death.

I would have to balance my mother and her drug-addicted vampire with a newly born demon. And I would have to do it carefully, or it would mean I wouldn't be able to get the information I needed, at worst. At best, one of them would just kill me.

I wouldn't let my friends suffer a mistake I made. Not with any of that. No matter if they wanted to. Not on an errand being run on the slimmest of hopes.

A few minutes outside Tylertown, I pulled off to the side of the road. In my ethereal sight the Dead Zone appeared like a red curtain, draping left to right in front in front of me.

I left the Camaro running, but went and popped the trunk. I made sure my shotgun and .38 were both loaded. The shotgun I set near the driver's-side door, on the floor by the seat. The .38 I stuck in my jacket pocket.

The trunk had a few of Nick's old knives. I hid them all around, inside the Camaro. The console, the glove box, between the seats. I wasn't going to ride around with Raphael without something in reach at all times.

Finally I grabbed the wilted flowers. Bits and pieces broke off as I carried them to the side of the road. The grass there was dusty, and dry. The wind picked up, and a few of the petals shook and dropped off, like faded yellow tears.

I laid the flowers in the sun, among the grass. It didn't seem fitting to leave them here, but it seemed better than carrying them with me, to where I was going next. Maybe I didn't want the reminder with me, maybe I just didn't want the dried flowers and the smell and the memory of the sun with me when I was chasing darkness.

Either way, it was time to find Raphael.

CHAPTER ELEVEN

It turned out, finding Raphael wasn't hard at all. He was actually waiting for me. As if he had known my decision, long before I had made it.

Tylertown was one of those one-stoplight towns. It was smaller than Grafton. The main street here was a few brick buildings and a gas station, and a few smaller shops and stores.

It was right at the edge of the Dead Zone. The crimson-lined border stretched a mile or so north past the town, then abruptly ended.

People walked around normally, inside the reddish area marking the zone. Like the haze didn't exist. So I drove on in and parked at the gas station, and went to fill up.

The air felt drier here. Less humid. Like some inner heat underground was slowly roasting everything topside. Maybe it felt that way because I had been driving with the window cracked. But I didn't think so.

Across from the gas station was a run-down shack dressed up as a roadside bar. Parked in a line in front of it was a group of Harley-Davidsons. They were large bikes, covered in chrome, saddlebags dusty from the road. There was a pink neon sign in the front window that blinked the word *Open* over and over.

I went in and prepaid, but I didn't grab any food. I didn't want to eat anything inside the zone. No matter what the expiration date said on the package.

The cashier took my money and gave a half smile. "Crazy what's happenin' down South, right?"

I looked at him for a moment. "Yeah. Sure is."

I walked back out to the Camaro. At the same time the door opened from the bar across the street and Raphael stepped out.

"Grimm?" he called out. "That was faster than I thought."

I set my jaw.

He waved to someone inside, then headed across the street. He was dressed much like yesterday, black pants, white shirt. The shirt was a V-neck polo today, stretched tight across his frame. The demon smiled when he got near.

"I knew you'd be here," he said.

"Yeah, well, don't be too impressed," I said. "You had a fifty percent chance of getting it wrong."

Raphael rolled his eyes. "So, how's this going to work?"

"You mean making a deal?"

"I mean making this particular deal," he said, his voice getting a little serious.

"Going to be tough, since I can't trust you," I said.

"Might be tougher," he said. "I'm getting to think I don't need you."

"You?" I said. "All you've done is get sent to hell. Since I'm the guy who sent you there, the ball might be in my court."

"Huh," he said. He cocked his head, as if what I had said had brought something else to mind. "So, you being the guy who sent me, maybe you know what I am now."

"What do you mean?"

Raphael held out his arm, in the sunlight. "I used to be able to feel the sun. It was like constant sunburn on my skin. Now I can't feel it at all. Doesn't even feel warm to me. It's just … light."

"It is November," I said. "The sun doesn't normally feel warm now."

"Maybe," he said. "But I've changed. I've seen other dead folk here. They don't heal like I do."

Most of them had probably died, in the night we had rescued Sarah and Johnny. Her curse had pulled them around from miles away. They had been helpless, in the cemetery. Whoever had made it out from there may have decided to just be long gone.

Raphael's hand massaged his chin, and he stared off into the sky. "Maybe I should kill one and see what happens."

"There's one I'd like to find," I said. "Feel free to do your thing with him."

He snorted.

The door to the bar opened again, and someone else walked out. A younger girl, in a medium-length gray skirt and a white blouse. She had dark hair, tied back behind her head, and a pair of glasses. Before the door closed she reached back inside and pulled out a tiny black attaché case.

Raphael waved her over. She crossed the street.

"Grimm, my new assistant," he said, grinning. "Belle."

She held out her hand. I stared at it, until she pulled it back.

"Don't be rude," Raphael said.

"I didn't know we were making friends today," I said. "I thought we were here to make a deal."

"Well, the last couple of deals I made kind of went sour," Raphael said. "The last guy killed me with a bat. I thought this time I'd have someone around to help me with the terms."

"So, you're here to, what," I asked her, "notarize the thing?"

"You could call it that." She smiled, politely. Her voice was the perfect mix of attentiveness and business.

"What would you call it?" I said.

"Simply? I would call it keeping your word," she said.

"I figured maybe we could trust each other that way," Raphael said, "if it was signed in blood."

"Well, forget it," I said. "I'm not signing anything, especially if your notary is from hell."

"You think you can get someone from this side you can trust?" Raphael asked.

"It's a standard term of service," Belle said. "Standard contract length. Six hundred and sixty-six days."

I rolled my eyes at the number. *Cute.* "I told you, it's not going to happen," I said.

Raphael lifted his eyebrows. "Then I guess it's no deal."

We both stood there, waiting for each other to call the bluff. Raphael knew I wouldn't trust him, so I wondered what made him think I would sign a document notarized by hell. Seemed like a surefire way to lose a soul.

Although, I wondered, if I was part angel, if I had a soul to lose. It would make it easier to sign the document, if I didn't.

Raphael moved first. He raised his eyebrows at Belle, then headed back to the bar. Belle stood there with her hand on her chin, tapping her mouth with her forefinger, looking at me, apparently thinking.

About halfway across the street Raphael paused. He felt pretty serious about legalizing our deal. Which didn't make a lot of sense to me, since he was the more untrustworthy one of us. A fact both of us knew.

Likely he missed the geas. And this was some way of getting some kind of hold on me. Raphael was my only shot at finding his father, at finding my mother. At least quickly.

I gritted my teeth. Bringing back Jen began with this step, and it looked like we weren't going to even take it.

Belle followed after Raphael.

I had woken with purpose today. An hour ago I had told myself if anyone could bring Jen back, it would be me. That I was the most stubborn ass this side of hell. And then, at the first roadblock, I was ready to turn away.

Honestly what was one more bond, with the geas to worry about? What kind of worry was a piece of paper, when I was going up against people who could order me to die? Six hundred and sixty-six days was far too long into the future for me to worry about something like that.

The Key stirred then, on my chest. Or so I thought.

I let the pair of demons get as far as the door to the bar.

"Wait," I said.

Raphael turned back and looked at me, a big shit-eating grin on his face.

"Show me the damn thing," I said.

The two of them walked back. Belle reached into her case and pulled out a piece of paper. It looked more like parchment, thicker than paper, and more of a light tan or pale yellow color.

On it were three lines, centered in the middle of the paper. Each line equidistant vertically on the page from the next.

I, the undersigned, will help Raphael Antonado kill the demon Azazel.

I, the undersigned, will help Fergus Grimm find my father.

Whosoever does not comply with the above agreement, from six hundred and sixty-six days from this day, his life shall be forfeit to the other party.

Under each sentence was a long black line, justified to the right of the page.

Belle pulled out a long stylus, almost a quill, from her case. She set the paper on the trunk of the Camaro.

"Relax, Grimm," Raphael said. "I'll even sign it first."

He leaned over and signed his name under the second sentence. The ink ran red across the page. His signature was large, with lots of curves, and a flourish at the end. Then he handed me the pen.

I picked up the parchment. It was thick and leatherlike in my hand. I flipped it over. There was nothing else there. Just those three sentences. "No fine print?" I asked.

"You've seen too many supernatural shows." Belle smiled. This smile was perfunctory, just another assistant doing her job.

I flipped it back over and laid it down on the car. Took a long look at it. Simple, right? And the devil was always in the details. But I wanted to kill Azazel anyway, and I needed to find my mother. It was hard not to see the downside on the page.

"It a bit uneven," I said. "Seems like you're asking me to do all the work. All you have to do is tell me where your father is. I have to kill a demon."

"Normal contract terms *are* eye for an eye," Belle mentioned, glancing at Raphael.

Killing Dominic would make talking to my mother a lot easier. "Fair enough," I said.

Raphael's lips curved in a feral grin. "I didn't think you'd want me along. But we can do that."

He took the quill back from me, lined out the word *find*, carefully initialed by the line-out, and then wrote a single word above it: *kill*.

"Good?" Raphael said, holding the quill out to me. The demon maybe had the faintest hint of a smile.

It wasn't what I wanted, but it was a fairer agreement now. I didn't necessarily need to kill Dominic. I just needed to find my mother. But it was the only thing in the contract I could see that had given Raphael an edge.

Well, that and one other item. "We're doing my thing first, right?"

"It's first on the list," Belle said.

That was it, then. I signed my part. The quill was top-heavy in my fingers, and the shaft was thicker than what might support a feather. Almost bonelike, so my signature ended up as more of a scrawl, but it was legible.

I don't know what I had expected. There was no large expulsion of breath from Raphael. He didn't pump his fist. Neither he nor Belle danced a jig. They didn't even glance at each other.

Belle did take the pen from me, and then she signed the last line. Just a single name, simple, with no flourish.

Belial.

It was then I started to get a bad feeling.

CHAPTER TWELVE

Belial. One of the great demons. I had learned about her from the research I had attempted over the years, looking for more information about the Key. Through the history of time her name had sometimes been confused with Lucifer's. They were maybe *1* and *1A*. Curious, she would be here brokering a deal between Raphael and me, to kill Azazel.

There was something more here. Something I couldn't see, and didn't know, but could feel in a way a person could feel the knife, right before the cold metal plunged into their back.

It could be simple. Maybe Lucifer had lost some of his standing in hell. Azazel had been a scapegoat, but after building five new cities for those in purgatory, the demon might now be the new King of the Underworld.

It would make sense, then, for the high demons left to pick a patsy. Or a couple of them. Raphael or me. Either one of us would do. Hell would have a binding contract between us, a lot to gain, and nothing really to lose.

I needed to know more about Belial, in the future. Even though maybe it was too late now. The damage likely had been done. The deed was signed.

"So, what's next?" Raphael asked.

"We have a few years to get this done," I said. "But I'm all for starting now."

"We riding in your car?" Raphael asked, frowning at the Camaro.

"Both of you are coming?" I said. "I just need Raphael."

Belle smiled. "I'm making sure the agreement is met."

I had been right. The devil was always in the details.

"Fine," I said. I opened the door and motioned for them to get in. Raphael, being a gentleman, had Belle get in the back. I held back from rolling my eyes. I didn't need or want to sit next to someone who was the right hand of Lucifer.

I started the Camaro. The pop station immediately came on, playing some boy-band hit. Raphael grinned, and I shut the radio off. I headed out and drove a short distance, until I passed the line marking the boundary between the Dead Zone and the rest of Mississippi.

I glanced over at Raphael and Belle as we pulled past the red curtain and back into the regular world. I didn't know what might happen, and turns out, nothing much did. Neither looked surprised, or disappeared.

Raphael looked over. "You turn on the AC?"

I pointed to the knob on the console. It was set to vent.

He turned to the backseat, to Belle. "Does it feel colder?"

Belle just shrugged. Some assistants, right?

I drove for a few more blocks, and then pulled over on an empty stretch of the shoulder. The gas station was still in sight, in my rearview.

I shut the car off. Raphael looked at me, puzzled.

"Now we get to do a little test," I said.

"There's nothing about any kind of test in our deal," Raphael said.

"I couldn't give a fuck about that," I said. "Let's go."

I got out of the car. A few bystanders, back near the gas station, looked our way. I walked around to the passenger side of the Camaro and stood on the grass by the shoulder. I did zip my jacket up a bit. He was right, it did feel colder.

I should have done this before I signed the agreement, but what I wanted to do wasn't possible for me in the Dead Zone. I needed to check, before I did anything, that none of this was a setup. If Oriax was a part of this. I wouldn't put any of this drama past Azazel. He loved a convoluted plan. And it would explain why Raphael looked like a demon.

Because he actually was one.

So I waited until Raphael finally got out.

"We going to thumb-wrestle?" he said.

"Nothing like that," I replied, then tapped into a ghost and summoned my ethereal blade.

Then I frowned. The sword didn't appear.

I tapped into the ghost again. A whisper of a memory came to me, of a drunk father coming home and beating on his wife. I pushed it down and pulled more, willing the sword to appear.

It did not. Was it a daylight thing?

"Something wrong?" Raphael asked.

My hand remained empty. I tried summoning the blade again, tugging large amounts of energy. Memories flew through me, of beating the wife until her nose bled, breaking my daughter's legs, killing the cat, all those pushed into my brain, one crowding the next.

I swallowed them down and forced the blade to appear.

But it didn't.

"Damn," I said.

"Whatever you're going to do," Raphael said, "it'd be nice if you actually did it."

I only knew the one test, to see if Oriax had disguised a body differently than what it was. If she had made Azazel into Raphael. Or Belial.

But if my blade wouldn't appear, what else could I use?

I had Nick's knives. I was outside the Dead Zone, so silver, holy water, those things should at least damage a demon. I had to hope it would disrupt any kind of changing spell.

"Hold on," I said. I opened the passenger door, leaned over, and pulled a knife from beside my seat.

"Really?" Raphael asked. "It's the first day of our deal and you're going to try to kill me? With that?"

"Relax," I said. "It's just a test."

I had him hold out his hand, palm out. I held my hand underneath his, and laid the flat of the blade on his palm. He held back from jerking, and both of us watched the blade sizzle against his skin. Raphael tightened his jaw and forced his eyes to look at me over the burning flesh.

In my ethereal sight, Raphael never changed. There was no flicker. No morphing body, nothing changed in his spark. No fake Raphael outside covering a hidden Azazel interior.

I hoped that was enough.

I leaned Raphael's seat forward, and reached out for Belle's hand.

"I'll pass," she said.

"You don't get a pass," I said.

"Then I'll wait a few years, and let everything settle itself out," she said.

"That's fine," I answered. "But I get the feeling you have a problem you need taken care of. And I'm the guy you want to do it. But I'm not going one step further until we do this."

Belle still waited.

"I'm sure you know about Oriax," I prompted. "If we're all keeping our words here, I need to know you're the person you are telling me you are."

She looked over my shoulder, at Raphael. Then she rolled her eyes and held her hand out.

I repeated the test with her, with the same result.

"Good?" she asked.

I raised both eyebrows at her. "You know the meaning of that word?"

One eyebrow arched, and the corner of her lip turned up in a little sneer. Just a little, but I caught it. Which again, wasn't very assistantlike. "What do you know about what a word means, Fergus Grimm?"

That seemed ominous.

"Hey, you should at least chrome these wheels out," Raphael said, behind me. "This car deserves better."

I took a breath and backed out the passenger side, so he could get in.

"You won't be in it long enough to worry about it," I said while we were changing places.

"Says who?" Raphael said. "It's a long way to Colorado Springs."

I walked around to the Camaro and got in the driver's seat. "That where we are going?"

"You think vampires don't like to ski?" he asked.

I fired up the car and pulled back out on the road. "Last I heard, it's a daylight activity."

CHAPTER THIRTEEN

Johnny lay on his bed, the room dark around him. There was a slight hum of the air unit in the background. A few thumps from someone with heavy feet, on the floor above him. Other than that, it was quiet, and warm enough he was sleepy.

Johnny had texted Gabrielle, coming back from Nick and Sarah's room. He had fallen asleep waiting for her to text back. It had been a long day. And so far, a short night. He felt a little out of place here. He was with his friends, but they all had their own thing going on. Their own lives.

Nick and Sarah were maybe together, maybe not. Now that Sarah seemed to reciprocate Nick's feelings, Nick struggled with what to do next.

And Grimm, well, was Grimm. Implacable. Johnny had been convinced he would die the way he lived, hardheaded and doing what he thought best, even if that thing was starving himself to death. Johnny had been surprised to see Grimm get up that morning. Surprised at the energy, the burning desire underneath his friend.

Surprised, but happy. Jen had been a large blow, one he wasn't sure Grimm could recover from.

His group of friends was different than most, Johnny thought. They had grown up together in a world where people moved a lot. They were small-town kids. They had learned how to rely on each other at a young age. There were bonds there, tying them together, that would always be there.

Johnny didn't know many people like them.

He woke later in the morning, after a couple of insistent bleeps from his phone.

Hey.

Hey, u there?

Sry with father.

Back now. U need something?

It was always funny to him, the deliberate manner in which Gabrielle spoke, and how bad her grammar was when she texted. It was a weird mix of shorthand and proper language.

I'm up now, he messaged. *Fell asleep.*

So lazy. Her reply. *Whatever do I c in u?*

Good looks. Funny. Great in the sack, he replied.

Funny, thats 4 sure. Followed by a laughing emoji. The one with tears coming out of the eyes.

Johnny shook his head. He was dating the heir of the largest vampire family on the earth. Someone who dressed to kill, and measured every work she spoke to maximum effect. And she had just used the roll-on-the-floor emoji.

The contradiction in her, the mix of the young girl she had been, with all the hopes and dreams of her childhood, and the serious, practical woman she was now, was maybe what he liked most about her.

Free for a call? he asked.

His phone rang as an answer. He had set it to a song, about a guy who wore sunglasses at night.

"You text like a fourteen-year old girl," Johnny answered, smiling.

"I don't see how," Gabrielle said. "When I was fourteen years of age, there were no cell phones. I communicated with letters."

"Maybe it's an innate skill," Johnny said. "Like, in the female DNA."

"Sexist much?" she asked, a smile in her voice.

"Not at all," he said. "I like your female DNA. How are you?"

"Things are settled down here, a bit," Gabrielle answered. "They are still not happy with me, for allowing the drug to be destroyed."

"It's not like you had much choice there," Johnny said.

"We both know that," she answered. "*They* do not."

They both knew she was talking about her father and his council of advisers. A close circle of vampires, and the humans that supported them. The humans were what a traditional vampire family called complements.

"How is the family?" he asked. "With Paris, and Rome?"

Gabrielle's father, Victor Dumont, led the vampire clan in Europe. With Dead Zones surrounding Paris and Rome, the family had taken a large blow. They had lost contact with at least half of their family, vampires and their human counterparts both.

The clan was still figuring out the damage. Luckily the Dumont family had been in England at the time the Dead Zones appeared there. They had been in a council, worried about what had happened in Grafton, and how they would move forward without the drug, and against the Antonados.

One of the good things that had come out of that, for both Johnny and Gabrielle. Otherwise, they all might have been in their estate, in Paris. As it was, they had lost a lot of close retainers, and some of their brothers and sisters, who had remained there.

"The family is still recovering," she said. "It will never be the same."

After Grafton, Gabrielle had left to go back home. She had to report to her father, of the damages done, the people lost, the drug destroyed.

She had also wanted to stay away from Sarah. At the time Sarah had been under a curse. Her blood would call to vampires, and get stronger over time. Johnny had stayed to help his friends, but Gabrielle had wanted to avoid that temptation.

And now the Dumonts were reeling from the devastating blow of Paris and Rome. They had lost large parts of their families, their homes, not to mention the financial loss. All of which helped them to survive, vampires and their counterparts, in this world.

Johnny didn't know when he would see Gabrielle again.

"How are you?" Gabrielle asked.

She wasn't just asking about how he was doing. She was asking about how he was *feeling*. Johnny was Gabrielle's counterpart, what some of the less-understanding people called thralls. Gabrielle had bitten him, a while ago. At the time, Johnny had joked that it was the getting to third base of the vampire dating world.

Managed properly, the connection between vampire and counterpart only enriched both. But let time linger between bites, and, well …

Johnny stopped his hand from touching the side of his neck. Where two puncture wounds had been, a few weeks ago. It had only been a few weeks, and he was better than the junkies he had seen. "I'm okay," he said.

"Tell me true," she said. "Are you?"

He waited a moment. Counterparts could move faster, heal a little better, use their senses more completely than regular humans. Johnny had felt more alive, after being bit. Life was more enriched, vibrant.

There was only a set amount of time he could wait, though. After a while, the need for another bite would grow, like an itch that he couldn't scratch. Gabrielle had shown him, before asking him to be her counterpart, what it would be like if something happened to her, or if they broke up.

Johnny shuddered at the memory. It had been in Grafton, in a house that no longer held a family. The human she had shown him was no longer human. He was someone locked in a basement, long tears down his neck, where he had dug in with his fingernails. His eyes had locked on to Gabrielle, and he had pulled at the chain keeping him there.

Gabrielle had shown Johnny what it was like to be lost. She explained her family did what they could, but when they found counterparts in this state, they had to kill them. There would be no coming back from the bloodlust when it fully took you.

Johnny had still signed up. And hadn't regretted it. But now his mind focused on where Gabrielle bit him, where his hand had been reaching, as if to scratch the spot. He pushed away the memory of that man with the gouges down his neck

He wasn't close to that yet. "Pretty sure."

"Good," Gabrielle said. "If the urge grows, then I will come there, no matter what."

She would not want him to become a junkie. A feral human, looking for a fix from any vampire. In their craze, those beasts would even bite other humans, hoping to relieve the desire, the need, if only for a moment.

Johnny didn't want that, either. But he didn't need Gabrielle to worry.

"So, when will that be?" he asked.

She sighed. "I don't know. A lot of people died in Grafton. With little to show for it. I am no longer the apple of my father's eye."

Johnny had hoped to be with Gabrielle after Sarah, but that had changed with Jen's death. He thought he would be helping his friends for just a bit while Gabrielle went home and confessed what had happened in Grafton. She thought Johnny would be safer with his friends, without the threat of someone taking her failure out on him.

The vampire families were more civilized than people thought. Still, at times there was a survival instinct in vampires, a predator/prey thing. Vampires who failed to have that killer instinct didn't remain long. Which was why, when Gabrielle had come back empty-handed from Grafton, without the drug, she was worried that Johnny would suffer for it.

And then the Dead Zones had appeared, and had raised the emotional stakes of that game.

"My father is not entirely displeased. Dominic's power has lessened," Gabrielle said. "And the line of succession broken, with Raphael dead."

Dang it. That was something he should have told her. But the phones hadn't worked in the Dead Zone, and things had happened fast after they left.

"Ummmm," Johnny said. "About that."

She grew immediately quiet. Intensely quiet. Finally, "Tell me."

"It's why I wanted to talk," Johnny said. "It's about Raphael."

"I fear to know," she said.

"Yeah," he said. "We saw him."

"You have got to be fucking kidding me." Gabrielle didn't curse often. And didn't shout almost ever. "That bastard is alive?"

"We found him in the Dead Zone," Johnny said. "Or he found us."

"How the fuck did that happen?"

"We don't know," Johnny said. "But he convinced Grimm that only he can help Grimm find Dominic."

Johnny told her the whole story. She had known about Jen, but Johnny told her everything that had happened in the Dead Zone, and everything afterward. What Grimm planned to do. His call to Nick.

"So the group of us here, we hoped you would know where Dominic might be hiding," Johnny said. "So we could go help Grimm."

"And you say Raphael is with him," she said.

Johnny noted where her attention was focused. "We're pretty sure, yeah."

"And you are sure he was dead?" she asked. "In Grafton?"

"The way Nick described it, there was no other way he could be," Johnny said. "Nick even pulled the bat out of Raphael's head. That body was cold."

"Dammit," she said.

"What are you worried about?" he asked.

"Do you think they are going to find Dominic," she asked, "or kill him?"

"To be honest, I don't know," Johnny said. "Grimm wants to find his mother. He thinks she can help him with Jen."

She was quiet again. For a long time.

"Babe?" Johnny said.

"What do you know about your friend Grimm?" she asked. "His powers?"

The way Gabrielle asked, her tone, told Johnny she knew a lot more than she had told him.

"What do *you* know?" he asked.

"I am afraid," Gabrielle said, her voice tiny. Johnny had never heard the like from her.

"Well, tell me," he said. "What can I do?"

"You can wait," she said. "I will have to tell my father this."

"Does that mean you might be coming over here?"

"It is likely," Gabrielle said. "And it may not be a good thing. My fear is, my father will want to be there himself."

CHAPTER FOURTEEN

The drive was long before it began, and felt longer now. It had rained for a good part of the day, a hard, pelting rain that slickened the road and had me driving slower than I wanted.

As much as I loved the Camaro, the car wasn't the best on cold, wet surfaces. I had to hold the gas steady and almost cruise out of every turn, after accidentally fishtailing a few miles back.

The windshield wipers rubbed against the glass. It was humid enough I had to turn the defogger on, and the hot, dry air dried out my eyes. Clouds darkened the sky to the west, dark gray clouds with black bottoms, under which curtains of water fell to the earth. We were driving right into the storm. The rain was so thick, cars around me had put on their hazard lights, something I refused to do.

It was quiet in the Camaro, other than the rubbing of the wipers and the drumming of the rain. Belle apparently felt no need to talk. Raphael had tried to turn on the stereo, once. I had turned it back off.

The baseball bounced under the rearview mirror as the Camaro jostled over the road. Raphael reached up to touch it.

"Don't," I said. That was Danny's.

Raphael sighed. His voice was a little tired, and a little angry. "I get that you hate me. I even hate you back. But it's going to be a long couple of years if you keep being like this."

"I wasn't the one who wanted to come along," I said.

He finally stayed quiet, turned to look out the window.

We fought through the storm and stopped on the other side, at a gas station. I filled up the tank and got some coffee and a candy bar. Raphael got a banana. I wouldn't have thought him a health nut.

We got back in the car and took off. The sky was still heavy with clouds. The rain had gone from a horizon-darkening curtain to a light drizzle. We weren't making great time, but we were in Arkansas. I was hoping to make it into Oklahoma before the day was out, and pushed the car accordingly.

"What can you tell me about Azazel?" Raphael asked.

He wouldn't get it. I didn't really care to talk at all, much less to him.

"Why don't you ask your friend?" My eyes flicked to the rearview mirror. "She's known him longer."

The hum of the car's engine filled the silence for a bit.

"Long or short," Belle finally said, "the time you know him doesn't matter. Once you've met Azazel, it is easy to say he is a man who cares not about what he says."

I held back a laugh. "This, from a demon from hell?"

Her eyes met mine, in the mirror. "Words matter," she said. "There is still honor among thieves."

"Sure," I said. "It's why you have contracts you have to sign with red ink."

She was right about one thing. Azazel couldn't be trusted. With anything, at any word. Everything he said or did had a purpose, and no one would ever know what that purpose was. Actions and plans behind schemes and designs, all in a pattern only the demon kept track of. I believed I finally understood that now.

Maybe if I really wanted to defeat Azazel, to kill him, I just needed to stop paying attention to him. To anything he did or said, and stop playing his games.

I snorted. Funny how the demon could get me thinking that whatever choice I made, it wasn't exactly what he wanted. Whenever I did finally come after him, in the back of my mind I would still wonder if I wasn't doing exactly what Azazel wanted me to do.

Hell, Raphael could be here because Azazel wanted him here.

"Some people trust him," I said. "Oriax. Sabnock. Vine. Malthus and Malphus."

"They will learn." Belle's lips curved in a tiny smile. "Ask Kimaris, or Buné."

Those were the two demons, friends of Azazel's, who had been locked up in the Key. Whom I had then killed, with an ethereal blade that no longer came when I called it.

Though with our agreement, I didn't feel the need to tell Raphael or Belial that little detail, at the moment. They were probably counting on me using that sword, and six hundred and sixty-six days were a long way from today.

"Why do you want to know about Azazel?" I asked Raphael. "You never were the type to care about that stuff before."

Before I had killed Raphael, I meant. Back then he had been short-sighted, and only concerned with how the world affected him. He had never gone out of his way to learn about things not directly in front of him.

"Death changes a person," he said. "I think it's changed me in more ways than one."

"I'm not sure it's an improvement," I said.

Raphael laughed. "Don't get me wrong, I'm still an asshole. But I'm learning."

That was a scary thought to me. He and I had always rubbed each other wrong. Mainly because he thought he could do whatever he wanted, to whomever he wanted to do it to. And his downfall had always been his short-sightedness. He never had thought about the consequences of his actions.

If he pulled back from that, even just a little, and learned to think, and plan ahead, he would be much more dangerous.

And I had enough dangerous things around me, at the moment.

"Have you wondered why I found you, Grimm?" Raphael asked.

"I keep thinking it's just my bad luck," I said.

"It's because of the last thing you said to me," he said. "Right before you killed me."

"I'm where all this ends."

I remembered those words. I remembered saying them and punching the end of a broken bat through Raphael's skull.

Raphael half turned in his seat. His face, for once, was serious. Studious, even. "Powerful words, right? Maybe one of the truest things I'd ever heard. You *are* where things end."

I shivered. He was right. I was where things ended. All kinds of things. Demons. Vampires. People. Raphael. Greg. Father Benjamin. Buné. Kimaris. My regiment. Hundreds, if not thousands, of ghosts.

Danny.

Jen.

What was I, that this was what I had become?

Killing Raphael had been a turning point for me. One where I had become someone better. Someone who didn't run from problems, but solved them. At the time, I had been elated, exhausted, and a little worried. I had wondered what was next. Maybe all of that would be how someone felt after getting to the top of Mount Everest.

It was just like evil, to find a new way to creep back into my life. Like cockroaches, or weeds. Maybe I would never be finished killing him. Maybe each time I did, Raphael would pop back up. Different. Stronger. Smarter.

Killing Raphael had been a long time coming. I had finally finished something. Only, it turned out that was just the beginning of the climb.

I could mope about it. Or I could keep killing the cockroaches when they came back. I would just have to learn how to make the killing stick.

Maybe the next time would be the last time. I smiled. That would be something to look forward to.

Raphael seemed unaware of the impact his words had had on me. "So, when I learned what had happened to me, where I had been sent, and who had manipulated me in Grafton ..." He grinned. "I knew exactly who I needed to end him."

I'd had enough of the conversation. It was getting dark outside, the real dark of night, instead of the false dark of the rain.

In order to keep him from talking, I turned on the radio. Found a rock station. Turned it up until Raphael winced. Grinned to myself, and kept driving. It was still a long way to Colorado Springs.

CHAPTER FIFTEEN

Sometime before midnight I pulled off at a hotel, at a random interstate exit. The radio was still playing. No one was talking. So I slowed off the ramp and headed down the road toward one of the few buildings open, a generic tan building, yellow sign, red letters.

The Camaro rocked back and forth over a pothole as I drove into the parking lot. I parked in front of the office window, a large square plate of glass on the front of the building. A young man slumped behind the desk inside.

"We stopping?" Raphael asked.

"Got to sleep sometime," I said.

"I can drive, you know," Raphael said.

"Not while I'm breathing," I said. I'd never be able to close my eyes with two demons in the car.

Plus, I had another reason for wanting to be by myself tonight.

I walked in and got a single room. The kid asked me if I needed a double, and I told him no. He looked at me funny, and then pointedly looked at my car. I just stared at him until he gave me a key. I gave him cash and walked back out.

Raphael and Belle stood outside the car. I opened the trunk, got my bags, and then locked the Camaro up.

"You get us a room?" Raphael asked.

"Nothing in the deal about that," I replied. "I'm assuming you all can afford your own place."

Raphael rolled his eyes and went in.

"I'll be out first thing in the morning," I said.

Belle's mouth curved in a tiny smile. She did that a lot. Like she knew something I didn't. It wasn't my favorite quality about her.

"I'm sure we'll be there," she said. "You should try to get along with us better."

"He killed a friend of mine," I said. "And you're a demon. This is likely the best you're going to get."

"Let me ask you something," she said. "What if Raphael waited until the very last day of your deal before helping you?"

I hadn't thought about that. Could Raphael screw me over by giving me just a day to kill Azazel? It shouldn't matter in the terms of the deal, but Belle had told me my thing was listed first. I hoped it didn't matter, but the truth was I wouldn't know unless it happened.

"I guess I would have to find a way to kill Azazel while I'm waiting," I said.

"And how's that going for you so far?" she asked.

My jaw tightened. I went to walk past her, but Belle held out her hand.

"Like it or not, Raphael might be the best way for you to get rid of Azazel," she said.

"That's something you have a vested interest in as well," I said.

"True," she said. "I'd like to point out, as the party backing this venture, it would behoove you to play well with all of us."

Behoove. A word I think I last heard from Azazel, in a motel room, before all this had started. I hadn't liked it then, and I didn't like it now.

"So, what are you saying?" I asked. "We do the 'enemy of my enemy' thing? Look who's been watching too many supernatural shows now."

"There is no need to be friends," she said. "Maybe just scale back the antagonism. Just good business, when you have to work with someone."

When a demon thought enough of your behavior that she wanted to give you a lesson in manners, that made a point all on its own. Maybe it was time to revise what I was doing with Raphael. I didn't like him, and I would kill him again, but maybe I didn't have to be a total ass about it.

Though it was kind of how he and I worked.

"Whatever you think you've got on me," I said, "you need to think about it some more."

"What do you mean?" Belle asked, eyebrows raised.

"I mean getting me to work with Raphael," I said. "Snide comments, little suggestions to guide me."

"It's just good business," she repeated.

"It's not," I said. "I understand why you picked me for this. Why you need my help. However you think you're going to control me during this, after this, just understand it's not going to work out how you think."

Belle smiled then. "You think?"

"I do," I said. "I haven't been successful in a lot of things. In fact, I've failed more times than I've won. But there's one thing you aren't taking into account."

"What's that?" she asked. "We'd be interested to know."

"I'm still standing here," I said. "And whatever the score is between me and the rest of the world, it's a lot closer game now than it was when it started."

Belle didn't have anything to say about that. So I headed down the walkway to my room, entered, and shut the door behind me. Making sure to lock it, I put the little latch across the jamb.

This room felt no different than any of the other hotels and motels I'd slept in over the past ten years. There was one large front window, with thick musty drapes drawn closed over it. A table in front of the drapes, with a hard padded chair set off to the side. The air unit was running, or actually rattling, blowing a warmish air into the room.

There was just the one bed, maybe a twin, maybe a queen. Big enough for me. It was covered in a blue bedspread, which had been tucked tightly into each corner. It was surprisingly well made, as if someone had taken care in here.

The fibers in the medium-length tan carpet lay in a uniform, criss-crossed pattern, as if someone had carefully run a vacuum over the floor. I dropped my bag off and used the bathroom, which was cleaner than most hotel rooms I'd been in, and smelled faintly of bleach. Whoever worked here took a little pride in what they did.

I ate one of the protein bars left in the duffel bag, working it into a paste in my mouth. It tasted like blueberry pancakes with a hint of syrup.

I had to wash it down with some water from the bathroom, a couple of times. The bar had turned my tongue a light blue.

Then I got ready. I sat in the chair by the table. And I focused on pulling out my ethereal blade.

Nothing.

I found a ghost in the distance. Something that cried a lot. I swallowed and tapped it and held its energy inside me. Forced it into my hand. Thought about pulling a knife, about needing a sword. I thought of killing Kimaris, and Buné, and how the blade had felt each time it appeared in my hand. Cold, but powerful. Heavy, but light. Metal, yet air. The energy of the blade.

Still nothing.

What the hell was wrong with me? If the blade didn't appear when I needed it, would the armor? Or the wings?

I kept working at it. I kept getting nothing. At some point the ghost dissolved under my pull, and I had to find another. After living through and pushing down a particularly unpleasant memory of a razor blade, a warm bath, and slit wrists.

Was I the person I believed I was? Had the ghosts changed me? Had their memories tainted me? Did I need to pull from something better, more pure, for things like the sword and armor to appear?

That didn't make sense. The sword had appeared when I pulled from the worst of the ghosts around me, both times I had used it. And it wasn't like good spirits lay around in abundance on earth.

The memories of the last ghost still reverberated through me. The self-harm one. How she had cried and cried, then slit her wrists in the tub, and cried some more. For some reason, my brain tied that to when Nick had shot Raphael, and how he had healed.

I stood up, before the bed. Opposite it was a dark oak chest of drawers, three wide and two deep. A flat-panel television on top, and a mirror behind it.

I pushed the television to the side. I took my jacket off, and laid it on the side of the dresser. Then I took one of Nick's knives out of its sheath, and held the point of it against my forearm. I wondered if maybe I was crazy. Or if the last ghost had tipped something over in me, had broken open the vault I had locked all the bad memories in.

I set my jaw and jabbed the knife into my skin.

Dark blood welled up around the point and dripped down my forearm. The pain was hot, and sharp. No smoke drifted up from the tip of the blade, or my arm. I took a breath and tugged the blade across my skin, parting a channel there. The drips of red became a river.

I pulled from the second ghost and healed. As I did, I flipped on my ethereal sight.

Little flickers of lightning began to stitch the skin together. Just like what had happened to Raphael. The electric tendrils concentrated around the cut, closing it up. For me the color of the tendrils was blue, like the clear water of the Caribbean.

The spark inside my chest was mostly blue, in the mirror. But touches of red flared through it, in brief moments. Here and there scarlet would glisten, like bright flares of a dying star.

Ruby in the skies with diamonds…. The words came to me, crazily, in that moment. Bastardizing some song in a way that didn't make any kind of sense. Maybe because my mind was in a million pieces, and what it tried to put together didn't have a chance of making sense.

Until a sudden realization brought one clear thought to my mind.

The knife fell from my hand.

I let out a bitter laugh.

I might have discovered the reason the sword would no longer appear to me.

It seems like Raphael and I were a lot alike. We had both changed, in the past few days. Maybe even becoming the same thing.

The question was why.

I swallowed, hard. Let out a big breath. Whatever was happening, I wouldn't figure it out now. I went to the bathroom and grabbed one of the white towels hanging there. I used it to clean up the pool of blood on the dresser, and felt a little bad for the person who had done such a good job cleaning a hotel room in the middle of nowhere.

I put the towel back in the bathroom. My arm was as good as new. I turned the light off there and walked back out to the main room.

Jen's ghost was sitting on the bed, watching me.

I stood there silently, and stared back at her. My breathing grew shaky. I couldn't get enough air. My hand balled into a fist, and I forced it back open.

Seeing her might have been too much for me then. Jen was everything

I wanted, and everything I couldn't have. I had promised myself I would bring her back, and here I was, in a car with Raphael, and I had just found out that I might be turning into a demon.

Still, it was Jen. And even as a ghost, she settled me down, just being here.

"Hey," I finally said.

Hey, she mouthed back.

"Can you hear me?" I asked her.

She shook her head, then repeated the words.

Can you hear me?

I shook my head.

She held up her first two fingers and used them to point at herself, at her eyes. Then she used the same two fingers to point at me.

"You're watching me?" I asked, slowly. Making sure my mouth formed each word correctly.

She nodded.

I slipped the Key out from under my shirt. The stone circles seemed to glow a little, in the room. "From here?"

She nodded again.

"Jen," I said, and then started to cry. If there was a moment I needed her, this was it. Warm tears streamed down my cheeks. A moment later she was floating before me, one of her hands near my face, her thumb trying to wipe the tears away. And I felt nothing.

She frowned, angry, and spun away.

I held back a scream of rage. So hard, to be this close to someone who completed me, and yet be unable to hold her. To help her. Or to be held by her.

Impossible to describe that kind of pain.

So I finally walked over to the chair, and sat down. It was hard. The pads had gotten thin with age. I put my elbow on one knee, and laid my forehead into that hand so that it would support my head. I spoke into the floor.

"I don't know what's happening to me," I said.

Jen couldn't hear me. But it didn't matter. If I said something, and she couldn't help me with it, she would be hurt. It was the type of person she was, wanting to be there for me. If there was one thing I could make sure of right now, it was to make sure nothing hurt her anymore. Especially by me.

I looked up. She was sitting on the bed in front of me, her eyes a mix of worry and great anger. Her jaw was set, her arms folded over her chest, her eyebrows lowered.

"Hey," I tried again.

She shook her head. Then she pointed at me, and then moved that same hand in a circular motion, like she was polishing a surface. Or washing a car.

I shook my head. "I don't understand."

She did the same motion. Pointed at me, then washed the car. Pointed at me, then washed the car.

"Tell me," I said, one hand wiping my cheeks.

Slowly she formed the words *You take care of yourself.*

"It's so tough," I said. "None of this feels worth it, without you."

Her lips thinned. She pointed at me, then washed the car.

"Jen," I said.

She pointed at me, then washed the car. Then drew a cross over her heart.

"Jen," I said again.

She slammed her fist against the bed. It actually passed through it. Then she pointed at me, washed the car, and drew a cross over her heart.

I got it.

"Okay," I said.

Her chest swelled, as if she took a deep breath. Then she arched an eyebrow, and waited.

"I will take care of myself," I said. "I promise."

She crossed her heart again.

"I promise, Jen," I said. "I do."

She nodded a final time, and smiled. Even for a ghost, it was a beautiful smile. One that would always and forever make me feel a little taller.

"This is going to be so tough, without you," I said. Bringing her back would be a miracle, and this was just the first step along the path. This would be the longest journey of my life, and I was doing it without the one person who could make me do anything.

I had no idea how I would keep going on. I would have to lean on my hardheadedness. I would have to count on it.

She repeated the cross over the heart action.

I frowned. "You know I promised. No need to nag me about it."

She smiled again, something mischievous, accompanied by a wink. Which had me chuckle.

"You did say you would haunt me forever." I reached out my hand. She laid hers above mine, and we did the best we could to pretend our fingers were entwined together.

Jen tapped her chest and crossed her own heart. Then she laughed. Soundless laughter, but I joined in anyway. My loud belly laughs echoing her silent ones.

It was a happy moment, and felt good. I felt good. Jen looked good, she always did, even as a ghost. She floated just above the bedspread. Little unseen currents picked up pieces of her hair, so that they floated above and behind her, blond-blue strands drifting in the night. There was the slightest scent of honeysuckle and rain.

"I'm bringing you back, you know," I said. Speaking slowly, mouthing the words.

I know, she said.

"You think it's possible?"

A shrug.

It seemed like something she wasn't thinking about, in a serious manner. Maybe she was just more worried about me. Or maybe she didn't want to have that hope, only to find out that bringing her back to life wasn't possible. Or that I couldn't do it.

"You should know better," I said. "I'm pretty stubborn about things."

She smiled again.

We sat there for a while, in the quiet early of the night. Enjoying being around each other, however we could get it, and for whatever it was worth. I got up and got undressed, and pretended to do a little striptease for Jen. It went poorly, but it got her laughing.

Still, there was a tension through the air. Of being with Jen, and not being able to convey the things I wanted to convey. Of wanting to hold her to me, and my arms passing through her. Of wanting the feel of her skin against mine, of her heartbeat, thudding hard in her chest, of her lips ...

Impossible to describe.

I finally turned out the lights and slipped under the tight covers of the bed. The sheets were cool and soft, and I worked my feet at the bottom until I untucked everything, so that my feet could be in the open air. I liked my feet free.

Jen lay next to me, floating. Pretending to put her head on one arm.

I stared at her and wondered when I would see her again. The image of her the night before, fading away, frustrated, ran through my mind. Neither of us could control the time we had to spend with each other, and I wondered if this time would be the last.

It made it tough for me to close my eyes and go to sleep.

I think Jen wondered the same thing. She seemed comfortable, lying there, but her eyes were sad. There was something she wanted to tell me, but like me, she was enjoying this moment for what it was.

"Hey," I said, softly. "Tell me."

Her lips curved, just a little. She held up her hand to her mouth, pointing her first two fingers down, like incisors.

It took me a moment. My brows lowered. "Raphael?" I said, slowly.

She mouthed the words *Of course*.

Was she worried about him? Or Belial? Or the contract?

Those things would all have their day. Now I would do what it took to bring Jen back. Then I would deal with Raphael and Belle. "One thing at a time," I told her.

She shook her head. She pointed at me, and then crossed her fingers over my heart.

You promised, she reminded me.

"I know," I said again, staring into her face, eyes open in worry. Her hand reached out, pretending to push the hair back from my forehead.

She was worried about me. Not the contract. But me.

Goose bumps shivered across my skin. Tears welled up in my eyes. God, I missed this. I missed *her*.

"Don't worry about me," I said. "I can do whatever it takes."

Then Jen pointed at herself, then made the incisor motion, and then pointed at herself a last time. Then she shook her head, her ghostly hair stirring in the air behind her.

I understood.

And I wondered if she needed from me the same thing I missed from her.

"Oh, Jen," I said. "You are definitely worth it."

CHAPTER SIXTEEN

The next morning there was no evidence of any storm. Sometimes weather was weird. A light rain could come through and leave roads damp for days. Other times a squall could blast over a town and the next day the sun came out bright and shiny and warm.

I woke up later than I wanted. It had been tough for me to fall asleep. I would close my eyes and my mind would start to race. I had been worried that this might be the last time I'd see Jen. It was impossible for me to not stay awake, watching her.

Sometime past midnight, she started to mimic being asleep. Maybe trying to help me relax.

But it didn't. An ethereal Jen had captivated me. I had lain on one elbow and watched her, the tiny currents of the room that moved her hair, that tugged and pulled at her clothes, the ethereal blue glow softly radiating from her form.

And her face, angelic with her eyes closed, a contented, peaceful repose.

Maybe she actually was asleep.

It didn't matter. Sleep could happen tomorrow. I lay awake and took in as much of her as I could. As long as I could.

When I woke up, it was with my arm folded weirdly underneath me, nerves pinched, hand asleep, and Jen gone. The room felt empty, without her glow. Her presence. It was just me, cold, lying above the blankets.

I let out a breath. Then got out of bed. I shook my hand and swore, as pinpricks of feeling came back. Then I took a quick shower and raced outside.

Today was a bright and shiny and warm day. The storm had left no trace of its passage. Everything looked new, under the sun. The air smelled fresh, empty of all scents except for a cool briskness, as I breathed it in.

Raphael and Belle waited, leaning against my car. Raphael looked at his wrist, like he was looking at a watch.

"I get it," I said. "I'm late."

"You tell someone to be somewhere," Raphael said, "be nice if you were there, too."

"What you tell people matters," Belle said.

I frowned at her choice of words, but I was going to try to make the best of the trip. "My bad. I'll get us breakfast."

Raphael's eyebrows rose, and he pulled back a bit, a little surprised.

I had thought about it last night. I had told Jen whatever it takes. Part of that would be working with Raphael. I needed to make sure that I did everything in my power to make that happen, that I didn't make a slight misstep somewhere that broke apart our fragile alliance, or – in my anger – miss a tiny detail that would make all the difference with bringing Jen back.

Raphael had killed Danny. He had tried to kill my friends. He had wanted to enslave me and my mother. The man was, in any way it could be defined, a monster.

But he was also my way to get Jen back. So I needed to do whatever it took to make that happen. I didn't have to be friends with the man, but I could scale back the antagonism a bit. I could try to make our relationship a working one, for the time I needed it.

Danny would understand that. I needed to figure out a way to under-stand it, too.

We got into the Camaro. It fired up like it always did in days like this, the chassis rumbling, the muffler just barely keeping in check a throbbing roar. Like the car was antsy. The gas pedal vibrated with three hundred and fifty horsepower at the ready. I pushed my foot down, we accelerated, and inertia pushed me slightly back into the seat.

We got back on the interstate. I turned on the radio, but kept the volume down this time. It was still playing the rock station, and as I remembered Raphael liked classical music, but I didn't go that far. A song about bells in hell came on, which got me grinning.

A few miles later there was an exit with a bunch of the buffet places I liked. Food for all types. We stopped by and ate. Raphael was a salad and fruit guy, though he took a piece of roasted chicken from one of the metal trays, and looked at it questionably, before taking a bite. Belle ate more like me, pancakes and waffles and sausage and eggs.

I guess demons, like humans, have all types.

I picked up the check. Then we went to a gas station. Topped off the tank and got my usual stuff for the day. I even grabbed a couple of bananas for Raphael, though they were soft and covered in black spots. At least I was trying.

We got back on the road and drove for a while. The rock station faded out into static. I inclined my head to the radio.

Raphael frowned, not understanding.

"You can pick the next one," I said.

"Okay," he said, tilting his head at me. "What the hell happened to the other guy?"

"What do you mean?" My eyes went to Belle in the rearview, who was smiling a little smile.

Go ahead and think you did this, I thought about the demon, the holder of contracts, the enforcer of agreements. *It'll make it easier, in the end.*

"The asshole who was driving yesterday," Raphael said.

"He's still there," I said. My hands turned the wheel a bit as we sank into a steeply banked turn. "Like you said last night. We both hate each other. That's never going to change. But we got this thing to do, so I'm going to try to do it."

"Yeah, well," Raphael said, "this new Grimm worries me."

"Take advantage while you can," I said. "He won't be there forever."

And he wouldn't. He would just be there long enough.

Raphael's eyebrows rose, as if he had a hard time believing me. "Fine," he said, and turned the radio knob so that the red line marking the station moved left. Into the bands where just old music played. Not old music, but *classically* old music.

Raphael's father liked similar music. I guess as much as he might want to, some parts of us never fall far from the tree. Something always stays rooted, close to where we began.

A piece came on the radio, a violin played softly, a plucking on a cello's string in the background. I was disturbed to discover I knew the song. Some canon piece they played at weddings.

A friend of mine had it played at her wedding. Lily Thompson. It was before our team had headed over to Afghanistan. She had married some guy before deployment. And had never made it back.

My whole team had died, the night I found the Key. The short of the story was a building had been blown up underneath us. We had fought creatures called rakshasas, zombielike in appearance, undying. We had gotten to the top and our master sergeant had blown the C-4 at the bottom.

It was the only time I remembered ghosts actually speaking to me. I had woken, trapped, lying in rubble. My entire team trapped in the same way. We all had lain under the rubble and talked to each other, joking. Happy we had made it. Trying to keep our spirits up.

I had been able to dig myself out. The first person I had gone over to, in order to free, had been Lily.

That's when I figured out I had been talking to her ghost.

Turns out, the only person who had survived had been me.

Lily's ghost lay on top of her body. What was left of her had been crushed by a huge slab of rock. What was left of her mind, all the jellylike substance in her skull, pushed out to the side of the stone. Like her head had been burst, like a grape.

Her nickname had been FlowerPower, after some cartoon. She had been like a sister to me. Something between us had clicked. She had told me once she wanted to take her husband to Williamsburg that Christmas. It was an old Colonial town in Virginia that they lit with candles during the holidays, where everyone drank out of tin cups. Old things, tiny and battered and dented.

She had been excited about that. Lilly had tried Coke out of a tin cup in Jamestown and she told me there was nothing like it. The tin was cold to the touch, and the soda tasted completely different.

I took a breath. The classical piece ended, and the station went on to something with a piano. I turned the radio off, holding the wheel tightly in one hand. Keeping my mouth tightly shut.

"There's the guy I remember," Raphael said. "Don't like classical music?"

"It's fine," I replied. "Just bad memories."

"To Pachelbel?" Raphael tilted his head. "Bad marriage?"

I looked over at him, for a long moment. He knew about Jen. "You're making this hard right now."

"Fine," he said, though his tone said he couldn't care less. Raphael waved his hand in the air. "My apologies."

"Sure," I said.

We listened to the piano piece. I didn't know it. Or the next song. I tuned out the music and focused on the road, and driving it. The Camaro responded and flew across the interstate, weaving back and forth through groups of cars, slower packs making their way together west. After we had navigated our way through each pack, the Camaro would accelerate away, free again.

We made good time that day, eating up the miles, as Colorado drew nearer and nearer.

CHAPTER SEVENTEEN

Nick lay back on the bed, arms behind his head, his legs crossed. The bed was lumpy, but he was still relaxed. Content.

Sarah was in front of the bathroom mirror, patting her face with a tiny round piece of cotton. They had gone out this morning and picked up a few things of what she called "necessities," and she was trying them on now.

"Can we get a guitar?" she asked, smoothing something over her cheek.

"What?" Nick asked. He had been lost in thought.

"I used to play one," Sarah said. "I've been missing it."

"I remember." When she started to learn, she had followed other singer-songwriters. She had posters of them on her walls, and would play out on her porch, all the time.

After Danny died, her music had gotten darker. Sarah had gone more goth. She had started wearing tight black leather, and the posters in her room had come down, to be replaced with pictures of vampire bands, he had called them.

He hadn't liked it much.

But maybe that was because she had left the group then as well. Had started partying with other boys. Older boys. Then Raphael.

Who was alive, again.

Nick swallowed away old feelings of anger and resentment. Sarah was here now. They were closer now than they had been, maybe since kids.

But they were together, and yet not together. They slept in the same bed, but they hadn't been *together*. Or even fooled around, much.

He felt like their relationship was like a brittle piece of metal. Nick thought they both were afraid it wouldn't hold, that one additional weight would cause it to shatter. So they both were scared to take everything an additional step.

And with Raphael back, Sarah was asking for her guitar again. Nick couldn't help the jealousy that ran through him. He *knew* it wasn't something Sarah wanted now, but it burned through him anyway.

So he did what he always did when an emotion like that rose up in him. He focused, and remained silent.

Sarah turned her head and looked at him. She had a pale red lipstick on that outlined her mouth in a subtle way, and a light eye shadow that caused her eyes to stand out, and her cheekbones to protrude, ever so slightly.

She saw something in his face, and her face softened. She came over and sat on the bed, reached out, and grabbed both of his hands in hers. Her skin always felt feathery-light to Nick.

"I miss playing," she said again.

Nick forced a smile to his face. Internally he rolled his eyes. He would get her a guitar, no matter what. Even if Raphael walked in through the door.

He had always wanted Sarah to be happy. He had always hoped it would just be with him. And it was so close.

"Sure," he said. He moved his hands so that he could close them firmly around Sarah's. Reassuring her. "We'll find one."

And they had plenty of money, thanks to Grimm. Though what Grimm had done that night, what he had to live through, with that ghost, scared him. Nick had no idea how that didn't leave a scar on a person. And it was something Grimm did a lot.

"What's the matter?" Sarah asked, mistaking the look in his face.

"I was just thinking about Grimm," he said. "About the memories he has to live through."

"Oh," Sarah said. It was something Nick and she had talked about, a few times. And Nick had learned Jen had talked to Sarah about it as well.

Jen had been worried about what doing that would cost Grimm.

Sarah got back up and went to the mirror. Nick couldn't see what she was trying next.

"You think that's something that changes a person?" she asked him.

"What do you mean?"

"I mean," she said, "if someone lives something like that, for years and years, does it change them forever? In a way they can't change back?"

The way Sarah phrased it, Nick didn't think she was talking about Grimm. Or maybe not just Grimm.

Nick had had a similar conversation with Grimm, back behind the barn in Alabama. Maybe a week ago or so now, though it felt like much, much longer. Grimm had a Bible out, like he was going to figure out who he was, and what he was going to do, by reading it. As if he could find out who he was by reading a few sentences in a book. Nick had tried the same thing once, looking for a reason why he had the powers he had.

He had told Grimm, *"Who I was was who I was. I was just looking for a passage somewhere, or a person somewhere, to tell me what I already knew.… I think maybe what matters first is figure out who you want to be. Then go be it."*

Maybe it was ironic, that Nick was having the same talk with Sarah now. He certainly felt like it was, that Nick was giving out life advice.

So he got up and went to Sarah. Put a hand on her shoulder, and kissed the back of her neck, right behind the ear. She closed her eyes and leaned back into him, and let out a tiny, low moan.

The metal held.

"You can be anything you want to be," Nick told her. "Once you figure out who that person is, just go be it."

She turned around in his arms, leaned up, and kissed him, hard.

The door to their room opened. Both of them jumped apart. Nick turned around to see Johnny paused in the doorway, one hand holding the hotel key card, eyes open wide. He looked like he wanted to back out.

"Ummm," he said. "Sorry."

"It's fine," Nick said. Though he still could feel the heat of Sarah's body, leaning against him. "What's up?"

"Gabrielle got back in touch," Johnny said. "We've got trouble."

CHAPTER EIGHTEEN

They sat around the room. Nick and Johnny in the chairs by the table, Sarah on the bed. Nick had a smear of lipstick on his lips, which Johnny couldn't help but grin at. Sarah noticed and smiled at Nick. She leaned over and tried to wipe Nick's mouth with her thumb, but Nick pulled his head back. So Sarah leaned over farther, held his hand with one hand, and wiped his mouth with the other.

Nick's cheeks reddened when he saw the lipstick on her thumb. He lowered his eyes at Johnny. As if daring Johnny to say something.

Johnny did his eyebrow waggle thing. Which everyone hated, but he kind of felt like it was his trademark.

Nick didn't appreciate the gesture. He frowned, just like every other time Johnny did it. Johnny grinned at himself. *Critics*.

It was time to get to the serious stuff. Johnny leaned forward, placing both of his elbows on his knees. "What I'm about to tell you can't go anywhere," he said.

"Who are we going to tell?" Nick said, his face still a little red.

"I know," Johnny said. None of his friends would say anything. But he wanted to make sure they knew how dangerous this knowledge would be, once they heard it. "This could get Gabrielle killed, just because she told me. Us, too. This is something only a few of the head vampires know."

"I get it, man," Nick said. "You know us."

"I do," Johnny said. "I'm just saying, is all."

"So tell us," Sarah said. Johnny wondered if she was a little frustrated too, after having their moment interrupted. The two of them were on this edge, where all they had to do was step across it and be together, but neither one of them could make the first move.

Maybe it was something the two of them couldn't acknowledge, or talk about, but then there had been a moment, and they had started kissing, and things had moved organically where they both would take that step together, and then he had interrupted them.

Which was unfortunate. And Johnny felt a little bad about it. But what he knew was important. He let out a breath. When he told them this, everything would change.

"We all know what Grimm is," Johnny said. "Or what we think he is, right?"

"He's part angel," Nick said.

Johnny held up a finger. "Right. And he's got this geas. It's why he ran from Grafton, because Raphael could order him to do things, and he would have to obey."

"This is nothing we don't know," Nick said. "The geas, Grimm, Grimm's mother. They both are controlled by it."

"Except his mother is the focus of the geas," Johnny said. "So she's even more bound by it."

"To Dominic." Nick blew out a large breath, thinking a moment. "Johnny, what's life-threatening here? We know it already. The bishop told us all of this."

"The bishop told you his *guesses*," Johnny said. "What I'm telling you, and I'm about to tell you, is straight from Gabrielle. It's fact."

Nick and Sarah exchanged a glance between them.

"I get it, guys," Johnny said. "But let me work through it. It's important."

Nick frowned at Johnny. "Go ahead, man."

"Okay," Johnny said. He went over the conversation he had had with Gabrielle, after Grimm called. And that Gabrielle had started to be worried when she found out Raphael was still alive, and that both Raphael and Grimm were looking for Dominic. And how Gabrielle had hung up with a promise to call back.

It had taken a day, but when she called next she had gone from worry to fear. Mixed in with the fear was a little shock. She was slow to answer questions, or even speak at times. Johnny had to lead her through the call. It took a few minutes just to get her to really say anything.

After he heard the news, he became afraid, too.

Johnny just glossed over a lot of that, now that he was talking to Nick and Sarah. He started out talking about the origination of the geas. How it had been created to bind seven angels to seven different vampire clans.

And they knew that over the years some of the angels had been killed. When that happened, other vampire clans had learned that the geas would pass on to an angel's child, should one exist. So they had started breeding them.

Nick motioned his hand in a circle, as if saying, *We know all this, get to the point.*

"Here's the thing," Johnny said. "The geas binds the parties both ways."

He explained what Gabrielle had told them. In order to make sure the angel never had a chance at freedom, each of the vampire clans had to have a successor to pass the control of the geas to. So at the time, each of the vampire families had selected who would first hold the geas. Before they turned them, they had made sure each of the holders had created plenty of offspring. The vampires had come up with a way to continue their family lines.

Nick made the connection. "That's when the families must have been created."

"Exactly," Johnny said.

For centuries the vampire clans had lived as families, as partners with humans. Gabrielle had called it a tradition, the rules the vampires had bound themselves to in order to be better than the monsters they had been called. Gabrielle had always believed vampires had become something more than just predators who fed on human cattle. She had believed she was part of something worthy.

She had found out all that had been a lie.

The only thing holding vampires to their human counterparts was the geas. Her father had explained this to her, when she told him about Raphael and Grimm.

"It was all a lie," Gabrielle had whispered over the phone. She was not handling the news well. She had believed she could have nobility as a vampire. That she was good.

"It doesn't have to be," Johnny had said to her.

"You do not understand," she had replied. "This was something I had *believed* in."

"Just because that's how it started," he had argued, "doesn't mean that it's the way it is now. You're an example of that."

Johnny had stopped talking to Nick and Sarah, lost in the memory of his conversation with Gabrielle. He was worried about her. And he had not found a way to convince her that she wasn't a monster. That her family wasn't evil. Everything she had learned about herself had been turned upside down.

Nick finally said something. "Is that it? That's what you are worried about?"

Johnny shook his head. "Oh no. That was just so you all would understand what I'm about to tell you."

Sarah laid her hand on Nick's leg, her eyes a little pinched. Wondering. Worried. Nick's face was blank, though he did lay a hand on hers.

"If a vampire has no one to pass control of the geas to," Johnny said, "the geas has something like a blowback mechanism. If a vampire dies while the angel they're controlling still lives, all the vampires, in each of the seven families, will die."

"Wow," Nick said.

"Really?" Sarah asked.

"Gabrielle said her father told her the demon gifting the geas to the vampires showed them what would happen," Johnny said. "After they had accepted it."

"Sounds like Azazel," Nick said.

"And that's not even the worst part," Johnny said. "All the angels will be killed, too."

They both got it then. If Grimm killed Dominic, or helped Raphael kill Dominic, he would be signing his own execution.

"Are we sure that Raphael wouldn't get the geas passed to him?" Sarah asked.

"I don't think he's a vampire anymore," Nick said. His face looked up a bit, thoughtful. "I don't know what he is now."

Johnny remembered Nick firing the shotgun into him, and how Raphael had healed, each time. The sparks of red lighting.

"The way he healed," Johnny said. "Reminded me of Grimm."

The room was quiet for a moment. They all were processing what Johnny had told them. Johnny still was processing it, himself.

"Well, you're right," Nick said. "It's a shitload of bad news."

"There's one final piece," Johnny said.

"Seriously?" Nick asked. "More?"

"Victor Dumont sent his angel to kill Raphael and Grimm," Johnny said. "Before they get to Dominic."

"Oh," Sarah said.

"And Victor is coming to America, to make sure the job is done," Johnny added. "Gabrielle thinks other vampires will come, from the other families. No one is going to risk what could happen. It's kind of an all-hands-on-deck situation for them."

Gabrielle had struggled to tell him the last part. About her father sending his angel. Clearly her mind had been on the news that had shattered the foundation of her world. The families were a sham, in her mind. But she had made sure Johnny heard what he needed to, to protect his friends.

Gabrielle was the person he knew she was. But she couldn't see it in herself, not yet. It was something she couldn't let go of. And Johnny worried about what it might to do her. He wanted her here, or he wanted to be there. He knew he helped her, in times like these.

All of their relationships were a little fucked-up. Nick and Sarah were too new, too fragile. She had slept through high school like she was punishing herself, and he had treated her with kid gloves. Neither one of them seemed able to put their past behind them, so they could move forward together.

And Gabrielle and Johnny. At one point Johnny had thought they had the perfect relationship. She was serious, intent. He was happy-go-lucky, taking things a day at a time. They complemented each other well, and were as devoted as any couple could be.

He would never have questioned her, before. He wasn't sure that he questioned her now. But before this day, Johnny would never have worried about her. She had been a bedrock for him, through Grafton. He had counted on that foundation more than he had realized

Nick pulled out his phone, and dialed it. Swore when it went to voice mail. "No one ever answers when you need them to."

"Grimm?" Johnny asked.

Nick nodded, and then looked like he thumb-typed a text message.

"We know where he's headed?" Nick asked.

"Yeah," Johnny said. Gabrielle had told him that as well, knowing that they would want to try to stop her father's angel. That they would want to save their friend. Her father would be angry, but she no longer seemed to care. "Denver."

"We got to get moving, then," Nick stood. "I'm going to go get us a vehicle."

"I'm pretty much ready," Johnny said.

"I'll pack up here," Sarah said. "Won't take long."

Nick tucked his phone in his pocket. "Sounds good. Outside in thirty?"

"We'll see you there," Sarah said. "Be careful."

Johnny watched the two of them look at each other. They were a foot apart, but they could have been a mile. The tension rose in the room, and Johnny wished he wasn't there, and knew whatever he did, it would interrupt what was going on.

Nick ducked his head then. "Will do."

Then he left.

Sarah watched the door shut behind Nick. Then she let out a deep breath. "It's so tough."

"What is?" Johnny asked.

"I know I've slept around," Sarah said. Her voice had always been delicate. Johnny remembered she used to sing, a long time ago. She had played guitar, too, and her voice would break at just the right moment in the song, where, when he was listening to it, it would almost break his heart. "I know what I used to be. It was easy to be with someone when I knew they didn't care about me."

"That's not Nick," Johnny said. Nick cared with great passion. Without holding anything back.

"Yeah," she said. "He's so careful around me, and sometimes I want him to just grab me, you know? But then I'm worried that what I've done, that he will see that in me, and that he doesn't want me, because of that."

"I think that's about the silliest thing I've ever heard," Johnny said. "Nick will always be someone you can count on."

"You think?" Her eyes were a little wet. "Right before you entered, there was a moment where I thought it was all right. Where we both were ready. And I was so excited, Johnny. And now I'm just scared that the moment passed, and we both missed it."

"Hey." Johnny grabbed her hands and held them in both of his. Waited until her eyes met his, and held his gaze. "You two are going to be great together. I promise, the next time I have earth-breaking news, I'll wait for you guys to come out of the room first."

A laugh burst from her, one that ended as quickly as it had begun. She pulled away from Johnny, and wiped her nose and eyes, sniffing a few times.

"How is Gabrielle?" she said, maybe trying to change the subject.

"Not great," Johnny admitted. He reached up and lightly rubbed a spot on his neck. "I'm worried about her."

Sarah had been the one who had liked Gabrielle from the beginning. Maybe because she had dated a few vampires, in Grafton. But she had treated Gabrielle like any other date Johnny would have introduced his friends to.

"She's taking the news hard?" Sarah asked. "About the families, and the geas?"

"Yeah." Johnny let out a breath. "I wish I could be there for her."

"Our relationships are fucked-up, aren't they?" Sarah said. And it was close enough to what Johnny had been thinking that he laughed.

"Sometimes," he said. "But sometimes I think they're all fucked-up, part of the time. It's the good ones that get through this."

"I think I've only seen one relationship I've ever wanted for myself," Sarah said. "Jen and Grimm."

Johnny tilted his head. "They were kind of perfect for each other."

"They argued sometimes," she said. "And hell, Grimm left for a decade. But when he came back, for Jen, it was like he had never left."

Sarah stopped then, looking at the mirror above the sink. Johnny wondered if she was comparing herself to her sister. Or her relationship to theirs.

Johnny couldn't help but do the same thing. Grimm and Jen were maybe what he had thought about when he first met Gabrielle. He might have thought, *I could have what they have, with her*.

That realization was a little surprising to him. But also something he understood.

"You know, it's the one thing I don't worry about," Sarah said.

"What?" Johnny asked.

"My sister," Sarah said.

Johnny had realized he had never seen her be despondent over Jen's death. Sarah had been sad, and she had cried and held Nick, but that was it. It wasn't eating at her. Maybe subconsciously Johnny had thought it was because Nick had been there, but maybe there was more to it.

"It's because I believe in Grimm," Sarah said. "I know she'll be back. That he'll bring her back."

"Really?" Johnny said. He wasn't sure if he believed it. It was enough for Johnny to just be there for his friends.

"Definitely," Sarah said. "It's just something that will happen. If there's anyone who could march into the afterlife and drag someone back, it's Grimm. And if there's anyone worth doing it for, it's Jen."

Johnny thought about it. Grimm was as implacable a person as he had ever known. As a kid, he had thought Grimm unstoppable. Until he had run.

And when Grimm got back to Grafton, Johnny had felt like Grimm was different. Less sure of himself. Haunted, maybe. Fearful, definitely.

Johnny wasn't sure Grimm was the same person now, either. Not like the kid he had been. But he did think Sarah was right. If anyone could bring Jen back, it would be the old Grimm.

And if anyone could maybe bring the old Grimm back, it would be Jen. Even now. Maybe especially now.

For all that to happen, though, Grimm had to stay alive. And Victor Dumont, his angel, all of the other vampire families, they all had a twelve-hour head start on Johnny, Nick, and Sarah. So the three of them had to get moving, to make it to Denver in time to help their friend.

CHAPTER NINETEEN

Once we settled in, the drive hadn't been that bad. It had been quiet, even, for the most part. Belle hadn't talked at all, and hadn't fallen asleep, either, just sat in the backseat and looked out the side window, like a statue. It was eerie, and got on my nerves, so I forced myself to not pay attention to her.

In the past I'd driven days without stopping for a rest. I had gotten good at it, running from Azazel. I knew exactly how many energy drinks, candy bars, and gas stops I needed every five hundred miles I drove. I'd pull up an atlas and know exactly how far I would get that day, and where I would stop.

It just took getting into a rhythm. And rhythms were best developed in the low thrumming of the Camaro's engine, the feel of the tires rolling along the road, and a peaceful, quiet cabin.

Throughout the day the radio played a variety of classical music. Sometimes the news, when a channel wasn't available. Raphael would turn the knob occasionally, bouncing around the lower end of the dial as we left the coverage of one station and drove into another.

He had kept to himself most of the drive. Maybe he was unsure of how to proceed with the new, friendlier me, or maybe he was thinking about seeing his father again, but either way I was happy for the silence. If I believed in an afterlife I would thank heaven for small miracles.

Though thinking about it, I *was* an angel. And apparently there was a hell, so I guessed I should believe in heaven. I just always had been a seeing-is-believing type of guy.

I had always wondered where the ghosts went, after I had lived their memories. Ten years after seeing my first one, I still didn't know. And while I said good riddance to the murderers and rapists, I also feared Danny was gone from this world, forever.

Which brought a certain level of urgency to bringing Jen back. She was on the edge of this world, about to fall out of it forever. Once she was gone, she would be gone.

The sun descended quickly through an empty blue sky. A dark ridge rose, far in the west, like a black wave swelling over the horizon. Right now it was the size of my pinkie finger, a fuzzy darkness running north to south at the edge of the earth, but as we drove along, the strip would grow taller and more defined, and ultimately become the Rocky Mountains.

My good luck had held for most of the trip, but it was failing me now. Raphael was getting restless. It started out with him shifting in the seat. Then he played with the window handle. Cracking the window to the whistle of the wind flying by, then rolling it back closed.

After that he pulled my phone out of the center console, where it had sat in the cup for drinks. Then frowned at me. "You leave something running on this, Grimm?"

"What?"

"It's dead," he said. He opened the glove box, and looked around the seats. "Where's your cable?"

I had packed it up in the trunk. I motioned toward the back of the Camaro with my head.

Raphael sighed.

My eyelid twitched.

He tossed the phone back into the console. It clattered against the holder. Then he fidgeted with the air vents, flipping them up and down.

"All right, man," I finally said.

"What?" he said.

I raised my eyebrows and stared at his hand, which was still holding the tab of the air vent.

He pulled his hand back.

"You try sitting in a car for ten hours without anything to do," he said.

"Whenever that happens," I said, "I'm not going to be flipping air vents and cracking windows."

"Whatever," Raphael said.

He tried to stay still. But it didn't last long. He looked out the side window, then the front, then the side again. A few minutes later his leg started bouncing up and down.

I blew out a breath. I wanted to press on a bit further, but there was no way to reestablish the rhythm I had been rolling with. Not with clown-boy next to me.

"So talk," I said.

"Really?" he said.

"Man, I'll take anything but this," I said, working my neck so it cracked. Little motions in the corner of my eyes, little ticks of sounds, that got on me.

"Then tell me about Azazel," he said.

It was odd, to be riding in the car with Raphael and talking about Azazel. Raphael had been someone I had hated for a long time, and still hated, yet the two of us were going to team up to kill Azazel. Who was one spot above Raphael, on my list.

"Why are you so interested in him?" I asked.

"Because I'm going to take everything he has," he said. "So I want to know everything about him."

"Big goal," I said.

"I don't like being made a fool of," Raphael said. "He played me back in Grafton. I thought he had been helping me, with the drug. That I was going to rule the world. Turns out, that's what he wanted."

"You know what they say about looking a gift horse in the mouth," I said.

"Yeah," Raphael said. "He's good, though. Smooth. A hell of a talker."

"See?" I said. "You know as much about him as I do."

Raphael waited a moment. He tilted his head, like he was weighing what he was about to say. Or maybe wondering if I would laugh at what he was about to say. When he spoke, though, his tone surprised me. It carried an edge of venom, of malice. "I think he loves to create things."

That was a different thought. One I had never had about him before. I was surprised to hear it from Raphael, who had never looked forward or back when he did a thing. He had never been a deep thinker.

"What makes you say that?" I asked, curious.

"He's got all these plans, right?" Raphael said, his eyes narrowed, like he was working all this out. "He steers people the way he wants them, to fit those plans. And people don't plan when they create chaos. People plan to build things."

"Huh," I said. What he said struck me in a way that resonated as truth. It was a side of Azazel I hadn't realized before.

Of course, running from the demon for six years hadn't left me a lot of time to think. Other than the *why me?* part of it.

Thinking about it now, Azazel had built the pentagrams and the cities. His new home. He created the geas. He had created everything in Grafton for the drug, and even had helped create Raphael. He changed everything he touched, almost as if what it had been wasn't his vision but someone else's.

"What's Lucifer have to say about this kind of thing?" I asked.

Belle met my gaze in the rearview mirror.

"Azazel breaks the agreement," Belle said. "That's all we care about."

I wasn't surprised to hear that. Azazel didn't pay attention to a lot of rules.

"He's probably broken a million," I said. "Which one are you worried about?"

Belle's mouth twisted. "*The* agreement."

"Wow." I exaggerated a roll of my eyes. "Thanks for clearing that up."

She sighed now, like I was bothering her. And I didn't care. I hadn't asked her to come along, and I didn't want to play nicely with either of them. That was her request.

"After the fall," Belle said, "there was one condition we all held to. No direct interference. We all gave our word."

"Oh," I said. No interference was an odd way to describe the past couple of millennia. It seemed like the world was getting worse, each year. "So you guys just sit down there in hell and take bets on where people end up?"

"You don't get it," Belle said. "You think this is an evil-good thing. It never has been that."

I waved at the road in front of us. "Well, explain it to me. We've got some time."

"Let me ask you," she said, "why are people good?"

"I like to think that's our natural state," I said. And as soon as I did, I glanced at Raphael. Who noticed the glance, and grinned back at me.

"Really?" she said. "You think you were born good? That you lived life in a good manner? Did nothing wrong?"

I didn't think that. I hadn't always done the right thing. But I had always tried. Before Grafton, I had thought I was good, running and keeping the Key from Azazel. But I had learned that being absent from my friends had put them in harm's way.

So, had I been living a good life? Was I a better person for running from Azazel with the Key than I would have been had I stayed and protected those I loved and cared about?

If I had done that, would Jen be next to me right now? Instead of Raphael.

I thought that might be the case. But I didn't know. All I could do was try.

"I have to hope so," I said.

Belle smiled, like she had scored a point. "Exactly. You have to hope. You don't *know*. You try your best and see where the chips fall. It's *only then* you find out."

I was exactly where I always was. Trying my best, but not understanding the rules of the game. Figuring out things, way too late. After it cost others.

"Seems rigged to me," I said. "If you don't know where you are at until you die, then how can you change? How can you get better? It's too late then."

"You are telling me you don't know the difference between right and wrong?" This apparently was a topic she was passionate about, and Belle leaned forward. Getting closer to me. "What if you knew God existed? Without a doubt. Maybe he grabs you and shows you heaven? What if you *knew without a doubt*, if you were good that's where you would end up? In some place with all your friends and family, having an eternal party?"

Would I have lived life differently? I didn't know. But I didn't think so. I was who I was. I did what I did.

"I think I'd be the same," I said.

"Bullshit," Belle said.

"Really?" I said, surprised at the curse. It was not in line with her assistant persona, the one she played at. And Belle didn't know me. What I decided or why. How I felt about things. "How would you know?"

"I've seen countless examples over thousands of years," she said. "Going to heaven because you know it's real is like giving someone a participation trophy for losing a game. There is no *cost* to it. There is nothing *real* about it."

I frowned at the thought. Did knowing a heaven existed actually cheat the system, or just identify the rules in place? "So Lucifer and God argued about cost?"

"Lucifer wanted people who made it because they were good despite everything," Belle said. "He wanted it to be clear. Not because they were good because they believed they would go to heaven if they were. He wanted people who were worthy without knowing a reward existed. He wanted people who paid a cost for being good. Who held to their word."

There was a story there, at least a parable. Something I had heard in church maybe, the few times I had gone. Maybe Father Benjamin had told it, once. About a test, and a bet, between Lucifer and God.

"Is that what you all do," I said, "just lay down some tests and see what happens?"

Belle's mouth twisted. "There is no need for a test. It is too easy for you humans to slide into a hole, and too hard to climb back out."

That sounded uncomfortably like what I had just gone through, after Jen died. I was still in the hole, and I was trying to get back out.

Though was *this* really climbing back out? Signing a contract with two demons? Working with Raphael, and Belial? Even if I was doing it for Jen?

What was it they said about the road to good intentions?

I avoided that train of thought. It wouldn't take me anywhere I wanted to go.

"So, what," I said, "Azazel ruined your party? What did he do, kill a puppy?"

"What do you think? He said one thing, and did another," Belle said. "He *interfered.*"

That sounded like Azazel. But what could he do to interfere? He had a million schemes. Which of those had really changed the structure of things, as far as heaven and hell were concerned?

It all came back to one thing. "You mean the geas, don't you?"

Slaughtering the forces of heaven. Capturing them and making them slaves. Binding them to vampires to do the will of evil.

Rumor had it, very few angels had been seen since. They were mentioned a lot less today than they had been, at least since the Old Testament. Today, if someone said they saw one, it was likely on the way to a mental institution.

"His actions forced a response," Belle said. "Before then, we were all letting things play out. We had all given our word, to see how they played out."

I hadn't been the greatest listener when I was young. Or the most consistent student. But if I recalled the stories correctly, there had been a whole lot of interference, back then. There had been a flood that had wiped out the earth. Sodom and Gomorrah. Plagues. That was how things had been played out, before the geas.

So, what event had happened after? What response would have been great enough to rile Lucifer and Belial? My shotgun was tucked beside my seat, side angled up. There was a cross scratched on the side, from Patrick. It had been his, before I borrowed it.

Oh.

"The response gave people belief," she said. "Hope." She waved her hand to the world outside the window. "And thus we are here."

Here. In a place where good people go to heaven and bad people go to hell. Supposedly.

"So, in your idea of a world," I asked, "what kind of people end up in hell?"

Belle shrugged. "Does it matter now?"

I guess it didn't. But I wondered. I wondered at what Azazel had pulled up, from below the earth. The large spark in Lake Pontchartrain. Other things, before then.

Azazel had mentioned hell had existed long before the fall. I had always assumed hell to be the place where you went when you sinned. But it didn't sound like Lucifer had always wanted to be king of everything evil. At least from how Belle spoke.

"You know, hell is littered with people Azazel has betrayed," Raphael said.

I wasn't surprised. If hell was the landfill of the earth, where everyone had tossed their trash, well, Azazel had done a lot of dumping there.

"Is there a support group down there?" My lips twisted in a snarky smile. "You a member?"

Raphael laughed. "Damn near," he said. "They greet you when you get sent down there. At least the ones that keep track do."

I wondered how many had forgiven Azazel. The Dead Zones didn't seem to have a shortage of volunteers. "Enough seemed to have joined him up here," I said.

"Yeah, well, trust me," Raphael said. "It's a drop in the bucket compared to what I've seen."

The demon had told me once that it was tough for him to be appreciated in hell. That most of the people who ended up there weren't the type to value the depth of Azazel's plans. But I was beginning to wonder if he was just the type of guy who didn't have friends. The one kid on the corner of the playground that no one would play with.

Azazel had told me he had more fun chasing me than he had in thousands of years. There was something about me that brought out the best, or the worst, in him. Maybe it was fear for the demon, knowing that he could die, that I could kill him. Maybe he feared if I killed him, all his games would end, there would be no one to carry them forward.

But he had enjoyed chasing me well before he had known I could kill him.

There was something that resonated between the two of us. He had known it the moment I picked up the Key. Azazel had followed his intuition about it, and that intuition had set me up to come back to Grafton. Then to New Orleans.

I wondered if there was some subconscious current I was following, even now. Some pull that kept the demon and me together. Maybe his plans weren't as intricate as I had believed they were, but maybe underneath them lay a magnetic attraction, a pull that tied us together. A force that only got stronger, the farther apart we were.

Right then a jet passed by, low overhead, from the east. It looked like one of the Lear jets that rich people own, and the plane left behind a long white trail as it screamed by, a roaring rumble following it.

"That's odd," I said. I didn't like odd.

After a few minutes a parachute opened up, high above us. It was white with red stripes crossing over the top, like thatch. Raphael leaned forward, looking up through the windshield.

"Probably some rich guy skydiving," he said.

"In the middle of this?" I pointed. Everything around us was open road and rounded hills, mixed with a few flat plains.

"What do you think, then?" Raphael frowned at me, cocking one eyebrow. "You think someone flew a jet across the earth to find you, and then once they found your car on the road in the middle of nowhere, someone jumped out of the jet to come get you?"

The demon snorted. "Got a big ego over there?"

I set my jaw. Said like that, the idea seemed far-fetched. Still, I didn't like it.

And I didn't like Raphael pointing out that I might be overreacting. But I was trying to get along now. Whatever it took, for Jen.

"Why just the one parachute?" I said.

"Why does someone rich do anything?" Raphael replied, and grinned. He had been rich once. "Because they can."

A big green sign rolled by us, pointing out it was only thirty miles to the next town. Maybe it was time to take a break. Get a good dinner, get some sleep. Trying to get along with Raphael was wearing. He had started fidgeting, and I had started some conversation to get him to stop, and that had ended up with me knowing more than I wanted to. What did I care about agreements and what had happened in the past? All I was worried about was improving the future. By having Jen in it.

But that's what I get, for trying to get along.

"I think we'll stop a bit early tonight," I said. It was getting dark out. "Get something to eat. Get a good night's sleep before we get to Colorado Springs."

"Fine by me," Raphael said.

I hadn't been asking, but I let it slide. Since it was good for business and all.

CHAPTER TWENTY

It was full night out by the time we stopped. The dark ridge of the Rocky Mountains hid in the inky blackness of the evening. The waning moon spread little light as it climbed the sky to the east, and stars began to blink into existence over us.

I pulled off the exit, coasting down to a stop at the end of the off-ramp, looking at our choices of where to eat. There wasn't a buffet place, so we went in and had a nice dinner at some seafood restaurant. One of those chain stores with crab and lobster specials, even though we were a thousand miles from any ocean. We sat at a round table with a white tablecloth and a large candle lit in the center. The napkins were thick and folded, and the silverware heavy.

Raphael ordered a bushel of crabs and attacked it with gusto. I found a pasta dish I liked, something with a lot of garlic and cheese. When the waiter brought it out, Raphael sniffed at it with distaste. Belle had a shrimp dish, and we all ate baskets of biscuits, warm and moist and served with a honey butter that was delicious and oddly enough, comforting.

I took the check and paid for it out of the money I had gotten from the crack house in Lewiston. I hoped wherever Jo's ghost was, it was watching me enjoy his money. Part of me had never shaken the memories that ghost had left in me, the snuffing of women during rougher and rougher sex, murders and rapes and the delight Jo had taken in it all.

Bile rose in my throat. My stomach bubbled with uneasiness. Whatever I had enjoyed about the meal got twisted up with those memories, and I swallowed several times, to keep it all down.

After the meal we hit up a hotel. I got a couple of rooms and told Raphael and Belle we'd leave early again. And I told them I meant it this time, after Raphael arched an eyebrow at me.

Belle took their key and walked away.

I went to grab my stuff, but Raphael stopped me, holding out a hand.

"What I told you, about the contract?" he said. "About me needing to be sure I could trust you?"

"What?" I asked.

"Give me a moment. Let me explain," Raphael said. "You know why I picked you, Grimm?"

I guessed he meant picking me to kill Azazel. I was sure that was because I was someone who could kill demons. Who *had recently* killed a couple. Sword or no sword. And that's what I told him.

Raphael's look was more thoughtful, though. As if he wanted to get a point across to me, but didn't know how to say it. "Hell is littered with people wanting a crack at Azazel," he said. "But when I figured out where I was, and who had done this to me, there was only one person I wanted."

Raphael liked his drama. I rolled my eyes. "I'm honored."

He grinned. "I'm under no illusion of who I am. Of what I've done. At some point you're going to come after me, for killing your friend. For what I did to Sarah, and Jen, and Grafton."

"Miss Tammie and Parker, too," I said. They deserved as much justice as anyone. Greg and Father Benjamin. All the people in my life who had been hurt or killed because of Raphael.

Or because I had left, and they had no one to protect them.

"Yeah," he said.

He and I were standing face-to-face, at the side of the Camaro. We were of a similar size, though he was a little taller, a little broader in the shoulders. We stood there and measured each other for a long, long moment. A slight breeze washed over us, and I shivered with the November cold of the mountains.

"You were saying?" I prompted.

Underneath his cheeks, the muscles of his jaw flexed. "We're enemies, Grimm. In the cleanest, clearest way. In the way enemies should be. There's nothing we hide from each other. In the end, it's going to be you, or it's going to be me."

"It *was* you," I said.

He laughed. "I missed this, Grimm. All the time you were gone, I missed how pure this was, between us."

"Miss it all you want," I said. "It'll end one day."

"It will," Raphael agreed, with a serious nod. "It's nice to count on someone for something. Even this. It is something I can depend on."

He looked up at the sky, and let out a breath. "It was never easy for me. I was built for something evil. I was a construct, I was never real. And I failed my father's expectations. Maybe I'm broken.... I had something inside me that always wanted to punish, to break, to lord over. To dominate."

Like I said, some of us never strayed far from our fathers.

"Cry me a river," I said. "You don't get to blame what you've done on being some kind of demonic Frankenstein."

My response was angry, vehement. I had stepped closer, inside his space.

Raphael tilted his head at me, like he was surprised. I was a little surprised myself. And likely more scared than angry. I had told Nick just a day ago I was broken. And here Raphael was telling me he felt the same way.

I was more alike to Raphael than I wanted to admit. We were just broken in different ways. I viewed bringing Jen back almost like I had once viewed the Key. Jen had become my sole focus. Everything I did, from when I woke to when I slept, was about her.

Just like when I had run from Danny. I had run with the purpose of keeping my friends safe. For punishing myself, for failing Danny.

When I got the Key, it had quickly become my purpose for living. I pretended I was protecting the world, no matter what happened to others I cared about. What I ran from. Or who died while I was running from Azazel.

This felt the same. In my world everything had become second, to Jen. The rest of the world, the demon cities, my friends, me. I just had to trust she was worth it. Because abandoning this path wasn't an option. I couldn't live every day, with her gone.

So if I was broken, it wasn't something that could be fixed. Not by me. Even now. There were cities of demons in the world. Something I might be able to do something about. My friends were sad, but they would be sad whether I was killed on this crazy journey or if I died wasting away in a motel bed.

Everything was one or the other, with me. I was either all in or all out. There was never anything I did in moderation. Running from Grafton, running with the Key, running to save Jen. All things I had done, no matter the cost.

"I get it," Raphael finally said. His eyes clear, focused. "What I'm telling you is the only thing I felt like was real in my life was you and me. Those were the only times I felt like I was the person I was supposed to be. I could trust that."

"Lucky me," I replied.

"Yeah, well," he said, "don't tell me you don't want Azazel dead, too."

Raphael was right. I wanted him dead in the worst way. But only after I brought Jen back. Then I would settle that score. Whether or not my name was signed on some contract.

Jen would come first. Or I would die in the effort. That I was sure of.

"It's why I wanted the contract, you know," Raphael said.

I tried to hide a look of surprise. Our thoughts had been along the same lines. I wondered if he knew what I would do once I found my mother. Once I learned what I had to do next.

I had some time yet to kill Azazel. And Jen was first on my list.

"It wasn't to protect me," he said. "You're going after Azazel, whatever I want. I've seen what you're like when you want someone dead."

"So it was to protect me?" I snorted. "Raph, I know you. I'm going to kill Azazel. You can bet on that. But you can't bet on me believing any of this bullshit you're feeding me."

"Oh, there's never going to be a world where you'll trust me," Raphael said. "But I figured the contract, bound correctly, would give you the confidence that I'm going to see my part through."

This was the strangest conversation I had ever had with Raphael. And there had been plenty, even just a few weeks ago, back in Grafton.

Death had changed him. It had made him more contemplative. He had never been one to go back and look at something, figure out what he did wrong, and then make a change. He had always been more hell or high water in his approach.

And he had gotten hell.

"It's why Belle is here," he said. His gaze looked past me, somewhere over my shoulder and out into the night. "I asked for her. I wanted someone here, to make sure I carried through on my part."

There was a moment of quiet. A car pulled by on the road, something old with a small engine that whined and a muffler that rattled far into the distance.

"Not to make sure you handled yours," he said. Raphael smiled then, a smile at some inner thought, or memory. His voice was quiet. "You see, I know myself, too."

CHAPTER TWENTY-ONE

I left the demon and grabbed my shotgun out of the side of the car, and my bag out of the trunk. I remembered the phone was dead, so I went back to the front of the car and picked it up out of the console. Then I headed to my room, next to Raphael's. Both of us were on the bottom floor.

The motel room was so much like the last few I had stayed in, it almost felt like home. I had traveled for so long, the shape and size were natural to me. Small square room, single bed, smaller than the queen it was supposed to be. Chair and table by the front window. Dresser with a television on it.

It was the same temperature inside as it was outside. Cold. Maybe management was saving on the electric bill. I turned the thermostat on the unit under the window, the fan kicked on, and a warmish air blew out into the room.

I plugged the cell phone into the charger, the charger into the wall, and laid all of it on the dresser, the phone facedown. The remote to the television was there, so I turned on the television and found a news channel. For a moment I sat on the bed and got caught up.

The station coverage was all New Orleans. A couple of anchors talked while a feed from a helicopter circled outside the city. Smoke rose from a building, here or there, but it was impossible to see what. The feed was from too far away.

Apparently the pilot wasn't comfortable, being even that close. A tiny explosion burst from a building, and the helicopter spun away.

The battle on the eastern front, on the interstate heading into New Orleans, had been called off. An uneasy truce rested there. A picture was shown of miles of barbed wire curling north and south from in front of the army camp, heading north and south. Hundreds of miles of it.

The navy had been called in, most of the Atlantic Fleet. A few aircraft carriers sat in the gulf, with their battle squadrons. There had been talk of a bombing run for a bit, but apparently a few of the nuclear-powered submarines, normally part of the task force, had disappeared.

Very little of the news was information provided by the government. No official statements, at least. A lot of these reports were from people. Individuals that raced in to grab footage and race back. Social media posts and videos.

What was being said, and what was evident through the footage being shown, was that everything in the battle inside the Dead Zone hadn't stayed dead long. And even the reports from the people who had been inside were hard to trust. They came from people in the bars outside the camp, or soldiers who were UA, or even AWOL.

I knew those terms, but the anchor explained anyway.

"No word on whether these unauthorized absences, or the soldiers who have been declared absent without leave, have anything do to with the reports we are getting about what the army saw in New Orleans, so this reporter will leave it up to your imagination...."

I put the television on mute. Then I got undressed and took a quick shower. The bathroom was nothing like the last hotel's. It was nice and clean, and a warm air had stirred up a thick cherry scent throughout the room.

I toweled myself off, wiping off cold drops of water. An air freshener sat on the shelf of towels in front of me, and while I stood there the freshener let out a plastic squeal and puffed a bit of mist over me.

I rolled my eyes. Now I smelled like cherry. Great.

I had hoped to see Jen when I got out of the bathroom, but the room was empty. Nothing but slightly warmer air and that cherry scent. I threw on a different pair of jeans. I wasn't sleepy, so I turned off the television and the lights, then sat in the chair by the window.

I waited for Jen. The room was dark, but a soft yellow glow edged in from the boundaries of the drapes, from the hotel lights outside. The glow outlined the walls of the room and left lumps of shadows here and there, where the light couldn't reach.

It grew late. I ran through a seesaw of emotions. Through the drive today, an undercurrent of the rhythm I had been in was wanting to see Jen, tonight. Part of me just wanted to get to this moment. All of me just wanted her to show, so we could do our thing together. Have our silent, ghostly conversation. Be close to her. *With* her.

I had been sure she would appear, and the longer she didn't, the more frustrated I grew.

Then I would reset and wait a bit longer.

Raphael's conversation kept playing back in my mind. Especially the part about being broken. He had been an experiment, some kind of bastard child born between Azazel and Dominic. I didn't know if they had used blood, or magic, or some kind of combination of both. I didn't even know if Raphael had a mother, but it made sense that he would have. He had human genes in him, from somewhere.

I was a blend of things myself. Part angel, part human. Created under some geas, just a curse of a different name. Raphael and I were much alike, in some ways.

I needed for us to be different in the ways that mattered. Because I didn't think Raphael could ever be fixed. If the two of us were both broken, and if we were more alike than I thought, then maybe I couldn't be fixed, either.

I needed a small part of me to believe I could be. After a bit I got up. Walked back and forth. Went to the bathroom, hoping again to see Jen when I came out. I did that more times than I could count, getting frustrated, and growing angry at myself because I was fidgeting.

I had to find a way to calm down. I sat back in the chair and forced myself to relax. I wasn't successful. I fingered the Key a minute, on my chest, the stone cool on my skin. Then I pulled it out and studied the amulet.

New lines ran across its face. Tiny lines. Almost individual scratches, scored just deep enough into the stone that I could tell they weren't accidental.

After I got the Key back from Azazel, the surface of the medallion had been blank. Like it was empty. The concentric circles of the stone, each of which used to spin to lock in different patterns, had become smooth, empty rings. As if the symbols for the demons had evaporated from the surface of the Key, after each demon had been freed.

But now there were these lines. Almost a spiderwebbing. I rotated the circles to see if I could make anything of the pattern, but nothing lined up correctly.

I found a ghost. Pulled from it. Almost didn't notice the slapping of a hand against a face, over and over, in the spirit's memories. Didn't notice the slight protest from the ghost, the way it fought me. That part had become normal to me now.

I blinked on my ethereal vision. A light golden glow radiated from the stone. The lines of each of the circle segments, though, was blue. The spiderwebbing lines glittered blue, too. As if something explosive rested behind it, and was trying to force its way out.

I worried that it was breaking. That its purpose had gone, and with its purpose the power that had kept the Key intact all these years.

I wondered if there was a way I could heal it. I tried to force the energy I held into the Key. I covered the cracks with my hand and pulled from the ghost and pushed into the Key, thinking, *Heal, stone, please heal.*

When it was opened, the Key had screamed in pain. Something had been taken from it. Maybe I could push something back in.

There had always been a bond between the medallion and me. I understood it as the bond between the Key and the Key bearer. I had always been able to sense where the Key was, along the thin line that tied us together.

I found the bond and pushed energy along it. It was studious, hard work. My jaw tightened so much it began to ache. The golden glow of the Key grew bright, so bright I closed my eyes, and I still pushed more energy into it.

Jen, are you there? I thought, along the bond. *Help me, Jen....*

I sensed something, a response, a cry, and pushed harder. Something lightly brushed against me along the bond, like the flick of a finger along my wrist.

I took everything the ghost had, straining with the effort, and the ghost disappeared, replaced with its memory.

That bitch had gone out again.

Slap.

To the fucking bar again. When I'm out there bailing fucking hay all day, feeding the fucking cows, too tired to do anything but collapse into bed when I get home. She was bored?

I'd show her a fucking board.

Slap.

Where was my fucking dinner?

"Please, stop," she begged. Tears in her eyes.

Slap.

I worked the farm all day just to keep food on the table.

Slap.

We were this close *to losing it all. And she's out at the fucking bar tossing back shots with some guy. Just enjoying a night out, she says. While I'm fucking working.*

My hand balled into a fist.

Something interrupted the memory. The Key, reaching out to me. Or something inside the Key it, at least. A force grabbed me and tugged me down into the bond between us.

Something large cracked. Like a slap of stone on stone. The booming force echoed loudly from the walls of the room. Someone banged on the ceiling, above me. Shouting at me to be quiet.

Then the tug from the bond became a powerful yank, like a physical force. Something hard grabbed my wrist and I fell out of the chair and onto the floor, onto my hands and knees. The Key dangled from my chest, glowing brightly gold and blue, the colors mixed together and swirling.

I gasped, and held on to whatever was tugging me. I found another ghost, somewhere, and put everything I had into my hand, holding tightly to whatever was holding tightly to me.

Then there was a sharp snap. Energy flowed back out of the Key, along the bond, and into me. Crackles popped through the room, like a transformer throwing sparks. Electricity raced along my nerves like I had been hit with a Taser.

I lost control of my limbs and fell face-first onto the carpet. I lay there awhile, shaking, even in the warm room. The carpet fibers, dry and scratchy, pushed against my cheek.

The Key was breaking. I was sure of it now.

I wondered if last night was the last time I would ever see Jen. I thought I had felt her, inside the Key, briefly. I was sure it had been her hand in the bond, grabbing mine. I had heard her scream, and I wasn't sure if she was in pain, or yelling at me to get out, or something else entirely.

I wasn't sure if what I did had repaired the Key, or if I had broken it further.

One thing was certain. The lines in the stone were deeper now. The etches had become scores, and had spread out farther across the surface.

The lines had started out like a crack on the windshield, where a tiny stone may have hit. The spiderwebbing had been small, the size of a quarter, like a starburst.

What I had done made it look like a fist-sized rock had hit that same windshield. The lines there thicker, like channels, and reached farther out across the Key. The scores weren't black, but a deeper azure color. They glowed, subtly, in the dark room. Even the concentric rings, which had been black, seemed a deeper blue now.

Even though the Key was breaking, my bond with it was stronger now. Before, it had felt like the light tugging of a fishing line. Now it felt like a large steel cable connected the two of us, tight, thrumming with energy. If someone physically pulled the Key away from me, my body would be yanked right behind it.

I could sense more between us along the bond. It told me all I needed to know. It was how I knew the Key was breaking. Like it was opening, slowly. Letting go. I could feel it.

I did not sleep well.

Which turned out to be a good thing.

CHAPTER TWENTY-TWO

I had been trying to sleep. I needed to. I would not see Jen this night, and maybe any other night. The Key was breaking, and I needed it to hold together, at least for another day, and possibly longer.

But sleep wouldn't come. Even though tomorrow I needed to be my sharpest. Tomorrow I'd find my mother, and all kinds of hell would break lose then. Not only from what might happen with her, and Dominic, but the demons with me. Raphael couldn't be trusted, no matter what he or Belle said about the contract.

So of course sleep, when it came, was fitful. At best. I writhed in my blankets, throwing them off, pulling them back on. Rolling to one side, then the other. Waking up with a puddle of drool on the pillow, like I had been knocked unconscious for a few brief minutes, before closing my eyes again. All those moments were mixed between long periods when I lay awake and stared at the ceiling.

Then someone was shouting in my ear. I might have been dreaming, and in the dream I was sleeping in a motel bed, the covers half on, half off me. I watched myself roll around on the bed, my eyes moving back and forth under my eyelids, in some deep REM kind of dream.

The shouts grew more urgent, in my ear. It sounded like Jen's voice. And then I saw her, or maybe dreamed her. She faded in next to the bed, and leaned over against my face, putting one hand on my chest, and screamed.

WAKE UP!

I jerked up, sitting straight up in the bed.

The room was empty. Jen was not next to me. The Key pulsed oddly on my chest.

The first thing I did was tap into a ghost.

Then the door to the hotel room burst inward, bringing the frigid Colorado cold with it. It had been opened with enough force that the top hinge broke off and the door pivoted and fell at an angle against the wall.

A figure stood in the doorway, outlined in the light of the parking lot, his face hidden in shadows. He took up almost the entire door. A large handle of a sword poked out from over one shoulder. Every feature of his black in the darkness of the room.

For a moment I thought the person was Kimaris. Come back from where I had sent him. I feared that I hadn't killed him, killed any of the demons.

Then the man spoke. His voice was guttural, and carried an Irish accent. His tone was tight and slightly hesitant, as if the man fought to say each word.

"Fergus Grimm?" Part statement, part question.

I drew from the ghost and rolled to the opposite side of the bed, dropping to the floor. I cursed. My shotgun was on the window side of the bed. All I had on this side was a semiflat pillow, and the coverlet.

Neither something to bring to a sword fight.

"Who wants to know?" I asked.

The ghost I had tapped went fast. Disappeared with a pop. It had been small, weak, and it had burst in a bubble of ethereal energy that I had inhaled as quick as breath.

The energy was enough, though. Enough for me to harden my skin. To strengthen my body. Whoever this was, I was going to make it a fight.

"Your father," he said.

Oh. Not a demon. But maybe someone deadlier.

"Be careful when you meet him as well." Words from my mother, the last time I had seen her. *"We are all under the geas."*

Oh shit.

"You're only about twenty-six years late, Pop," I said, casually. "Better late than never?"

He stepped into the room. One hand flicked out and turned on the ceiling light.

His face was much like mine. A five o'clock shadow, a few minutes past needing a shave, spread across his chin and cheeks. His hair was black, with a few streaks of gray, and curly, though fairly short. Almost like a Caesar cut, just tight to the sides, curls on the top.

His cheekbones were strong. And his eyes were a brilliant blue. His teeth were perfect, even, and white. They were easy to see because the man had on a barely controlled grin, like part of him was ... *proud*?

"I had heard you were a smart-ass," he said. His eyes were pinched, and conveyed the immense amount of strain he was under. I guessed from holding himself against the geas.

There was only one reason he was here. It was to kill me.

"Smart-ass, funny," I said, grinning. "I've been called worse."

I could feel the geas he was under, just like I could feel the curse that had commanded my mother. Like I could feel the geas in myself, when it was directed at me. A tiny *thump-thump*, like the beating of a heart, pulsed inside my father. I wondered, if he was killed, if his geas would pass to me. Like it would if my mother died.

My father's smile grew slightly wider, the lips thinning as he fought the command of the curse. The grin looked fake, with the geas, but it also felt real. A sense of commonality, maybe, between us. Or pride. "Your mother thinks much the same, about me."

It was interesting, to think of my mother and father as a pair. If my father thought he was funny, my mother likely wouldn't think the same thing. She hadn't found me funny, either. She was all business, wrapped inside precise, elegant motions. Maybe because she held her emotions tightly wrapped inside, protected from the world she endured.

I tried another ghost. Found it was busy already. My father had tied himself to it. So I reached out even further.

I had never fought someone who could use ghosts before. Who was like me. At least, not with ghosts actually around.

This was going to complicate things that were already complicated enough.

"Who sent you?" I asked.

His eyes looked left and right, like he was calculating what he could answer, and what he couldn't. "I belong to the Dumonts."

Gabrielle's family.

Why would they want me killed now?

I was going to kill Dominic. Doing that would only help the Dumonts. One less crazy vampire clan for them to contend with.

Though maybe it wasn't Dominic they were worried about. Maybe they didn't want my mother free. If I killed Dominic, and Raphael couldn't hold the geas, would it pass to someone else? Or would she be free to help me? Or go after the vampires whom she had been enslaved to for hundreds of years?

Either way, probably something they wanted to avoid.

"If you're telling me you're here to stop me from killing Dominic," I said, "it's probably going to make me want to kill him more."

"As it should," he answered, jaw muscles flexing.

"I don't have long, do I?" I asked.

Meaning, how long could he hold out against the geas?

He shook his head. "Not long."

I wondered how he had found me. Likely he had sensed me pulling from the ghost, trying to heal the Key. If he had an ethereal radar, like I did, then it would have pinged loudly there.

But he would have needed to be near the area. And the Dumonts were based in Europe.

"It was you," I said. "The skydiver."

People did fly in from all over the world just to kill me, it appeared. I would definitely rub this in to Raphael, if I lived.

"It was," he said. "I will not be the only thing trying to stop you."

His accent made the words seem a little mystical. Like a prophecy had been read aloud. But my entire life could be filed under urgent, so this to me seemed pretty normal. The world I lived in was either flight or fight. I was just in the fight part.

"Have time for a question?" I asked.

"Maybe one," he said. One of his hands inched its way above his shoulder, to the handle of the sword there. Like his arm was moving in slow motion.

"Can you bring someone back from the dead?"

His eyes opened wide, as if the question not only surprised him, but terrified him.

"Son," he said, "whatever you do, you don't bring your mother or me back. *Ever*. Understand?"

His hand found the hilt, and began a slow draw.

"I don't," I said. Why had he thought I would bring either of my parents back? They were both alive. I didn't understand it.

A slow raspy drawl of steel against hardened leather told me the sword was free. I wouldn't have time to get a clearer answer.

"What now?" I asked. Though I knew.

My father grinned. "Now you try to run."

His accent had made *run* sound like *ruin*. Which maybe was appropriate to the spot I found myself in.

CHAPTER TWENTY-THREE

I ran to protect my friends. If it was just me, it was just me. And I was cornered, so running wasn't an option. Not at the moment. So I soaked in ethereal energy from the ghost, pulling it all in, and charged my father with the pillow.

At the last second I threw it at his face and ducked under the swing of his sword.

The blade was quick, but maybe not as quick as it would be. Each swing was slowed by my father, as he fought the geas. The emotion was in his face.

An outsider would see us as two faster-than-light motions, as blurs. But in the fight I noticed the long pause at the end of each of my father's swings, then the slow reverse of the blade. Always a pattern. The swing, then the wait, then the beginning of the next swing.

It gave me openings. Small openings, but openings nonetheless.

It was all I needed.

I got inside his arm and grabbed his shoulder, flipping my father over me as I turned on my hip, tossing him deeper into the room.

He crashed through the bathroom wall.

I dove for the side of the bed and grabbed my shotgun. It had been lying against the wall, between the nightstand and the bed.

I pumped it and stood up.

My father was already back. His sword swatted the barrel and the gun rattled through the doorway and into the parking lot.

My hand stung. I used energy to harden my skin.

My father walked across the bed, head lowered against the ceiling. Body folded a bit. His face and hair had bits of drywall in them. He swung the blade again, kind of an angled slice, and I held up my arm and put as much energy as I could into my forearm.

There was a bonelike *thunk*. The sword stuck into the bone of my arm. Pain shot through me, but I was used to pain. I had hardened my arm enough to keep my hand from being severed, but my father's strength, with his ghost, still cut into me.

My father put his foot on my chest and yanked the sword free. Kicking me off.

I screamed and healed my arm as I fell backward, over the chair by the window. My father jumped over me; I rolled to the side. His sword punched through the chair.

I rolled again as the table went through the same treatment.

Welcome to Furniture R Us, where every piece of furniture you buy has a guaranteed sword cut in it, or your money back.

I scrambled across the bed. My father swung again. I somehow flung the palm of my hand up and knocked the flat of the blade aside. The bed took a heavy slice, the sword opening up a cottony wound.

Every piece, or your money back.

What followed was a tense few seconds. My father weaved his sword in the air above me. At random, he flicked the blade toward me. Each swing not at full strength, as he fought the geas. Each time the sword flicked out, I was able to slap it away.

It was only a few seconds, but it felt like forever. This game of patty-cake with a sword couldn't last forever. Somehow I needed to get outside and get my shotgun, before I made a mistake.

Hell, even maybe get to the Camaro and flee.

I slipped at the last second. Or my father's fight with the geas did. The palm of my hand pushed the sword down, and my father went with the motion, twisting the blade in the air and chopping deep into my thigh.

My leg gave out, and I tumbled down.

I was used to pain, but my father's sword was dark and cold. My leg felt numb, and I fought back a scream. I just pulled ghost and healed. The muscle in my quads had been cut in half. The ends of muscle had snapped back from the slice. And the axlike chop had stuck in my tibia.

It fucking hurt.

I needed to get back up.

I pulled ethereal energy, feeling the torn muscle stretch itself back out, the fibers probing around the sword stuck in my leg, trying to find a way to knit themselves back together.

"It is good that you know how to heal yourself," my father said. The words seemed important to him. "That you know how to live."

My father's foot came down on the center of my chest, pinning me against the floor. He yanked the blade out of my leg. Blood spurted across the dresser, but the wound started to close, the muscle to knit.

His face was sad. He steadied himself, his boot sliding across the top of the Key.

Which pulsed against my chest, as if in response to the fight. As if the Key was a heartbeat, and beat against me.

My fingers rested in the air, outstretched and empty. This was a perfect time for my ethereal blade to appear. Or the armor. Hell, anything.

Even a hand. Where the hell was Raphael? Was he that deep a sleeper?

My father lifted his sword high above him. He tried to hold the blade in the air and give me time, but his foot still held me against the floor.

I gathered as much energy as I could, and tried to push my father off. But he pulled just as much to keep me pinned. I grabbed his foot and tried to twist it. My back arched off the floor, and I roared with effort. A ghost disappeared and I tapped another. And another. I saw, on the ethereal radar, my father match each of my pulls with one of his own. I felt, through his foot on my chest, the command of his geas throbbing to a heartbeat kind of rhythm.

Kill-kill, kill-kill, the curse thumped out. *Kill-kill, kill-kill, kill-kill* ...

The same throbbing in the Key, on my chest. I screamed with a deep rage. I pushed so hard against my father's foot that my wrists snapped, and my hands slipped off. An edge of my father's lips curled up. As if he appreciated the fight.

"We all have a time to die, son," my father said. Which was an odd thing to say, before killing someone.

The sword descended.

I pulled. The ghost was giving out. I might be done if I couldn't find another. Frantically I tried to reach out, trying to find a ghost my father hadn't tethered himself to first. Some kind of energy from someone …

And someone responded.

Here …

A warmth spread along my chest. The Key. Jen reached out to me along the connection between us. At the same time a blue glow lit the underside of my father's foot, radiating from the stone. I reached an invisible hand back along the bond. Like I had earlier.

Jen's hand grabbed mine.

The connection locked in.

The crack of a bat, and a baseball traveling far over right field. I jogged a few steps and then stopped, watching the outfield slow down as well. I looked over to the dugout and winked at Jen, who leaned against the rail with her hat on backward, blond ponytail hanging below the cap …

What the hell? I wondered. I usually lived someone else's memory. Was something living one of mine? If so, who? Jen? I frowned, puzzled …

Then a bright blue-white light burst through the room. I forced my eyes shut, and pressed them tighter as the blaze burned brightly against my lids. What felt like thousands of volts of electricity passed through me. An explosion rocked the motel. The whole building shuddered.

The pressure holding me against the floor was gone. So was my father's foot. A high-pitched tone rang through my ears. The rest of the sounds in the room were muffled. Clumps of things hit the floor, like heavy bags of sand.

I opened my eyes and blinked a couple of times. It had been a second or two, at most, but it had felt like forever. The part of the room that was still there was lit like an overexposure. What had been white was now black, and what had been black now looked like a glow of deep azure. Like I had stared at a brilliant blue sun for too long.

Jen? I waited for an answer, but the bond felt silent. Empty. I tried reaching along it, stretching far and deep into the Key, but all I felt there was a spacelike emptiness.

JEN?

What had happened? Was the explosion something I had caused? Some lightning power Jen had called up? Or had it been us, together?

Whatever it had been, it had kept me from getting a sword in the chest. And my father was gone. I wasn't sure if it had killed him, but I didn't think it had. My luck didn't run that way. My father would be someone I saw again. I was sure of that.

I picked myself up and dusted myself off. Raphael stood in the doorway, holding my shotgun loosely. The end of the barrel smoked, as if he had recently pulled the trigger. His eyes were blinking, like he was trying to get his sight back, and he shook one of his hands, as if something in the gunshot residue had hurt him, after he pulled the trigger.

The ceiling above me had disappeared. A great chunk of the outer wall and windows were gone as well. The edges of the wall were blackened, burned. Bits of brick and wood and drywall and glass were littered out into the parking lot, all over the cars. As if a bomb had gone off.

A bomb of lightning.

The smell of ozone flooded the room. The hair along my arms lifted away from my skin, floating in the air. As if I was a charged particle.

Weird.

"Where the fuck were you?" I asked.

"What do you mean?" His eyebrows narrowed. "I got here as soon as I heard something."

The whole fight had taken seconds, then. Sped up because my father and I were both using ethereal energy. It had felt much, much longer.

I struggled over to Raphael. I took the shotgun from his hands. As I did, a tiny spark jumped from my hand to the barrel, and Raphael jumped.

"Dammit, Grimm," he said. Then, "What was that?"

I didn't answer.

Jen had been in the Key. Like Danny, she had given me some of her energy. And unknowingly, I had taken it, and used it, like I would use a ghost. The steel-like cable connection I had felt earlier wasn't so much a bond between me and the Key, it was between me, the Key, and Jen.

I had struggled to find a ghost. I had needed something to stay alive. Had Jen lent me some of her power? Had she given me her own ethereal energy, through our bond? Had our powers just ... mixed?

Whatever it was, whatever had happened, I had unleashed it all. Uncontrolled.

Was she gone? Like Danny in Grafton, when he had passed all his energy to me? My heart started to race, and I felt along the bond like I would reach out to a ghost. The connection was still there, between me and the Key, and I hoped that meant Jen was, too. I hoped I wasn't imagining it.

I didn't know what I would do if I had used her up. We were a pair. Each of us would do anything for the other. If Jen could call her lightning from the Key, if she had found a way around the prison she was in, then she would give everything she had to keep me alive. Even if it meant her end.

Somehow we had bonded. Somehow our powers had combined and become something different, something greater than each of us apart. I had to have hope that she was still there. I hadn't lived any of her memories, the way I had lived the lives of other spirits. The way I had lived Danny.

Maybe what we had done exhausted her. I had seen her after a fight, the amount of power she could pull down from the skies, the massive strikes of lightning. Jen had needed rest, each time. Recovering. Recharging.

I'd have to figure out how to fight my father when he showed up. Or my mother. I would need to keep ahead of them, pulling from spirits. There was no way I'd risk *this* again, Jen giving me her power, from her tap to the plane.

I would give my life to bring her back, but I would not let her use life up. Not to save mine. What the Key held of Jen was everything that was left of her. I couldn't risk losing that. Losing her, the person I wanted most to save. I wasn't worth it.

My breathing, which had been rushed, settled a little. I would have to be careful, in the future, of pulling from her again. In fact, I was going to have to avoid it. I needed my sword, my armor. I needed to learn why those things that had quickly become natural to me now avoided my call. I had only used the sword a few times. It was funny how fast I had gotten used to having it.

What a fucking mess this was going to be.

I was exhausted. Drained. Scared.

"We've got to go," I said.

He nodded. "Was that Cronan?"

"Cronan?" I asked.

"Yeah," he said. "The angel for the Dumonts. I met him once, with Gabrielle."

Cronan. My father's name. Odd, I had spent more time around my mother, and I didn't know hers.

"Then yes," I said.

"He went somewhere that way." Raphael motioned with his head, out past the parking lot, toward a group of trees.

"He's alive?" I asked. I didn't know whether to be happy that I hadn't killed my father, or scared that he didn't appear killable.

"From what I could tell," Raphael said. "Whatever that explosion was, it threw him far and fast."

I looked for his partner in crime. "Where's Belle?"

"Hiding," he said, and then shrugged at my questioning look.

My jaw set. Belial was one of the more powerful demons. It would have been nice to get a hand. From either of the demons riding with me.

I searched for my bag, and found it covered in broken pieces of the ceiling and wall by the side of the bed. I spent a few moments looking for the cell, but the dresser and television were in so many pieces I had no hope I'd find the phone. Miraculously my car keys were still on the night-stand, which had somehow been left untouched.

Raphael waited while I gathered my stuff. At one point he took a long sniff and looked at me funny. So I looked at him funny back.

"Why do you smell like cherry?" he finally asked, grinning a bit.

I shook my head. Found a shirt in my bag and put it on. While I did, I placed my hand over the Key, briefly. It was cold, under my palm. Quiet.

Jen, I thought, along the bond. And waited for an answer.

And waited.

I might have caught the faintest scent of honeysuckle. The feel of a breeze with a hint of rain. The soft, trembling fingertip reach of a human at the end of her limits.

I hoped I wasn't making all that up.

I walked out to the Camaro, taking a moment to brush a few pieces of drywall off the hood. The outer wall of the motel had bulged outward. Large cracks radiated from the hole in the building that used to be my room. Some of the other motel doors had opened, and faces peeked out of windows.

I threw the bag in the trunk and tucked the shotgun beside the seat. "Let's go."

"Why are the Dumonts after us?" Raphael asked.

"Us?" I asked. "Or me?"

His grin told me he knew the difference. "Does it matter?"

"Probably not," I said. Part of me wanted to leave Raphael and go after my mother. Especially since I knew where they were. I wanted to run and get things done, and not have to deal with Raphael and Belle.

But there was a chance I would still need Raphael. To find my mother in Colorado Springs. Or to find her, if she and Dominic fled before I got there.

Why would the Dumonts want to protect Dominic? Why would they want to kill me now?

"Weird," Raphael said, apparently thinking along the same lines. "Them trying to protect my father."

Belle appeared then, walking around the corner of the building, as if she had always been there.

"Nice of you to show up." I had the door to the Camaro open, and one hand on the hood.

"My sole purpose is to make sure the agreement is met," she said. Not explaining further.

My hand tapped the hood of the car as Belle and I locked gazes.

"Hard for the agreement to be met," I said, "if Raphael or I am dead."

She saw where I was going. "Do not be fooled, Fergus Grimm. If you fail, another will come."

"Hell of a plan." I shook my head. "No wonder your side is losing."

"So you say." She frowned. "Is this something I forced on you?"

"You mean the contract?" I asked

"I mean your word," she said. "Did you say or promise something you feel like you cannot do? Did I place that burden on you?"

That didn't make sense. I had killed demons before. I wanted to kill Azazel. I planned on doing it. I was just planning on doing it after I got Jen back.

We all got into the Camaro. I started it up and backed up, slowly. The car rocked up and down as we navigated the debris-filled parking lot.

I swung the Camaro onto the main road. Behind us was the warbling sound of sirens. In the distance now, but getting closer. It seemed like I had been hearing those a lot lately. I was almost used to them.

CHAPTER TWENTY-FOUR

We drove for a bit in silence. It started out cold in the car. The leather seats were stiff from the temperature. I trembled in my seat. I couldn't tell if it was from near death, exhaustion, or just temperature. But I could do something about one of them. I turned on the heater. The air blew out of the vents, chilly at first. I had to wait for the engine heat to radiate through the system.

Finally, after a few minutes of driving, the car began to warm up.

The night was dark and so was the road. A slight mist came off the blacktop and hid everything underneath. The crescent moon, thin in the sky above, gave off no light. Only half of it appeared above us; the other half of the pale face obscured in shadow. I found it hard to pick out the white lines by the shoulder, even with the headlights on full.

And my mind was elsewhere.

For some reason, I could not summon the ethereal blade. Maybe earlier in my life, I hadn't needed it. But I spent my days among demons now. I needed it more than ever.

I didn't know why it had stopped appearing. I didn't think it was something that angels could just call, or something I could call because I was an angel. I had summoned the sword before I had believed any of that.

Did other people's powers work that way? Could they do them, and then something would happen where they no longer could anymore? Would there be a day Nick tried to walk a shadow and found out he couldn't? Or walk into one, and never be able to walk out again?

That didn't seem right. So I didn't think so. But what did I know?

I had definitely changed, after Jen's death. I had become something self-contained. Again.

I hadn't cared about my friends, or at least the ones still alive. Had I seen the result of that when I cut myself and watched my body heal, a day ago?

There had been no mistaking the bloodred streaks among the ethereal blue glow I was used to seeing heal me. I was changing, but why? Jen's death? Had it put me in a darker place, an evil place impossible to get out of?

I gripped the wheel of the car, tight. I slammed the gas pedal down to the floor, even as dark as it was, and as misty as the roads were. Shadows flew by us, of trees and signs on the side of the road.

Jen's death *had* changed me. But what had changed? Was it something in me, or something I did?

Then a thought occurred to me. When I first summoned the sword, I had needed something to kill Kimaris. But I had needed to kill him to save Jen.

I had used the sword to kill, but I had summoned it to protect.

Now I just wanted the sword to kill. *Needed* it to kill. I wasn't trying to protect anyone.

Was that why it wouldn't come? Because of what I was going to use it for?

If so, that was going to be a problem. Swords were used to kill. That's kind of why they were built. No one walked around announcing, "Hey, look at this great sword I made to collect alms for the poor."

There were rules to using my powers, then. Rules to being an angel, maybe.

Neither my mother nor my father had shown the ability to summon an ethereal blade. But they both had carried swords, and used them for killing. I wondered if there was something in their genes, in the back recesses of their minds, hinting to my parents of what they used to be, maybe even what they both could be, if they were but allowed.

I was nearing a piece of truth about myself. That calling the sword wasn't just an on-off thing, it was something done with a purpose. It needed a reason. A *good* reason.

Belle had spent a good bit of time trying to convince me that true good could be revealed only when a person performed a deed selflessly. That to know a reward existed cheapened the act. She was convinced a person was cheating by doing good things just because they knew heaven existed. That if a person knew what happened at the end, we couldn't really tell if the person was selflessly good, because they were just paying the price of the ticket in.

I didn't know if that was true. And I didn't know if the rules were laid out like Belle thought they were. What I did know was, when I wanted to help others, the sword had appeared. When I wanted to protect others, the armor had appeared.

When I wanted the sword to kill someone, or wanted the armor just to save myself, neither had come.

That logic seemed pretty clear-cut to me.

I *had* changed, after Jen's death. I had cared nothing about myself, and had cared maybe less for my friends. I had given up wanting to protect those I cared about, of being the person Danny would be proud of.

I was on the right track. Being able to summon the sword was tied to the reason why I needed it. And in this moment, I wasn't the right person to summon an ethereal blade. At least, the person I had become lately.

I needed to go back to being the person I had been, right before Jen died.

And that was going to be tough, because I seemed to only be that person because of Jen. She had been the catalyst, the person I would stand taller for. Be better for.

Now? I was the type of guy to ride with a demon who had killed one of my best friends. I was the type of guy who made compromises, in order to see things through. I was the type of guy who would do anything to rescue Jen.

Anything but maybe the right thing.

I had – once again – reverted to the person I had been when I was running with the Key. Running from Azazel. I was again a person willing to sacrifice anything to keep the demon at bay, for one more day. How much longer until I became the same exact person as back then, until all I cared about was just getting through the day?

The back of my mind screamed at me that I was being too hard on myself. That I was a better person than I was crediting myself for. But the conscious me knew I was an all-or-nothing type of guy. I was all in or all out. And right now I was being more of the all-out guy than the all-in.

I was going to have to think about this. And come up with an answer soon. Because whatever the reason, I needed that blade, that armor, to survive what was around me.

"We driving all night?" Raphael asked.

"Huh?" I asked. He was staring at me, one eyebrow raised. As if he was wondering what I was thinking.

Then what he said registered.

"At least to Denver," I said. If my father was alive, I wanted to put as many miles between us as I could.

"You don't look like you're going to make the next mile," he said.

I didn't acknowledge what he said. I just kept driving. I happen to look like that a lot. Didn't mean I wouldn't power through it. It was what I did.

"You going to tell us what happened back there?" Raphael was feeling talkative.

I glanced at Belle in the rearview. I didn't want to say anything with her in the car. Nothing about what I was thinking, or what had happened. For as much as she had talked about acting selflessly yesterday, she hadn't taken the opportunity to back those words up with action.

I didn't like people who hedged their bets.

It said a whole lot about Belle, if I was more willing to talk with Raphael, than her.

"What's there to say?" I said. "The Dumonts are after us now. It'd be nice to know why."

"My father and Victor have never gotten along," Raphael said. "I would think he'd be happy to have him killed."

"Apparently not," I said. "And they sent their number-one killer to do the job, right? So the Dumonts are serious about it."

I was beginning to think it all had something to do with the geas. There was the way my father had looked when I asked him if he could resurrect someone.

"Whatever you do, you don't bring your mother or me back. Ever. Understand?"

When I was near my father, I had felt the geas. Just like I had felt the curse back in Grafton when I was near my mother, or Dominic. The power commanding my parents resonated in me, biding its time, ready to take control of me, when needed.

Dominic and Victor Dumont would both be in Colorado Springs. Two people who could control me with the geas.

Two other people bound by it.

I had wondered if both curses could control me. What would happen to me if Dominic ordered me to turn right, and Victor told me to go left? Which order would I be forced to follow? Or would my body tear itself in two, trying to follow both?

There was something there, with why my father had been sent to kill me. Something to do with the geas. Everyone in Colorado Springs had something to do with it. And my father hadn't been terrified being brought back from death. He had been terrified of *me* being the one to do it.

What did that mean? His fear hinted at a purpose I couldn't even begin to guess.

It circled back to the geas. Everything now was about it. It was the only thing that tied us all together. Me, my mother, my father. Dominic, Victor Dumont, and Raphael. It was the only thing that made sense.

I rubbed my eyes.

"What do you know about the geas?" I asked.

"Not much, other than I could control you with it," Raphael said. "My father first told me about it when I was sixteen. That was when–"

I cut him off, curtly. "I know when it was." That was when he had killed Danny. "That bill will come due."

"You mean it'll come due, again," Raphael said. He arched an eyebrow. "You know, you have killed me once for that."

"Once just wasn't good enough," I replied. Then I glanced at the rearview. "But I wasn't asking you. I was asking her."

Belle glanced over at me, but the demon didn't answer. There was something between us now, from when I had gotten on her about not helping when my father appeared.

"Nothing to say?" I said.

It remained quiet in the car. And I think maybe that got to me. I was riding a knife's edge of hope, trying to rescue the woman I loved. Thoughts churned around in my mind. The not-good kind.

The Key was breaking. I was running out of time, and I felt the loss of every minute. Like time was a broken hourglass, the bottom shattered, the sands running out of the top and getting blown away by a screaming wind.

And more pressures piled on. My sword wouldn't be summoned. I was maybe more demon than angel. I had pulled power from Jen, and that could only lead to her disappearing like all the other ghosts I had pulled from.

I had Raphael and his demon friend as company. His demon lawyer, just below Lucifer in terms of power. A strong demon who had hidden from a fight when she could have helped.

And a fucking contract. Another time limit. Another hourglass, waiting to break.

Belle could talk all she wanted about enforcing the agreement, but she hadn't stayed around when the going got tough. How long would she stay next time? Long enough to stab me in the back?

I needed answers. And I was tired of all the bullshit. I slammed on the brakes and pulled the Camaro off to the side of the road. The car fishtailed back and forth, nose down to the ground, until we stopped.

Raphael cursed and braced himself on the dashboard. Right after we stopped, an eighteen-wheeler rig rocketed past us, the driver laying long and hard on the horn, the wind of its passage buffeting the car and rocking it.

I switched the Camaro off and got out. The air was bitterly cold, and all I wore was my shirt, but I didn't care. I took the shotgun from by the seat and walked over to the other side of the Camaro. Yanked open the passenger door, and pointed the barrel at Belle.

"Get out," I said.

Raphael held his hands out. "Wait a minute."

"You want to go, too?" I asked him.

He went quiet.

Belle sat there, and looked at me. "I am here to–"

"Ensure the agreement is met." I said the words with her. "Yeah, I'm sick of hearing that. If you're not going to provide actual help, I don't need you."

She looked at Raphael, or the back of his head.

I pumped the shotgun.

"That won't kill me," she said.

"It'll get you the fuck out of my car," I said. "I don't need you enforcing me. Or ensuring some fucking agreement. I've taken care of Raphael before, so I don't need you for that, either."

"You are so *sure* about that?" Belle said.

I leaned closer, into the back of the car, making sure Belle caught my gaze fully. So she would not misunderstand my intent. "I'm going to ask you one last time. What do you know about the geas?"

Her mouth was closed, but her jaw muscles worked on the sides of her face. Like she was thinking about how much she knew. Or maybe how much she should tell me.

"We don't know that much," she finally said.

"You mean you haven't found out anything at all? For the past three thousand years?" I shook my head. "I'm not buying that."

"We do know some," she said. "Azazel bound the seven most dangerous angels he could find. The seven he hated the most. At the time, we all were happy about it, really."

"Even though he broke the agreement?"

"Even though," she agreed.

"So all these lectures about the agreement, then," I said, "seems kind of like bullshit."

"It's a lesson we learned," she said. "Pray you don't learn it, too."

Selfless good deeds, my ass. When angels had been enslaved, everyone in hell all stood by cheering. It was only after the fact, when they realized what Azazel had done would cause a response, that they had gotten angry. When they had realized they could be played just as much as the other side.

Azazel always set you up with something small, at first. If they had realized their mistake at all, it was only after it was way too late to do anything about it. I was living proof. And if I knew that, after six years with the demon, then Belial and Lucifer should, after six thousand.

I rolled my eyes. "That's what Azazel does."

"We should have known better," Belle said, understanding the admonition. "Sometimes judgments get clouded in war."

Raphael motioned to his seat belt. I nodded okay. He unclipped it and swiveled to look at the backseat. Funny how two people who hate each other can learn how to work together. Apparently he was interested now as well.

"The geas?" I asked again.

"We don't know this for certain," Belle answered, slowly. "But it makes sense, to us, for Azazel to have protections involved in the curse itself."

I rolled my eyes. *Of course.* It wouldn't be a curse unless Azazel had a few traps inside it. "What do you mean by protections?"

"Azazel would want to protect himself," she said. "And in order to do that, he would want to make sure no one would try to break it."

She meant he wouldn't want a few angels, trained to kill since birth, liberated from the geas and free to hunt him down.

"By breaking the geas, you mean what?" Raphael asked. "Killing my father?"

Belle looked at me, and then looked at Raphael. As if trying to make a decision. I wasn't sure if she didn't want to say something in front of him, or in front of me. Or perhaps she was just figuring out how much information to parse out.

Raphael tilted his head at Belle, as if waiting for her answer.

I was getting a worse and worse feeling about the *agreement*.

"Likely not that, by itself," Belle finally said. "But killing him, with no surviving heir to pass control of the curse to?"

Her head tilted back and forth, side to side, as if she wasn't wholly confident in the answer. "That might be a condition he would place on the holder of the geas. To always have an heir."

Interesting. Even more reason for Dominic to figure out a way to have Raphael. A son to pass the geas to.

"Why not tell us this earlier?" I asked.

Belle's eyes once again flicked to Raphael. "I am just here to enforce the agreement. To make sure you keep your word."

"So, what was all that about being selfless?" I asked. "Something you preach, but don't live?"

Belle didn't answer.

"Figured," I said. I couldn't trust her, or Raphael, but knowing it and experiencing it were two different things. It would be much easier going this alone. "Maybe it's just not in your nature, right?"

"I had a family," Raphael said aloud. "Brothers. All killed before I was born."

Which would have made figuring out how to have an heir extremely important to Dominic. It wouldn't be hard to add all of that together, and come up with Azazel. I shouldn't be surprised, how far his plan had reached back, but I found that I was.

"The geas wouldn't pass to me now." Raphael kept talking. Understanding. "Because I'm no longer a vampire."

"So Dominic doesn't have an heir, then," I said. "So, what happens if we kill him?"

"It's not like Azazel came and told us everything," Belle said. "And if he had, it's not like we would have trusted what he told us."

I placed the barrel of the gun firmly on her chest. Right in the middle. The veins in my arms, and hands, all tight from the strain of not pulling the trigger.

She looked at the shotgun, then looked at Raphael. He raised his eyebrows.

"The bound angel likely dies with Dominic," Belle said. "That makes a morbid kind of sense."

It did. And it would keep Azazel safe from an unbound angel. And if one less angel walked the earth, so much the better for Belle's side. Which told me how much of the lesson they had really learned, down there.

"Funny, how you hid that from me," I said.

It made what I wanted to do almost impossible.

I just needed five minutes with my mother. But there was a good chance Dominic wasn't going to let me have that time. Even if he was lucid, and not fighting off the withdrawal from the drug Raphael had injected into him. So I had been okay with the idea of killing the vampire, because it would have made it easier for me to get the information I needed.

But now I was stuck. Dominic likely wouldn't let me talk to my mother. But if I killed him, she would die as well.

What options did that leave me with?

This thing had gotten messier. More dangerous. My father was here as well. Victor Dumont, too. With an army of his vampires.

Were they here to stop me from killing Dominic? From loosing a bound angel? Something there didn't make sense. I couldn't shake the feeling I was being played. I just didn't understand how. Or even who. Raphael? Belle? Both?

Why?

I took a breath.

I took another.

Then I spun around and walked off the shoulder, into the thick grass on the side of the rode. *"Fuck!"*

I stumbled across something plastic that crinkled under my foot. I kicked it, but it didn't fly too far. Just *wuuushed* through the thick grass in front of me, until it stopped.

"Fuck, fuck, fuck," I muttered. Trying to figure out how to go forward. My mother had brought me back from the dead. I wanted to learn how she had, for Jen. But there seemed to be no way I'd be able to talk to her.

The Camaro's suspension creaked. A moment later Raphael stood next to me. "Got tougher, didn't it?"

I didn't answer. What kind of world was this where one of the people I hated most came out and tried to comfort me? I didn't know this new Raphael, and the longer this drive went, the more Belle tried to work me, the more uncomfortable I felt about all of it. There was nowhere I could turn, no one I could trust, and it was beginning to wear on me.

"So let's shoot her, then," he said.

I snorted. That was the Raphael I knew. "Wouldn't help."

"Yeah, but if it makes you feel better," he said.

"Sometimes I wish that was all it took," I said.

"So, do we need her, then?" Raphael said. "I told you I'm good, as far as our agreement goes."

"Shit, I don't know," I said. "But I don't trust her."

Then I focused on Raphael. "Or you."

Something about all of this wasn't right. It didn't fit. I just couldn't see what it was. Truth was, Raphael wasn't the only person who had been bad at looking into the future. I had been bitten enough by things I hadn't seen.

And there was something large here I wasn't seeing. I just didn't know who was going to betray me. If it was going to be Raphael, Belle, or the both of them.

The demon just grinned.

"Hell, Grimm, that seems to me that would be normal for you," he said. "Who *would* you trust? Who *have* you trusted?"

"There is that," I said.

"So let's tear up the contract," Raphael said, lifting one shoulder and letting it fall. "And just go with it. I'm game if you are."

I didn't think Belle would just let that happen. And she wanted to be close by. As hard as it was to have both of them around, here was the only place they could be. Whenever the betrayal happened, I had to be around so I could stop it.

If they were unseen, the knife might fall, and I'd never see it coming. I shook my head.

"So, what are we doing?" he asked.

"I don't know," I said. "But *we're* not doing anything."

"Sure," he said. "I get it."

He was entirely too comfortable with going along. Almost to get along.

I didn't trust him. But I couldn't figure out what Raphael was up to. He wanted to kill Azazel, sure. And he had always wanted to kill his father. But he had never been agreeable before. It was almost too much.

The thought made me grin.

Raphael looked at me, suddenly curious.

I didn't explain, just headed back to the car. Raphael followed. We both got in, me putting the shotgun back in its place by the seat. Belle sat quietly in the back, like she had known she wasn't going anywhere.

I went to start the Camaro, wanting to get the heat kicked on again. It was freezing outside. It occurred to me I had a bit of good news, out of everything that had just happened.

My father had been afraid I would try to bring him, or my mother, back from the dead.

Regardless of why he was afraid, or what he was afraid of, the fact that he was afraid did mean one thing to me.

Bringing Jen back *was* possible. And it was possible for *me*. It was something I could do. I had thought it was possible, and had begun to believe I could do it, but now confirmation had come, from my father's words.

Which really was all I should be worried about. Whatever Raphael and Belle wanted from me, I had six hundred or so days left to get it to them. The Key would likely break long before then. So there was plenty of time to fulfill the contract, after rescuing Jen.

The Camaro fired up with a roar, and I spun back out onto the road, and into the night.

CHAPTER TWENTY-FIVE

Nick woke from the backseat of the sports utility vehicle he had stolen. It was a four-door, black, with large wheels and tinted windows. A big inside cabin, with a bench middle seat, and a smaller third bench behind that one. It smelled like sandalwood, though the air freshener in the vents had a "new car" label on it.

Still, it was big. Nick had wanted something with plenty of room. He had been tired of being cramped, on the road.

Johnny had been driving, but the truck was stopped now. Quiet, but idling. They were sitting in a parking lot, with a few vehicles around them. It was dark out, and it felt like early morning, or after midnight. It was cold enough outside that the windshield had fogged, so Johnny had the fan on high. There was the sound of hot hair blowing up against the glass, creating two half-moon patterns there in the fog.

Nick looked at the blue digital clock on the dash. Three thirty in the morning.

He had been sleeping for just a few hours, then.

"What's up?" he asked.

Johnny nodded to the right. Nick struggled to push himself up in the seat, looking that way.

They were in a motel parking lot. In the back of it. The motel itself looked like it had been hit with a wrecking ball, from the inside. The walls had exploded outward, and peeled back some, cracks running through it like a spiderweb.

The explosion, if that was what it had been, had been on the bottom floor of the motel, somewhere in the middle of it. It looked like it had knocked out all the power there; none of the motel lights were lit. Even the parking lot. What Nick could see was in the headlamps and beams of the nearby emergency vehicles.

A firetruck was parked off to the side. A few cop cars beside it. All with their lights off, as if they had been there awhile. There were some state road trucks as well, the white equipment trucks with the yellow road signs on the back. The area was roped off with caution tape. A number of workers were walking through the lot, picking up debris.

"A few cops sped by me, on the interstate," Johnny said. "I took a chance and followed them here. I thought wherever these cops were going, Grimm was likely at."

The firemen were hanging around the outside of the wall, by the hole. Cops hung back a little farther, talking to people various states of dress: pajamas, robes, jeans, and shirts. Quite a few of those held travel bags.

"It's not a bad bet," Nick said.

"Yeah," Johnny said.

The passenger door opened. Sarah got in, huddled in a jacket. A blast of cold air came in with her. She twisted in the seat to face the two of them, and brushed part of her hair back.

"I talked to some of the people," she said. "The firefighters know it's not a gas leak. They just can't figure out what happened. Someone said they thought it was a freak lightning strike."

Nick looked up at the sky. It was black, and clear, with a sliver of a moon falling to the west. No clouds.

"Sounds like someone we know," Johnny said.

It did sound like Jen. But there was no way Grimm would have brought her back and not reached out to his friends. Nick didn't know what had happened here, but he would bet Grimm had been part of it, and things probably hadn't gone the way he had expected.

"Yeah," Sarah agreed.

"You think he got ambushed?" Nick said.

"Maybe," Sarah said. "I can't get into the room to see anything."

Nick smiled then. "That's what I'm for."

He looked across the parking lot, at the hole in the motel wall. Deep into the shadows there. And then shifted.

There was always a slight tug when he walked the shadows. It was like the snip of a thread, like Nick had to cut away from wherever he was standing, in order to move to the next. It wasn't painful, or powerful. He was always just aware of it as a sensation.

Then he appeared, deep in the motel room. At the back corner, by the bathroom. He instantly wished he had brought his jacket. It was colder than he had thought outside. His bare skin instantly goose-bumped, and his breath came out as little clouds.

So Nick worked quickly, going through the back of the room first. His eyes always instantly adjusted to the dark, like they had been made for the night. He knew to others, the room would be lumps and shadows. To him, it was like everything was well lit, even though it was dark. He had trouble explaining it. Everything was still black, but he could still see like it was daylight. It was just a black kind of daylight. It was easy for him to see the sunken, shattered floor in front of the bed. The coverlet on the mattress, gathered together on one side. Little bits of the wall and ceiling lying everywhere.

Voices came from outside the room. People discussing what had happened. Someone mentioned things had gone to hell since New Orleans happened.

Nick thought a truer statement probably hadn't been uttered.

There was a shirt hanging on the back of the bathroom door. He grabbed it. Then he made his way through the middle of the room. There were piles of splintered particleboard in front of the bed. Nick guessed it had once been a dresser. He moved his hand through that, finding square pieces of plastic, and glass.

A television.

There was a pillow, a bit farther up by the door. And a strong smell of ozone, throughout the whole room. Nick was more careful in the front of the room, watching outside and only moving when he was sure no one was walking by. He moved, not by walking, but by moving from shadow to shadow.

He did it that way so that no one would see his motion. Some humans had that sense, seeing something flicker at the edge of their vision, in the darkness. So Nick had perfected his shadow-walking. He would remain still, let the shadow swallow him, and then reappear in a different part of the darkness, farther away. Nick was a statue in one place, then a statue in another, and in that way he went from standing in one corner of the room, to kneeling by the bed, to lying down by the back wall.

On the far side of the bed he found a charging cable. As if to charge a phone. Part of the cord was charred, and attached to the bottom half of a cell phone. He stuck that in his pocket.

Nick searched for a little bit longer, but found nothing else of value.

He looked briefly at the truck. Johnny hadn't moved it. Which made it easier to walk the shadows back.

Tug, cut. And he was in the backseat again. His glasses immediately fogged up, from being out in the cold, and then instantly in a warm place. Nick took them off and wiped them with the shirt.

Johnny's eyes were open, as if he had been staring at the seat the entire time.

"It's weird, man," Johnny said. "You kind of just appear. There's, like, a blur, and then you're there."

Nick raised his eyebrows, as if saying, *It's just what I do.*

"Find anything?" Sarah asked.

He pulled out the burned cord, the half a phone, and held out the shirt.

The shirt was black and had a superhero logo on it. It still smelled new, mothball-like, as if it had been bought from a store and hadn't been washed yet.

Grimm had worn something like this, coming into New Orleans.

"I think it's Grimm's," Nick said.

Johnny rolled his eyes at the half of the cell phone. "Well, at least we know the reason he's not answering."

"Yeah," Nick said.

"Think he's okay?" Sarah asked. Her face looked worried, and Nick thought she wasn't just worried about Grimm, but about her hope for her sister.

He tried to comfort her. It still was weird for him. This not-quite-a-friend, not-quite-a-boyfriend thing was another world between them. He had trouble navigating this world. He wanted to be just the one, but didn't know how to get there. He wished it was more like walking shadows, where he could just want to be somewhere, and then he was there.

But sometimes distances had to be crossed in a slower manner. Sometimes you had to walk them, and trip and fall, and climb, and get there when you got there.

Nick motioned yes with his head. Not trusting his voice, in the moment.

"Grimm'll be fine," Johnny said. "He'll be the last person standing after a nuclear war. It'll be him and the cockroaches. And the cockroaches probably will be worried."

Sarah smiled a little at that. Even Nick found a grin on his face. Grimm was scary when we wanted to be.

He could be a lot of things.

"The wall burst outwards," Nick said. "The door was missing, too. I'm thinking someone or something surprised him, and then was thrown back out. Violently."

"It wouldn't be Raphael, right?" Johnny said. "You think they're traveling together?"

"I don't know," Nick said. "Nothing else in the room but what I found."

"So, where'd he go, then?" Sarah asked. "Grimm?"

"Denver is west of here," Johnny said. His hand tapped the steering wheel. "Couple of hours, maybe, if we fly."

"Want to change up?" Nick asked him. They had all taken turns, driving nonstop, trying to catch Grimm.

Johnny tilted his head back and forth, like he didn't know. Finally he unclipped his seat belt. "Sure."

They changed seats. For a moment Nick had gotten up, half-crouched in the vehicle, one hand on Sarah's shoulder to balance him. It seemed like an electricity tingled under his palm, between them, and the two of them locked eyes while Johnny scooted on by.

Nick winked.

Sarah smiled, and lightly patted his hand. Her eyes were moist. Though she had told Nick she wasn't worried about her sister, that she believed in Grimm, she had to be worried. And held that worry in, the best she could.

Nick got into the driver's seat, scooting the seat back a hair. He buckled up and adjusted the mirrors. He turned the defogger down so the hot air wouldn't blow against his face.

Then he drove them off. The truck's engine was strong and the vehicle rolled easily out of the parking lot and onto the road. Nick punched the gas and the truck accelerated with a long, slow pull onto the interstate ramp.

Sarah ran a hand through her hair. He recognized the motion as one of her nervous tics. Something she did when she was thinking.

"Going to sleep?" Nick asked her.

"Me?" Sarah shook her head. "I couldn't."

"Want the radio on?"

"No," she said. Her mind still distant. "Thanks, though."

Nick drifted the truck into the left lane so he could pass a row of eighteen-wheelers in the slow lane. There were a bunch of trucks, their tail-lights burning bright, pair after pair, as he passed them, long trailer after long trailer, the drivers pushing their rigs hard against the steady climb to the Rockies.

Each truck rumbled loud as they passed it, and then faded behind them, headlights bright in his rearview. The silver panels had a big blue name on their side, some supermarket, food and clothes being shipped to stores around the country.

Funny, how the world could go to hell, or – Nick thought – hell could come to the world, and people still had to eat. Buy clothes. Probably pay bills.

They passed the last rig then. Nick set the cruise control to eighty-nine. One under twenty above. He hoped the police would be busy elsewhere for a bit, and he had something that might help Sarah. "You asleep, Johnny?"

"Not yet," he muttered, after a bit.

"Look in the third seat," Nick said. "There's something for Sarah there."

Johnny gave Nick one arched eyebrow. Then unbuckled his seat belt and climbed into the back. He grumbled a bit, wanting to know what he was looking for, but he ended up recognizing it as soon as he saw it.

"Oh," he said. And pulled a guitar case out from between the seats. Where Nick had tucked it, earlier.

Sarah's eyes lit up.

Nick grinned.

Johnny brought it up, sliding it carefully across the backs of the seats. Sarah took it from him and unzipped it. The case was cheap and soft, and lay against the shape of the guitar like a cloth.

While Nick was out looking for a vehicle in New Orleans, he had shadow-walked a music store. Or a pawnshop. It looked like it could be either. He didn't know much about guitars, but saw this acoustic one and had taken it. Along with a case.

And because it was for Sarah, left some money on the counter.

Sarah took the guitar out. It was a light chestnut color, but Nick had grabbed it because of the picture on its face. A tiny blue stream wound across the guitar, from the neck of the guitar to its base. A range of hills perched above the river, and a brilliant sun sat in the bottom-left corner, above the highest mountain.

She turned in the seat, putting one leg to the side, and set the guitar on her lap. Sarah tuned it with little plucks of the strings. She would pluck, turn the knob, and pluck again. At first they were little *tinks*, but after a few minutes the strings vibrated at the right pitch, and soft notes drifted inside the truck.

The music made Nick feel lighter. The air seemed easier to breathe. All of a sudden the three of them on a road trip, and not tired from a long drive, racing to save Grimm.

Sarah began to hum, in harmony with the guitar, and the sound resonated up and down Nick's spine. She looked at him and smiled, and he smiled in return.

She played. Something soft and smooth and slow. The song was a little broken, here and there, as Sarah remembered how to play it. She started hesitantly, and then fell into a rhythmic playing of the strings, her voice humming in counterpoint. Then she played a little more, and a little harder, and her humming became a crooning, and then the crooning a song.

Her voice had always been a little ethereal. Angelic. It was full of emotion, yet fragile, and would break at just the right note. Nick thought he had fallen in love with her the first moment he heard her play.

Nick glanced at the rearview. Johnny lay back on his seat, eyes closed, arms folded around him, but his fingers tapped lightly on his chest. In rhythm. His lips curved in a slight smile.

Sarah's face was focused, concentrated, her eyes closed. She played and softly sang, and played some more. Nick turned back to the road and focused on the drive, listening to his girl sing, smiling inside.

There was still some distance between them, but the most memorable journeys took the greatest number of steps.

CHAPTER TWENTY-SIX

Snow had begun to fall as we closed in on Denver. The sun had begun to rise in the east, bright orange in my rearview mirror. The sky around us was a pale light blue, dotted by the thousands with white snowflakes. It hadn't taken long before I had to turn on the wipers. They rubbed against the windshield in long, slow arcs, leaving behind a tiny pile of snow to the left of each blade.

I had looked at the map early in the drive and decided to cut southwest before getting to Denver. We'd save some time, angling off the interstate, heading southwest to Colorado Springs. And while not an interstate, the state road was large enough to handle the weather, a four-lane expressway. I thought I had made a good choice. It was a shorter drive, and maybe going off the interstate would throw my father off the hunt.

If he was still behind us. I had to bet he was. No matter how much he fought it, the geas would drive him.

It wasn't long before I found taking the shortcut hadn't been the best decision. The morning brought a snow, thick big flakes, and after a bit I had to slow the Camaro down. The first sharp turn, where the car had slid into the opposing lane, convinced me to take it easy.

The flakes were wet and packed easily, and soon a couple of inches existed everywhere. The snow turned the shoulder, the median, all the pine trees and fields into a white canvas that sparkled as the sun rose.

The highway led upward in the hills before us, the road's surface bleak and white, sparkling where rays of the morning sun caught bits of ice. In front of me was a canvas, the Camaro was the brush, and together we left a long, dark streak that cut everything behind us in two.

It was a ghostly road, leading to an ethereal end. Everything was wide-open, and at the same time everything was marred. It would have been beautiful, had I not been riding with a pair of demons.

Raphael was catching a nap. Belle hadn't done much of anything. She stared at the window, perfectly content with whatever plan she had for me.

I hadn't figured that out yet. And having to focus on driving didn't allow me the time to think much about it.

Belle had mentioned Lucifer. She and the head demon seemed to be together on this. Once, Azazel had told me he saw Lucifer as much as I saw the other guy. Then I thought that meant neither existed.

Now I wasn't sure. If what Belle was saying was real, then she and Lucifer were standing together against whatever Azazel had planned. So Lucifer, the actual real devil, might actually be real. Which meant, possibly, that the other guy was, too.

What Azazel had told me had felt true to me, at least it had the ring of truth. But maybe it was just something I wanted to believe, because to actually believe in a heaven and hell, to believe in those places, the creation of the places, and the creator, would mean that my entire life, everything I've done, I would have to view all of it in a different light.

It all came down to which of the demons I wanted to believe. Azazel? Or Belle?

The answer wasn't clear.

Azazel would always lie to me, not for the fun of it, but always with some ulterior purpose. I was sure Belle was the same, even with all that talk about honor among thieves, about honoring the agreement, about words mattering.

Especially if by keeping something from me, Belle could get what she and Lucifer wanted.

There was no good option, for me. No real information I could act on, or trust. No facts to act on, and no one telling me anything I could have any confidence in.

I guess I could believe one thing or the other. Without facts. Without being certain.

But that kind of thing wasn't me.

A tall sign broke over the white-coated trees ahead. The top of it announced gas prices, food, drink. A large truck stop, a few miles up, it appeared. A good place to get some breakfast and some coffee.

Maybe a lot of coffee. I was pretty beat.

Raphael woke as I slowed down. He stretched a bit, and looked surprised by all the snow.

"Going to be cold out," he said.

I wondered if demons felt the cold. Azazel spent so much time pretending to be human, I always wondered what was real, and what was an act. Whatever, neither Belle nor Raphael had a thick coat, and I just had a light jacket. Something to put the .38 in.

The gas station was long, and wide, and surrounded by large windows reaching from the ceiling all the way down to maybe a person's hip. Thick panes of glass, through which there were candy aisles and rows of chips and nuts, bags of beef jerky. Even refrigerators along the back wall, holding sodas and water and crazy-colored cans of energy drinks.

To the right was a breakfast place. Booths and a long counter with stools in front of it. Like a diner.

I swallowed a bit, thinking of Miss Tammie.

I parked the car by the diner and got out. The thick flakes of snow immediately coated me, sticking to my hair, melting on the skin of my arms. It was cold, but there was little to no wind, so it wasn't frigid. I shut the door and walked over to the double doors in the middle of the gas station. The doors separated the diner side from the store.

The station was warm. A smell of sausage carried through the air. There were bathrooms right in front of me and I went in and used one, splashing water on my face, running my fingers through my hair.

I looked a mess. Dark circles under each eye. Hair curled in places, spiked in others. I still was too thin, I wasn't eating enough, and what energy I used I usually pulled from ghosts. If someone didn't know me, they would think me a junkie.

Which wasn't far off the truth.

I needed a good meal, or a bunch of good meals. I'd grab one, or a couple, here.

Raphael came in then. Stopped to look at me looking at myself in the mirror. He was still dressed in black slacks and a white button-up shirt. Very non-truck-stop clothes. He grunted, rolled his eyes, and walked by to use the bathroom. Which settled the whole "is it an act or real?" thing I kept wondering about.

I left and headed to the diner. Sat in a booth, where four laminated menus lay on the table. An older waitress walked up, blue shirt, white apron, gray-black hair back in a bun. Her name tag said Betty. I ordered some biscuits and gravy, some eggs, and a thing of pancakes.

"You can pay, right?" she asked, after writing my order on a white pad, then sticking the pen back behind her here.

I flashed some of the folded twenties out of my pocket. "Not angling for much of a tip, are you, Betty?"

Betty shrugged. "Sorry, we've been getting some odd folks here."

Raphael slid in, across the table from me. He glanced at the menu and frowned. "Have any fruit?"

Betty pursed her lips. "It's on the menu," she said.

The demon scanned down it with his finger, then shook his head when he reached the bottom right corner. "I'll take the fruit bowl mix, then. And an egg-white omelet."

"I don't know if we have egg whites," she said.

"Look," Raphael said, "there's a hundred dollars in it for you, if you can come up with some."

"Okay, then," she said. "Coffee?"

"Please," I said. "Plenty."

"I'll be back." She walked off.

"She didn't write down your order," I said.

"Egg whites aren't hard to make," he replied, shaking his head.

Weird, having this kind of conversation with Raphael. Just weird.

I looked outside. Belle sat in the back of the Camaro, staring out the side window. "She not hungry?"

"She didn't say." Raphael grabbed all four menus, tapping them on the table to keep them together, and then set them against the wall. Then he took a napkin and wiped the surface down.

Weird.

Betty came back with a very black pot of coffee, and a couple of white coffee cups on saucers. She set both cups down, and poured the coffee into it. The liquid steamed, and the aroma of roasted beans hit me.

"Cream?"

I shook my head. Raphael nodded. "Half-and-half, if you have it."

Betty smiled to herself, as if she had won a bet. "Be right back."

She left the pot of coffee there.

I raised the cup in both hands and took a breath of the coffee, goose bumps rising on my arms, and along my spine. The first sip was bitter, and black, and both acrid and tasty on my tongue. The first cup of coffee sometimes was everything in a day.

Raphael waited until he got his half-and-half. It came in little white plastic cups, barely larger than thimbles, with pink tops. He carefully peeled the tops back and poured two into his cup, then stirred everything with a spoon in slow, perfect circles.

It hadn't been long ago that I shared coffee with Jen. Flavored brews, lattes, sometimes mocha, sometimes vanilla.

Life was definitely different, with her. Without her I had reverted to my base self. Just what I needed to survive. Maybe not so much what I needed to really live.

Betty brought the food out. My meal was on three different plates, all thick, white, and hot to the touch. Like they had come fresh from the dishwasher.

The biscuits were dripping with gravy, and I dug into them. The gravy was warm, the biscuits were moist and slathered with butter, and as I ate I found spicy pieces of pork sausage. It was delicious.

"That stuff looks like a heart attack," Raphael said. He only had his fruit bowl, a mix of sad-looking grapes, strawberries, and melon. He stabbed each piece with a fork, and ate that separately.

"I don't argue with delicious," I said. I could always heal my arteries, if they needed it. Which, if I had been a regular person, they might have, after the years of fast food, peanut butter cups, and meals like this.

Betty came back with Raphael's omelet. It was large and pale yellow. Flat on the plate. She laid it in front of him and waited, raising both eyebrows.

Raphael sighed and pulled out a hundred-dollar bill, and handed it over.

Betty smiled, taking the bill, and left. I may have imagined it, but her walk seemed like it had a little extra spring in it.

We went back to eating, both of us quiet. Raphael carefully cut his omelet into strips. Then he would roll each strip up, stab it with his fork, and eat it.

I just dug into mine. When I couldn't eat any more biscuit, I switched over to the pancakes. The sugary maple syrup mixed perfectly with the melted butter. I ate those until I had to lean back and take a breath, trying to find more room in my stomach. It was delicious, and with a little regret I slid the empty plate aside and started on my eggs.

They were a little cool by now, but still good. Scrambled, with hash browns mixed in. Onions and bits of sausage, too. All sautéed in butter and melted in cheese.

Good stuff.

I finally got to a part where I felt full. I pushed that plate off to join its brother. Taking short breaths. My stomach felt a little tight.

I had needed that food.

I refilled my cup with the pot of coffee, then sat back and drank the hot brew. The snow still fell outside, heavy, and there was maybe an inch covering the Camaro, except for the center of the hood, where the snow had melted. Other than that, even the windows were covered. Maybe a little movement in the backseat.

"I wonder if she's still staring out the side," I said.

"Who, Belle?" Raphael paused with a grape halfway to his mouth. He still had a good amount of the fruit bowl left. "Probably."

"I can't figure you two out," I said. "I guess it doesn't matter, though."

"What's there to figure?" he said. "I told you why I got her, didn't I?"

"Yeah." I rolled my eyes. "So I would trust you."

"That's for real," Raphael said. "I meant it."

"I'm sure you did," I said. "I'm just not sure how you thought that would help."

"Grimm." He laid his fork down. "In all our time together. Everything we fought about. Was there one time I came at you from behind? That I tried to fool you into something?"

I thought about it. He was right. We had been two kids who just flat-out hated each other. I hated him because he had been a narcissistic know-it-all rich kid who wanted everything his way. I didn't know why he really hated me, but in my mind it had always been because I was the first kid who had stood up to him.

"No," I finally said.

"No," he echoed. "Don't let me being nice here fool you. I still don't like you, Grimm. I've always hated you. But when we finish things between us, it'll be best man left standing. It'll be straight."

Raphael was saying that now, but he had spent half the drive telling me how much he had learned in death. How he had changed. How he was going to be different. And instead of going after Azazel, he was using me in a scheme to kill the demon. It wasn't the Raphael I was used to.

He couldn't have it both ways. Either he was changed or he wasn't. What wouldn't change is me trusting him. I just flat wouldn't.

"There's not much more here I can say or do," Raphael said. "You're either going to trust me or you're not."

I raised my eyebrows. "Decidedly not."

"That's on you, then," Raphael said. "But if you're going around looking for ways that I'm going to betray you, you're wasting time and energy on something that's not going to happen. Time and energy better spent on other things."

"I've got energy to spare," I said.

Raphael snorted. "Didn't you just see yourself in the mirror?"

"Whatever," I said.

"Whatever," he mocked. "When the time comes between us, Grimm, I'm going to put that on your headstone."

I shook my head, glancing at the ceiling. *Whatever.*

Raphael drained the last of his coffee, then poured himself some more. Did the same thing as he did before with two half-and-half cups, and the circling of the spoon.

"Let's get to it, then," he said.

"Get to what?"

"Colorado Springs," Raphael said. "We need to figure that out."

"What makes you think I'm figuring out anything with you?" I asked.

"Man, we've got to have a plan," he said.

"Why?" I said. "So you know what I'm going to do?"

His eyebrows lowered. "Look Grimm, trust me or don't. But come up with something for this geas thing before we go in. My father is going to have whatever is left of his forces there, and I'm not having you blame me for getting your mother killed."

He set his cup down. Our gazes held for a minute. This seemed to me like a way for him and Belle to figure out what I was going to do, and then stab me in the back when I went to do it.

He looked at me. "I told you, I'm playing this straight.'

Sure.

The problem was, I didn't really have a plan. I didn't know what I was going to do. I needed five minutes to talk to my mother. Hopefully she could answer me. After that, I wanted to leave. I didn't have an idea of what to do about the geas. Part of me wished it would call to me, so I would know where they were. So I could just *get there* and find a way to talk to my mother. Without Raphael or Belle.

I couldn't kill Dominic now. And I didn't want Raphael to do it, either. Especially if the geas would kill my mother.

But there was the contract. It was likely Raphael was going to be just as bound by it as me. Which meant – if I asked him not to fulfill his side, then in six hundred and some odd days Belial would be coming to get Raphael, to bring before me.

He wasn't going to want to be a part of that.

Of course, the contract might not even be real. I wasn't sure how it could be held up. But it had felt real. And Raphael had lined out and initialed his part, like it had been a legal document. Did that stuff count in the real world? Would it hold up in some court in hell?

Fuck. I was going around in circles. No plan. No way out. Just a desire to see one thing through, to bring Jen back before the Key broke and she was gone forever. I leaned against the back of the booth, and slid down a bit in my seat. Slumping.

I never had a plan. I didn't have anything other than going in, guns blazing.

Raphael had picked up his spoon and was slowly stirring his coffee. The tip of the spoon circled around the ceramic bottom and produced a scrawling type of ringing, claylike tone.

"Let me ask you something," Raphael said.

What did I have to lose? "Shoot."

He smiled. "You think my father knows I'm dead?"

I didn't know where he was going to go with this. Dominic had fled

Grafton before I killed Raphael. My mother had rescued the vampire, and taken him as far away as she could. When I left, with Jen and my friends, most of the town had been burned to the ground. What was left had still been burning.

"I don't know," I said.

"So there's a chance he could think I'm alive?" Raphael said.

"I told you," I said, "I don't know."

"Here's what I'm thinking," Raphael said. "Let's just go in through the front door."

He wanted to take me to the one place where Dominic could control me. Seemed a little obvious. There was only one way that could end. I shook my head. "Nope."

"Here me out," Raphael said. "Let's go in, pretending you're under the geas to me. Let me make something up to my father, if he's lucid enough."

I thought about it. "Prodigal son returns home?"

"Sure," Raphael said. "Call it that."

I perked up a bit. Sat a bit straighter in the booth. It had a slim chance of working. If Raphael could get us into his father's place, without any fighting. If he could get me near my mother, just for a minute.

Of course, that would mean I would have to trust someone newly born as a demon. "That's asking a lot of our new ... relationship."

He arched an eyebrow. "It's going to have to be your call."

The only other plan wasn't really a plan. Trying to sneak into Colorado Springs, a place where Dominic had lived forever, and finding a place to hide. Using a little ghost, and hoping my mother would come to me. Without orders to kill me, or a geas to pull me to her.

And if I did do something to alert my mother I was in town, if she could find me using her ethereal senses, my father could as well.

That would be a hell of a reunion. And one I certainly wouldn't survive.

"I hate to say it," I said, "but that's a better idea than anything I can come up with."

"So let's do it," Raphael said.

"What about the contract?" I said. "Killing your father?"

"In the beginning you just wanted to find him, right?" Raphael said. "So you could find your mother?"

"Yeah," I admitted.

"We have time to kill him, before my side of the contract is due," he said. "If I can keep from doing it, I'll give you that time."

I shook my head again. The idea had a chance of working, but it also easily put Raphael next to his father. Who he wanted to kill. "That's hard for me to believe. How the hell can I trust that?"

"Grimm." Raphael locked eyes with me. Back in Grafton his eyes had had a crazy kind of wobble to them when he got angry.

Now they were clear. Focused. Determined.

And mean.

"I promise you this," he said. His voice guttural, as if he had been holding this in for a long time. "I will fucking kill you. I will tear your limbs off. I even hope to kill your friends, too. But I'm going to do it my way. You and I are going to stand toe-to-toe and see who is better, one day."

Those words felt very real. As real as anything I could trust from him.

"You know," I said. "We've had that fight before. And we both know who came out on top."

"Sure," Raphael said. "Don't bet against the underdog. I did, once."

And lost. The words weren't said, but we both understood they were there.

Was that how he looked at it now? That I was a greater power of some kind? Was he studying me, and figuring out how to kill me, when the time came?

Was I underestimating him? With all the fear of betrayal, and the lack of trust, I hadn't asked that question. Was Raphael someone I should fear?

I went quiet then. Nervous, maybe.

A lot was going to play out, in the next day or so.

I might have my answer by then.

CHAPTER TWENTY-SEVEN

More people had come into the diner, throughout our meal. Probably people taking a break from the snow. Betty got busy, but stopped by to replace the coffeepot with a new one. She asked us if we wanted dessert, and Raphael shook his head.

"Have any pastries?" I asked.

"We got a tart," Betty answered. "Lemon with cream cheese."

"Bring it here," I said, smiling. Feeling better, for some reason. Maybe it was because we had something resembling a plan. Even if it was Raphael's, and it was something I couldn't trust. Or maybe it was because, in a day or so, I'd have some kind of answer.

Or I'd be dead. There might have been a finality to that. A feeling of relief. Of peace.

Betty brought back a thick slab of something, with a yellow kind of filling in it. There were sprinkles of what looked like orange peel over the top. I grabbed a forkful and it was tangy, with a strong taste of lemon, sweet, with a hint of marmalade from the orange peels.

Raphael swirled his spoon some more, drinking only occasionally. His gaze had gone out the window, following the snow.

"Looky there," he said.

Belle had gotten out of the car. She walked, businesslike, into the station. Went to the women's bathroom.

"I do believe you've upset her," Raphael said.

"You telling me you guys get along great?" I said.

"Probably not," he said, then waited a moment. "It's a different world down there."

I was curious. "In what way?"

"In any way you can think of," he said. "No rules. Survival of the fittest, all of that. These things that came up to the Dead Zones, they came up because they are fleeing what's down there."

"Sounds like any version of hell I've heard of," I said.

"Yeah," Raphael said. "Me, too. But it's different, living it. Being there."

Things were always different when they became real. People always had an idea of what something was, and then were surprised that when they experienced it, it was always much worse than they had imagined.

It was like they had no idea of what cost truly was. Like their choices in life were always a game, they were *for pretend*. Consequences were always imaginary.

Until they weren't.

Belle came out of the bathroom and walked over to our table. Took a seat next to Raphael, who scooted over a bit. I watched their interplay, wondering if I would be able to tell if they were working together against me, or both working against me, individually.

How the hell could I tell something like that?

Betty came by with another cup. Belle thanked her and ordered a small breakfast. Egg over easy. Toast.

If I was a regular in hell, I'd certainly eat something more than that when I got out. Not just once. Every meal. Every time.

Betty brought the breakfast back. I finished my tart, scraping the plate with my fork and then licking it. Belle winced at the scratching sound.

I waited, seeing who would talk first. That person would reveal something to me. Whoever spoke, and whatever they said, would be an actual clue to what they wanted.

At least, so I believed.

Belle finished her breakfast. Raphael was quiet, mentioning none of our plan to her. Even though I hadn't asked him, one way or the other. She sipped her coffee and pressed her napkin lightly to her mouth, folding it carefully over before dropping it on her lap.

"So," she said, "are we staying here all day? Or going?"

Aha, I thought. *Gotcha.*

So, what did I have?

"You worried about the agreement not being met?" I asked. "Don't we have, like, six hundred and sixty-four days?"

"And six hours, fifty-two minutes, twenty-eight seconds," she said. "And yes. That amount of time remains."

Raphael raised his eyebrows.

"So, what's your hurry?" I asked.

"It's cold in the car," she said. "And I don't want to sit here all day."

"What, you got other agreements to go ensure?" I said.

Raphael grinned.

Belle blew out a breath, and shook her head.

I liked that I was getting under her skin. It meant something. At least, it meant there was something there to find.

"The snow is going to slow us down a bit," I said. "No need to rush."

Though we couldn't stay here all day. If we did, I'd have to face my father again. And I didn't know how many times he could hold back from killing me, before the geas caused him to slip.

Or me, from killing him.

"Fine," she said. "I'll go back to the car. Can I have the keys?"

I didn't pull them out."I know how important keeping your word is to you," I said with a smile. "And I promised someone I'd help prevent global warming."

She picked her napkin up, placed it firmly on her plate, and left.

"She didn't leave a tip," I commented.

"I forgot what an ass you can be," Raphael said, a big grin on his face. Apparently he also had issues with Belle.

"Sometimes I do, too," I said. "But it's nice to bring him out, once in a while."

"So, we doing this?" he asked.

Unfortunately his idea wasn't bad. "Might as well," I said. "I've got nothing better."

And I didn't. I was going to roll the dice, but stay aware.

Raphael knew exactly what I was thinking, and his grin spread wider. "Going to be hard for you, isn't it?"

"Trusting this?" I motioned between the two of us. "Always."

"Like I said, just trust that I'm going to kill you one day," he said. "Just not today."

"You should have that notarized," I said.

He laughed. "Who says I don't?"

Raphael got up then, and left a large tip under his plate. He was feeling generous. I finished my last few sips of coffee, letting the bitter remnants stay on my tongue, lukewarm.

All I had to go on was my gut. And it was telling me I could trust Raphael. Which made me question my sanity. I had learned to go off my instincts. I usually trusted what I felt. But sometimes my feelings were wrong. Sometimes I might have believed too much in them. Or maybe, myself. Especially where Azazel was concerned.

My instincts were never enough with *that* demon.

They were only a shade better with Raphael. At least we had a history, though. We knew each other, as much as two enemies could. Intuition was something that would get better, the more you understood a person. I believed, I *hoped*, I could trust mine enough about Raphael to get me in front of my mother.

Though it was still a roll of the dice.

I would also have to hope Raphael wouldn't kill Dominic. I needed my mother alive.

I had never really known her. I didn't know how I felt about her. We had talked for just a few minutes, in total, in all the time I had known she was alive. But something in her called to me. After she had brought me back from the dead, when I had woken with the white scar I still had over my chest, I remembered her sitting there, in a chair beside the bed.

Nervous.

Her hand shaking, as she had reached out to smooth back a little piece of my hair.

She had not killed Jen when she had had the opportunity to do so. Some part of her was me. And that meant something.

My mother was trapped, like I had been. Both of us were trapped in a life we never wanted. She had been forced to kill for evil, protect that same evil, and even while doing that she had kept some part of herself good. Pure.

I remembered when I had seen the scars over the backs of her fingers. Her arms. It reminded me, only fighters had scars like those.

My mother was a hell of a fighter.

"How do you survive?" I had asked. *"How do you not become them?"*

"You find a little part of yourself," she had answered. *"You tuck it away, where nothing can get to it. You hope the smaller part is greater than the evil."*

I wondered if my mother had meant me when she said that. If I was the part of herself she had tucked away, hoping that I was greater than the evil that had us all trapped. If I could be the one to break the geas.

I would have said yes, a week ago. When I had believed I was an angel.

I didn't know how to answer that now.

I pulled out my pack of twenties, selecting five bills, and left them tucked under my plate. Raphael wasn't the only one who could tip well. I gave a half wave to Betty and got up, heading over to the gas station side.

There I got an energy drink, then put the drink back in the fridge. Got a tall coffee cup instead, filling it with one of the tall brews they had lined up on a counter in the middle of the store. Something Ethiopian dark roast that was supposedly super-caffeinated. I put a lot of cream and sugar in it, figuring I would ride the sugar high until it crashed. When it did, hopefully the caffeine would pick me up.

The shelves were mostly empty, at least in spots. I frowned when seeing the boxes of peanut butter cups were all empty. I had to settle for candy bars. Then I wandered over to the electronic section, where there were radios and headsets and little televisions for truckers, as well as Blu-rays of movies and audiobooks.

No cell phones, though. That place where they would be hanging from, empty. I needed to call Nick and let him know what was going on, but the world seemed to be conspiring against me.

I might have to call after everything was done. If I was still alive. Even if I felt like I should call my friends, there was just no way to do it.

I walked up to the cash register and rang up my stuff. I asked to prepay twenty for gas.

"Which pump?" the man asked, packing the candy bars into a white plastic bag. He was an older man, balding, with a spotty beard and a perpetual frown.

All the pumps outside were empty. There just wasn't any traffic on the road. "Twenty." I liked the symmetry. "Twenty on twenty."

He followed my gaze. "You're not parked there."

I stared at him, eyebrows raised.

He finally rang it up. "Someone else gets there, your loss."

"I'll risk it," I said. "You guys got any prepaid phones?"

"We don't," the man said, but didn't fill me in on why. I felt like he was paying me back for the risk-it comment.

"Why not?" I ended up asking. And stood there a bit longer, holding the money in my hand. I wasn't going to give it to him until he answered.

He got the message.

"Things don't come like they used to," he finally said. "With New Orleans, and all. Got to wait on some things."

I guess that made sense. The world was different now, with the Dead Zones. I was sure that trucks and trains and planes all were on a different schedule now. The normal routes had been shaken up, and now things were needed in different places. Emergency supplies. Food, water. Bandages. Armies to support.

And peanut butter cups to deliver. Funny, the things that went first in a crisis.

"Thanks." I gave him the money, grabbed the bag, and walked out.

Feeling a bit irked, I revved the engine of the Camaro and backed up fast, hitting the brakes so that the car slid to a stop next to the pumps. It was a race, but I happened to beat no one else to pump number twenty. That would show the old man.

During the slide Raphael braced himself against the dashboard and looked at me with a raised eyebrow. I got out of the car and waved to the guy at the counter. His frown was still obvious, out here by the pumps.

Some days I *was* an ornery fuck. Today was going to be one of those, it seemed.

CHAPTER TWENTY-EIGHT

Nick finally pulled off the interstate. The snow was too much. The storm had come out of the west and dropped a blanket over everything and everyone. It was so thick across the top of the road that everyone had slowed down, and there was only the light windlike brushing sound as he passed other cars, and the wet sound of slush on the road.

After a while, he passed fewer and fewer cars, as the storm got worse. At first he had been happy, having a large sports truck with four-wheel drive, but moving along at five, or ten, miles an hour just dragged on and on. The green mile marker signs had flown by at one or two a minute, and now it was taking fifteen minutes to get to the next one.

It was still dark out, but it was the not-quite dark of morning. Almost six in the morning, actually. A light blue glow had risen in the east, the early sun's rays reflecting around the curve of the earth and catching the three of them.

Sarah had stopped playing the guitar, after a while. She had smiled at him, putting the guitar away, tucking a piece of her hair behind her ear. Nick hadn't wanted to try the radio, after that. It seemed like the music he heard from it would be cheaper, somehow.

But the countdown to Denver had slowed, and Nick felt every minute of it. He tried to push the truck, but every time he did the rear end would get squirrelly, and then he had to slow back down. He was fighting the road, fighting his nature, fighting the need to get to Grimm.

Finally they came up on a vehicle that had slid off the road. A light blue sedan, with the shade things in the back and side windows that people put there to protect their babies from the sun. The sedan was a little slanted off the shoulder, and tilted slightly into a ditch. Enough snow covered the sedan that in a bit it might be hidden from sight.

A thin man stood between the car and the side of the interstate, waving them down. The headlights of the truck had caught him, even though he was hard to see in the snow.

Sarah looked over at Nick.

"I will," he said.

He slowed them to a stop. Nick put the truck in park, put on the emergency brake and the hazard lights, and got out. It was cold out, like stepping into a meat freezer, and wet. The flakes plastered immediately to his face, his glasses, and his hair. Nick went around to the back of the truck for a jacket. It wasn't a winter coat, but it was all he had.

He shrugged it on. The hazard lights made a little ticking sound next to him, as the yellow lights blinked on and off. He stood in maybe six inches to a foot of snow, his shoes instantly soaked with the icy slush underneath the wet powder.

The thin man immediately came over, his arms huddled around himself. He didn't have a jacket, either, just a thick brown sweater and jeans. His voice stuttered a bit, maybe from the cold, and he tried to control himself as he spoke.

"Th-th-th-th-thanks for stopping," he said. "We were worried."

"It's fine," Nick said. "How bad is it?"

"W-w-we hit something and just slid right off," the man said.

Nick understood how icy roads worked. "How bad is it?"

"It was crazy." The man shook his head.

"Hey," Nick said, and waited for the guy to look at him. Then Nick said the next words carefully, slowly. "How. Bad. Is. It?"

"Oh." The man's eyes opened. Like he was trying to process the question.

Nick had seen people like this. People in shock. Likely the guy had a wife and a kid or two in the car. They had been trying to get somewhere, maybe Grandma's for thanksgiving, and he had pushed too far. Gotten worried at the snow, but kept pressing.

Then maybe he had hit a patch of black ice and lost all control of the car. Spun the steering wheel and found the car wouldn't respond. The man had probably sat then and wondered if he had killed his family, steering a loose wheel helplessly, watching the car slide left and right across the interstate until it had crashed into the side.

"It won't move," the man said. As if that explained everything.

"Let's check it out," Nick said. He walked down the side of the truck. Sarah looked to be waking Johnny up, inside. He had fallen asleep hard, finally.

He would need every ounce of energy, if this storm was any indication. They all would. It promised to be a rough one. Almost as if the weather knew what the day was going to bring them.

The blue sedan was still running, exhaust fumes puffing steady from the muffler.

Nick popped open the driver's-side door. With snow all over the windshield, the inside of the car was dark, but the bubble light at the top threw a bright glow from the top. There was a tiny lady in the passenger seat, roundish, with both cheeks red from crying. Her hair was pulled back in a bun.

There was a baby in the backseat, sleeping in a car seat. Maybe six months old, with the tiny plump face all newborns had, and wearing a blue cross-stich cap. A young girl sat next to the baby, maybe five or six. Her hair was long and braided in pigtails.

"Who are you?" she asked, in a curious little-girl voice.

"Nick," he said.

"You gonna help my da?" she asked.

"Sure," Nick said. He focused on the thing man. "Mind if I try?"

"N-no," the guy said.

Nick got in. The guy was thin but shorter than Nick, so he adjusted the seat to get a little room for his legs. The car was a front-wheel drive. The gas tank showed half-full, and none of the dashboard lights were on. So maybe they had been lucky, with no damage to the engine. The car felt a little slanted. The front right nose of the sedan dipped a little into the trench by the shoulder.

He left the door open. Told the man to step back a bit. Nick released the emergency brake and put the sedan in reverse. Goosed the gas. The left wheel grabbed a little traction, but the right wheel spun free. The car rocked just a bit.

That was enough. Nick had driven in enough snow in the hills around Grafton to know what he needed to do, and he didn't want to lose what traction the left wheel had. He didn't have any sand or salt.

He got out of the car. The man looked a little blue.

"Get in the car and get warm," Nick said. "But crack the windows, would you?"

"Crack the windows?" the man repeated.

"Yeah," Nick said. "Just a little. You know cars make carbon monoxide, right?"

The man's face turned white.

"I'll be right back," Nick said. "Don't do anything."

"Okay," the man said. Then repeated, "Okay."

He got in. The sedan door closed with a light latching sound. Then there was the quick hum of power windows, and the windows lowered around the car, just an inch or so.

Nick looked away from the road. There were trees, a little bit away. They looked like blue spruce. Pine branches would help get traction for the car, but man, there was a lot of snow between here and there.

He waded through the snow to the front of the car. Bent over and wiped the ground by the front right tire. It looked to be an inch or two off the ground, and had spun loosely there.

He walked back to the truck. Johnny was standing at the back, putting on his jacket.

"Can we get them out?"

"Think so," Nick said. He ruffled through their bags. They had a few shirts and jeans, but he didn't think what he had would get them enough traction, even if he stuffed it all tight underneath the tires.

Damn.

"We got to get some tree branches," he said. He pulled some knives out of his bag, a few of the larger serrated blades.

Johnny looked where Nick had looked earlier. "Damn, that's a bit away."

Nick's feet were already wet, and cold. "Yeah."

They walked down to the sedan. Nick poked his head in and told the guy what he was going to do. The guy asked if he should come along.

"Just stay here," Nick said. "Keep your family safe."

Johnny and Nick slushed their way off the shoulder, and onto the field beside the road. The snow varied between ankle height and midway up their shins.

"Man, my feet are cold," Johnny said.

"Yeah," Nick agreed. Not having much to add.

Johnny grinned. "I'm looking forward to when they go numb."

Nick snorted. His feet were still just wet and cold. Like he had stepped into an icy river. "That makes two of us."

They got to the trees after a few minutes. Nick handed Johnny one of the blades, and both of them cut down as many branches as they could reach. The pine trees were weighted down with snow, and each time they cut a branch down, the rest of the tree would shiver and shake snow on top of them.

Nick swore after the third or fourth time a clump of snow landed on the back of his neck, chilling his back. And he had to keep taking his glasses off and drying them.

"This sucks," Johnny said, tugging his collar tighter around his neck.

The green branches were flexible, though, and should help the car get out. They grabbed as many as they could, and dragged them all back.

The sedan waited there, exhaust puffing along. Sarah stood next to the passenger's window, it having been rolled down more, leaning over and talking to the woman inside. She waved at the two of them.

Nick and Johnny laid the branches down under the front right wheel, cramming as many as they could underneath and behind it. Then they put the rest behind the front left wheel, and laid a few behind those, so the car would have something to grab as it backed up.

Nick walked back to the truck and got in, backing it a good distance away from the sedan. Giving it plenty of room. Then he came back and knocked on the driver's window.

The man rolled it down.

"The two of us are going to push your car," Nick said. "We're going to rock it back and forth. Each time it rocks back, *lightly* push the gas down."

"Okay," the man said.

"Repeat that to me," Nick said.

"What?" the man asked.

"For heaven's sake, Stan," the lady said.

"Stan," Nick said, "I want you to repeat what I said."

"Um," he said. "You guys are going to push the car, try to rock it. When it goes backwards, I'm supposed to push the gas."

"Lightly," Nick said, and waited.

The man nodded. "Lightly."

"That's important," Nick said. "It's going to be a feel thing. When it grabs, you're going to feel it, and then you should press down harder."

Nick waited for the man to acknowledge what he said.

The man waited, blinking, apparently happy sitting in the car.

"Stan," Nick said, "repeat it."

The lady shook her head.

Stan frowned. He glanced at his wife, then back to Nick. "I'm going to push the pedal, *lightly*, when you guys push the car back. I'm going to feel the traction, and if it feels right, then I need to push the pedal harder."

"You got it," Nick said, giving the man a thumbs-up. "Now let me see you put the car in reverse."

Stan grabbed the shifter in the center column, and worked it until the red line on the dash was pointed to the *R*.

"Okay," Nick said. His feet were feeling frozen, bigger than the shoes they were in. He looked over at Sarah, and motioned to Stan. *Watch him.*

Sarah smiled and gave Nick a thumbs-up.

He and Johnny went to the front right of the car. Braced their legs on the opposite side of the trench, and leaned up against the car. Sarah took a couple of steps back from the passenger window.

"On three," Nick told Johnny. He counted. One … two … three. They pushed on three. The car rocked. Stan did not hit the gas.

Nick counted again. One … two … three. Johnny and he pushed on three. The car rocked back. Stan goosed the gas, and one of the branches spun out from under the tire.

They did it again. Another branch shifted under the tire. There was a gravelly rub from the left side of the car, as the tire there found blacktop.

They did it another time. Sarah called out encouragement, to the inside of the car. And, finally, another. Stan hit the gas just enough. The car spun backward, some of the branches flew out the front and hit Nick's legs, but the car backed out onto the road.

Where Stan hit the brakes and slid to a stop.

Nick brushed the snow off him. He grinned at Johnny. "Feet numb yet?"

"I think I'm losing the left one." Johnny's return smile was half-real, half-forced. His left leg was deep in the trench.

"You boys need to stop the whining," Sarah said. Though Nick noted she carefully stood in a place he had previously walked in.

They headed back to the truck. Nick stopped by the passenger window and leaned in. The lady had been talking to Stan, but she stopped when he appeared.

"Look," Nick said, "follow me to the next exit. Be careful. And remember, if you start skidding again, take your foot off the gas and steer into the skid."

"Steer into?" Stan asked.

"Yeah," Nick said. "If the car points right, steer right. Left, then steer left. Always *gently*."

"Okay," Stan said. "Thank you."

Nick shook his head. "No problem."

"Can we offer you anything?" the lady asked, looking between Stan and Nick.

"No need," Nick said. "We have what we need."

And maybe they could use the good karma. A lot would ride on these next couple of days, for Nick and his friends. If this bettered their chances, it was worth it.

The baby giggled from the backseat. Awake, with eyes a crystal blue. Drooling a little, like all babies did.

It was worth it anyway.

"Thanks for the help," Stan said again. "Amazing what some people know, and what some people don't."

"We were glad to," Nick said, a little uncomfortable with the praise.

And he was glad. Nick smiled to himself. Here they were, on a life-saving mission for Grimm, and Jen. Just a week after barely surviving a postapocalyptic encounter with a bunch of demons in New Orleans, and the Dead Zones had appeared.

Sometimes it was the little things in life that made him realize what it was all about. Or maybe what it should be. The playing of a guitar. Helping someone on the side of the road. The giggle of a happy baby, without apparently a care in the world.

It was these things to hold on to when the world went to hell.

Nick needed to be better at remembering that.

CHAPTER TWENTY-NINE

Nick got back in the truck. Sarah winked at him from the passenger seat. She already had the heat on high, and even though the snow had fallen heavy on the windshield, enough had melted that Nick could see the sedan in front of them.

In the middle seat, Johnny already had his shoes and socks off and was rubbing his feet vigorously with a dry shirt. They didn't look blue, but they did look wet.

"Man, it's cold out there," Johnny said.

"Kind of a weird state for vampires, right?" Nick said. "Who would have thought Dominic would set up shop near the Rockies?"

"Where else would a vampire go?" Johnny said, handing the shirt forward to Nick, with a pair of socks. "It's not like they can hang out at a beach all day."

"Good point." Nick took the socks and the shirt and did what Johnny had done. He put his legs to the side of the seat, pointing his knees toward Sarah, and took off his wet gear. His toes had gotten a little numb. They might have been the slightest bit blue, and he took a minute to rub the digits hard, until they started to tingle.

"You see the baby?" Sarah asked.

"Yeah," Nick said, still drying his feet. "Cute."

What would it be like to have kids? Nick wondered. And to have a family, with Sarah. Would they have a sedan somewhere, a house with a white picket fence? Children that went to school, and who he had to help with homework? A dog?

Those thoughts had never occurred to him before. He knew what he felt for Sarah, but when she had been with Raphael, his only thought was to get her free. Nick hadn't really ever thought Sarah would feel something real for him, and now that she appeared to …

Well, thoughts like babies came creeping around.

"All mannnn," Johnny kind of sang the words, drawing out the sound of the *N*. Nick caught Johnny waggling his eyebrows out of the corner of his eyes. "Nick and Sarah, sitting in a tree. K-I-S-S-I–"

Nick tossed the shirt at Johnny. It was wet enough to smack against his face.

"Ugh," came Johnny's muffled voice.

Nick didn't look at Sarah, though. He focused at his feet, his cheeks heating up a bit. So he saw her hand lying on his knee and pat it, softly. He looked up and found Sarah smiling at him. Her cheeks were a little red as well. Like she knew what he had been thinking, and had found it interesting.

Goose bumps rippled along his skin. He smiled quickly back, and ducked his head again. Pretended to work on his feet. Getting the dry socks on, and rubbing them some, to heat them up.

After that he got the truck moving again. No one had passed them on the interstate, at least, not that he had noticed.

Johnny had his phone out, and took a look. "Looks like five miles to the next exit."

"Tell them, if you would," Nick said. He stopped the truck to the left of the sedan, and rolled down Sarah's window.

She leaned out and spoke to them for a bit, then leaned back in and rolled up the window. "He said okay. And thanked us again."

"I'm thinking we should stop, too," Nick said, pulling the truck forward. "At least for a bit. Until we see what happens with the storm."

They were both quiet.

"Makes sense," Sarah finally said. "We don't want to end up like the sedan."

"Ten bucks says they were headed to Stan's mother-in-law's place," Johnny said.

Nick thought of Stan. Way out of his element. Of his knowledge sphere. But trying anyway.

"I'd probably need some really steep odds," Nick said. Stan was definitely going somewhere he wouldn't normally go.

"On ten bucks?" Johnny said.

"I'm a sure-thing kind of guy," Nick said.

They drove for a bit in silence, to the slushy sound of tires against the road, the crunch of new snow whenever they drove over it.

The sun had risen, and while the snowfall was thick, it was daylight thick. White flakes fluttered through the light blue skies, no longer floating down out of the dark of night. It made driving easier, and maybe a bit faster, though Nick carefully watched the sedan in the rearview. He was careful to not go faster than Stan could keep up.

It took an hour to get five miles, that way. But soon they came up on the exit ramp, with signs giving all kinds of sleeping, eating, and fueling options.

"Coffee would be good," Johnny said.

"Yeah," Nick said. A good dinerlike breakfast would hit the spot. Maybe not the best for vegetarians, though. "You okay with that?"

"We eat pancakes." She grinned. "Dork."

Nick pulled off onto the shoulder at the end of the ramp, and waved Stan on by. His wife waved back at them as they passed. It looked like they were headed to a gas station.

Nick then pulled back onto the road, driving them over to one of the breakfast places, picking one out at random. A place that advertised pancakes and waffles, stacked high with whipped cream and maple syrup.

"Is that waffles and ice cream?" Johnny asked, leaning out the side. "Man, I'm getting that."

Nick saw what he was talking about. A big poster on the side of the building, of a stack of waffles, soaked in butter, topped with ice cream, with chocolate syrup dripping off the side of the plate.

"It's on, then," he said, putting the truck in park, shutting it off, and pushing the emergency brake in.

Sarah shook her head. "No bellyaching," she said. "Literally."

"Mine never hurts," Johnny said with a straight face

"Except for that last time," Nick said.

"Pretty much never," he said.

"Pretty much?" Sarah turned to look at the middle seat. "Didn't you tap out, last time?"

Nick liked that she was on his side. It felt good. Even on something as silly as this. It felt more than good, it felt right.

"Bad sprinkles," Johnny explained. "They got to be fresh."

The three got out and headed in. As soon as they walked through the doors, Nick immediately caught the sweet smell of maple syrup, as well as the buttery scent of caramelized pancakes.

Johnny inhaled deeply. "Ahhh… Heaven."

There was a waitress at the front, a young girl with black hair and twinkly eyes. Her name tag told them her name was Pam, and for them to have a Waffly Great Day. She seated them in a booth and ran down the specials.

"That one," Johnny said, when she got to the waffle ice cream stack.

"Make that two," Nick added.

"Make that three," Sarah said.

"Yes!" Johnny pumped his arm. "We have a new contestant."

"You guys doing an eating contest?" Pam asked.

"They are," Sarah said. "I'm not."

"Gotcha," Pam said. "I'll see what I can have the cooks come up with, special, then."

Pam left, but came back quickly with three glasses of orange juice and three cups of coffee. She poured the coffee quickly and asked if they wanted cream.

"Definitely," Johnny said.

Nick shook his head. "That takes up stomach space."

"Oh God," Sarah said. She laid a hand on Nick's lap. "This day is going to be wild."

"You telling me." Johnny tapped his cell phone, which he had laid on the table. "Gabrielle is coming in today."

"Really?" Sarah asked.

"She'll be in later tonight," Johnny said. "Flying into Denver International."

"Whoa," Nick said. "Gabrielle and Johnny, sitting in a tree–"

"Yeah." Johnny shook his head. "Let's not do that around her."

Nick grinned.

"I mean it," Johnny said.

"Sure," Nick said, covering his grin with his cup of coffee. "We picking her up?"

"If we can," Johnny said. "I figure we'll be looking for Grimm. Or finding Grimm. Or pulling Grimm out of some kind of fire."

Pam came back then, and dropped off a tiny tin pitcher of cream. The metal was frosted on the outside, as if it had been sitting in a freezer. Johnny grabbed it and poured some in his coffee.

"We can figure it out as we go in," Nick said. "The way the weather is looking, we're not going to get to Denver until later this afternoon or evening."

"Maybe Grimm will call us by then," Sarah mentioned.

"There is that," Nick said. "Although the way that guy is around technology, we'd do better looking at posters in a post office."

"Seriously, though," Johnny said, "how are we going to find him?"

"I don't know," Nick said. "Our best chance is probably Gabrielle. If she knows where Dominic is hiding, we can find him that way. Might not be bad to pick her up first."

Pam came back, carrying a large tray, on top of which were three plates. One of the plates was like the poster outside, with a stack of waffles, ice cream and chocolate syrup on top. The other two looked like miniature architectural nightmares, waffles stacked twice as high, double the ice cream, and enough chocolate syrup to bathe in. The waitress actually grunted when she set the tray down.

"Holy moly," Johnny said.

"If you guys are having a contest, you should mean it, right?" Pam waggled her eyebrows, which was Johnny's thing.

"Man, Gabrielle is going to be really disappointed in the weight you gained today," Nick said.

"I forgot about that," Johnny said, almost in a whisper. Like he had just realized it.

"Are you meeting someone?" Pam asked. "You probably shouldn't eat all this, if you are. I've seen people go into food comas after one of these."

"I'm sure she's more into your personality, anyway." Sarah squeezed Nick's leg. "What are looks, right?"

Nick sat back and enjoyed the consternation on Johnny's face. Then Nick took the big fork to the side of the plate and cut down the side of his waffles. Each of them opened up softly under the fork, and were thick and fluffy on the inside. Steam rose, and Nick could smell the butter.

He used the fork to stab the pieces he had cut and picked it up. Syrup and melted ice cream dripped everywhere. Somehow he got it all into his mouth. Vanilla ice cream, chocolate syrup, butter, and waffles. Heaven on his tongue.

Nick munched as best he could, and spoke with his mouth full. "You probably wouldn't like this anyway."

Then Nick swallowed and put together another bite.

Johnny looked at his plate. Raised his eyebrows, hopefully. "Truce?"

Nick took another forkful. Chewed and swallowed. "We both know you're not eating as much as me. The only question is how bad your little tummy will ache when Gabrielle lands."

"Dammit." Johnny sighed. "Life's not fair."

He started eating. His face lit up after the first mouthful. Then alternated between sad and delighted, as he ate through his stack. Delighted in the taste, sad for the waist.

"She is going to be disappointed," Johnny said, digging in for more. "But this is pretty much worth it."

CHAPTER THIRTY

Colorado Springs wasn't what I expected. Somehow I had an image of the town, that it would be a village nestled in the mountains, next to a couple of ski lodges, tucked underneath a pair of white peaks among the tree lines.

Not a fair-sized city, with a skyline perched before the Rockies. Apartment complexes and business buildings, city blocks built among trees, so that it looked like the buildings had grown out of the forest.

Everything was easy to see. The sky was bright and blue. The sun was high overhead and brilliantly yellow, though the thick white clouds that had dropped the blanket of snow still hung behind us, north in the rearview mirror.

"Not what you expected?" Raphael asked.

"Not a place I'd have picked a vampire to hide in," I said, steering the car into the city. Traffic had picked up, and we were in a pack of cars, most of them covered in the gray-white slush and bits of salt from the road. We all rode along at the same clip, no one in a hurry to press their luck after the morning's weather.

"Olympic City, USA?" Raphael grinned. "I used to come out here a lot, as a kid."

"I still don't see it as a hideout," I said. "I was expecting something more like Transylvania."

"This has everything he needs," Raphael said. "Heavy tourist population. Enough business and industry to be able to get the good stuff. Even defense contractors, if you want to arm up your troops."

Food. Entertainment. Weapons. It made sense, that way.

We entered the heart of the city. Signs for radio stations, lawyers, attractions, and ski parks hung off the shoulder, and it seemed like we passed one or two every hundred feet or so. Tall structures, not quite the skyscrapers of New York or Chicago, but big nonetheless, surrounded us. They were high enough they hid the sun, shadowing the road in front of us, like I was driving into a tunnel.

Raphael pointed. "This way."

I pulled off the interstate and merged onto a state road heading west. A sign told me we were heading into Old Colorado City. The tall structures around us got smaller and smaller, block after block, until we began to pass older two-story buildings, built with horizontal wooden panels. Each building was narrow and painted in a solid color, with the bottom story different from the top. Most of the first-story exteriors were brown, paired at the top with blues or reds or grays. Sometimes the color alternated.

The bottoms of the buildings were specialty stores, coffee shops or fancy eateries. People walked by, mostly as couples, wrapped in jackets, breath coming out as a warm white mist. Some of the people stood in front of stores, peering in. A few of them had scarves hanging from their shoulders, and all of them had some kind of hat on, either a wool cap, a cabbie hat, or something knitted. One guy stood in front of a coffee shop, a long scraggly beard and wild hair, and wrapped in a sleeping bag. He faced the store and held a cardboard sign in one hand.

"Man, I liked this place," Raphael said. "The Gold Rush built this neighborhood, back in the eighteen fifties."

I shook my head, exhaling loudly.

"What?"

"I didn't figure you for a history student," I said.

"What do you really know about me, Grimm?" Raphael asked, his voice all of a sudden low.

What did I know about him? He had been a vampire once. A demon now. He had been a spoiled brat of a kid, a bully, and touched with crazy.

A killer. Now he was a little more careful, a little more thoughtful, and the crazy, if it was there, was a lot more hidden.

The killer wasn't.

"Not much," I said.

"So what if I liked it?" he said. "People leaving, dreaming of finding a fortune. With just a little luck, striking it rich."

"You were already rich," I said, with a little frown.

"It wasn't about the money," he said, not catching my tone. "It was about the discovery. The thrill of the find."

I raised my eyebrows and looked both right and left. The same buildings existed on both sides of the street. I wondered about when they had originally been built, these tiny stores that had once been homes, built by young men and women and families coming out here to find their fortune. Likely finding poverty, hardships, and death instead.

As if on cue, we drove through an area advertised as the Ghost Town Museum. A billboard described it as a town left behind in time, where everyone just disappeared, leaving everything they owned behind. Come experience it, the sign said, and feel the ghosts that still walk through their homes.

I quietly snorted. Grafton should be here. A more modern town, sure, but dead all the same. What people hadn't left had become vampires, before I killed them all.

Before I had killed the guy next to me.

"So, is your father here?" I asked. "Is that where we're headed?"

"Now?" Raphael chuckled. "They wouldn't let us in now. We'll have to go up there at night."

He leaned forward, having caught something in his sight, and followed it with a turn of his head as we passed by. "I just wanted to see this place again."

Dammit.

The Key throbbed gently, on my chest. As if sensing my mood, and trying to relax me. I might have mistaken it, but it felt a little warm to me now. As if the stone was leaking heat.

It felt a little fragile, under my hand. Like a cookie baked without enough butter, it felt like it would crumble if I picked it up. The bond between still remained, strong and thick, and I took a little reassurance from it.

I guess I didn't mind waiting until tonight. It might be the last chance I got to see Jen. I would take it.

Just keep holding on, I thought into the Key. *We're almost there.*

My jaw set. I didn't know what I was going to do, what to ask, even if I could talk to my mother. And if my mother had the answer. Part of me thought bringing someone back to life was just a matter of scope. I had healed Jen before, I had healed myself. It was just that principle, on a much larger scale.

But that seemed too easy. There had to be a trick to it, some kind of ritual like the witches, or some key word. Some phrase of power.

I had fumbled through many things in life, but I didn't want to take that same chance with Jen. I had one shot at this. The penalty would be too great if I failed.

It took some time, and we waited at a number of traffic lights, but we finally got out of Old Colorado City. We started passing some suburbs. There were large shopping centers here. Places where we could get food and clothes.

And we would probably need heavier jackets. At least, I did.

I drove us into the parking lot of one of the large chain-mart stores. A wide gray-white building with its name proudly displayed in big blue letters on the front, and quad doors to the left and right. One side for the clothes and pharmacy, the other for the food.

The parking lot was a mix of cars and piles of snow. The snow lay mainly around the islands, and in a few cases a shopping cart had been caught up there. As if someone had unloaded their groceries and then abandoned it.

"You're telling me we can't go to your father's hideout until night," I said.

"That is correct," Raphael said.

"It would've been nice to know that earlier," I said.

"I didn't think I'd have to tell you," he said. "How many vampires you think let people in during the day? Especially people that might wish them ill health?"

"Sure," I said. It wasn't something I thought about. It's not like I'd stormed many vampire strongholds. Actually there had been the one. Raphael's place, on the Hill in Grafton. But I'd had more to work with then.

"I guess we got some time, then," I said. "I'm going to get some stuff."

"Like what?" Raphael asked.

I plucked at my jacket. "A winter coat, for starters."

He waggled his head back and forth, like he was thinking about something. "All right."

I hadn't been asking his permission. But maybe he was just agreeable today. Either way, Raphael got out when I did. He actually pulled the seat forward so Belle could get out as well. She had been so quiet, it was almost like she hadn't been there.

The bright sun was in the process of melting the snow in the parking lot, but it was cold enough that it wouldn't all melt. Tonight the roads would be pretty icy. The three of us walked into the store, feet getting wet in the slush on the pavement, white wisps of breath coming from each of us, as we exhaled.

I had always thought Azazel pretended at being human. But maybe demons did need to breathe. Eat and sleep. Even use the bathroom.

I guessed, thinking about it, that I needed all that stuff, too. And I was an angel. Or part angel. Demons were just angels who had fallen. So maybe eating and sleeping and foggy breath all made sense. Maybe we were more the same than different.

That made me wonder what the difference was. Could it just be who was good, and who was evil? Was it just murderers and rapists and thieves? I didn't think so. I had seen too much, with the memories of the ghosts I had lived through, to believe hell was full of only the people who had performed those horrifying acts.

In a person's life, was the one moment, a lever, a switch that flipped a person from good to evil? Did they realize it, when it happened? Or did they look back, in the end, and wonder how they had gotten *here*?

There was a greeter at the door, an older man with square black glasses, and far too little hair on his head. I nodded a hello as we passed. I walked by the carts. I didn't think I'd need one, although Raphael did grab a basket. Something caught his attention, and he dovetailed away from us quickly.

I headed to the men's section, in the middle of the store. A number of other people walked through the store, carts packed high with jugs of water, milk, eggs, flour, flashlights, and batteries. The staples bought after every storm.

I got to the men's clothes. The circled racks were packed too tight, and I had to turn sideways and shuffle through a section of flannel shirts. But I got to a few rings of coats I liked and started trying on a few. I would pick one up, test the feel around the shoulders, how snug or loose it felt.

Belle suddenly appeared. I almost jumped.

"It's funny to me," she said.

"What?" I said, mistaking what she was talking about. The coat I had picked out was something thick and flannel-like, red and blue on the outside, with a dark blue liner inside.

"You trust him now," Belle said.

I put the coat away, having to cram in among the other coats on the rack.

"You're wrong there," I said. "I don't trust him. But I *do* know him."

I left it unsaid, but I was sure she understood. I didn't know her at all. Other than the fact that she was a demon. Which wasn't a ringing endorsement.

"You humans always fall back to that. What you *know*," she said.

"Are we back to that?" I said. She seemed hung up on humans knowing that heaven existed. "What did you say before? Knowing is a form of cheating?"

"Knowing the answers invalidates the test," she said. "You don't get it, but you will. And when you do, you'll realize we were right."

"What don't I get?" I asked. "I make decisions based on what *I've* experienced. You're asking me to take something on faith, from *you*. I mean, isn't there a reason you guys are down there?"

I pointed to the ground with my forefinger, a slight grin on my face.

Belle's face looked pursed. Her eyes were narrow, eyebrows lowered. Like she was deciding what she could say, or what she might be able to say, to convince me. Finally she came out with something. "You've heard of Job?"

It wasn't a question.

The story of the man tested by God. Sure, I'd heard of it. It was a lesson every kid learned. Endure as much as you can, no matter what happens to you. I had always thought it was a story to let people know the world wasn't fair, and you better get used to it.

"Wasn't that the guy you all took everything from, trying to break him?" I said.

"You all always think that," she said. "It was never about breaking a man's spirit. It was about showing the world, as long as a person knows heaven exists *without a doubt*, his spirit *cannot* be broken."

"Well, you don't have to worry about that, with me," I said. I hadn't seen a lot of evidence about heaven, or where good spirits went. I had seen a whole lot of bad ghosts, though, and bad people, and demons and monsters. Believing in hell, that was easy. Believing in heaven was another story.

Belle's voice carried an edge. "Trust him, then. See what happens."

"I don't get why you keep saying that," I said. "You think we're planning something together?"

"I can see it," she said. "You can, too. If you paid attention."

I really didn't know what she was talking about. Belle made it sound like Raphael and I were planning some great takeover of the world. All we had decided was to put off killing Dominic. Raphael might or might not be trustworthy, but his plan was the only thing that might buy me enough time to get to my mother.

At some point we would have to kill Dominic, though. That was part of the agreement. And then my mother would likely die, no matter what. Could I let that happen? I didn't think so.

What else could I do?

"So, what's your alternative?" I said. "Make it something I can believe."

She was quiet.

"Yeah," I said. "You and Lucifer don't have anything, do you?"

Her jaw flexed.

I found another coat. Something that made a riffling sound as I moved the arms and legs. *Nope*. I quickly put it back.

Belle remained in front of me. "You and Raphael act like we sat you down and made you *sign* it."

"I certainly didn't ask for it," I said.

"You think you're the *only* person to want to avoid their deal?" Belle shook her head. "You think hell isn't littered with people who have signed a contract, and then gone back on their word? How do you think people get there?"

She looked at me. "Almost everyone down there can trace back what happened to them, what got them to hell, and every story begins with *If I had only done what I said I was going to …*"

I had had enough of the badgering, and the lectures. Especially by a demon from hell.

"Come on, Belial," I said, maybe too loudly. "What the fuck are you bothering me for, really?"

"Sir," a man in a blue vest called out from the clothes-changing area. A thin, tiny man with a whiny voice. Helping an older lady. "Please watch your language."

"Sure," I said. And then stared at the man in the vest. Until he glanced away, and focused on who he was helping.

Maybe my language was a bit rough for the Midwest. Maybe I wasn't using the right words for where I was. But I had other things to worry about.

"There is no *alternative*," Belle finally said. "There is *the agreement*, and there is *not*. There is your *word*, and there is *not*."

"Always back to the agreement," I said. "That's not tiring."

She locked her eyes with me. "You should try seeing what happens, over thousands of years, and not being able to stop it."

Was that what she was complaining about? Having to watch people come to hell? Was it getting too crowded down there?

"What does it matter to you anyway?" I asked. "If I break it, or he breaks it, what does any of that matter to *you*?"

She stepped closer to me. "You will refuse to understand, even if I told you. Which I cannot."

"Because it'll be cheating?" I asked. "Because if you help me to know, you'll be breaking your own rule?"

Her eyes opened slightly, like she was surprised I got it.

"Give me a hint, then." I casually tugged a dark coat off the rack. The jacket was thick, with a good liner. I hefted it with my hand. It had a nice weight to it. "Try me."

"Fine," she said. Her eyes narrowed. "Your word has power. *Words have power.* Before everything, there was nothing. Words were first."

"Before everything, there was nothing?" I blinked. "What's that even mean?"

"It's a hint." She let out a sigh, small and slight in the noise of the store. *"Think,"* she said. *"Take the next step."*

What would the next step be? If I was right, and Belle couldn't tell me, because of some rule she and Lucifer had about giving people knowledge, then where was she trying to lead me?

And why? Was it knowledge of the afterlife? Or was it knowledge of what your decisions were costing you, in *this* life? Was the information Belle held something that would influence a decision I was about to make?

Why would she, or Lucifer, care?

What did it mean, that before everything, there was nothing? Was she talking about creation? *The* creation? I searched back through my mind, through random church memories of a kid from a halfway house. What were the first words spoken in the Bible? All I could remember was the words everyone knew. "Are you talking about 'Let there be light'?"

I guessed I got it wrong, because Belle's lips twisted in a sneer. "'In the beginning was the Word,'" she said.

That didn't ring any bells for me. So I raised my eyebrows and waved both hands, making a *how was I supposed to know?* kind of motion.

Belle sighed. "Your lack of knowledge isn't surprising."

"That's hardly a revelation," I said. "It's not like I had a lot of time in my life for school."

"One day you'll understand the things you lack in understanding now," Belle said. "That day will come."

I rolled my eyes. "That makes perfect sense."

"Take the next step," Belle said again. Like it would be easy to connect the dots she was giving me.

It was more likely I could paint the Sistine Chapel than put those lines together and come up with the answer she apparently wanted.

"Whatever," I said. And instantly regretted it, with Raphael and his talk about putting the word on my headstone.

I didn't know why Belle was bothering with this. With me. Maybe her role really was making sure the agreement was met. That both Raphael and I came through with our promise. Weird, to think a demon responsible for something like that. Like keeping a promise.

Maybe not completely out of the realm of sanity, though. I tried a compromise. "Look, whatever you think I have planned, trust me when I say I'm just flying by the seat of my pants."

"You ask about alternatives." Belle's voice was soft, low, but still carried. "You should understand there is none. There is only our word. And there is Azazel, twister of words."

Was twisted another word for liar? If so, it was something we could agree on. "Sure," I said. "I plan on killing Azazel, if that's what you are asking."

"I only ask you to fulfill your word," Belle said, shaking her head, like she had already decided I wasn't going to. "It is all I can do."

It was hard for me to believe, but Belle obviously felt constrained by something. A code, a law, a curse, something.

"By it," I asked, motioning between the two of us with my hand, "you mean talking to me."

"You and *him*," she said. I assumed she meant Raphael. "I won't reap your soul when this is over. It's not my job to kill everyone you love, should you fail to do what you have agreed upon. It is my job, when I see you walking further from your word, to point out the agreement must be met."

"So you are like a dorm monitor?" I said. "You just point out when I'm breaking a rule?"

"I am here to enforce the agreement," Belle said. "And you two walk around conspiring to break it, and for what?"

I defended myself. "We're not conspiring anything." Although maybe we had been. But we weren't declaring war on anyone. Just delaying.

She waved her hands. "You both want Dominic dead. You both want Azazel dead. You have given your words on this, and yet you are choosing to do anything but what your word demands you must."

"We haven't *chosen* to do anything," I said again, using her words against her. For some reason I held the coat in front of me, like a protective shield. Belle had gotten more furious, through the conversation.

"I can *see* it," she insisted. "You *are* choosing."

"What the hell are you talking about?" I said.

"Has he mentioned tearing up the contract?" she asked.

I paused. Raphael had said something like that. But it had been offhand, not something he had meant.

"We've talked," I admitted.

"Words have power," she snarled, and almost spat. "Words *matter*. I keep telling you this. Trust your enemy, if you must. *Know* your enemy, if that is what you count on."

She took a breath and let it out. Then stepped back. "But know this. You will always only get only what you deserve. Job understood that part right."

With that, she walked away.

That was a strange conversation to have with a demon, I mused.

And I wondered what she meant. She claimed to be able to tell I was going to break the agreement, when the truth was, I hadn't decided that yet. At best, I was just going to put it off a bit.

I finally picked out a coat, then headed over to the electronics section of the store. Bought yet another cell phone and a monthly card. I was buying so many of these lately, I should invest in the company's stock.

The lady there rang the coat and the phone up for me. She was an older lady, portly, with thin gray hair pulled back so tight on her head her scalp was visible. When she was done she handed me both, stuffed in a big white plastic bag.

I surfed around in the bag and pulled out the phone. "Would you know how to set this up?"

"Eh?" the lady asked. Her attention had already wandered to somewhere over my shoulder.

"The phone," I repeated. "Would you be able to help me get this set up?"

She stared at me for a moment, then the phone, before shaking her head. "I don't work back here much."

Which meant I was going to have to figure it out. I hated electronics. Dammit.

"Thanks," I said.

I walked out of the store. Raphael leaned back against the wall by the double doors, waiting on me. He held a couple of smaller plastic bags in one hand, the bags hanging by thin plastic handles that stretched a bit under the weight. He also had a new jacket himself, something sharper than mine, and black. Raphael ignored the greeter, standing across from the demon, checking receipts of people leaving.

"Ready?" he asked, pulling himself off the wall.

"You know how to set up one of these?" I asked, waving the plastic phone package at him.

"Shit, Grimm," the demon said. "I had people do all that stuff for me."

"Figures," I said.

We walked out of the store. As we did I pulled the jacket out and put it on. It smelled a little like canvas, felt a little snug around my back, and still had a tag hanging from one sleeve. I yanked that off. I took the phone and phone card out, then stuffed the empty bag in the trash.

Raphael followed suit, except that his jacket seemed to fit his form perfectly. It hung from his shoulders like it had been tailored. I bet it was a demon thing.

We headed across the lot. Belle stood out there by the Camaro, arms around herself, keeping warm. Neither Raphael nor I had bought her something warmer, and she hadn't asked for a jacket. Something about that struck me.

The parking lot was still slushy and cold. Shopping carts still lay abandoned on the little islands. We got into the car. I fired it up and turned the heater on high. I was going to wait until the air heated up before moving.

"So, is midnight a good time?" I asked.

"I like a well-timed entrance," Raphael said.

"Then I'm going to grab some sleep," I said. Actually I hoped to see Jen again. And I needed to get the phone set up and call my friends. But sleep would be nice, too, after last night.

I would be careful to not use any ghost. I didn't want a repeat of the activities of the evening before.

"Sure," Raphael said. "Let's find a place close to some restaurants. I could grab something to eat."

By that, I guessed he meant something healthy to eat. Not the pancake powerhouse I'd had earlier. He was going to get a rude surprise, because all the road held was diners and fast-food places.

"Okay," I said.

We drove around, and found a hotel off the state road. A major chain hotel, ten or so stories high, with a few gas stations and chain restaurants nestled around it. As good a place to stop as any.

I went in and got us all rooms. For some reason I got three this time. Raphael and Belle took their keys without saying a word.

I grabbed the phone package out of the car, and my bags. I'd have to figure out how to get the cell working and talk to my friends. Let them know what was going on. Not that I really knew, I guessed. On the very eve of finding my mom, I had one half-ass plan, one demon I hated, another demon telling me I was screwing things up, both of whom I couldn't really trust.

If I was honest with myself, all of it felt pretty regular. It was kind of how my life worked.

CHAPTER THIRTY-ONE

Johnny sat in the back of the truck, waiting for the message to come back across. The three ellipses surfaced, disappeared, then surfaced again. Like a bubble about to burst.

They all were waiting in the bottom level of the short-term parking lot of the Denver International Airport. The truck was tucked tightly into a parking space just a hair too small for it. Sedans, coupes, trucks, all of different shapes and colors, parked around them, as far as they could see. It was five or six stories high, and Johnny wondered how many people flew every day, for this many vehicles to be here.

Night was falling, the outside grew darker by the minute. The fluorescent lights of the lot were spaced farther out than they should be, so that shadows were everywhere, against every car, in the cracks between every wall and floor.

Nick had parked so they had a clear line of sight to the elevators. His friend sat in the driver's seat, hand occasionally tapping the wheel. They had gotten to Denver without too much of an incident. Stopped at a truck stop to use the bathroom and fill up the truck, then raced to the airport to meet Gabrielle.

Delayed, the text finally said. Then an emoji of a woman shrugging, both hands in the air.

Where? he texted back.

Chicago, Gabrielle answered. *B a few hrs.*

Shit, he said. *We're here, waiting in the parking lot.*

Sry babe, she said. *U k?*

It took Johnny a second to understand that. *I think your texting is getting worse*, he typed, *How do you shorten a two-letter word to just one letter?*

Johnny followed that with a laughing-out-loud emoji.

Wtv, was the answer. Followed by a rolling-the-eyes emoji, and a laughing-out-loud one.

They had texted back and forth, over the past day. Gabrielle still didn't seem right, but it was hard for Johnny to tell over text. The news about her family, and the geas, had surprised and shocked her. Not only because she had a deep desire to be noble, to be something better than what the world perceived her to be, but because of what had happened to her, as a teenager.

She knew now why she had been forced to have a kid at thirteen years old. And her baby had been taken away, hidden from her. She had been told it was to keep their line pure, to keep the Dumonts in charge of the family, to uphold their traditions. And she had clung to that, as dramatic as her experience had been. As much as she still missed her babe today.

They hadn't even told her if it had been a boy or a girl.

After hearing the news about the geas, Gabrielle knew that the only reason that had happened to her was a way to protect her father. Keep him alive, because of the threat of the geas. A selfish self-preservation had been the reason for her rape. For being robbed of her baby.

It had only been a day, but she had recovered, fast. Johnny sensed a new resolve in her. And something hidden, dangerous, like a sheathed blade.

It'll be good to see you again, he texted.

Yeah …

The ellipsis again. The little word bubble that meant someone was typing.

U find Grimm?

Waiting on you, he answered. *Found a hotel, in east Colorado. Looked like it had undergone a small war.*

O.

We think it was him, Johnny typed. *Just not sure what happened. Could it have been your father's angel?*

Likley, she answered. Misspelling the word. *Father sent him by leer.*

Leer? he asked. *Lear jet?*

Y was the response. And another roll-the-eyes emoji.

I need to see one of the letters you say you wrote as a kid, Johnny replied.

Wtv, plus the rolling-the-eyes face, came back to him.

Johnny imagined she had gone through a lot of paper, back then. Possibly her spelling was so bad, it made her hyperaware of what she said, and how she spoke. Or maybe she just texted more than he did. She seemed to pick up new slang every day.

So when you getting here?

Midnight, she said. *There. One perfectly typed ward. Happy?*

Johnny snorted. Sarah raised an eyebrow at him, maybe wondering what he was laughing at. Johnny waved her off. The three-ellipses bubble was back on his phone.

Fuck, came the response. *WORD.*

Johnny laughed then, out loud. Nick and Sarah both looked at him now.

"She's the worst speller," Johnny said.

Nick's eyebrow rose.

"Just weird, right?" Johnny said. "She speaks very precisely. And every time we text, she sends this messy jumble."

Sarah took the phone from him, read the messages, and started laughing.

"See?" Johnny said.

Sarah looked at the phone again. "Oh. Midnight?"

"Looks like it," Johnny said. "They got delayed in Chicago."

"Damn," Nick said. "I could use a coffee, or something."

"They usually have something in the airports," Sarah said.

"I guess I can get something," Nick said. "You guys want anything?"

"I'll come along," Sarah said. She looked at the phone again, like it had buzzed in her hand, and handed it back to Johnny with a smile.

Boreding, the text from Gabrielle read. *Miss U.*

Johnny shook his head slightly, then smiled and tried things her way.

Miss U 2. But he held back on sending it. The way it was written, it was like he missed the band. So he retyped it.

Miss you too. That he sent.

Johnny did miss her. He reached up and slid his hand across the surface of his neck. Where she had bitten him, originally. The soft feel of his fingers against the skin drove the bite wild. It itched like crazy, so bad he wanted to dig into it with his fingernails.

But he held back.

For some reason the itch was worse now than before. Maybe it was a cumulative thing. Maybe the desire got worse, over the years. He didn't know. But he was willing to pay the price. Gabrielle was worth it, to Johnny. They had been apart this long before. He would make it again.

A final buzz in his hand. One last message.

In seat, she said. *Think about it?*

Johnny knew what she meant.

And possibly, maybe that was why the itch was worse now.

Gabrielle wanted to turn him. She was worried, in the world they lived in now, with all the danger to Johnny and his friends, to Gabrielle and her family, with all the Dead Zones, that she could lose him forever.

He had just never seen himself like that, though. He didn't know if he could bite someone, suck their blood, use them to feed. It didn't feel like something he *could* do.

Which was odd. Since he was happy to have Gabrielle use him in the same way he didn't want to use others. But Johnny felt like it was something he shared only with her. Something he gave her, when she needed it. A bond. In return, he was healthy, strong, fit. Quick. He would stay younger, for longer.

He was perfectly happy to keep it that way. When he offered Gabrielle his blood, or she bit him, it was an intimate thing between them.

If she turned Johnny, they would no longer share that moment. That bond.

And he worried that would change their relationship.

Johnny understood her worry. If he happened to be killed, helping his friends, that would change it, too.

He just didn't know.

"Hey," Nick said, waving his hand in front of Johnny's face.

Johnny looked up. Apparently Nick had asked him something, and Johnny hadn't responded.

"You good, man?" Nick said.

"Yeah," Johnny said. He was good, for now. He was helping his friends, and that meant a lot to him. He had been different, as a kid, than a lot of others in Grafton. One of the few black kids. One of the few black people, in that town, other than Parker.

He had come to the orphanage, or the halfway house, or Parker's, whatever they called it, later than the rest of the kids. He had been twelve years old then, and until then he had been moved from home to home, never fitting in, until he got sent to Grafton.

Johnny hadn't known then that he was supposed to develop a power. That's what the halfway homes like Parker's were for. For parents who didn't really care about their kids, unless they inherited their parents' powers. When they did, the parents would come get them, and call it an adoption.

Johnny had never developed anything. The halfway homes for supernatural babies got sick of waiting for him to "come of age." He had rebelled some, in every place he had gone, having no idea why he was being moved around, or the attitude with which people had treated him. Johnny had developed a tough skin, and a sense of humor, to fight the looks others gave him.

He had had the feeling Parker's was the last place he was going to have a chance at.

Danny and Grimm and Nick had taken him to the group right away. He had met Jen and Sarah, and they had pulled him in as well. Johnny had slowly relaxed and become himself around them. He had become the jokester of the group, someone they all counted on in a tough moment. There was a home with them, a place, and he didn't want to give that up yet. He wanted to be there for his friends, like he felt they had been there for him.

Even Parker, as gruff as the man had been, had treated Johnny squarely.

"We're getting some coffee, man," Nick said. "Take a little walk. You want some?"

"Sure," Johnny said. "A latte, if they have it."

"You got it." Nick got out of the truck, leaving the keys in the ignition. Sarah reached out and patted Johnny's knee, her eyes a little worried.

Johnny waggled his eyebrows at her. And Sarah smiled, then got out after Nick.

Johnny and Gabrielle had been together awhile, and happy, almost all of the time, in the past few years. Only after Grafton had they separated, and had things gone sour. Not really between them, but around them, and enough had happened where it might have changed their relationship. Or at least, how they both perceived it.

There were three couples in their group. Himself and Gabrielle. Nick and Sarah. Grimm and Jen. Only one pair of them had been happy together, at any one time. The other two had always had to endure something, go through a bad spell. Like the world had to be just right, for all six of them to make it.

He wondered if that was fate, or just a coincidence.

And grew worried it was neither.

CHAPTER THIRTY-TWO

Nick focused on the coffee shop board, looking at the white letters on the black background, describing all the different combinations of lattes and mochas and cappuccinos he could order. The barista at the cash register waited patiently, as if she had seen this kind of indecision on many a customer.

An older man stood by the large espresso machine, packing the portafilter with grounds, making drink after drink in a mechanical motion that seemed to be muscle memory now. The dark roast scent of coffee, strong by the register, stirred through the air and gave Nick a jolt of energy all by itself, each time he took a deep breath of it.

They had never had this kind of place in Grafton. He had always had coffee at Miss Tammie's, and it had always been strong, black, and bitter.

So Nick gave up and turned to Sarah. "What do you want?"

Sarah smiled at him, reaching her hand out and grabbing his, loosely. Squeezing it just a bit.

"Let me get a medium mocha, with coconut milk, and put it in your largest cup," she ordered. "Extra whip." As if she had made the order a million times.

"Medium cup in a large," the barista said, as if she had done that a million times.

"Please," Sarah said, then raised her eyebrows at Nick.

He sighed. "I'll take the mocha thing, but make it regular. And a large cup."

"Large coffee in a large cup?" the girl asked, making sure of his order.

Nick smiled, and thanked the girl. "Oh, can I get extra coffee in it?"

"You mean an extra shot?" she said.

Nick looked at Sarah. Sarah smiled again. "He does."

"Does he want an extra pump of mocha, too?"

Sarah squeezed Nick's hand again. "Sure."

"Oh," Nick said, remembering Johnny. "A big latte, too."

The barista grinned at them, then rang up their order and took their names. She carefully wrote them in black ink on green-and-white cardboard cups. Nick paid, left a tip, and the two of them walked over to the side and waited.

There were still a lot of people in the airport, even this late at night. Plenty of customers walking the stores that were still open and accessible to the families and friends waiting for their loved ones to get off flights. For a bit, Nick and Sarah browsed a place that sold books. The front of the store had stands of all the best sellers, in every genre. There was a candy aisle, magazines all sitting in a row against the wall, and a rack where newspapers still were sold.

Nick browsed those for a bit. Every front page was about the Dead Zones. The American papers, like the *New York Times* and the *Washington Post*, concentrated on New Orleans. But there was something called the *Guardian*, from Great Britain, that talked about the Dead Zones in Paris and Rome.

Some creature flew the skies over Paris. People wanted to call it a dragon, but Nick looked at the pictures and wasn't sure. Every picture, taken in the night, during the day, or even from high above, was blurry and shadowed.

It seemed more manlike than dragonlike, though it was as large as a city block. The creature had made its home in the top of the Eiffel Tower. After a few weeks, planes and helicopters stopped flying in. The creature was something like 50–0 versus the French Air Force.

Towers had grown out of the earth there as well. At each of the points of the pentagram, and at every inner angle. People had watched them, day after day, swell out of the earth, growing taller and taller as the weeks went by. They were big and red with black spots, like cancers, bulbous and protruding out of their walls.

Lately a line of earth had begun to swell between each of the towers and its neighbors. Thousands of miles long. Like a countrywide fence, or embankment. Like the demon there was building a fort for the largest army the world could hold.

Nick shook his head, reading that.

The Dead Zone in Italy was still in flux. There was still fighting going on. A large group of Catholic priests, bishops, and followers was camped to the north, in the tiny corner of Germany between Italy and Spain. The camp gathered believers by the day, and were arming themselves, calling the movement the Last Crusade.

Germany was having some issues with the large armed contingent inside its border, and had sent forces there to keep an eye on the Crusaders. There was a lot of tension there, with the Crusader camp between the Germans and the Dead Zone.

But believers still came.

Sarah and Nick walked around. Sarah got a magazine, something with a guitar on the front page, and a promise of the tablature of a new pop song inside. Nick bought some peanut butter cups, and planned on eating them in front of Johnny.

"Hey." Sarah tugged on Nick's hand, pulling him out of his thoughts. "They called our names."

Nick blinked, came back to the present, and smiled at her. Her hand was warm and soft in his, and he thought he could feel a tiny bump at the end of her fingers when their fingertips touched. Bumps that would become calluses as she kept playing.

"I liked your music," he said. "It's been forever since I'd heard you play."

Sarah blushed. "It's been forever since I've played."

Nick swallowed, and caught her eyes as she looked over at him. There was a tenuous moment when he felt like their gaze might break, when both of them wanted to run away, but then it held. "It's what had me fall for you when we were kids," he said.

"Oh," Sarah said.

"I was kind of always angry, you know?" His voice low, almost rumbling in his chest. "But every time you played, I'd feel this peace inside. And I'd have these goose bumps, I'd have to take these large breaths, like my chest was too small for what it was feeling inside."

Sarah's gaze did dart away then. Nick kept his hand from holding hers too tight. He just let it stay there, hanging in hers. After a moment her gaze returned.

"Do you want me?" she asked, softly, in her ethereal, little-girl voice.

"God yes," he exhaled. "But I'm afraid."

"Me, too," she said. "I was afraid, because of who I'd been with–"

"None of that mattered to me," Nick said.

"Good," Sarah said. "Good … this, it's the most real thing I've ever had."

"It's always been real for me," he said. "And there's a lot of times when I just want to grab you, pull you close and feel your body against me, and just get it over with, you know?"

Nick's chest swelled. Somehow they were standing closer together, and his face was right in front of hers, and he kept his voice low. "But I don't want to just sleep with you, to sleep with you. I want it to mean something."

Somewhere over the words between them, he heard a male voice call out his name. Then Sarah's.

"It'll mean something, no matter what," Sarah said then. Her voice as soft as his. "I'm afraid, too. But I think we need to get past it. I think we need to take the next step, and see what's after that."

He moved his head up and down, a slow couple of times, not trusting his voice. His heart beat faster, his breaths came shallower, and he kept swallowing.

"Yeah," he finally said. All of a sudden Sarah was looking into his eyes, he was looking into hers, and that was all either of them could see or feel. Everything else fell away.

"Nick. Nick. Nick and Sarah," the male barista called out a final time, raising his voice and looking over the few people standing around.

Nick waved his hand. The barista let out a breath and called out both their drinks. Nick didn't hear the words, just nodded.

Sarah smiled then, maybe a little sad, and maybe a little hopeful. Nick did grasp her hand then, hard. She squeezed his back.

CHAPTER THIRTY-THREE

They were walking back to the truck. The overhead lights weren't spaced right, and the parking lot was dark, like in a spy movie, with shadows along the concrete columns and between cars. Nick preferred the shadows. He felt like they were his natural element, but he also found it odd. There was a feeling that danger hid out in the parking garage, and he couldn't quite shake it.

He and Sarah had taken their time coming back. Not really talking, just enjoying being together. Maybe even taking a small step forward in their relationship. They had gotten out of the elevators, Nick had spotted their truck, and they had just taken a few steps when Nick's phone vibrated in his pocket.

Nick handed Johnny's latte to Sarah and fished the cell out. The screen proclaimed it an Unknown Caller. He slid his thumb across the red bar on the screen. "Hello?"

Grimm's voice came over the line. He sounded frustrated. "You know how hard it is to get one of these damn phones set up?"

Nick exhaled a large breath. "Man. We've been looking for you."

There was a pause before Grimm said anything. "You have?"

"Yeah. Hold on." Nick pushed the audio button on the phone, and held the cell up between him and Sarah. "Putting you on speaker. Sarah's here."

"Hey, Grimm." Sarah leaned closer to the phone. "You okay?"

"As okay as I can be, I guess," Grimm answered.

"We found this hotel that had its wall blasted out," Sarah said. "We were worried."

There was another long, long moment of silence.

"What are you guys doing in Colorado?" Grimm finally asked.

"Man, we're coming to help you," Nick said. "We're in Denver right now."

"Denver?" Grimm replied, slowly.

"Yeah," Nick said. "We're waiting on Gabrielle right now. She's flying in. Then we were going to look for you."

"Why are you looking for me in Denver?" Grimm asked.

Nick answered Grimm's question with a question of his own. "Aren't you here?"

"No," Grimm answered. "I'm in Colorado Springs."

"What the hell are you doing there?" Nick asked.

"You know what I'm doing here," Grimm said. "I'm looking for my mother."

"And she's there?" Nick looked at Sarah. Her eyes were worried, and open. "You've seen her?"

"No," Grimm said. "But in an hour or so, I will. Why do you all think she's up there?"

Nick paused a long moment. His eyes flicked back to the airport, where Gabrielle was probably landing now. He worked his jaw, thinking.

Did Gabrielle lie to them?

Nick couldn't believe she would do that to Johnny; he had seen them together. As much as Nick hadn't liked Gabrielle, hadn't liked Johnny becoming a thrall, he had been happy for his friend, because he had found someone who obviously cared for him. Gabrielle misleading Johnny would be like Sarah lying to Nick.

"Ummm," Nick finally said. "Something here is fucked."

"I don't get what you mean," Grimm said, his voice edgy. Like he hadn't had a lot of sleep.

"Gabrielle told us Dominic would be in Denver," Nick said.

"That doesn't make sense," Grimm said. "I'm with Raphael. He's the one who brought me to Colorado Springs."

Nick's jaw flexed. As soon as he had seen Raphael, he knew the guy would cause them trouble. He wished he had just kept shooting him, back in New Orleans. At some point, Nick felt, Raphael's pieces would have stopped putting themselves together.

"So one of them is lying," Nick said.

"Yeah." Grimm's voice was thoughtful. And deep, as if he held a great anger in check. "Yeah."

"The question is who," Sarah said. "And why."

"Gabrielle wouldn't lie to you all, right?" Grimm asked. "Not to Johnny?"

"That's what I would think," Nick said.

"Raphael would fucking lie, though," Grimm's voice trailed off. "Dammit."

Nick found himself wondering what the past few days had been like for his friend.

"You okay, brother?" Nick asked.

"I'm pretty far from okay," Grimm said. "But I'll make it."

That was Nick's friend. As hardheaded, determined, and implacable as any force on earth. Grimm was always all or nothing. All in or all out.

Sarah raised her eyebrows at Nick and pointed to the phone. Her mouth formed the words *Tell him*.

"We've been needing to talk to you," Nick said. "We've got some news. About the geas."

"I know," Grimm said, then a moment or two later. "At least, I *think* I do."

"Really?" Nick tilted his head, and put the phone speaker closer to his mouth. "What do you know?"

"Killing Dominic will kill my mother," Grimm answered.

Nick shook his head. Which his friend couldn't see. "That's not it. Where'd you hear that?"

"Belle," Grimm answered. "Belial. Another fucking demon."

Nick had once gone to church. He had done his studies, trying to figure out what his power was. If he was good, or evil. So he knew about Belial. That was a heavyweight demon. What the hell was Grimm doing riding around with her? Nick shook his head. "That's not all."

"What do you mean?" Grimm asked.

"Gabrielle told Johnny if you kill a vampire before killing the angel they are bound to, the geas will blow back and kill every vampire that ever was a part of the geas," Nick said. "Every angel, too. All of them."

There was a long moment of quiet then. Long enough that Nick wondered if he had lost connection with Grimm. Then his friend finally spoke.

"Sounds just like Azazel," Grimm said. "Scorched earth. Something so dark and twisted and scary, every vampire would be afraid of crossing him."

"Yeah," Nick said.

"So there's no way to free the angels," Grimm said.

"Pretty sure," Nick said.

The elevator opened, behind Nick and Sarah. A couple of people got out, maybe people who had just debarked their plane. The guy was slumped, tired, and overloaded with luggage. The woman had the strap of a large purselike bag over one shoulder, and a baby resting on the other.

Grimm's voice was small. "Then there's no way I can be free of it either, then."

"We don't know that," Nick said.

"Fucking Azazel always has every base covered," Grimm said, his voice edged with anger.

"Man, we can figure this all out," Nick said. "Maybe we come down there, get you out, and we think about it."

"You don't understand," Grimm said. "There's a contract involved."

"A contract?"

"Yeah," Grimm said. "Long story. But I basically have a couple of years left."

"We can figure out a lot in that amount of time," Nick said.

"Fucking Belle," Grimm said.

"Belial?" Nick asked.

Grimm didn't answer.

"Grimm," Sarah said, "get in your car. Come back up here. Let us help you."

"I'm starting to wonder what I really control," Grimm said.

"You're not making sense," Nick said.

His friend kept talking. "When have I ever done something right?"

"Grimm," Nick said, strongly, "what are you saying?"

"It's like my whole life has been some fucking script," Grimm said. Like he was wondering aloud. "Like I have never had a choice."

Nick looked at Sarah. Her eyes were open, and worried, and maybe a little moist. Like she could feel the sadness and rage and confusion coming from their friend.

"Grimm," Nick said, and then there was no response. *"Grimm."*

A long exhale came from the other side of the line. A large breath that wound down to nothing. Then Nick's friend's voice, tired and small. "Yeah?"

"Can you wait for us to get there?"

Grimm snorted. "There's no time."

"What do you mean?" Nick said. "You just said we had two years."

"It's just me that has that time," Grimm said, and then stopped. Like he didn't want to tell them anything more.

"Grimm, what?" Nick said. "Fucking tell us."

His friend stayed quiet.

"Be a man about this," Nick said. "We're your friends."

"It's the Key," Grimm said. "It's breaking."

Jen, Nick thought. That was why Grimm felt like he didn't have any time.

One of the coffee cups slipped from Sarah's hands. It hit the ground, the top popped off, and coffee splattered all over the concrete. Nick jumped back, just in time to keep his shoes from getting sopped.

"Grimm," Nick said.

"Don't," Grimm told Nick.

"I'm sure we have some time, man," Nick said.

"I'm not sure of much anymore," Grimm said. "Time, though, Nick? I'm going to be short of that."

Nick hit the mute button with his thumb. He looked at Sarah. "I could get there, shadow-walking."

Her head tilted to the side a little. Tears hung at the corner of her eyes. Sarah still held the other cup of coffee, loosely, like she didn't realize she hadn't dropped both.

But she nodded at him, slowly. Understanding that Grimm was their friend. That they all were in this together.

Nick unmuted the phone. "Grimm–"

Grimm cut him off. "I've got to go. You guys take care of yourselves up there."

"We're coming, man," Nick said. "Hold on."

"It'll likely be settled before you get here, Nick," Grimm said. "Probably was always set up that way. Fucking demons."

They both were quiet.

Nick looked at Sarah. She didn't know what to say. Stay or go. Nick tried again. "Let me come down, brother."

"If I was you, Nick," Grimm said, "I'd stay up there. Keep Sarah and Johnny and Gabrielle safe. Live what you can, while you can."

"Don't say shit like that," Nick said. He was going to hang up, make sure Johnny and Sarah were okay, and then start shadow-walking to Colorado Springs. No matter what Grimm wanted, he would get there in time to help his friend. "Wolverines, right?"

Grimm chuckled. The sound of it was dark. "Wolverines, brother. Wolverines."

A last moment of silence, across the lines.

"You guys take care," Grimm said again. And hung up.

CHAPTER THIRTY-FOUR

Nick slid the phone back into his pocket. Behind Sarah the elevator opened, and a small group of people got up. More unloading from the flights that had just landed. These looked like businessmen, in dark suits a little wrinkled from the flight, back from some conference. All of them looked young, fit, and used to travel.

They each held a bag and a briefcase, and stood with their backs straight. A few talked among themselves, and one of them waved to Nick. He waved back, absently. The group stopped outside the elevators, looking out into the parking lot. Like they were looking for something, like a taxi or an Uber.

"You and Johnny going to be okay?" Nick asked Sarah.

"We'll follow you, once we get Gabrielle," she said. "Just hurry."

"I will," he said. They both started walking to the truck, navigating through the thin aisles always created when a bunch of cars parked too close together.

"What did he mean by the Key was breaking?" Sarah asked.

"I don't know," Nick answered, turning his hips sideways to get between opposing side mirrors.

The door to their truck opened, and Johnny got out. He must have just seen them. He grinned and held up his phone. "Gabrielle just landed."

"Yeah, we got some news, too," Nick said. "Grimm called."

"He okay?" Johnny asked.

Then he stopped, his hand still in the air, holding his phone. Forgotten. Johnny's eyes tracked past Nick and Sarah, toward the bank of elevators, and then opened wide.

A whisper of danger touched along Nick's spine. Sometimes he could feel the warning ahead of time. It could have been just instincts, or supernatural reflexes, but sometimes he felt the shadows just spoke to him. Directed him. Like they could see into places and times he couldn't, and signaled him moments before something bad happened.

He never questioned those moments. He just acted on them.

Nick grabbed Sarah with one hand and yanked her to the ground. She bounced off the side of one of the cars, and as the two fell between the cars and into the shadows, he didn't think, he started to shadow-walk.

Gunfire erupted behind them.

He didn't think about what he was doing – *instincts, right?* – but Nick still had a hold of Sarah as they fell into the shadows. When he walked, he brought her along with him. Even as bullets smacked into the cars around them, pinging off engine blocks, shattering glass.

Like always, he felt the tugging sensation of pulling from one place and going to another, then the cut as they transitioned. Maybe a harder tug this time, and a heavier tug. The two of them came out of the shadows and hit the concrete behind the truck, so that the vehicle was between them and the gunmen.

"Was that …?" Sarah asked, next to him, trying to fathom what had just happened. "Did we …?"

Nick had never tried to bring someone with him when he walked. But he just had. He nodded.

The blast of gunfire and the sound of bullets *thunking* into the panels of cars echoed up and down the parking garage. High-pitched whines repeated as bullets deflected off the concrete and winged off into the night. Whoever the businessmen were, they had brought automatic weapons with them.

And had landed at the same time Gabrielle did.

Or maybe instead of. Maybe Grimm was wrong, and it was Gabrielle who had been the liar.

Johnny screamed and fell to the ground. Nick watched Johnny's phone bounce off the concrete and slide underneath the truck. He reached up and pressed the top of his chest, and dark liquid welled up between his fingers and spread out across his shirt.

"Johnny!" Sarah screamed out.

Johnny turned to look at them, his face as pale as it could be. He blinked once, then twice, and tried to say something.

"Stay here," Nick told Sarah.

He needed to take care of this, fast. He shifted.

Tug, cut.

Nick was in the back of the truck. He didn't bother with getting the flak jackets. He found his vest of knives, slid it on as quick as he could, leaving it unbuttoned. Then he grabbed the shotgun he had kept after New Orleans. A Remington, with a sidesaddle of buckshot.

Then Nick went to work.

Tug, cut.

He blinked through the parking garage, around the truck, quickly stepping out of the shadows and shooting the lights in the ceiling above him. Bullets struck around Nick, even as he disappeared, and car alarms started going off in the garage. First a couple, then more, until the garage was flashing hazard lights and beeps and boops and loud crying wails. It was a special kind of madness, which added to the confusion.

Nick didn't get all of the fluorescent lights, but he got enough that the darkness in the garage spread to the elevators, and the group of men there.

The team of men saw him, and shot at him, but each time they were an instant too late. He was already gone, across the way, in another direction.

Tug, cut.

It all happened in a couple of heartbeats. Then he was around the side, reloading. A couple of the men sounded panicked, and one man shouted orders above them. Nick heard something like "make sure he's down."

Nick would make sure they were down. All down. Permanently.

Tug, cut.

Only a few seconds had passed, but darkness descended through the garage and blended with the night outside, so that shadows were everywhere. A kind of darkness where Nick could see, and his enemies couldn't. Where he could be everywhere and nowhere, see everything and do anything.

Nick's kind of place.

He blinked to the back of them and pulled the trigger. The leader flipped forward into the group, a spray of blood leading his dead body. A few of them started to swing Nick's way.

Tug, cut.

Nick stopped shooting. He started flicking around the elevators, and each time he did, he pulled a knife out of his vest and let it fly.

Tug, cut, throw.

A man screamed, reaching up and behind him, to the knife sticking out of his spine.

The attackers started randomly firing everywhere, carelessly. They had compact submachine guns, and changed out magazines as soon as they emptied them. Another guy tried to call out Nick's location, but he was way off. A few of the guys started stepping forward, guns held out in front of them.

Tug, cut, throw.

A second man fell to the ground without making a sound. Except for the thump of his head bouncing off the parking lot, and his submachine gun skittering along the concrete.

Tug, cut, throw.

Another scream, and a man fell forward onto a car.

And then another.

The last man ran. But Nick finished him off by blinking in close and severing the man's jugular from behind. Nick stood there for a second, breathing heavy, and wiped the knife across his vest.

"Sarah?" Nick shouted.

"Here!" she called out.

"Johnny?"

Silence.

"He's not moving," Sarah answered instead, her voice worried.

The elevator dinged then. The doors opened, throwing light in front of it.

Nick shadow-walked to the corner and peeked around. More young man came out, in the same suits, this time, though, already with their guns in hand. As if they had heard the gunfire and come running. They grew panicked, seeing the bodies in front of them.

"First team is down," one of the men said, finger on something near his ear.

"Roger that," the same man answered, to whoever was on the other end of the earpiece. Then he motioned to the rest of his team.

"Stay here," the man said. "Stay hot. Boss is coming."

Dammit. Nick had just a couple of knives left, and a few shells.

Tug, cut.

Sarah gasped when he appeared next to her, behind the truck. He held up his forefinger to his lips. "More coming," he whispered.

Then Nick scrambled around to the other side. Far off, he could see a few heads of the second team, by the bank of elevators. He checked his friend.

Johnny's eyes were open. They fluttered when Nick appeared. Blood covered Johnny's shirt and formed a large pool that he lay in.

Johnny's chest wasn't moving. At least, not that Nick could tell. And his pulse raced. Like Johnny's heart was trying to find something to pump.

"We'll wait here. Support teams coming," Nick heard the leader of the second team say. "Stay focused on G2, and stay hot."

Nick looked up, then swore. That was the number and letter on the column in front of the truck. He grabbed his friend by his armpits and pulled him around to the other side of the truck. Johnny's feet dragged through the puddle of blood, and pulled some of it along with him.

Then Nick shadow-walked into the back of the truck, grabbed a few extra shirts, some shells, and a pair of ratcheting straps. Then Nick blinked back to Sarah.

"He's lost a lot of blood," Sarah said.

He pressed the shirt on Johnny's wound. He asked Sarah to hold it there, tight. "We've got to get him to a hospital."

"Can we?" Sarah asked. "Does he even have the time?"

Johnny's mouth moved, but nothing came out. His hand flapped weakly to his side. Nick tugged one of the straps underneath his friend, circling it around Johnny's back and pulling it through the handle of the strap on top of his chest.

"We've got to find it," Nick said.

Sarah leaned over Johnny, placing her mouth next to his cheek. "Hold on, Johnny. It'll be okay."

Johnny's head moved around, and he blinked a lot, as if he was having trouble seeing.

"Spread out," the leader of Team Two called. "Stay hot."

Nick wound the strap through the metal ratcheting handle, and then pulled the strap tight over Johnny's chest. Then Nick made sure the balled-up T-shirt was directly over the wound, and under the strap.

Sarah pulled her hand away as Nick worked the handle of the strap mechanism up and down a couple of times, the strap tightening around Johnny's chest with each click of the handle. Nick got the strap snug, then ratcheted the handle a couple more times. On the last one, Johnny arched his back and gasped.

"Hopefully that holds," Nick said, looking back at the elevator bank. "Be right back."

He went after Team Two. They hadn't stayed hot enough, and learned the same lesson about Nick that Team One had. Nick fished a knife out of the back of the last man, the leader, who lay facedown in front of the elevators. Nick cleaned the blade, wiping it on his sleeve, and then shadow-walked back to the truck.

The T-shirt under the strap was turning red, but the blood loss had slowed. Johnny was hanging on, but barely. Nick didn't know how, but he hoped his friend could hold on a bit longer. He hoped he had bought them all time, that Teams Three and Four and whoever the fuck else out there would be more prudent now.

Maybe those teams would get out of the elevators, see the dead bodies of all their friends, and go ahead and decide now was the time to use all those vacation days they had saved up.

It would save them all the trouble.

He and Sarah struggled to get Johnny in the truck. Bullet holes traced the passenger side, up and down in a wavelike pattern, and one hole was right on the handle of the door. Nick fought to open it, and when he did the two of them wrestled Johnny into the middle seat. Even so, Nick tried to position his friend carefully.

Johnny's hand flopped at Nick. His friend tried to focus on them, and his mouth moved once, but then something like a sigh escaped Johnny, and nothing else. No words.

"Nick," Sarah said, worried. She bent over and put her ear on Johnny's chest.

"Hear a heartbeat?" Nick said.

"I don't know," Sarah said, pressing her head hard against Johnny's chest. "Maybe."

"Pull back," Nick said, pulling Sarah off. The side of her face was covered with Johnny's blood, some of it wetting her hair. He ratcheted the strap again, and Johnny kicked his foot out.

Maybe that would hold. Maybe.

"We got to get out of here," Sarah said, her hand on the side of Johnny's neck. Maybe attempting to feel a pulse.

Nick glanced back through the windshield at the elevator bank. "Fuck."

More teams had come out there. At least two of them. Leading the groups, though, were a man and a woman. They looked Asian, and they were dressed a little different. Each had a white, blousy shirt on, and a dark, pleated skirt down their legs. The skirt was high and tight on their waists. Their hair was long, and tied simply behind them in a warrior's knot.

The two looked mature. More elegant. As if they had come from a time and place where fashion had been different, and they were trying to blend in. They walked slower, with a certain gait. Like a predator hunting prey.

Vampires, Nick thought. And not part of Gabrielle's clan. A different family?

They had real trouble now.

"Sarah," Nick said.

Sarah's hand was trembling, against Johnny's chest. Her eyes wider than normal. "I don't–"

"Sarah," Nick repeated, cutting her off.

Sarah blinked and focused on Nick.

Nick pointed at the elevator bank, staying low. "Vampires."

"Oh," Sarah said.

The female vampire pulled alongside the male vampire. She touched his sleeve, briefly, and he paused. She touched her ear and spoke, listened, spoke again. Like she was communicating with someone else out there.

How many fucking people with submachine guns could be here? Nick wondered. How could they just fly an army in? Were there more vampires than just this couple, too?

If so, they were in trouble. Hell, they were already in trouble. But there was trouble they might be able to get out of, and the kind of trouble that would put them all six feet under.

And one of them had at least one foot in the grave already. Nick avoided looking at Johnny. He would do his best to get his friend help, and if he failed him, he would not fail in his vengeance.

Nick crawled to the back of the truck, quickly, and got what was left there. He handed another Remington to Sarah, and passed over her flak jacket as well. Then Nick grabbed the last of his knives and restocked his vest.

"It's going to be tough for me to take on the vampires, with the small army out there," Nick said, shifting around behind the seat in order to take off his knife vest.

He was worried. Vampires could shrug off bullets. Nick couldn't. If he got into any kind of prolonged battle with one, all the rest of the attackers had to do was shoot.

"Let's just go," Sarah said. "Drive out of here."

Nick shook his head. "We wouldn't make it." He put the flak jacket on, tightening the straps and getting the fit of the jacket right. Then he slung his homemade knife vest over it. The combination was bulky, but he was as protected from gunfire as he could be, and he could still get to his knives.

Which was the important thing, since it was all he had that might hurt the vampires. He caught Sarah's look. "Look out there. We'll never make it. It's going to be them, or it's going to be us."

Sarah's hand was still pressing the bandage down on Johnny's chest. "Nick ..."

Nick knew. His friend breathed out his last. If they didn't get help immediately, *right now*, Johnny would die. And they couldn't leave right now. There was a small army out there in the parking garage, with more somehow coming, and leading the way were an unknown number of vampires.

There was still a boss out there, somewhere, if the female vampire speaking into her earpiece meant anything.

"I know," he said. He shook his head. "Fucking Gabrielle."

"We don't know she did this," Sarah said. Her eyes opened wide, and she motioned with her head to Johnny. As if asking Nick to be careful to blame Gabrielle, where his friend might be able to hear. Even though Johnny was dying because she had set them up.

"The fuck we don't," he said. "One of them said to make sure Johnny stayed down. They came here for him."

"We don't *know*," she said again.

He sighed. Behind her, through the windshield, more heads appeared over the cars. Coming from the banks of elevators, and the stairs next to them. Troops massing for the assault.

"Fine," he said, checking what knives he had left, snugging each one hard into its sheath. Everything had happened so fast, a minute or two, maybe, but it still felt like hours had passed. Nick's heart raced from adrenaline, and his breaths were deep, even, but fast. Ready.

He chewed his bottom lip, and an idea occurred to him.

"I'm going to pull a Grimm," he said.

Sarah's head tilted. "A Grimm?"

"Get in the driver's seat," he said. "Get ready. I'm going to go out there and cause as big a distraction as I can. I'm going to get them all looking another direction. When I do, pull this truck out and drive like crazy for the nearest hospital."

He handed her his phone. "Call 9-1-1 on the way. Hell, call them now. Maybe you'll meet the ambulance on the way."

Sarah looked at the elevators. "I don't like it."

"Hell, me, neither," he said. "But it's a shot. It's the best shot we have of helping Johnny."

She nodded. "I get it. But you have to promise me you'll be safe."

He put on a grin. It was more fake than real, but it was what he had. "Can't kill a shadow."

Sarah took a breath. Her hand found his and gripped it hard. "If it gets Johnny help, then we do it. But not if we lose you."

She squeezed his hand, one more time. Making sure he understood.

Her gaze was so intense, Nick looked away, down. He could only give her a slight up and down of his head. Nick's breath came out ragged, and all of a sudden he didn't want to leave Sarah.

"I understand," Nick said, his voice rough. "I'll do my best."

"Okay, then," Sarah said, making sure Johnny's seat belt was tight. "We'll make it."

She snuck into the driver's seat, and found the keys.

Nick took a last, deep breath. This might be the last time he saw his friends. It might be the last time he saw Sarah.

But he was about to do something he was good at. Something he excelled in. Quick, sudden violence. Without mercy or compassion or quarter.

It was what he did, for his friends. For Sarah. Nick picked up the shotgun, made sure the sidesaddle was loaded up with shells, and told Sarah, "Let's do this."

Tug, cut.

CHAPTER THIRTY-FIVE

I hung up the phone. I had the feeling my friends were in trouble, and that I was the reason they were in trouble. They had come here for me. They were in Denver because they thought I was there. And the back of my brain told me they were in real danger. It was an instinct, or a hunch, that I had trouble shaking. My thumb hovered over Nick's number for a long moment, until the phone screen went black.

Chances were, all I was feeling was guilt. How could I even help them, from Colorado Springs? Supportive words over the phone? Maybe something like *"You got this, buddy"* or even *"Go get them, tiger."*

A snort burst out of me. No matter if my friends needed me or not, it would take hours for me to get to them, unless I could somehow fly. It didn't matter if my friends were okay, eating bowls of ice creams together, or in the fight of their lives, there was nothing I could do about it. Not now. Not with me here.

They were on their own. No matter what bad feeling I got. No matter what bad feeling crawled up from the back of my brain and screamed at me to check on them. We had just talked.

I fought the feeling a moment. Calling Nick back right now felt foolish. But I had trusted my gut for a long time. That same gut was telling me my friends were in danger. And I was arguing with myself about looking foolish. I could call back. It was the very *least* I could do.

I punched up Nick's number on the phone. It rang, a tiny thin ring that repeated over and over, until the call finally went to voice mail.

I waited a moment and tried again, with the same result. A third time.

The thing crawling out of the back of my brain grew larger, swelled into a monstrous worry. The feeling became a tangible thing, and spoke to me. Fear screamed loud, echoing through my mind.

My friends were in trouble. Dying. Dead. And that I had done nothing to stop it. In fact, it had happened because I had left them. I hadn't been there when they needed me.

Grafton, all over again.

For a moment I held the plastic case of the phone in my hand, feeling the heft of it. How heavy the connection felt. It was such a small device to carry so much weight. I was an anchor, dropped into the depths of the ocean. All I could do was sink into those cold, murky waters and drag all my friends to their icy, abysmal doom with me.

I took a breath and blew it out. It was just the guilt I was feeling. That was all.

But maybe it wasn't.

I had promised to myself, many times on the road to New Orleans, to take care of my friends. To make sure they were okay. All my friends. And after years of being on my own, I discovered I had liked taking care of them. I had felt, finally, I was doing something I should have been doing all along.

And yet I had run from my friends, after Jen's death. Even though they all had helped me get into the Dead Zone, the first chance I got, I had abandoned them. As soon as the road had turned dark for me. Just like I had run from them before, after Danny. Running was a pattern I couldn't seem to break. It was a part of me I had trouble getting rid of. A demon I couldn't purge.

I couldn't summon my sword anymore. Maybe the key wasn't about how I could summon it, but *when*. I was thinking about the blade like it was something I had always been able to do. Like I had been summoning it my whole life.

The truth was, that power had come just recently. Which told me there was a specific set of rules to the blade. Conditions that had to be met, before it could be called.

"Words have *power*," Belle had said. "They *matter*."

She was there to enforce the agreement. A binding contact, based upon something I said. I had guessed it might have been the ghosts I lived that robbed me of the sword. Ghosts like Jo, and his memories that I had lived. Turning my ethereal color from blue to blue with hints of red.

Then I had blamed the contract. It was the contract's fault, me entering into an agreement with demons. The road to hell was paved with good intentions, and my contract with a demon had robbed me of the power of the sword.

But there had been an agreement, long before I had made the one with Raphael. An agreement I had made on my own, with someone I loved. Back in a garage, after a cop had shot me. When Jen and I had sat, backs against the wall, talking together, on our way to New Orleans.

"Just promise me," Jen had said. *"For me."*

"Sure," I had answered, back in that garage. Telling Jen what she wanted to hear. *"Sure."*

Jen wasn't quite buying it. She knew me too well. "Your word, Gus," she said.

"Okay," If that was what she wanted, I'd give it to her. I blew out a deep breath. Felt the promise lock in. *"You have it."*

Son of a bitch, I thought. Punching my leg with a fist. More words came back to me.

"If you don't, Gus, I'll haunt you. As a ghost. Forever."

Those words had been Jen's.

The promise had been mine.

She was here.

I was, too. But my sword wasn't. My *powers* weren't. It was just me, with the something I had once given … gone.

"Your word, Gus."

I remembered rolling my eyes back in the garage, and playing along. Saying them for Jen, and maybe even believing what I was saying, even though I was just giving *her* my word.

"You have it."

The truth chilled me to my core. Had I stayed strong? Had I protected my friends?

Had I kept my promise, and kept swinging, after Jen had died?

The answer was clear. I had not. In fact, it had been everything my friends could do to keep me going. Even worse, I had left them. Sure, I had believed they might be safer. But that wasn't the same as protecting them. Not by a mile.

And now they had followed my trail to Colorado. They were the ones trying to help me. Trying to protect *me*. And that action might have brought them into danger. It had just sounded off to me, Gabrielle wanting to meet them in Denver. Gabrielle telling Johnny that's where I was going.

There was something really wrong there.

My fist tightened over the phone, until the plastic of the case creaked.

I had promised to protect my friends, and I didn't.

"Words have power," Belle had said. She had been talking about the contract when she gave me that warning. She had no idea there had been a contract I had broken long before her speech.

I had promised Jen I would protect my friends.

I had given Jen my word.

And then I had broken that promise.

Hadn't even thought of what I had said to Jen, after her death. I had given up. I had descended into grief, crawled into that hole, and not let anyone else in.

Maybe I had believed my friends would be okay, that they could take care of themselves. That they were better off, *safer*, without me. But I had traveled that road before. I *knew* where that road led. I had seen the evidence, in Grafton.

Words have power.

And I had broken mine. And in the breaking, I had become something less than who I had been before. Something who couldn't call the sword. Or the armor. The tools I needed, to be strong enough to protect those I cared about. Those I had promised to protect.

People who needed protection now, even if it meant I couldn't save Jen.

Now I stood in front of the motel bed, a guy looking at himself in the big mirror on top of the dresser. His reflection was too thin, too tired, maybe a little too desperate. He needed more food and sleep than he could get in a week, let alone what he had gotten in the past twenty-four hours.

The reflection was running on fumes and pushing himself to his own end game. To a place where he believed he could magically make everything better. Instead of being with his friends, protecting them, the reflection rode with a couple of demons in order to have some kind of crazy conversation with his mother, where she would tell him all he had to do was *X, Y, and Z* and *poof!*...

Jen would be brought back to life.

All the reflection had to do was leave his friends, ignore them and any danger that might happen to them. Surely they were safer, away from me. After all, all the reflection did was fail. I had failed Danny. I had failed Jen. I'd fail my other friends at some point, too.

What a bunch of bullshit.

I punched the mirror. The glass crunched and spiderwebbed under my knuckles, transforming my pathetic reflection into a thousand more splintered images, each one tiny and shattered and alone. A few triangles of glass, tiny slivers, cracked away and bounced off the top of the dresser.

My knuckles bled. I let them bleed. My chest heaved in and out in deep, measured breaths. Angry breaths.

What the fuck was I doing? Who the fuck was I? What was I letting happen to my friends? Who was I sacrificing, all in the name of getting Jen back?

I wasn't doing this for Jen's sake. I needed to admit I was doing this for a more selfish, destructive reason. I was doing all of this for me. Not because living without her was impossible, only because I didn't *want* to live without her.

I collapsed back onto the bed. The mattress sank under me. I lay there, thinking, the coverlet hard and lumpy under my back. I tapped a local ghost, briefly. My knuckles healed in a spastic, chilling tingle.

The truth of it was, I could live without Jen. I had proven it, these past few days. I had eaten and slept and driven, I had fought and survived, I had argued and screamed and yelled. I had driven and lived in the presence of one of my worst enemies, and another high demon of hell.

Funny I could do all of that with my enemies, and yet I couldn't do those same things with my friends. Maybe it was easier to be angry at Raphael than share pain with my friends. It was easier to take it all on myself. All the pain and loss and fear. To not involve them, because involving them meant sharing. Not just the pain. Not just the fear. But the *loss*.

But keeping my friends away was costing them. And costing me.

Saving Jen was a lottery ticket of all lottery tickets. A Powerball I would never hit. But my friends were alive. They were *here*, on this earth.

And they needed me.

I hadn't changed from Grafton. The first time I had left. I could blame the ghosts I had lived for not being able to summon the sword, that living every memory of every evil act I had lived had changed me. A bad apple always ruined the bunch, and I had lived through a lot of really bad apples.

The truth was, the memories of the ghosts were just another excuse. I had run away from Grafton a decade ago. The fear that led me to leave my friends, it was just despair. Leading me in the wrong direction.

My living those memories, sure, they were horrible experiences. Things I shoved into a vault. But I couldn't blame them for not being able to summon the sword, or the armor, anymore. The ghosts weren't responsible for the tinge of red I saw in the energy healing me now, instead of the pure ethereal blue.

It was always easier to blame something else than take that the responsibility that the fault was yours.

Blaming others was a subtle, insidious thing that led to a hidden, vicious kind of damage inside. The kind of damage that robbed you of a personal strength. When you blamed someone, you let yourself off the hook for your own actions. There was this little voice, speaking from the back of your head, saying that none of this was your fault.

And that had changed me. That was the evil inside. What I hadn't felt, even as the dark voice whispered at me to leave my friends. To come on this journey to save Jen.

It wasn't these evil memories I lived, of all these ghosts, that had created the slow corrosion of my broken promises. It wasn't the spirits who had caused me to fail my friends. It was easy to blame the memories, all these evil acts I lived. They were a thick oil that coated me, stained me, a darkness hard to clean.

Insidious, how it had worked, now that I saw it clearly. Somehow it had always been easier to blame something else, anything else, than take responsibility for my actions. My decisions.

I had given my word to protect them. And I had failed. *That* broken promise was what had changed me. Despite all the little arguments I had told myself on this journey, each choice I had made had changed me a little more from the person I had promised Jen I'd be.

All the evil memories I had lived, all the stacks of the memories of murderers and rapists and pedophiles, those evils seemed so dark and hideous when I balanced them on the scale against one broken promise.

But that's what made it insidious. Breaking my word was worse than everything I had lived in ghosts. Hell, Belle had hinted at it. And lying to myself had changed something in my core, betrayed a truth I once had held evident about myself. It had done so slowly, so I couldn't understand the change.

I wasn't the man I believed I was. Who I wanted to be. Who I had thought about when I was young. The kid who had told the sheriff in Grafton that I would keep finishing things, because he couldn't stop my friends from getting hurt.

How could I be that person again?

I needed to keep faith with my word.

What was happening here, with Belle and Raphael, could wait. Belle had lied to me. Sure, she was just enforcing her contract, but she had withheld some truth as to what would happen if the contract was fulfilled. She had told me her side wasn't evil, they just believed in withholding information about heaven, so that people could live their lives without that influence, and thus be properly judged good, or evil.

It wasn't that far of a stretch to figure out Belle would have been happy to withhold other knowledge from me. Like the destructive blow-back of the geas.

It set up nicely. I had seen the tendril connecting my mother to Dominic, and though I couldn't see the one connecting me, it still made a demonic kind of sense there would be one there. And if some part of the spell tied us all together, and the blowback would kill all the vampires involved in the geas, as well as what angels were left, well, that only helped Belle's side.

That also gave Raphael the revenge he was looking for.

Sure, Raphael had promised me he'd wait one year before killing his father, if I needed the time. Sure, he had told me it would be an honest fight between us, at the end, to settle that score.

That's what he wanted. Or what Raphael's ego wanted. Him versus me, one versus one, last man standing. It wasn't hard for me to believe him then.

I snorted. Maybe I knew better now. He likely had oceanfront property nearby he wanted to sell me, too. While we were in Colorado.

It was time for me to start keeping my promises. It was time to start doing the *right* things, and not just the things I wanted to do. I lived around a lot of evil. It was time to stop compromising who I should be, who I wanted to be, in order make sure I did the *just* thing.

It was time to be the person I needed to be. The person I had promised Jen I would be. Even if it cost me the person I loved most.

The Key thrummed a little then. I put my hand on it, and felt it shiver and shudder a little, like whatever held it together inside was crumbling, bit by bit. The spiderwebbed cracks ran across the Key, and seemed larger now. It looked like a ball of lightning had been carved into the stone. All of the lines glowed a deep blue, but they cut into the Key so deeply the stone felt fragile in my hand. Like it was falling apart.

Life wasn't fair. It was far easier to stay beat down than get back up. I had seen more evil than most, and I could lie in a bed, and had done so, and try to let the world wash away. I tried to give up, and honestly thought I had.

But somehow I had never completely given in. I had found a way to keep going after Danny. I had found a way to keep going when my team was killed, back in Afghanistan. I had found a way to keep going while Azazel was chasing me. So I would find a way to keep going now. Even if it took Jen from me.

Especially then.

I wiped my eyes. My fingers came away wetter than I thought they'd be. And when my hand pulled down, Jen sat next to me.

She glowed in the room, a soft, transparent blue. Like me, she looked sad. Her eyes shimmered, and her lips twisted in a little grin, with one of the corners turned down.

"I don't know if I can save you, Jen," I said into the mirror, loudly. Mouthing the words.

She laid a ghostly arm on mine. Neither of us could feel the other, but a well of support stretched across our bond, from Jen. A peaceful, content type of energy passed into me, and centered me. It was a sad energy, quiet, and I took solace in it.

"I don't know if I can live without you, either," I added. "But I think I have to try."

That was the razor's edge of it. I had promised to take care of my friends, no matter what. But in order to make sure they would be okay, I would have to do something that could cost me the Key, and leave me without Jen.

The Key *was* breaking. Maybe a day left before it fell apart. Maybe a week. I didn't know, I wasn't an old stone carver and spell crafter from four thousand years ago. All I knew was every day that passed was another day the stone grew more crumbly. Each time I brushed my shirt, I found more tiny bits of dust and rock, where they had rubbed off.

Without Jen, I would be alone. It would be just me, even among my friends. Nick and Sarah. Johnny, with Gabrielle. I would live and I would protect them as best I could, and I would do it alone. I would go to bed alone, wake up alone, I would get up and get the same black coffee I always got, and not the lattes and the flavored drinks and the coffee cakes Jen and I got together.

There would never be a time when I would look up into the night sky, and know she was somewhere looking at the same stars, each of us knowing we were thinking about the other. There would never be another time we would sit on a couch, resting against each other, watching some lame movie. There would never be a time we would ride in the Camaro, her hand on top of mine, her hair whipping in the wind.

A part of me would be ripped out forever, and burned. I would live with a hole inside me, an emptiness that could never be filled. If I left now, I was maybe passing on the one chance I had to save Jen. To be with her again. For us to be what we should have always been. A couple who could change the world.

But people lost loved ones every day. Would they do what I was doing now, if they had the choice? What made me so special, that I believed I could march into the afterlife and drag my Jen back from death? Who was I trying to fool?

I still felt her in my arms. Of holding Jen as she died. Her body warm, soft, shaking. She had felt smaller then, like she had been disappearing from the earth, even as hard as I had tried to hold on. Was it me that had kept her here?

Had she willingly entered the Key, or had I trapped her there?

Was the Key breaking because it wasn't made to hold a human spirit, or was it breaking because Jen was supposed to be somewhere else, and I was keeping her here? Was it not breaking, but trying to release her instead?

I didn't know. Danny had stayed here, on earth, after his death. At least, I thought he had remained, because his ghost had appeared when I needed him. I didn't know if he had been waiting there, or if there was a place he had come from. I didn't know even if he had returned to that place, or disappeared, after he gave me his memories.

But he *had* shown me then that I needed to keep up the fight. Keep going on. That we all helped each other, when we needed it. That Danny was proud of being a part of my life, and helping me when no one else could. Even if it had cost him his life, and even if, later, it cost him his afterlife.

I had told Sarah I tried to live life more like Danny would have wanted. But that had been a lie as well. Because Danny wouldn't have run from his friends again. And if his friends needed him now, that was where he'd be.

I knew what I had to do. If the choice was between helping my friends and a crazy wild-goose chase for my mother, then that wasn't really a choice. My friends helped me. I would help them. Because picking each other up helped us all keep moving. Helped us all to keep growing.

Kind of a simple concept. It was these little things, helping each other, that helped us withstand the evils that were around us. Every time we helped each other, it kept us all going. When someone died, we closed our ranks and pressed on harder. To us, giving up allowed evil to win faster. If we kept getting back up, though, we could keep standing against it. We could form a beacon that would call to others, and build our foundation, grow our strength.

Maybe evil never actually left this earth. But it could be withstood. And if someone was hard enough, and strong enough, and supported by enough of those he loved, then maybe he could beat it.

Like me and my friends.

I was weaker now. I had abandoned my friends in my quest to rescue Jen. They had propped me up. In turn I had protected them, and now that my foundation was gone, I was toppling over. Without them, I would become more like the evil I fought. Weak. Fearful. Angry.

Kind of like the person I had been becoming.

It was a hard lesson. It wasn't a fair lesson. But it was the one I needed to hear. At least I would learn it trying to save those I loved, and cared about. I could look myself in the mirror, after that. I would be sad, and I would be alone, but I could face myself again.

I buried my head in my hands. If I flipped a coin right now, it would land on its edge, and stay there. It took a while to realize I was sobbing.

I looked up, finally. Jen still sat beside me. Tears ran down her cheeks as well, little luminescent silver drops, trickling down her ethereal skin and falling into open air.

"Them first, right?" I said.

She nodded.

"So hold tight, okay?" I said.

She nodded again. Her hand came up, pointed at me, pointed at her, and then she balled her fingers up tight and tapped her chest.

You and me, she was telling me.

"I know," I told her back. Wanting her to stay here in this room with me and never leave, wanting every last moment of whatever I could get with Jen, and yet knowing I had to go. "Forever."

CHAPTER THIRTY-SIX

I stood up then. Tapped a ghost and asked the sword to appear. Felt the blade in my hand. It was shadowy and ethereal in the room, transparent enough the pale coverlet of the bed showed from underneath it.

There was something new, though. Tiny blue arcs of lightning raced up and down the blade. The bond between us pulsed, the connection between Jen and me tight. She was giving me what she could. Still in the fight.

Or maybe she and I were just together now, forever. In everything we did.

But not everything. There was a line we could not cross together. One she could cross on her own, if she used too much of herself. Or if I used too much of her.

"Jen," I said aloud, my voice concerned. Understanding that using too much of herself would cause the Key to break. Or, like all the other ghosts I used, cause Jen to disappear.

A warning came back from along the bond then. A slight anger. As if Jen was telling me she knew what she was doing.

I would have to depend on her knowing her limits.

And I laughed, something dark, and yet also uplifting. Which of us had ever known our limits? Both of us would keep swinging, until every ball was slammed out of the park, the bat broken, the crowd gone.

On that thought, it was fitting, what I was about to do next.

I burst out of my door and walked to Raphael's room. Opened his door without knocking. I may have even broken the handle.

He sat in a chair, a book in his hand. His eyes opened a little as I walked in. As if a little surprised.

"Did something break in your …," Raphael started to say, but then his voice trailed off as he looked at me. Realizing something was different. His head tilted. "Grimm?"

I held the sword up. Tiny electric blue motes streamed off the blade, like steam. The smell of ozone was heavy around me. A buzzing sensation filled the room, as if thousands of volts of electricity hovered over all the walls.

"I'm going to ask you this once," I said. "And I want the truth."

"I've told you," Raphael said, concerned but trying not to be, about the sword. "I'm playing this straight."

"So keep telling me," I said. "Gabrielle told my friends your father is in Denver. She also told them that's where we were going. Why would she do that, if you're telling me he's here? If you brought me *here*."

There was a zap then, a snap and crackle, and blue sparks dripped off the tip of the ethereal blade and scattered across the carpet. Jen, punctuating my words.

"My father would be here," Raphael said. He carefully closed the book and set it on the small nightstand next to the chair. "In Colorado Springs. It's his safest haven. I don't know how or why you heard what you did."

"Why is Gabrielle in Denver, then?" I asked. "Why would the Dumonts come here?"

Raphael's face paled.

"Shit," he said. "They've called a Conclave."

"What do you mean, Conclave?"

"It's a place where the vampires would meet," he said. "All the families have a place to host them. There's one in each country, seven of them."

"And I'm supposed to believe you didn't know about this?" I said.

"Grimm," Raphael said, "why would I bring you here if I didn't think my father was here? What's in that for me?"

"I don't know," I said. "Maybe some deal you made with Belial."

"Belle?" Raphael snorted. "There's no deal with her." He paused, looking at me a little oddly. "Except for the one you and I have."

"So I'm supposed to take this on faith," I said. "From you? Either you've been wrong, or you've been lying to me. Neither of those options inspires me that you know what the fuck you're doing. Or that you'd even be any kind of help."

"I'm telling you, I didn't fucking *know*." Raphael stood. His face twisted. "If that Dumont bitch is in Denver, with her father, then a Conclave has been called. All the vampires will be there. How the fuck would I know that was happening? You think anyone reached out to me? You think I have some kind of emergency line in hell, where I get told that shit?"

He looked past the blade, into my eyes. He was furious. "Grimm. Do you really think, with the drug in his system, my father would *want* a Conclave called?"

Shit. Raphael made some sense with that. Dominic wouldn't want anyone around he couldn't control, in his weakened, drug-crazed state. Especially the Dumonts, who were the reason Dominic had been kicked out of Europe, and had to bring his family to the Americas.

So maybe Dominic didn't call the Conclave. Maybe Victor Dumont had instead.

Which meant my friends *were* in danger.

I had heard enough.

"I'm headed to Denver," I said. "Whatever contract we have, it's going to wait."

"Denver?" Raphael said. "Then I'm coming with you."

"Not my way, you're not," I said. I wasn't planning on driving. I didn't think driving wouldn't get me there fast enough.

He stood, his arms folded across his chest. "Grimm, you can leave, but you can't ban me from Denver. I'll still be coming. So don't you think it's better I go somewhere you know I'll be, instead of you just wondering where the fuck I'm at?"

He was right. At least, if he was going to go anyway. Whatever deal we had between us, I wanted to make sure to keep my enemy if not close, then somewhere I was aware of. Somewhere I could find him, if I needed to.

"Fine." I tossed the keys to the Camaro to the demon. I tossed him the phone as well. "Keep this on you."

"Sure." Raphael frowned. "If you're not driving, then how *are* you getting up there?"

"Don't worry about it," I said.

"I'm not worried. Just curious," he said, and then after a pause: "It seems like we both have changed, haven't we?"

I didn't like the new Raphael that thought about these things. We both had changed. Not only since we had fought as kids, but even since our last battle in Grafton.

Would we keep changing? Were we both morphing into something greater? Were we each like some kind of solitary silkworm, crawling along our individual, cocooned paths of life, growing into some kind of Frankenstein butterfly?

"Stay curious," I finally said.

"Whatever," he said.

Maybe it was that moment that I knew it. Here, in this room. That Raphael would be someone I would have to deal with. That he would be a *danger*.

I had always been scared of him, since Danny. I had overcome that fear when I killed him in Grafton. But he had changed since then, in death. I had changed since then, in life. Something told me we both were on a collision course, something different than the battle I'd had with Azazel.

Something maybe more intimate. An organic struggle. Him or me, until one of us killed the other to such a degree we could never come back.

So I wanted to make sure we were on the same page, before I left. "Just so you and I are clear, if you're not telling me the truth about anything, or if you try to hurt any of my friends, I'll make sure you stay dead next time."

Raphael smiled. "That's the Grimm I remember."

His smile grew larger. "And prefer, truth be told."

I had wasted enough time already. If my friends were in danger, I needed to get to them.

"Let me know where you're at," I said.

"Of course." Raphael inclined his head, as if between equals.

There was something eerie here. With him. Us. But I didn't have time to focus on it, or figure it out. I made a good-bye type of motion with my hand and headed out to the parking lot.

CHAPTER THIRTY-SEVEN

I stepped outside. The wind had picked up and whipped around my shirt, and blew gusts of sparks off the blade. I felt along the bond for Jen, mentally held her hand in mine. Tried to squeeze it, and tried to feel her squeeze in return.

The two of us had always had this connection. It was unique. We knew we belonged together, from the very first time I had seen her, and she had set next to me, in middle school. Her smile, *oh man, her smile*, there had never been anything like it for me. She could just look at me, out of the corner of her eyes, and I would stand a little straighter.

She was the one pillar I couldn't be without. The one person who could always prop me up. The person I needed to lean on, right now, when my friends were in danger and helping them could cost me what I loved the most, in this life.

A warm reassurance came over me. Like I was doing the right thing. There was power, along the bond, strength. Fight. Everything I needed and everything I wanted right beside me, forever.

We both knew this could be it for her. I didn't know what would happen to her ghost if the Key crumbled away. But I hoped she would be proud of me, for doing what I had promised her I would do.

"Hang on, babe," I said aloud. The words drifted away without an echo in the parking lot. They were too loud, too sharp, in the freezing night air around me.

The sky was the deep blue-black of twilight, darkening slowly into true night. The waning moon struggled to rise in the east. The snow had stopped, the skies were cloudless, and the night city lights of Colorado Springs hid the stars above me. The sky was just purple and resonating with a chilly coldness only a barren sky could bring.

It was the cold of the Colorado Rockies; the cold of thousands of tons of snow locked up on peaks poking high up in the atmosphere; the cold vacuum of deep, empty space. I shivered from the icy chill of abandonment, of being alone in the universe, of vengeance not taken. Or at least, postponed.

I didn't have my jacket on, and I didn't go back and get it. I had wasted enough time. Instead, I let the sword disappear. For a moment the image of the blade hung in the air, the dark parking lot by the motel shadowy underneath the sword's silver translucence.

The sword faded away, leaving a framework of electrical arcs behind, little blue traces racing across the disappearing surface of the ethereal metal. For a brief moment there was a cage of electricity, an outline of the blade, which hung in the air. Then it, too, was gone.

I turned to face the north, and the dark spot in the distance I imagined was Denver. I closed my eyes and stretched out over the ghostly radar, toward the north, finding points here and there, blue and red points of people long dead along the road connecting the cities.

If Nick could figure out a way to cross an entire state quickly, so could I.

I tapped into one ghost. Like all the others, it resisted me. Fought me, for a quick moment. Then I subdued it and pulled ethereal energy through the spirit.

Me as a ghost, a woman, standing in a kitchen, knife in her hand. All I could think about, or the ghost I was living could think about, was all these fucking kids running around and screaming. Here I am, late for work, and they won't get their clothes on. They won't eat their fucking breakfast. They just keep running around and screaming and screaming and screaming and my boss is going to fire me if I'm late one more time....

There was the usual disgust, the bile rising in the back of my throat, but I still pushed that memory down, into the vault with all the others. I was tired of living these memories, of being a part of the darkness of the world. I was angry that I had to keep pulling from these terrible souls, living these horrifying acts, some so bad I threw up afterward.

I didn't understand why these spirits remained. Why they started to fight me. It had happened first after the factory fight, back in Grafton.

The first time the ethereal wings had appeared.

And although I didn't know it at the time, the very beginning of the road that would lead me to understand who I was. Or who I could be. Something I had never believed in, an angel.

Maybe being an angel was less about who I had been born, but more of how I lived. What I chose to do, in the life I had. Perhaps it was some combination. Did the ghosts fight me – not because I was using them up – but because of what I was becoming?

I always had the feeling the spirits hung around on earth. Most were reluctant to leave. Some of the worst ones, like the ghost of Jo, back in Lewiston, did everything in their power to stay. They preferred limbo to disappearing.

Unless maybe they weren't just disappearing. Maybe they were sent to a worse place. When Danny had shown up, and given me the power he held, and then faded away, I sensed nothing but happiness from him. As if he had known where he was going, and helping me was just a stop along that journey.

By experiencing their lives, I was seeing who they had been. Good and bad, or in most cases, good *or* horrifyingly bad. I was doing that while I was accessing the ethereal plane, because I needed the power there.

Could it be that accessing the ethereal plane and using the power was just the result of what I was actually doing? That by living the spirits' memories, of everything they had done in their lives, I was tabulating up the good and the bad each of those spirits had done? That the real power was in the judgment of their lives?

That meant, as an angel, I played some kind of judge, jury, and executioner role. That every ghost that remained on earth lived here in limbo until it was judged and passed on to its next life. Which was why they fought me so hard, because hanging around here was better than where I was sending them.

Did I believe that?

Maybe I did. I didn't know that I trusted in the idea of heaven, with its pearly white gates and peaceful souls kicking back on clouds, but I did believe in justice.

I had told Jen I wasn't an angel once. That I had done things I wasn't proud of, through my life. And I believed that, even now. If being an angel meant doing the right thing every time, being altruistically good, then that wasn't me.

But an angel of vengeance?

That was a concept I could get behind.

I pulled more from the ghost. It fought me harder, transparent arms swinging wildly in the air. I focused more – not on the drawing of the power – but on the experience of the memories. Judging them in my mind. Pushing the spirit down into the earth, toward where I imagined hell to be.

The woman had stabbed a kid, maybe by accident. But then she had looked at the knife and snapped, stabbing the kid over and over.

I pulled even more.

The woman's spirit fought me then, as hard as she could. The stream of energy lessened, like a river drying down to a trickle, so I strengthened my resolve and yanked harder. The other kids ran from the woman in fear, screaming not in play, but in true, horrified terror. The women chased each one down, until she was in the front yard of an old house, stabbing the last kid over and over.

I swallowed the bile down. Then I crammed the memories into a vault and labeled the vault True Evil, and then pulled everything from the ghost. Banishing her spirit to whatever came next.

Strength radiated along my bond, from Jen, then. Strength and satisfaction.

I always thought angels should be a force for good. That they were pure. Holy. But maybe angels were people, too. Maybe they made mistakes, and some of them became demons, like Belle. Maybe some of them had regrets, and tried to do the best thing they could.

Maybe the good I did wasn't the "help the old lady across the street" type of good. Or "feeding the hungry" kind of good. Maybe the kind of good I did was justice. Or even vengeance.

I kind of liked the sound of that.

A burst of blue energy left my feet and rolled across the parking lot. Bits of blacktop burst out of the ground as the wave passed into the distance. An ever-so-small rumble of thunder accompanied the wave, a long, resounding note of bass that raised the hairs along both my arms.

Then something flapped over my head, fluttered about, and spread to my left and right. Wings. Ethereal, and semisolid in the corner of my eyes. Not quite transparent, with a little heaviness to each, like a favorite blanket. My weight rebalanced in the balls of my feet, each of my heels pressed hard into the ground, bracing my body under its transforming scale.

"What the hell?" A question, from Raphael. The demon stood in the door of his hotel room, a puzzled, incredulous look on his face. As if he saw, for the first time, what he would go one-on-one with.

I winked.

Then I took off.

Not running. Flying. I leaped into the air and poured ethereal energy into my wings. I ran out of the first ghost and tapped another. Pushed away the memory of a snort of coke into the evil vault.

The currents of wind swirled around me and punched under my wings, buffeting them and tossing me around. I flew faster and heading north, fighting the wild currents pushing against me.

I was a mile above Colorado Springs. The city below had dwindled into tiny yellow and white lights. Cars ran north and south on the interstate, arcs of headlights traveling across the roads, followed by red brake lights, like pairs of demonic eyes.

I was maybe a mile up. The air was knife-cold against my skin, and I tried to burn ethereal energy through my body, to keep me warm. A jacket would have been nice.

I hadn't thought that part through.

Gusts of wind kept slapping me. It was like I was a kite, with a tiny string pulling me north against a heavy headwind. The air and I fought each other. The wind pushed hard against me, catching my wings and twisting me sideways, until I straightened them out and kept going. North.

Miles flew by. But I needed to go faster. I needed to be in Denver *now*. I took energy from every ghost I passed, pushing more power into my wings. I found out that if I folded them back, and laid them down, like a fighter jet, I would fly faster, and encounter less pushback from the air around me.

Maybe I was most like a missile. Or a rocket. I was moving so fast I was sure people only saw me as a blur. I took everything from ghosts until they popped, until I almost glowed with energy, and streaked across the skies.

Even as fast as I was moving, it wasn't going to be fast enough. If my friends were in trouble, they needed me *now*. I could feel it, an urgency in my chest telling me to hurry, the quick beating of my heart. I forced myself to think of my promise. To always protect my friends. No matter what.

I would have to be more than what I was now. I had to try to be something I had always needed to be. Maybe something the world needed me to be. Definitely something my friends, those I cared about, and those who cared about me, needed me to be.

I began taking huge pulls from every ghost around me. Large mists of ethereal motes streamed up from each one, until long streaks of blue energy strung throughout the sky, through the air from every ghost, and into me.

Some of the ghosts became resigned. They stopped putting up their huge fights as I tapped them, and a few even submitted when I banished them. I even felt something like sorrow, for those. I, of all people, knew where a road of bad decisions could lead a person, where it came to *this*, for them. To a place where I lived their memories, weighed their lives, and then they were dismissed forever.

I still needed to be faster. I needed *more*.

My chest warmed up, where the Key tucked against it. Hot, like the burning rays of a sun on a hot summer day. I reached along the bond for Jen and then …

The two of us were high above Grafton, in our usual spot. The water tower. We sat next to each other, quiet, feeling the wind whisper by us, hearing the rushing of leaves in the trees below. The town lay underneath us, tiny dots of people walking the sidewalk, small matchbox cars heading up and down Main Street. Jen ran her hand down my arm until our palms met, our fingers intertwined, and her hand tightened in mine.…

The landscape blurred underneath me. The dark spot I believed was Denver swelled from over the horizon. The darkness was fuzzy at first, then slowly resolved into one luminous light at the edge of the earth. Like a human-powered sun. As I flew toward the glow, the light dissolved into individually lit skyscrapers, tall buildings, car headlights, and windows of homes and stores. And even, to one side of Denver, the blinking flashers of large jumbo jets taking off and landing.

I had always felt like Jen and I were meant for each other. That somehow I had ended up with the one person in the world who could make me the best *me*. That together, we would be much greater than either apart.

We had to be careful with this, though. With Jen and me, using her powers. Being so close to finding my mother, to a chance of bringing Jen back. I needed her to let me know how much was too much, and neither one of us was good with something like that. Neither one of us knew our limits.

Be careful, I thought. I knew she would rebuke me for the thought, and smiled when the bond radiated a reprimand at me.

She was okay, I thought, with what we are using now. We were okay. We would be okay, as long as we were careful.

Still, I had to say it. Or think it. *Hang on, Jen.*

Then, silently, to my friends.

You guys, too. I'm coming.

I summoned the sword back into existence. The blade sliced through the wind, the gusts blowing a trail of electric blue sparks behind me, little pops of lightning bursting every few miles, as if Jen had gathered so much energy she couldn't hold it all. Below people would look up and see a blazing comet, a long blue ethereal mist trailing behind it, streaking across the night.

Jen and I, together. If not in the way we wanted, at least in some way.

So I corrected myself.

Hang on, guys.... We're coming.

CHAPTER THIRTY-EIGHT

So this is death ..., Johnny thought. There had been pain, at first. It had happened so fast he hadn't recognized what was happening. Gabrielle had texted him.

I'm here. We've landed. See you soon.

He got out of the truck, excited, but also having that little *off* feeling. Like something wasn't right. It was only a few seconds later, after he had been shot, that he realized what that feeling was telling him.

The texts were grammatically correct.

He would have snorted, had he been able to.

Instead, he lay on the concrete, bleeding out. The stone floor was stiff against his back. Nothing moved like it should, not his hands, his legs. Johnny only noticed the temperature when he thought about it. He grew cold, slowly, and in stages.

The bullet had taken him somewhere in his chest. It had been a sharp, piercing hot pain. He thought it had hit a bone, cracked a rib or something, and that the bullet was still in his chest. Johnny didn't think it had hit his heart, but a lot of blood had soaked into his shirt, warm and sticky on his chest, in sharp contrast to the cold concrete underneath his back.

Muffled pops sporadically fired, all around him. It was hard for Johnny to hear, like someone had pushed cotton into each of his ears, but the pops sounded like gunshots. There was a wavering tone, the sound traveling up and down in scale, like a police siren, or a car alarm, or alarms. He struggled to lift his head to see something, anything, but the muscles in his neck didn't seem to have the strength.

Gabrielle, he wondered … *what happened?*

Johnny and his friends had been set up, but he didn't believe Gabrielle had done it. Likely her father. Victor Dumont had never liked him, and though Johnny thought this trap had been set for Grimm, first, Johnny was sure he was second on the master vampire's hit list.

This floor was fucking cold. Like an ice block, sucking all the heat from his back. He flopped his hands around, trying to push himself up, but all they did was twitch.

Is that Sarah, screaming? Is she okay? Is Nick okay?

The cotton thickened in his ears. What a way to go out. All the stuff Johnny had seen, had lived through, Grafton and New Orleans and then even the Dead Zone, and he would end up biting it in an airport parking garage in Denver. Where he and his friends had felt safe. They were going to wait for Gabrielle, then help Grimm. That was where their attention had been focused. That danger. Not this.

Dammit.

Nick appeared above Johnny, first. Said something out loud, but Johnny couldn't quite make it out. Then Nick disappeared again. Funny how that shadow thing worked.

A warm liquid heat rested at the bottom of Johnny's throat. He wanted to cough and clear it out, or swallow it down, but he could do neither. His throat worked, but nothing came up or went down; the heat just rested on top of his stomach.

Nick came back and pulled Johnny back behind the truck, dragging him across the concrete. It didn't hurt that bad, but things had started getting harder to see. Objects had gotten fuzzy in Johnny's eyes. He tried to blink the fuzziness away, but the clouds and shapes just got darker and more tangled.

He thought Nick and Sarah were still above him, though. They were talking about him. The cotton in his ears let him hear that much. Words about Gabrielle. About the teams of vampires around them.

Johnny tried to tell them it hadn't been Gabrielle, but he couldn't tell if words actually came out of his mouth. He couldn't hear them, if they had. Something got tugged underneath his back and wrapped around his chest. There was a ratcheting sound, a tight compression tugged his chest tighter, and a shooting pain burst from his ribs.

He arched his back and screamed. Johnny's vision got worse, darker, until all he saw were the shadows. Nick and Sarah. He felt himself getting moved, then lifted. He thought he ended up lying in a seat. Was he in the truck now? Why was it just as cold as the concrete floor?

His friends were talking again. The words were more muffled now. Something about pulling a Grimm.

Was their friend here? Had Victor gotten them all, then?

What a shitty way for all this to end.

It was hard to tell who was Nick, and who was Sarah. They both were dark shadows in a darker world. The larger shape disappeared, though. The smaller shape went to the driver's seat. It sat there, one blob of a hand patting a blob of its leg in a quick, rhythmic motion.

Johnny blinked. He wanted to say something. He wanted to tell whoever was driving that Gabrielle wouldn't betray them, that it was her father, always her father. He wanted to hang on, another moment. But even the top of his body was cold now. Johnny thought he would be shaking from the chill now, if he had been able to.

His heart raced, an odd beat of trembling underneath his chest. As if the muscle was looking for something to pump, spurting along what blood it found. He thought, the only reason he was still alive now was the connection he had to Gabrielle, from being her counterpart. Soon, though, that bond would give up, that power would leave.

Johnny had never been the strongest, nor the bravest. He hadn't even been the brightest. He had no superpower, really. He had never developed anything, and had been tossed from halfway house to halfway house his whole life. He thought, with his friends, with Gabrielle, he had overcome all that. But maybe this was how it was always going to end, for him.

He felt more than heard the truck fire up, a rumble underneath his seat. There was a rocking motion, and then the truck shot backward. Momentum pushed Johnny back into his seat, and then his seat belt tugged tightly around him, briefly. A deadened squeal of the tires worked its way past the cotton in his ears.

The truck rocketed forward, as the shadow driving punched the gas.

Everything grew dark around Johnny. The fuzzy dashboard lights of the truck. The lights out the windshield, out in the garage. The black sky outside that.

The muffled sounds in his ears drifted away into a quiet, peaceful silence. The cotton in his ears hardened into concrete plugs, and he no longer heard anything going on around him. Johnny wanted to break the silence with a word, a good-bye, anything.

Johnny felt his lips move, but heard nothing coming out of his mouth. He wanted to talk to that shadow driving, to keep talking about everything and nothing, because he felt like as long as he kept talking, as long as he could form words and speak them, he was living.

But the quiet, when it descended, was all.

CHAPTER THIRTY-NINE

Nick went back in like he had done for Teams One and Two. He wasn't averse to doing the same thing over and over, if that thing worked. There was a comfort in patterns, in repetition, when you were good at a thing.

Nick was very good.

Teams Three and Four were a little better prepared, though. They stood in six groups of four, each company separate from the other. In each of the groups of four the mercenaries stood back to back, each of the soldiers a ninety-degree angle from the two men standing next to him. And each of the individual groups had rotated a little, so that none of the soldiers would shoot into another group.

Though their margin for error was tight.

Each of the mercenaries held submachine guns high in front of their chests, the stocks firm against their shoulders. They were ready, they had stayed hot. Each of the mercenaries, or soldiers, pointed in a different direction, so that Nick couldn't pop in and out of the shadows and take shots, stab lone mercenaries, and whittle them down like he had done before.

So each company of four would be a harder nut to crack. And together, the groups would be maybe impossible for Nick to take on. And he hadn't even factored in the vampires.

His pattern wouldn't work, no matter how good he was. Nick shrugged to himself, though. He wasn't trying to kill them all. Well, he wasn't *only* trying to kill them all. The first thing was the distraction. Cause a big enough havoc, and get everyone looking his way.

He waved a final hand to Sarah in the truck. Then Nick shadow-walked to the corner of the elevators. *Tug, cut.* He came out of the shadows right next to one of the groups of four. There was a mercenary looking his way, and the man's eyes widened slightly as Nick stepped out of the darkness of the wall.

"Boo." Johnny must have been on his mind, because Nick waggled his eyebrows. Then pulled the shotgun trigger.

The man's head exploded. Immediately afterward the groups fired, gunfire chattered around Nick, but he was already disappearing back into the shadows. He popped over behind a car, screamed aloud, and fired blindly, then walked again to another spot and did the same thing, making sure to keep everyone's attention away from Sarah and Johnny.

Bullets kicked into the cars around him, shattered more glass, plunked into the side panels. Nick kept low, and fired once more, until he heard the squeal of the truck peeling out of the parking space.

Go, Sarah....

Nick ducked under the car and fired a few shots. One of them took out the legs of a soldier, and that guy spun in the air and dropped to the floor. Nick shadow-walked to the other side of the group and fired again, taking out another man in the same group, just as that man glanced at the man who had fallen.

Nick thought maybe he could win this thing. He fired another round into the same group, and then–

A vampire collided with him. The male vamp. Nick bounced off a concrete pillar, and the shotgun flew into the distance. Nick blinked away into the shadows immediately, but he had picked a spot close to the female vampire, or she had figured out Nick's pattern, because as soon as he stepped out of the shadow she was there and grabbed him.

Jesus, they were *fast*. Nick struggled against the vampire's grip. The vamp tugged Nick toward her. Nick gave in to the motion and ducked under her arm, pulling a silver knife out of his vest and slicing her along the rib cage.

She hissed and let go of him. One hand went to her stomach, where a grayish mist or steam drifted up from the cut.

Nick backed into the shadow of a car, then turned and winked at her. Her mouth twisted in a snarl and she leaped at Nick.

Tug, cut.

He stepped out of the shadows and shot at another company. Everything had taken seconds, but the groups of men had drifted closer, like all people did when something was out there they couldn't see, but feared. The submachine guns chattered away, and bullets flew everywhere.

Nick blinked and went to pull the trigger again, but chance intervened. He had come out of the shadows right where a stray bullet was headed. It caught his flak jacket and spun him over the hood of a car.

An instant later the male vampire was on him. He grabbed one arm. The female appeared and grabbed the other. They held Nick spread-eagled on the hood of the car, keeping him in the patch of light there.

The female grinned. The gray steam still rose off her midsection, less of it now than before. She held up a hand, and the chatter of gunfire slowed to a stop.

The male vampire looked across the car at her. Nick looked over his shoulder. The truck was flying down the aisle, toward the exit in the parking garage, accelerating away from all of them. Hopefully in time to save their friend.

Go Sarah, go…, Nick thought, grinning. They would make it, at least out onto the road.

Then there was a tiny boom, a high-pitched squeaking of tires chirping across concrete, and the truck took a hard right turn before flipping end over end. The tumbling, crashing sound of the truck echoed down the garage as the vehicle rolled over and over, only stopping when it bounced off a low concrete barrier.

It was like a missile had punched into the side of the vehicle.

Oh Jesus, Nick thought. *Sarah …*

"Friends of yours?" the female vampire asked. Her voice carried a slight British accent, clipped and short.

Nick screamed and fought the hold of both vampires. Their hands held his wrists tight. No matter how much he twisted or kicked, he couldn't get free. Both the male and the female allowed him to struggle, to kick and drum his heels on the hood of the car, smiling at each other. Waiting.

Nick finally stopped, chest heaving. His attention turned to a man who had walked out of where the impact had happened from the truck. Tall. Thick in the chest and shoulders. Curly black hair. With a thick-handled sword poking up from his back.

The man walked over to the wreck and yanked open the side door to the truck. Actually he tore it open, and threw the door away. It banged and clattered on the floor of the parking garage. Then the man ducked into the truck, did something, and pulled out Johnny.

Then he repeated the same motion, and pulled out Sarah.

They were small figures, far enough away that Nick could tell who they were but not what kind of condition they were in. The man held each in one hand, almost like kittens, and dragged them both this way.

Nick waited, almost lifelessly, to see if they were alive. All his anger and fury and darkness had dissipated, left. All he had left was the wonder of what he would do if Sarah was dead.

He understood Grimm a bit better then.

The rest of the mercenaries, or soldiers, or whatever the fuck they were, all came closer. They circled Nick and the vampires in a semicircle, guns out, all the barrels tilted a little to the floor. Facing the new guy. As if they all were unsure what was going on.

"We did not ask for your help," the male vampire called out, as the man neared.

"You do not command me," the man said, simply. He had what Nick thought was an Irish accent. The closer he got, the more familiar he looked to Nick. And then Nick got it. The man looked a little like Grimm. Just a larger, broader, older version of him.

"And you do not command *us*," the male vampire hissed, even as the female vampire put out her free hand to her friend.

"What does *he* want?" the female asked the newcomer.

The man stopped a few feet away. Johnny hung limply from the man's hand, a few drops of blood dotting the concrete underneath Nick's friend. Sarah hung the same way, hair over her face, and Nick though he caught a glimpse of her eyes open, for a quick moment.

The man waited a long moment, steely-eyed, facing down both vampires and the group of soldiers behind them.

Nick hung there, trying to pay attention, trying to see if Sarah was okay.

The female took a breath and let it out. "Cronan, if you will, tell us what Victor wants."

"*He* wants what you two have fucked up," Cronan said. "*He* wants his daughter to stop hanging around this one."

The big man shook Johnny in midair, then tossed him to the floor. Johnny landed badly, with a thumping, thudding sound. His legs and arms folded awkwardly underneath him, and he didn't move. "Mission accomplished there."

Nick struggled again, yanking against the vampires' grips. The strength in their fingers made their fingers feel like iron bands around his wrists.

"This the shadow-walker?" Cronan asked.

"*We* have him," the female answered instead.

Cronan looked over the garage, his head stopping at the bank of elevators and all the dead bodies there.

"Impressive," the man said. His accent on the word making it sound a little off.

"Thanks," Nick said. "I haven't finished the job yet, though."

The male vampire reached out and smacked Nick's temple. There was a flash of stars as Nick's head bounced off the hood of the car. For a second everything was black, and Nick shook his head until his sight came back.

When it did, he was looking at Sarah. In that brief moment Nick saw that she was looking at him, her eyes almost hidden by her hair.

Sarah winked, then closed her eyes again.

Nick took a breath. Relieved. Sarah was okay. They had a chance.

Enough car alarms were still going on that the bottom floor of the garage was like a disco floor, pulsing lights and wavering wails of sounds. The big man paused a second and closed his eyes. A pulse of energy left him, a little blue-white wave, and as it crossed over the lines of cars, all the alarms shut off, one by one.

Then Cronan stepped closer where the vampires held Nick, and motioned for them to pull Nick up off the car.

"You do not command us," the male said again.

"Maybe I don't." Cronan grinned a dark grin. "Maybe I could just kill you instead."

This new person was someone to fear.

A long moment later the two pulled Nick up and placed him before the man. Each still held Nick's wrists, and he had to catch his balance against the front of the car.

Up close Cronan looked so much like Grimm it was hard for Nick to not think of his friend.

"I admire humor in the face of death," the man said. His accent on *death* made the word sound like *deeth*.

Nick glanced at Johnny. "You would have liked that guy, then."

"You understand this wrong," Cronan said. "I did like that guy."

"Then why is he lying there, dead?"

"Some orders cannot be ignored," Cronan said simply. As if that were all.

Fuck, Nick thought. Another one of these angels under the geas. Dumont's angel? Gabrielle's?

"I'm going to have to kill you, you know," Nick said.

Cronan's eyebrows rose. He looked at the male and female vampires. "Let him go."

"We're supposed to–" the male vampire started to say, before shutting up under Cronan's glare.

A moment later, both vampires let Nick go.

"There is a time of death for all of us, young shadow-walker," Cronan said. "So even if you could kill me, my time is not here, in *this* moment."

"Says you," Nick said.

"Says me," Cronan said. His eyes intensely boring into Nick's, uncomfortably so. "We only give our lives for those we have to protect."

This was an odd conversation. And it wasn't serving any purpose, for Nick. "You might want to call that person here, then," he said. "Because that time is near."

Cronan grinned at Nick. The man laid Sarah on the floor next to him, a little off to the side, between Cronan and the soldiers. The man took a weird kind of care with her, and when he was done he stood before Nick, a small smile on his face.

"You've got this shot," the big man said. "Now take it."

CHAPTER FORTY

It was an odd phrasing of words. As if the man was telling Nick they had this opportunity to strike. As if the man knew Sarah was okay.

Nick wasn't going to look a gift horse in the mouth. And he wanted to make a move, but he waited to see if Sarah would move first. Something clicked in his mind, and he realized now why Cronan put Sarah between the angel and the soldiers. So Nick wanted to make sure Sarah knew where he was.

Sarah let go of the power she carefully controlled. A black explosion rocked the garage. Dark tendrils burst from Sarah and struck out toward the soldiers. One by one they dropped, quickly falling like deflated balloons, as if something had sucked out their insides and left just a wrapper of skin.

The tendrils also struck both vampires, but they didn't deflate. Maybe as undead the two had no real life force to suck out. One did knock the female vampire hard enough that she had to take a step back. One also brushed Cronan. The big man was too near Sarah, and he swatted the tentacle aside with a hiss.

The black arms whipped wildly around, but never touched Nick. Like a protective shield surrounded him, a bubble the tendrils avoided. Nick marveled at Sarah's strength. She had told him the curse had broken something in her control. That she hadn't used to be as powerful as she was now. That her power hadn't been what it was now. And that she feared whatever she had become.

It was time to move. Nick slipped a knife into each of his hands. Plunged one into the center of the chest of the male vampire, who screamed. A large pouring of gray mist shot out of the wound. Nick missed the female vampire. She was a step back and was able to twist aside, so the knife barely nicked her.

Nick ducked down toward the shadow of the car after that, so he could blink away. But he was too slow, and didn't expect Cronan to blur forward and grab Nick in mid-duck. Then the man picked Nick up and tossed him through the air.

Nick twisted and shadow-walked as he passed through a dark area. He came out in shadows, and felt himself slam back against the wall there. It knocked the breath from him.

Dammit. Nick had thought the angel was on their side. Cronan obviously had kept Sarah alive, and placed her in a spot where she could have the greatest affect. So why would he fight Nick now?

And why would Cronan pick Nick up and then throw him through a dark area, when Nick was about to shadow-walk anyway?

Then Nick got it.

The geas was compelling the angel in some way. Cronan was trying to work around it, where he could. Nick didn't know what to do. That line was likely something the angel would have trouble walking. It would be tough, and any mistake made by Cronan would likely be deadly.

So Nick would do what he could to make sure he and Sarah made it out of here alive.

Tug, cut.

Nick appeared right beside the elevator banks. A moment later he held one of the submachine guns in his hand, picked up from one of the many dead soldiers lying around.

The tendrils were still out and wildly flailing around. They struck Cronan over and over, and the man grabbed Sarah. The tentacles whipped around him, a dark spot shot into the air each time one hit Cronan, and the big man winced and ignored them as best he could.

Then Cronan tossed Sarah against a car. The side panel buckled. Sarah fell to the floor, and the tendrils all disappeared.

Whatever the angel could control, it wasn't going to be enough. Nick yelled and pulled the trigger of the submachine gun. A stream of bullets zipped out and struck Cronan, bouncing off with tiny metallic pings. The man turned to face him.

Afraid the ricochets would hit Sarah or Johnny, Nick stopped firing.

An elevator dinged. Its doors opened. Gabrielle stepped out. She wasn't the carefully composed woman Nick had always seen before. Her skin was cut and bleeding in a number of places. Her hair was ripped out on one side of her head. Her clothes were torn and ragged and colored with a dark, viscous blood.

The two of them locked gazes. "Is he …?" she asked.

Nick shook his head, pointing to where Johnny lay on the garage floor. The two vampires stood behind his friend, who was still on the floor.

Gabrielle's eyes widened. Her irises trembled. And her mouth contorted in a rage unlike anything Nick had seen in her before.

Then she screamed and ran toward Johnny.

The female vampire was the first to meet Gabrielle and stood maybe a second before Gabrielle ripped her head off with her bare hands. It happened so fast Nick couldn't discern how it was done. The male vampire had just pulled the dagger out of his chest when Gabrielle took it from him, reversed the blade, and planted the blade in his skull.

He collapsed, twitching on the parking lot floor.

Nick blinked over to Sarah. Her forehead had a large cut on it, the temple had turned purple, and the cut bled a lot. Her pulse was steady, though, and Nick let the breath he was holding escape him. She was just knocked out. Then he thought, *It's been a crazy few weeks when I'm actually relieved someone I care about is only knocked out.*

Gabrielle knelt next to Johnny, cradling his head. She was crying and keening and smoothing his hair over and over. Nick felt a little embarrassed. He was happy Sarah was alive, and Johnny was lying dead on the floor, just a few feet away.

Cronan walked up. He moved stiffly, as if he was controlling each part of his body, or holding himself back. Gabrielle focused her eyes and her hate on Cronan.

She looked at Cronan. *"You."*

"I did not kill him," Cronan said.

"Like that matters. I know my father," Gabrielle said. Her voice took on a tone of command. "And I will deal with him later. You will die *now*."

Cronan stood before Gabrielle. Nick didn't know what he expected, but something along the lines of the man dropping dead came to mind. Grimm had told them of the time Dominic had ordered Grimm's heart to stop beating. He had been trying to talk them all out of going to Raphael's mansion, because the geas was something Grimm couldn't fight. Whatever his body was told, it would do.

So Nick knew about the geas. And so he expected Cronan to fall to the floor, lifeless. But the big man just kept standing there, wearing a little grin. Waiting. Gabrielle stared at him until the beginnings of a frown spread across her face.

"Shouldn't you be dead?" Nick asked.

"Yesterday I would have been," Cronan said. "Today I am fine."

Nick looked at Gabrielle. Her arm was clutched tight around Johnny's head, his face pressed into her bosom. The vampire's eyes narrowed. "He has taken my control away."

"He has," Cronan agreed.

"So I am no longer his heir," Gabrielle said.

"You are not," Cronan said.

"So he always meant to kill me," she said.

"I believe it was your friendship here that did you in," Cronan said.

"To us?" Nick asked.

Cronan lifted both hands, as if to say that answer was above his pay grade. "It seems likely."

"The world is falling apart," Gabrielle hissed, "and all *he* can worry about is his little kingdom."

Cronan's smile lessened. "He sees it as an opportunity."

"You know I just wanted to leave," Gabrielle said. "None of this was needed."

"I did," Cronan said simply. "Your father sees this now as well."

Gabrielle waited a long moment. "I see."

"You know your father," Cronan said.

"He loves no one," Gabrielle said. "He trusts no one."

Cronan made a little motion with his shoulders. As if to say, *What's there to debate?*

"You cannot kill me," Gabrielle said.

"I *could not* kill you," Cronan replied, his voice lowering. He had gotten stiffer, his body ramrod straight. As if he fought something Nick couldn't see.

"Oh," Gabrielle said. She looked down at Johnny, kissed the side of his forehead, near his temple. Then gently set him down and got up.

"What's going on?" Nick asked.

"He's been sent here to kill us," Gabrielle answered.

Cronan said nothing, just stood there, as if frozen.

"So why hasn't he?" Nick said. Cronan had had plenty of chances.

"Because he's fighting it the best he can." Gabrielle looked at Nick. "Because he believed one day, if I had taken over for my father, things might have gone differently."

"So he's fighting it?" Nick asked. "The geas?"

"The geas," Gabrielle agreed. "But he will lose to it, soon. Best get ready, Nicholas."

Nick focused on Cronan. The man's jaw was tight enough Nick could see the tendons. His arm reached up to the hilt of his sword, but stayed there, as if held in check by an immense will.

Nick pulled out a couple of his knives, and stood in front of Sarah.

"I am sorry," Gabrielle said.

"Me, too, young vampire," Cronan said. His hand trembling. "It was a fond hope. But it was likely always to end this way."

Gabrielle attacked.

And she was fast.

Just not fast enough.

She had a large blade, larger than a knife, smaller than a katana, but similarly shaped. Cronan took a hundred cuts from the female vampire. She attacked in berserker-like fashion, without care for herself. The man protected himself, and fought back at times, but it was obvious he was holding back. He took some hard shots from her, and got out of the way of others, but he stayed standing.

And Nick could quickly tell the fight was swinging Cronan's way. The big man stayed standing, absorbing shots, healing the bigger cuts, but always in a rhythm. And while at the beginning of the fight, all the blows landed were from Gabrielle, just a few seconds in Cronan began to respond.

The big man's fist connected then, a large blow that rocked the slim vampire. She backed up beside a large concrete column, and Cronan followed her in.

Nick jumped in.

Tug, cut.

Nick stepped out of the shadows with a silver knife in hand. He swiped at Cronan's back. It hit the man's shoulder and bounced off as if the man were made of metal, the blade throwing sparks. The whole motion threw off Nick's balance and he stumbled forward.

Tug, cut.

This time Nick was ready for how fast Cronan was. The man spun around, looking for Nick. As he did, Gabrielle took the time to slice into Cronan's hamstring, and the big man cried out, falling to one knee.

Gabrielle and Nick worked in tandem that way. Nick distracting, Gabrielle cutting. Cronan was able to heal each cut, and spun around in an effort to keep both of them in check. Gabrielle worked to get in closer, and Nick blinked faster, trying to keep Cronan off balance.

And it worked, for a little bit. Until the man lost control, and fell all in to the geas.

Then a large crack split the air. Gabrielle's blade spun through the air until it stuck into the hood of a car. She tumbled to the floor. Nick had just stepped out of the shadows next to Cronan, and a large hand grabbed Nick by the shoulder, lifted him up, and spun him around.

The big man brought Nick's face close to his and smiled. All of Cronan's teeth were white, but a few of his front teeth were a little short, and crooked. As if one or two had been broken, when the man was young.

Nick swung his blade into the big man's elbow, and Cronan winced before slapping the blade away with his free hand. Then Nick struggled harder, kicking at the man before Cronan swung Nick against the concrete pole. Nick's head thunked against the column and the world got really dark, and a lot shaky.

When he looked next, he saw a couple of Cronans. He gave the finger to both of them.

The first Cronan laughed, but even as he did, he reached up with his hand and pulled his sword out from over his back. It was hard for Nick to focus on the blade.

The man held the sword back a moment, still, high in the air. "I bet my son likes you," he said.

"Why bet," the second Cronan said, "when you can just ask him?"

The first Cronan started. He dropped Nick and twisted around.

Nick landed, catching himself against the column. His feet seemed to dance a bit on the concrete, and he had to concentrate to remain standing. Nick blinked until the second Cronan resolved into a younger Cronan. A touch smaller. A touch less broad in the shoulders. A whole lot more tired-looking.

Grimm.

Nick's friend held a sword of his own in his hand, like the one he'd had in New Orleans, only this one had traces of lightning running up and down the blade.

Nick held himself against the pillar. "Grimm?"

"Hey, Nick," Grimm said. "Sorry I'm late."

"Son," Cronan said.

"Pops," Grimm said with a grin.

Nick knew he had recognized Cronan, and now he knew why. He watched his friend step forward, holding his sword in front of him. "You get too much of me and decide to pick on my friends?"

Cronan grinned in return. "You know it's not my time yet."

That was the second or third time Nick had heard that from him. It was like an argument, where someone kept saying the same thing over and over, without really explaining it. Like he was going to believe in something despite any evidence to the contrary.

Grimm looked sad. "I don't think the geas gives you that choice, though, right?"

Cronan took a large breath, then nodded, once. "You understand, then."

"You can walk away now," Grimm said. "This doesn't have to go any further."

"You know I cannot," Cronan said. "I can only leave if my life is threatened."

There it was, Nick thought. The answer. Cronan had given it to them.

"Well," Grimm said, "let's see what we can do about that."

Cronan grunted, arched an eyebrow. "You would kill your own father?"

"I don't want to," Grimm said. "But if you're going to make me make a choice, I'll put you six feet under in a heartbeat."

Cronan smiled. "Then let the fight begin."

Nick's friend struck. Cronan parried and responded. Blue sparks blew off at each clash of the swords. The movements became a blur, each of the men moving faster than Nick could follow, and then some force detonated between the two. Cronan flew back over a row of cars, crashing into one and dropping down out of sight.

Nick looked at Grimm. Blue arcs traced out from his weird-looking sword and flicked all over the ceiling and the floor. What was left of the lights above exploded in showers of sparks. Grimm shook his head, and looked at his sword for a moment. It looked like – to Nick – that he was speaking to the blade. Then Grimm stopped talking and set his jaw. Like he had gotten an answer he didn't like.

Nick wondered what was going on there.

Grimm came out of it and looked at Nick. "You good?"

Nick was still holding on to the column with one hand. As if he was holding himself up. "Good enough," he said.

A roar or a bellow echoed along the garage. A screech of metal followed, of something heavy being dragged along pavement. The car Cronan had landed against shifted, then crunched up against another car. One big hand reached up and grabbed the hood of the car, pulling the large man into view.

Cronan shook his head a few times. Like a dog coming out of the rain. Then he bent back down to the floor. Like he was looking for something.

Grimm looked at Sarah, leaning against the car, and at where Gabrielle and Johnny lay on the floor. The vampire had begun to stir, her hands pushing herself up off the floor.

"Everyone okay?" Grimm asked.

Nick motioned no, with a tiny left-right motion of his head. "Johnny didn't make it."

Grimm tilted his head for a moment. Then he closed his eyes. When he opened them he patted Nick on the shoulder. "He's still alive, Nick."

Nick had seen Johnny, folded up like a rag doll. "Grimm, I'm telling you, Johnny's dead."

Another roar came from Cronan. Something not quite angry, something that held the excitement of a worthy opponent. A real challenge. Some kind of berserker thing, maybe. More cars were thrown back and forth, crashing together.

There was a shout of exaltation then, and Cronan reappeared, holding his sword in both hands. His face was contorted in something like glee, wild and crazy and looking forward to a fight.

Grimm grabbed Nick and pushed him backward, towards Sarah and Johnny and Gabrielle. "I'm telling you, he's alive. Keep him that way."

Grimm leaped over the cars, toward his father.

Nick looked at Johnny. At Gabrielle. At Sarah.

"I did not kill him," Cronan had said.

Cronan had seemed to like Gabrielle. The two of them had had some kind of understanding. So maybe he hadn't killed Johnny, maybe he had found a way to resist the geas. Maybe Johnny still hung on to something. Maybe the powers Gabrielle had gifted his friend with were enough to keep him alive, a bit longer than any human should be able to live.

Nick ran over to his friend, to see if he could keep him that way.

CHAPTER FORTY-ONE

I had made it in time. That was the first thought in my mind, after landing in the parking garage. Though maybe, after seeing the damage there, I had *barely* made it.

My friends were still alive, though hurt, bad. Sarah and Johnny and Gabrielle all lay scattered in a semicircle around a sedan at the end of one of the rows. Johnny had some strap tight around a bloody shirt on his chest, and neither Sarah nor Johnny moved, but I couldn't find a ghost for either of them. That was promising.

My father held Nick in the air, against a column. I had sensed other ghosts being tapped, as I flew up here, and I wasn't surprised to see him. Though I had hoped my mother was here instead.

He was so different from her. Outgoing and loud where my mother was cool and calm. Physical and brutal where she was elegance and precision.

I recognized that my father still fought the geas, in the stiff way that he moved, in the tense set of his jaw as he spoke. In the way he had slowly drawn his sword, holding Nick against the column, giving my friend as much time as possible to escape, for something, anything to happen.

That anything happened to be me.

I wasn't sure what my father's plan was. I didn't know why he didn't want to kill any of us. He didn't know my friends. He really didn't know me. But he fought the geas as much as he was able. The curse pulsed heavy around my father, in my ethereal vision. The tendril connecting him to Victor was thick, like a pipe, and waves of the command rippled down the cable and washed over my father.

He would succumb. I understood what my father was trying to do. I knew where he was at, under the geas, even though I had only ever felt a part of the power that controlled him. For him to resist this much must have taken an immense power of will.

When my father broke, he would be dangerous. Deadly. He had been fighting long before I was born. He knew tricks I had never seen. Like seeing what ghost I was going to pull from, and getting there first.

So it was going to be a fight. We both could restore ourselves using ethereal energy, and he was a master of manipulating that power. I had faced him before, and gotten away by luck, and because of Jen. And that was when he was fighting the geas.

If my father broke tonight … *when* my father broke tonight, it would take everything I had to protect my friends. I didn't know if I could get him to leave, without killing him. As much as I didn't know my father, I also didn't think I could kill him. I didn't have that in me.

But I had faced my mother once, and she had quickly disarmed me. Without even really trying. I had learned a lot since then, and I believed in trial by fire, but I didn't know if I could stop him.

But I had to try.

My father turned around to face me. We spoke. We both held on to our ghostly taps.

Then we crossed blades. Everything happened in an instant, a blur of time and motion. And then I found out that I did have something my father didn't.

I had Jen.

Somewhere in the middle of crossing blades, she came out. The sword fight was a blur; it was everything I could do just to get my blade in front of each of my father's swings. There was a rhythm in his movements, and a power in every stroke. They were powerful and fast and jarred my shoulder when his sword connected with mine.

I couldn't keep this up for long. My entire arm tingled with a numbness, even with the ethereal energy. The ghost I had tapped into was quickly dissolving away in memories of snorts of coke, and that wasn't helping, either.

My father could sense it. I saw it in the curl of his lips, the narrowing of his eyes. I stepped back from his latest swing, heavily pulled energy from the ghost, and jumped back with a wild overhand swing.

Except I hadn't been the only one pulling energy then. There was another tug of ethereal energy inside me, from my chest, from the *Key*, and a buzzing along my skin. It was like thousands of volts of electricity had charged up in my body, and rested in my arms.

All that voltage exploded as soon as my father's sword parried my swing, in a sparkling shock wave of an electric burst.

A brilliant blue sky over Grafton. A yellow sun, the scent of honeysuckle. A faint taste of peanut butter and jelly, from our lunch. And Jen and my arms locked together ...

My father flew back through the air. He crashed into a car and dropped below it, shattering the windows and leaving a man-sized dent in the side. The shock wave shoved another car on top of him, and he disappeared underneath it.

I paused then. *Jen?*

A slight satisfaction radiated along our bond.

I smiled, inside. *You know I got this, right?*

The satisfaction turned into something like a smug dismissal. I almost could feel her roll her eyes. So I rolled mine in return.

Nick held himself up, one hand on a stone column. His knife vest was shredded, and missing a lot of knives. His flak jacket looked in one piece, and though there was a lot of blood covering him, I couldn't tell if any of it was his.

A loud squeal echoed through the garage, of metal being dragging over concrete. One of the cars where my father had fallen rocked to one side. He was down, but not out.

"Everyone okay?" I asked Nick.

"Johnny didn't make it," he said. His jaw tight.

That didn't feel right to me. I hadn't seen his ghost. I reached out again. No ghosts above any of my friends. And none above Gabrielle, though I wasn't sure I would feel any.

I blinked on my ethereal vision, and looked over at my friends. I saw Gabrielle's spark in her chest, a dark purplish white. Sarah's buzzing white spark, and a tiny spark, mostly white, with a few dots of purple, in Johnny's chest. "He's still alive, Nick."

Nick's eyes flicked to their friend. "Grimm, I'm telling you, Johnny's dead."

My father roared. Or bellowed. Something jacked up and full of energy, as if he was preparing himself for a real fight. One of the cars tipped over. More rocked as he looked for something on the floor, until he shouted in glee and grabbed his sword from where it had fallen. His eyes were wild and crazy, mad.

The geas had gotten him.

We were all in terrible danger.

Nick would have to take care of Johnny. I would have to trust them all, and hope that I could chase my father away. Who was fully under the geas, and who had orders to kill us all.

I hoped I didn't have to kill him. I hadn't known him long, but I wasn't really the parent-killing type.

Ready, Jen? I asked, along the bond.

A faint agreement resonated back to me.

I found a new ghost and started pulling. I told Nick to keep Johnny alive. Then I leaped over the first row of cars.

If my father wanted a fight, I would give him one. If he wanted death, and that was the only way to keep my friends safe, I would give him that as well.

I knew, as well as anyone, what life was like under the geas. I would have to hope that I was freeing my father from that, at least.

CHAPTER FORTY-TWO

Nick raced over to where his friends were. He couldn't help himself, he checked on Sarah first. She breathed normally, her heartbeat slow, like she was asleep. Nick tried but couldn't wake her. So he quickly pulled her up and sat her against the side of one of the cars, putting her so that the car was between them and the fight.

Not that the car would be much protection, if it came to it. Nick watched a car get thrown through the air. It smacked into another car and rolled over the tops of the rest of the vehicles in the row. When it finally stopped, the car was upside down and rocked back and forth on top of another car's crunched roof.

He couldn't see Grimm, but from wherever he and his father fought came horrendous sounds. Glass shattered, thick plastic crunched, and a metallic gong sound reverberated in the air. All this, and their fight had just started. Part of Nick wanted to help, but Grimm had told Nick to keep Johnny alive.

Nick had to count on Grimm to hold up his side of the bargain. And even as he thought that, another car flew through the air, this one tumbling end over end along the concrete and wrapping around a column. The column shifted, then broke in two.

He turned away and checked on Johnny. He had no pulse, and Nick had no idea how Grimm knew what he knew. But he trusted his friend, so he cinched the strap a little tighter around Johnny's chest and pulled him around next to Sarah, offering a prayer to anyone who wanted to hear it.

Nick wasn't really a believer. And he wasn't really not a believer, either. But he believed in playing the odds.

Gabrielle was next. She was off to the side, where Cronan's fist had flung the vampire. Her arms still moved in little motions, as if she was deep in some unconscious dream, fighting to wake. Both her hands lay flat on the floor, palms to the concrete, as if she was gathering herself to burst out of unconsciousness.

Nick picked her up by the armpits and dragged her around to his other friends. He leaned the vampire up against the car, next to Sarah. Then he slapped Gabrielle.

She came awake instantly and into a scream, fangs out. She moved as if to strike Nick and then froze. Like she was processing an understanding of where she was, who he was, and what she was about to do.

Nick waited a moment, ready to shadow-walk if he had to. Gabrielle blinked a few times. Then the vampire's eyes cleared.

"Grimm tells me Johnny is alive," Nick said.

He had never liked Gabrielle. Maybe because of all the vampire movies he had watched, growing up. Likely it was more Raphael, and Sarah being with him for a bit. He thought, even with that, it was rational to be wary of those who could suck out your blood.

But his heart went out to her, as she recognized what he told her. Gabrielle's eyes softened, and glistened with a wetness he didn't know vampires had in them.

"Impossible," she finally said. "I'd know."

"Grimm wouldn't lie," Nick said. "I don't know how he knows, but it's what he told me."

"Your friend is here?" she said.

There was another wrecking ball sound of one vehicle being thrown into another. Followed by a roar that sounded like Cronan. There might have been a blur around the column, maybe Grimm or Cronan. Nick hoped it wasn't Grimm. He had seen him get hit by a car once; at the time it had almost knocked him out.

"That's Grimm right now," he said. "We're not going to have a lot of time."

Gabrielle crawled over to where Johnny lay. She grabbed his wrist in both hands, and was silent for a long moment. The crashing of cars stopped, and the garage went eerily silent.

Then Gabrielle sobbed. One quick inhalation of breath. As if recognizing something she had feared wasn't true.

"We need to get him to the hospital," Nick said.

"He doesn't have the time," she said. "It's amazing he's still hanging on now. His heart isn't beating at all."

"Can't you bite him or something?" Nick said. "Turn him into a vampire?"

Gabrielle's mouth twisted. She shook her head, and her hands clutched Johnny's in a white-knuckled grip. Tears streamed down her cheeks. "He doesn't want that."

Nick looked at his friend, who lay there, as good as lifeless.

"I was hoping to convince him, in time," she whispered, her voice trailing off.

A loud boom echoed over them all. The floor shook, and a wave of dust and dirt blew out over them all. Nick couldn't see, and hunched down until the wave past. He took a breath and coughed, then pulled his shirt over his mouth.

The dust settled in little ticks and tacks of rocks hitting the floor. It finally cleared enough to see. Cronan and Grimm had been at the other end of the building. Most of the floor above them had collapsed, and the floor itself above lay slanted down to their floor, like a new ramp had been built in the garage, holding rows of cars and rubble. Dust still settled a bit, around that area.

Nick made sure Sarah was okay, then checked on Gabrielle. She was cleaning the dust and debris from Johnny. The scene reminded Nick of a widow, kneeling above the coffin of her husband, brushing her hand along his unmoving face. "No way we can get him to a hospital?"

She shook her head. "I don't know how he's hung on this long."

Nick thought he knew. Johnny had always been there for his friends. He wouldn't want to just go out now. He would want to see this through. No matter what.

And whenever Johnny and Gabrielle had talked about it, surely it was in the context of living their lives out peacefully. She surely hadn't asked him, *Hey, if you're almost dead, and your friends are in life-or-death danger, do you just want to check out?*

Fuck it, his friend might hate him. But Nick made the decision. He told Gabrielle to do it.

Her jaw set, as if she was going to defy him. She was going to respect Johnny's wishes. Even if it cost him his life.

"Let him be mad at us," Nick said. "Let him be mad at me. But let him do it alive."

CHAPTER FORTY-THREE

If someone had told me this morning I would be playing catch with my father tonight, I would have laughed. I mean, I hadn't even met the man until the day before. But what kid didn't want that memory?

However, if that person had added we would be playing catch with cars, I would have understood.

I leaped over the first row of parked vehicles, toward where my father had found his sword, where I had first heard his scream of rage. When I had known the geas had gotten him. And right before I jumped I had looked at Johnny for Nick, so I had taken my eyes off my father for just a brief moment, but that moment was all my father had needed.

A car met me halfway through my jump.

I pulled a lot of ghost and hardened my skin right before impact. The car spun through the air and took me with it, after which all I saw was the ceiling circling the floor circling the ceiling. At least, that's all I saw until I hit another car. Then there was a huge metallic crunch, glass shattered, and I ended up being on the inside of a sedan sandwich.

I was nauseated, and a little dizzy. I held back from throwing up, and it took a moment to push the one sedan off me. The car tipped over and fell to the floor. I checked myself quickly. Nothing seemed broken, and I actually still held my ethereal sword in my hand.

My father stood down from me, along the same aisle, rows of cars and trucks to our left and right. His eyes strained with a type of madness I comprehended. I had been there. It was the fury of being utterly helpless against a force impossible to fight. The geas.

Though part of my father loved the fight. Just like me. I had run for a long time, but deep inside there had always been something in the "it's him or me" in a fight I understood, and even wanted. Something about the test, about having to be enough. My father apparently was made the same way, or I was made from him. So even if his eyes strained and his jaw was clenched, his grin was real.

I let my ethereal sword disappear. Like back outside the motel, electrical arcs hung in the air, suspended in place where the blade had been a moment before. This time, though, the electrical blue storm drifted toward my hand, running over my fingers and arm, before disappearing as well.

I felt powerful. Like I was two people.

Maybe I was.

I sucked in more ethereal energy, feeling the strength in my limbs, the power. Like I had drunk forty gallons of workout drinks. Like I had just bench-pressed a couple thousand pounds, as my warm-up rep. I kept pulling on the ghost …

… and I lay on her, thrusting over and over, pushing her face into the pillow, wondering when my brother would come back from work, and if I even cared. She had always wanted me, she knew it, I knew it, and now my brother would know it…

I set my jaw. Those memories got put into the True Evil box. Why the fuck were a lot of these memories of ghosts always about raping someone?

I pulled the last of the ghost. Until it popped. It seemed like the spirit's scream echoed from miles away in the real world.

Good riddance.

I liked my first day as the Angel of Vengeance. Something about how my powers worked seemed right to me now. Before, I had always just taken enough to survive, and left the ghosts in this world. Now what I did had a purpose. I would look at their memories, I would judge them, and I would send them on their way to hell.

Or wherever it was they went.

With that ghost gone, I looked for another. The first one I found, my father was already tied to, so I found another. He saw what I was doing and tied himself to that spirit just before I had begun my tap, so I found yet another one.

When my father moved to tether that ghost, I quickly circled back and went to the first ghost I had found and tapped the first one.

This was going to be tricky to do, in the middle of this fight. Looking and tying to ghosts seemed second nature to my father, while I had to think about it. Which took my attention out of what was going on around me.

So I almost missed the second car my father threw at me. One of those electric gas-saving cars, tiny and blue. I saw it at the last second and slid to the side, hearing it tumble and tear across the concrete behind me. My father grinned even larger and bent over to grab another vehicle.

I shrugged. If my father wanted to play catch, I could do that.

I grabbed a car of my own. One of the Subarus that populate the Northwest, four-wheel cars built for bad weather. I had never liked them. They always looked like a more modern station wagon to me. So I was happy it was nearby.

I had trouble lifting the car. The first couple of times I tried, the panels of the car ripped under my grip. The bumper tore off, and then my hands kept slipping.

So I tipped the Subaru on the side and grabbed part of the undercarriage. Even the thicker part of the frame buckled as I lifted the car. But I got enough grip, and threw the car toward my father with a loud grunt.

Who had already thrown another car.

Both vehicles met in midair. A loud boom echoed from the collision, and glass and bits of car burst outward from the cars in a wave. The cars spun around each other and fell to the side.

I got another car. One of those car-truck blends, with a hatchback. This time I was quicker, and got my car up first. My father had just started picking up a larger truck, something with the double tires in the back, and had to lift it twice to get it up.

So the hatchback I threw caught my father full in the chest, right after he had picked his truck up. The hatchback flew into my father and took him off his feet, the truck he was holding dropped to the floor, and he got swallowed by the wreckage.

I jumped that way, just as my father powered the hatchback off him.

Pushing it off and standing out of the wreckage. I was still in midair as he twirled in the circle, holding the crumpled car in his hands like a discus thrower. I had almost made it to him when the hatchback came rocketing back toward me.

It collided with me in midleap. Again I spun in a circle, carried back at the speed of a rocket, until the hatchback and I hit a concrete column. That column shattered, and I fell to the floor with the car lying across me. A low groaning sound came from the floor above, and a large crack spread out there, splitting away from the broken column.

My father roared, from down the row. Maybe because he still fought the geas. I understood the desperation, the need to scream, the fury at the helplessness of being caught under the direct command of the curse.

I rolled out from between the car and the column, brushing the dust off myself. My father stood where he had before, next to the dually truck, both fists clenched tight at his sides. Brows lowered, eyes rolled up to the back of his head with effort. I wasn't sure he even saw me.

I headed his way. His eyes found me. Stiffly he reached for the truck.

I walked toward him, summoning the sword. The dually headed my way in the air, and got cut in half. As my blade sliced through the truck, a tiny burst of lightning from the sword blew each half of the dually to either side of me.

My father's paused. His eyes widened a bit. Maybe in fear.

"You can leave now, if you want," I said, moving closer.

"You know that's something I can't do," my father said.

"Then it's only going to end one way," I said.

"It's not *my time*," my father screamed back.

"You've said that before," I said. "I don't think it means what you think it means."

He grinned then. His arms were so tense with the strain under the geas that veins had popped out along his forearms, his forehead. He pulled so much from his ghost that the wisps of blue streamed wide to him, like a river. With all that energy, he easily picked up the dually.

"Maybe it doesn't mean what you think it means," he said.

Then he threw the truck. I stepped aside, but I didn't have to move much, and it flew past me like a hundred-mile-an-hour fastball. I took a step toward my father and realized he hadn't been aiming at me.

He had been aiming at another column.

There was a snapping sound, then a larger groan and a loud rumbling. Like the whole building was shifting. The floor shook underneath my feet. And then thousands of tons of concrete, blacktop, and vehicles fell on top of me.

I gathered enough energy to stay standing as all of that stone collapsed around me. One ghost popped, then another. I had to keep finding them, until at least everything stopped falling, and the world stopped shaking.

Dust was everywhere. I wondered if the whole garage had come down. I blinked on my ethereal vision and found the sparks of my friends, still where I had left them, at the far end of the garage.

So not the whole building. Just part of it. I coughed, feeling the press of brick and metal all around me. I still held my sword, and used that to try to slice whatever was on top of me in half, but it was like using a tiny knife to cut into a tree.

My father still stood where he had thrown the truck at me. He might take a second or two to make sure I was trapped, maybe take those moments to fight the command of the geas, but after that he was going to go after my friends. Even now he turned a little in that direction. Toward Nick and Sarah and Johnny.

I needed to get out of this.

I let the sword disappear, trying to push and force my way through the tons of weight on top of me. It was like trying to bench-press a building. I screamed and roared until dust clogged the back of my throat, which made me cough some more.

Something tingled along my bond with the Key.

I focused on the bond. Jen was here, with me, just like she had been when I fought my father back in the motel. My hand stretched toward her, along the bond. Felt her hand grab mine.

In that instant I saw Jen. As a ghost. Inside the Key. She radiated blue and gold, glaringly bright. I wasn't sure if I saw her now because I had my ethereal sight on, or because I was imagining it.

I didn't imagine the funnel, tying Jen to the ethereal plane. The tap, where she could pull power through. Somehow she had found what tied her there, to the plane, and she was pulling energy through it, combining all that energy with her powers, and with mine. Blending the two of us together.

At the cost of using herself up, and being gone forever.

I now understood how Jen had created the bursts of lightning from my sword. How she had created the ball of lightning, back in the motel. And it was something I couldn't stop. It was something only Jen could control.

The voltage powered through me. Gained strength. Like I was a huge capacitor, and Jen was charging me with hundreds of thousands of volts. Even as she powered me up, the tap tying her to the ethereal plane narrowed.

Is this what you do? Jen said to me.

I was shocked to hear her voice, almost enough that I didn't respond. But the narrowing tap worried me. It was all I saw under the thrumming of the electricity in my body. Somehow she had mixed our powers together, and built something new.

Jen, I told her, *don't do this.*

Hush, she said back, grinning at me. Like this was all a game for us.

You don't know what you're doing. What's going to happen to you.

I know we are going to save our friends.

Jen–

I said, hush.

The world exploded around me.

All the rubble and the cars and the concrete burst outward as a bubble of electricity shot out from me. Anything within a few feet of me turned instantly into vapor, or melted to the floor. The floor itself softened and sank, under my feet.

But the rubble, the concrete, the cars … all gone.

My father paused. In his face was real fear. I didn't know what he saw, but I took advantage. I summoned the sword and launched myself at him, flying at a thousand miles an hour.

We collided. He twisted to the side at the last moment to avoid my blade. A burst of lightning propelled us out of the garage. The pair of us flew through the air together, both of us wrestling each other, until a mile or more later we crashed into one of the long-term parking lots.

More cars and trucks. We smashed into them and tumbled through trucks and vans. Somewhere during the tumble my father and I separated. I plowed through the ground, though, until finally coming to a stop in the middle of a row of blacktop.

I picked myself up, shaking my head. Bits of rock and pavement fell off me. I stood in the middle of a large crater in the ground, teardrop shaped, deep where I was standing and black and burned along the edges. The teardrop-shaped hole dwindled behind me, a long tail pointing back the way we had come. It looked as if a comet had crashed into the parking lot.

The sword had disappeared again. Cars rocked on the ground to my left and right, as the earth still shook. Gravel rolled around in my mouth. It tasted like cold stone, and I spat it out the best I could before pulling myself out of the small pit. I found another ghost and tapped it, looking for my father.

A tiny crumple of metal located him for me. I watched as my father pulled himself out of the side of a van. His eyes were clear and focused again, as if he was under less strain.

He glanced at me. Glanced once behind me, as if looking at the garage. Then he bowed his head, once. Perhaps acknowledging the loss.

Then he fled.

CHAPTER FORTY-FOUR

I watched him go. I had gotten the geas to admit defeat, and allow my father to flee. I took a shaky breath and let it out. It was a small victory.

But the *cost*. My fingers shook, and I felt along my bond for Jen, until a satisfaction swelled back from the other side of it.

Only then could I breathe. Jen was still here. Still with me.

Had she used the same ethereal energy I was using? Could she do that? Use the ghost I had tapped for her energy, and in that way not use herself up? Did we have a chance? Did *I* have a chance still at saving her?

Another shaky breath followed the first. I fingered the Key. Maybe making sure I still had it. A gesture without much thought, like occasionally tapping my back pocket to check if my wallet was still there.

Part of the Key broke off in my hand.

A tingle of fear ran along the bond, from Jen.

My heart beat faster. I studied the piece of sandstone that had broken off. It was white around the edges, as if it had aged a million years in the past few minutes. As I probed the piece, it crumbled in my hand, like sand, and slipped past my fingers.

Jen ...

"Son," my mother said from behind me. As if she stood right behind me.

Startled, I stepped forward and turned at the same time. My sword flickered into my hand, blue sparks dripping onto the blacktop. I banished it immediately, the blade came back, and this back and forth happened a few more times before I was able to make it go away permanently.

I didn't want to use any more of Jen's power up. Not with the Key one or two battles away from falling apart. I would fight my mother with something else. Anything else.

After all, she had said back in Grafton that the next time she saw me, it was likely because she had been sent to kill me.

That wasn't the case, though. My mother continued to stand a few feet away, both feet apart, hands behind her back, as if she was at parade rest. As relaxed as someone so precise could be. I checked her with my ethereal vision, quickly, seeing the ropy tendril stretch far behind her, into the night. The chain of the geas.

"Mother," I said. Formally, maybe catching it from her.

She smiled. It wasn't an easy smile, as if the whole process was something she was unused to. As if the muscles were unused to performing that motion. But the smile was real and made it all the way to her eyes.

There was a sadness there as well. But I was happy. Thrilled. Here was my mother. The person I needed to talk to the most of anyone. Who could help me, and Jen, right when we needed it the most.

"The battle was well fought," she said. "You have become something greater than the sum of your parts."

It was weirdly put. Did she mean greater than the sum of her and my father? Or could she see Jen, inside me?

"You know, your father named you Fergus," my mother said, her eyes still tracking where my father had fled.

I watched her. Her gaze was lost in some memory. Biting her lower lip. She was always so precise in what she did. Every motion having a purpose. It was odd, her looking so … human.

"I never gave you a name," she continued. Her eyes shimmered a bit. "I gave you to Parker. He named you Grimm. He told me once he had a book of fairy tales he would read to you, and you would sit there and listen, and never cry, never laugh. Just so … focused, maybe. So he started calling you Grimm. And that became your name."

I stood there, uncertain. Unsure. Watching my mother be a real mom. "Why are you telling me this?" I asked.

She took a breath and let it out, slow. "A son should know who named him," she said. "And why. I think names matter. I wonder, sometimes, if I had named you, as I should have, if you would have turned out different. Happier. Less dark."

A moment later: "Maybe you would put less of things on yourself. Stop blaming yourself, at every turn. Evil exists, son, it just does. We can fight it, or we can fall to it."

I *was* fighting it. I didn't understand what she was trying to tell me. I did blame myself, only because people always got hurt around me, in ways I thought I could have stopped, if only I had looked ahead.

Maybe looking ahead wouldn't be enough. Maybe being around my friends, they would always be hurt. Someone I cared about might always die. No matter how strong I was.

"I need to ask you something," I said.

She nodded. "We have the time."

"Did you really bring me back to life?" I asked, motioning to my chest. "After the whole sword-through-the-heart thing?"

"Of course," she answered, then tilted her head to the side. "Why do you ask?"

She blinked. I recognized the motion. She was looking at me with ethereal vison. As if examining me. There was a subtle glow of blue in her irises when that happened. I wondered what she would see….

My mother caught her breath, blinking again, back to our normal sight. She shook her head, slightly. Just a little back-and-forth motion. "Oh … son."

I fell apart.

I lost where I was physically in the world. I'm sure I was crying. For a long time I didn't know what I was doing. My mother grabbed me and guided me to the edge of the pit. Set me down so that my legs dangled loosely off its edge. Then she sat down beside me and put her arm around my shoulders, tucking my head onto her chest.

Worry and concern came from Jen. From the Key. Then admonishment. Anger at me, either because of what I was thinking or what I was doing now.

It all didn't matter, though. Nothing mattered. Saving Jen had been the slimmest of hopes, and now that was gone. I sobbed and sobbed until it was hard to catch my breath, and then I started over again.

We stayed like that for a while. More of the jumbo jets circled over-head. I didn't think they were landing at this airport anymore.

"I failed her, Mom," I said, finally. "She needed me and I failed her."

My mother patted my shoulder with her hand, softly. "This is what I am saying, son. It is not your failure, if you keep trying."

"I don't know how I can keep doing this," I said.

She let me get the rest of it out. What had happened, with Azazel in New Orleans. About what I had learned about him as the creator of the geas. About the geas itself, and what breaking it would do to my mother, my father, myself.

I told her about the Key, and what I had done to Jen, after she died. What had happened with Raphael and Belial and my friends, what I had discovered about myself, during the trip. How words mattered.

And finally about coming here. About needing to follow through on my promise to Jen, to myself, to protect my friends. No matter the cost to me. Or to Jen.

Jen ...

The bond was still angry at me.

I took a breath. And another. They were shaky, quivering things. Frag-ile. It was quiet around us. Though in the distance there were sirens. Always sirens around, wherever I was. Always danger. Always something I had to fight through, to save, to protect.

It was a hard life. And in the days after Grafton I had leaned on Jen. She had helped navigate me to a greater understanding of myself. Of what I was. Of who I was responsible for. She had given me the strength to keep going.

And I needed that more than ever. I needed *her* more than ever.

Finally my mother spoke.

"Do you remember asking me how I did it?" she said. "How I survived, in this life?"

I remembered. The moment had burned itself in me, and came to me occasionally. Especially after living a particularly bad ghost.

"You find a little part of yourself," she had said. *"You tuck it away, where nothing can get to it. You hope the smaller part is greater than the evil."*

"I have done horrible things in this life," she said. "I like to believe that some part of me is good. Some kernel inside that fights against what I am enslaved to. But that is not what I was talking about when I told you that. The little part of myself I hid away, that was you."

I didn't get it. And she saw that I didn't.

"We all have strength, son," she explained. "But there is always something greater. Stronger. Something that will overwhelm you. That will take every ounce of inner strength you have. Life on this earth is a crucible, and it will *always* beat you down. There is no one person, not you, not me, not your father, who has the determination and will to survive everything this world can throw at you."

I was quiet. It seemed to me my life had been more overwhelming than most. There were millions of different kinds of lives in this world. There were families with white picket fences in some suburb somewhere, buying groceries, walking the dogs, sending the kids off to school. I didn't think the world was such a crucible, for them.

But maybe I was wrong. Maybe both parents worked and were behind in the bills. Maybe one of their kids, little Tommy or Susan, had tonsillitis. Or needed braces. Or chemo. Maybe there were different pressures for everyone, in whatever life they lived.

I just knew about mine, though.

My mother kept on. "So, you were what kept me going," she said. "Whenever it got to be too much, I thought about you and endured. And just that thought would be enough."

She swallowed. Her voice grew hoarse. It was the most human thing I had ever seen from her. "My life … it has never been easy.…"

Then her breath caught, and she reached up to finger her throat. Where the crooked white line encircled her neck. My mother paused a long moment, as if remembering some particular evil. And then she continued.

"But thoughts of you always got me through. You've become greater than anything your father and I had hoped. You are so different, so … *more*." My mother looked away then. Her hand moved from her neck to her eyes and made a quick wiping motion there.

"We had you in desperation," she continued. "For a plan that only had the slimmest hope of succeeding. A last gasp for those we had been, once."

The slimmest of hopes. The words raised the hair on the back of my neck. I had started this journey on that same thin thread.

"Our only goal was to free you of this geas," she said. "It was our only hope. Ending this cycle of enslavement."

"I don't understand any of that," I said. "I'm still trapped, under the geas. You both are still commanded by the curse, too. You're no better off than when you had me."

"Maybe," she said. "Or maybe I am not finished yet. Maybe the plan isn't … complete."

"The plan?" I said.

She looked at me, smiled, and stayed silent. It didn't feel like the geas was keeping her from telling me any of this. So I waited. And her eyes softened, but she didn't add anything.

My mother was hiding something all her own. Just from me? Or from everyone?

I shook my head. "Whatever."

"I tell you this so you know I understand what it is like to live in fear of losing the one thing that gives you the strength to go on," she said. "That fear is something I am intimately aware of."

Parker… The man's face came back to mind, scars so thick on his face his mouth couldn't close properly. And all he had done was be responsible for me. Then I had run away. Leaving my mother no way to trace me, to find me. To make sure I was okay.

A memory of him, rocking on the porch, late at night. One of the last times I had seen the man, before he died.

"Nights like this," Parker had said, his voice soft, almost a whisper, *"feel better on my scars. Cools them a bit."* There was a long pause and a sigh. *"Or so I imagine."*

I understood the kind of anger, the passion that could cause someone to leave those kinds of scars. I felt so sorry for Parker now. I had then. It had been my fault. Unknowingly, but I had caused them all.

My mother's jaw was set. As if she was going through her own memories. Then she shook her head, slightly, and focused on me.

"At least your Jen is still with you, son," she said. "Take strength in that."

"For how long?" I asked. "The stone holding her is crumbling by the day. And if that's not enough, she's using her powers, too. And we both know what happens when we use up a ghost."

A touch of indignation, from Jen's side of the bond.

"It's a race," I said, "to see if the stone breaks first, or Jen uses herself up."

The indignation turned to anger, thick and powerful along the bond between us.

"I'm not wrong," I whispered to Jen.

My mother tilted her head, in that manner that told me she was curious. Then she blinked, looking at the stone.

"It is … odd. I cannot see her spirit," my mother said. "Are you able to talk to her? Is that what you just did?"

"No ... yes. Maybe," I said. There was just the once, when we had been trapped under the collapsing floor of the garage. "Once."

"You can feel her, then?" she asked, and when I told her yes, she said, "What do you feel right now?"

"Anger," I said. "Anger at me."

"So she is aware?"

"Absolutely," I said. I smiled a small smile. "And still tells me I'm wrong."

There was a long moment of silence, and I became aware of the sirens again. They were close, but not close enough. Like they were staying far from the garage, and the terminal. My mother and I were far out in the long-term parking, out on the edge of the airport, and only farther out could I see the lights of emergency vehicles flashing.

Odd, that they got no closer.

"So your Jen knows," my mother said.

I snorted. "Of course she knows. Or thinks she does."

The anger, if anything, swelled larger along our bond. I pushed it away, looking at my mother. I drew a shaky breath. "We came up here, knowing it might be the end for us. For *her*. But you being here, I had this crazy hope that everything might be coming together. That it all might work out. That because we had come to protect my friends, because I had followed through on my word, everything was going to work out."

I snorted. "Dreams of a kid, right? Thinking this was some book, some movie, where all I had to do was the right thing, learn a lesson, overcome an evil. Then there would be some big reveal, where you appeared and told me how to save Jen, how to bring her back. Make her safe."

I couldn't take it anymore. I *had* done the right thing. I had followed through on my promise. And it had all felt *right*. I had rescued my friends. I had driven my father away. And my mother had appeared, and for a brief moment I had thought everything was going to be okay.

Until my mother had seen Jen, and shaken her head.

I screamed loud into the night. It felt like the scream carried all the way to the Rocky Mountains, echoing off the tall peaks there and reverberating, just a thousand times louder. I pounded my fist into the cracked blacktop around me, until something broke in my hand. And I kept pounding.

My mother had leaned back some. Saw something in me then. Something that worried her, maybe.

Something wrong? Or just something misguided?

Jen's anger lessened, turned into concern. She tentatively poked along the bond. At the fury that swirled inside my chest and roared to come out. I brushed her away and pulled my fist to my chest. The pinky finger dangled, and blood ran down the side of my hand. I squeezed it into a fist and let the pain shoot through me.

The anger came back from Jen, powerful. Pounding. Like someone was banging hard to open a door.

"Son," my mother said.

I squeezed harder. Craving the pain. It was what my life was, after all. Why not let it be permanent? Might as well get used to it.

"Son," my mother said again, louder. She grabbed my shoulders and poured ethereal energy into me. Healed my fist and my finger in cold snaps of pain.

Then she slapped me across my face. Not something light, as if to wake someone asleep. A full-of-force slap that rocked my head backward. That knocked whatever it was I had been doing or feeling out of me and left me stunned.

The bond smiled at that.

"You *do not* despair," my mother snapped.

I felt like a child, before her. Embarrassed and ashamed and a little sulky. She was furious at me, her face set. There was little light between us, but enough to see the crooked white line around her neck, the one she had just recently fingered. Her skin carried a countless number of the pale scars, crisscrossing over each other, so many that even with our healing ability, reminders had been left.

"You think you know evil," she said, her words short and clipped but full of force. "You have lived it for a few short years. I have lived it for *hundreds*."

My face flushed under her gaze. I looked away. Though she continued, her words loud, her breath hot against my ear.

"You are so ready to give up now." Each word precise. "*Now*, when the world needs you the most."

Giving up was a strong way of putting it. I had only been angry. Furious. And I had bottled a lot of it up. Some of it had just leaked out, is all. Maybe the display had been childish, but hell, I wasn't perfect.

I rolled my eyes. I was far from perfect. Borderline psychotic, maybe, after that display. Pounding the ground until the bones in my hand broke and the skin split. No wonder my mother was worried about me. I would be, too.

She called it despair. Maybe she was right. Maybe I had been giving in. Just a little.

But it just didn't seem *fair*.

"You have listened to nothing I have said," my mother said. "You are *greater* than what your father and I ever conceived you could be. You are capable of *more*. Your Jen is *alive*. That should be *enough*."

Enough, that was a funny word. Jen hung on only by the barest of threads. The Key would fall apart under a hard sneeze. What my mother called enough, I called the last string of an unraveling tapestry, the end of the strand fluttering in the wind. One sharp, short tug would dissolve Jen away.

"Is it, really?" I asked. Not looking at her.

"I am telling you, *yes*." Her words firm. Resolute.

I didn't know that I believed her. I would always be in this state, somewhere between belief and disbelief. Perched in the middle, with no real clear idea of which way to swing. There were very few things I was sure of, and those were in danger of being taken from me.

"There should be *something*," I argued. "There should be a reason to keep doing this. I am *prepared* to keep going. I have promised Jen that.

But I don't have to be happy that I might have to keep going without her."

"You still aren't listening, then," my mother said in return. "There is a *something*. I am telling you, *you are more* than you think. More than you know, more than any of us know."

"So I can take more of a beating than most," I said. "What's that even mean, here?"

"There is the despair again," she said. "I cannot bring your Jen back. I can't begin to tell you how to do so. I can't even see her, in the sight."

My mother pulled my head around so that I had to look at her face. So that our eyes locked. Hers were blue and driven. Her voice forceful. "But she *exists*. You *exist*. You are *together*. That should be enough for you. But selfishly you want more. You want more, and you want it to be *easy*."

I snorted, and waved my hands around. Pointing to the crater, the garage. "All *this* is easy?"

"Easy," she said, her voice firm. Resolute with knowledge and experience I didn't have. "Evil has existed in this world for a long time. It has swelled over the earth, without real opposition, for thousands of years. It will be difficult for anyone to take it on without loss. But you are up for it, son. You were *born* for it. The pendulum shifts our way, again."

My mother had told me much the same thing, back in Grafton. That it was time for good to win again. That was before New Orleans, though. Before Azazel had created his cities. Before the world had discovered hell on earth really could exist.

Before Jen had been killed.

"With these Dead Zones, evil has launched its final blow," she said. "I can feel it. *See* it. The closer evil comes to losing, the harder it fights. I hear it, like some rabid hyena, yipping, backed into a corner."

Her hand squeezed mine, hard. "It is time, then, for our side to counter."

"You say that like there's some kind of balance," I said. "Like a scale with too much weight on one side, so we finally put more on ours."

"The world is not balanced, son," my mother said. "It is not *fair*. Or *even*. There is only stroke and counterstroke, until one side is no more."

She took a breath. "Evil is everywhere now. It has chalked up victory after victory. But good remains. It endures. It gathers its strength, like a tiny ripple rolling across the middle of the ocean. The ripple absorbs the winds. It swallows other waves, draws strengths from oceanic depths, until it has grown into this titanic, tidal force."

I paused a moment. "I think you believe something about me that isn't true. I think you want it to be, and you want it so much that you are trying to convince me, like you've convinced yourself."

Her mouth twisted. "Despair is a powerful tool of the other side, son."

I moved my shoulders up and down. Accepting what she told me, but not really believing it. "Call it what you will."

"Who else is fighting these demons?" she asked. "What other force remains, stands against them, *here on this earth?*"

I immediately thought about the Templars, and Bartholomew. Greg, Father Benjamin, even the bishop in New Orleans. Tabitha and the witches in Lewiston. Miss Tammie, taking care of the children, before she had been shot and burned back in Grafton. Parker. Frank Herder, who had covered Mrs. Cooper's body with a blanket.

Then, for some reason, I recalled the little face in the van window, back in the rest stop where Kimaris had attacked us. When every other person had been killed there, a tiny kid had remained, in a blue van with a *Believe* bumper sticker on its back.

There were bits of good, all around. Pieces of good everywhere, maybe. I thought it more likely those pieces would come and go, like people did. Some would die, others would be born, and all would try to hold out against the evils of the world. And most would fail. I mean, I lived the memories of the spirits who had turned. People who had given in.

How good could a person see, when that was all they experienced? All they lived?

"Mom, I'm barely able to make it to the next day," I said. "I'm just trying to save my friends. That's all."

"So start small," she said. "And then lengthen your reach. It is how things should work. Find yourself. Protect your friends. Then the world."

My mother flinched then, as if someone had stabbed her in the stomach. Her jaw tightened, her eyes closed, and she bent over, her hand going to her midsection.

I felt it, too. The geas. But whereas before, when Dominic had wielded it with an unmatched power and precision, this command was wild. Shaky. Insanely powerful and pounding. Not like the beating of a heart, but an arrhythmic pulsing instead. Like the vampire was screaming it at the top of his voice, and yet whispering at the same time.

Come, come. Come, come…

My mother fought the curse, standing in little, jerking motions. "He wakes."

"And then there's that," I said. "How can I save anyone when we are tied to *that*?"

The geas was focused on my mother, and seemed to ignore me. I only felt the wash of its call over her. Bits and pieces of her elegance fell aside as she fought it. She was always precise in each motion, but her body was taut with tension now. Not precision.

Her jaw flexed. Her eyes squinted. The muscles in her face, her arm, her neck, popped out. Her mouth still moved, though. Enough for her to talk. "Trust me. A wave rolls across the ocean, son. It is time it came to shore."

I snorted. Still, Dominic's command beat like an arrhythmic heart, varying in intensity and pull. "What does that even mean?"

"Son." She gripped my hand, tight enough that my knuckles cracked. Like she was using me as an anchor, trying to keep herself here as long as she possibly could. "There is a power to words, you said. So promise me. Do anything but despair."

I held her hands tight, feeling her fingers slip slowly through mine, like I was holding a thousand-pound weight over the edge of a cliff. I would have promised it, just to ease my mother's fears, but I couldn't. Even with her looking at me, pleading with me. Even with the encouragement from Jen, along the bond.

My mother saw my answer in my eyes. "Then promise me you'll continue the fight."

"That's one I've already made," I said.

"You promise me," she said, through clenched teeth. Her fingertips sliding out of mine, as if someone else was pulling her hand away.

"Okay," I said. "I promise."

She took a breath then, a large breath. One of her feet turned around under her body and pointed west. She had to fight these last words out. "Come. To. Conclave."

"Where Dominic and Victor are?" I frowned.

"Trust. Me."

Her hands slipped away from mine before I answered. Before I could tell her I did, my mother was already twenty feet away. Thirty. Sixty. Flying over the ground as fast as ethereal energy would take her, toward a gathering of vampires, toward Dominic and Victor and my father, and whatever else waited for her.

And now, I guessed, waited for me, too.

CHAPTER FORTY-FIVE

I watched my mother run for what felt like a long time, but was actually just a second or two. She covered the earth quickly, a blur across the lanes of the highway, away from the terminal. West into the night.

And then she was gone.

The bond thrummed underneath me, anger and concern all wrapped up in a question.

"I know," I said. And I did. The Conclave was no place for me. Not one, but two master vampires would be there. They both controlled a geas that could bind me and force me to their will. And one seemed like he was going insane, from what I had felt through my mother.

What emotions flew through me, as I watched my mother disappear into the dark? Some response to a hidden maternal instinct? Some connection tying mother to son? I couldn't say. My insides were knotted up with mixed emotions. The fear of losing Jen. A shame at feeling hopeless. And confusion at what my mother was trying to get across to me. For all my mother had just said, and for the things she had tried to do, she was someone I really didn't know.

But I remembered Grafton, when I had woken up with a freshly healed scar over my chest. How nervous my mother had been, sitting near me. How she had wanted to push a lock of my hair aside, but couldn't bring herself to do it. Her hand had lifted, and then drifted back down, of its own accord. And she had looked away.

I was the reason she could keep going, though. She had told me that. How someone could be so hard, so deadly, and yet hide a small part of herself away from Dominic, from the geas, said a lot about what I meant to her. I had to trust that.

And then the look on my mother's face, the desperate effort she poured through herself just now, to stay and fight the geas another moment, to stay one last moment with her son, had sunk into me. I knew what the geas felt like, even though I only felt a part of it. I knew the single-minded battle of trying to hold myself still, against the geas. Much less stay and try to say anything.

I couldn't promise her I wouldn't fall into despair. I had lost too much already, with Jen, and I didn't know what would happen if I lost what little I had left of her. If I lost the few friends I had left.

A feeling of hopelessness swirled over me, and I forced myself to think of something else. The feeling drifted away, but hung over the back of my mind like a cloud. It hinted at me that I was missing something.

And I was. I would go to the Conclave. I had made a promise, and I needed to keep it. I would keep my friends safe and show the world what would happen if they came after them.

But I needed to be more. I *should* be more. There were two more people that needed me. My mother. My father. Not just because they were angels under a geas, but because they were my parents. Even if I didn't know them, they were family. My family.

I was taking a lot on myself. More than I should, maybe. But if I needed to grow, if I needed to become more, then my promise needed to grow and become more. If I was going to become greater, then I needed to evolve, so what I promised needed to become greater.

Only in putting that kind of pressure on myself could I become what my mother saw in me.

The bond vibrated hard then between Jen and me. A protest. Or wanting acknowledgment.

I smiled.

I could be what Jen believed of me.

The bond relaxed. Jen probably was shaking her head. As if telling me, *About time*.

I couldn't promise to not despair. But I could keep digging myself out of the holes I found myself in. I could keep fighting. And I could protect those close to me. Those were all promises I intended to keep.

I was taking a lot on myself. But a part of me needed to make this right. Once that part of me had been small, but it was large now, something that had grown with every recent realization I had.

A mother deserved no less from her son. She played a larger game than I had guessed, something she had hinted at back in Grafton, but could never just tell me. Her words kept circling in my mind, that it was time for good to win again. But whatever secret she held, the geas kept it locked tight.

My father had battled the geas, too. He had told me it wasn't his time, even while he tried to kill me and kill my friends. Still, he had fought its control as much as I had ever seen anyone fight it. Whatever my mother had planned, my father was in on it as well.

"A wave rolls across the ocean, son. It is time it came to shore...."

So I didn't know the plan. I guessed instead. The geas bound her, bound my father, bound me. Maybe she was counting on me to break it, in some way. I wasn't sure how I thought that would be possible, when I was just as much under the control of the geas as she and my father.

"Trust me...."

"Promise me...."

"It is not my time...."

I didn't understand enough, though. And I had spent enough time here. I had another promise to keep. The garage sat across the highway from where I stood. The building slumped to one of its corners, one side completely collapsed. Cars and trucks lay among the rubble like they had poured out of each floor.

I took off that way, stopping only briefly at the highway leading into the terminal. Six lanes of roads heading in and out, and not quite a mile away there was a line of police cars and emergency vehicles parked across both lanes. Blocking the entrance and exit.

Off to the side were a couple of large sport utility vehicles, black trucks with tinted windows and letters on the side. I couldn't make out what the letters said. A few cars lined up at a checkpoint, trying to head out. Cops held the vehicles there. It looked like they were searching each one thoroughly. Trunks were popped, hoods were up, dogs sniffed around.

Other people walked the perimeter, some wearing three-piece suits, police wearing tactical gear.

I didn't understand why they weren't speeding to the terminal, sirens blaring. But maybe they were playing by Dead Zone rules now. Set a perimeter and see what the hell they were dealing with, before sending anyone in.

I headed toward the garage, quickly climbing up the rubble and hopping off onto the floor my father and I had flown off from, just a short time ago. I found my friends quickly. They were all huddled by a car near the banks of elevators. It was the second floor of the garage, and a lot of the lights were out, leaving a dull empty light to reveal them to me.

Gabrielle sat cross-legged on the floor. Her hair hung over her forehead and hid her face. Johnny lay in her lap, his head in the crook of her arms. His eyes were still closed.

"She bit him," Nick said. He looked tired, but not surprised to see me. Next to him was Sarah, leaning on him a bit. Her eyes were a little unfocused, as if she had taken a blow to the head.

Gabrielle's shoulders shook in tiny motions.

"I told her to," Nick added. "But I don't think it helped."

The memory of Mrs. Cooper came back to me. The last time I had seen her, when Rand and Jacob had turned her into a leech. She had lost too much blood and couldn't make the transition to vampire. Her brain had become inert, and when she was reborn as undead, all she had was an undying thirst, with no thought to control it. She would have had no human spark then, just the weak purple of an undead light inside her chest.

I flicked on my ethereal vision. Johnny's spark remained, though it wavered in his chest, light and dark, light and dark. Like a candle's flame, guttering under small gusts of wind.

"He's still alive," I said. I let out a breath. I had made it in time to protect my friends. To keep them all alive. I had lost Danny, and I had lost Jen—

Anger and denial from the bond …

—but I would not lose Johnny, too.

Gabrielle looked up at me. Tears ran down each cheek. Johnny's face was wet, underneath hers, and her eyes held only the deepest despair.

I recognized that emotion. Understood it. And understood how hope could sometimes only make that feeling worse.

I had healed Jen a few times. Once in the King's Lodge. Once outside the church after Kimaris. But I had failed her in New Orleans.

More anger, from the bond. I recognized the reason. Gabrielle's despair was catching. But I would always beat myself up for New Orleans. It was kind of how I worked.

The anger eased up some. Like Jen could feel what I felt, or thought.

I wouldn't let Johnny go now. I knelt next to Gabrielle and laid a hand on Johnny's chest, above the strap that seemed to be cinched around a couple of T-shirts there. His chest was both cool and sticky.

I closed my eyes and reached out, ethereally. His heart had all but stopped. The muscle seemed to slightly quiver under my prying. I pulled a little ghost and eased its energy into Johnny's body, letting it flow from my hand into his chest.

There was an awareness from Johnny. I sensed it. Like someone was watching me, from far away.

I took more ghost, feeling the spirit fight me, the more energy I took. It would be one of those. I clamped down and pulled harder, forcing the energy into Johnny, wanting him to heal. The power flowed over his skin and started to stitch flesh together, bind fibers of muscles, knit bone.

The ghost fought me more. It actually tried to close down the funnel between it and the ethereal plane. The spirit bore down, and the energy between me and the plane slowed down to a trickle. I set my jaw and tugged harder, breaking the funnel open again.

Blood. Johnny was close to out. I poured more energy into him, forcing his cells to multiply by the tens, the hundreds, the millions. I closed off all the punctures and the tears and the holes, and massaged his heart muscle until it pumped once, twice.

The spirit screamed at me. Tiny explosions echoed from its memories. There was a sound of a dog yelping. I tried to push the memories down and work on Johnny some more.

A bullet was lodged in a rib; then a moment later it popped out, the wound closing behind it. Blood cells multiplied and filled arteries and veins, carried oxygen to Johnny's body, his brain. I made sure that stream was steady. Mrs. Cooper, and what had happened to her, stayed in the back of my mind as I worked. As I fought the ghost. As I tried to balance everything I was trying to do and keep Johnny alive.

Johnny took one gasping breath, arching his back. Gabrielle had enough sense to loosen the strap and tug away the shirts underneath it. The cotton came away with the smacking sound of partly congealed blood.

One breath was all Johnny had. A wheezing sound came out of his throat, trailing off into nothing. His heart quivered and stopped beating again.

From the bond came worry. And fear.

The ghost tried to tie off its funnel again. Laughing at me.

Fuck it.

I took everything the ghost had. The funnel burst and the ghost burned in a bright blue flame. The trickle of ethereal power swelled into a roaring waterfall of energy that slammed into me....

I stuffed more firecrackers under the dog's collar. The creature's eyes stared at me, blank and fearful, but I only laughed. For a moment I wondered why it didn't bite me, why it trusted me this far.

Kicking the dog had gotten boring. So I had figured something better out. I stuck more firecrackers underneath, taping them on with thick black electrical tape. The creature yelped when I tugged the tape hard enough for it to break. Then I grabbed my lighter and flicked it once, twice, until a flame popped up over my thumb. The dog pulled away then, but I held the collar tight and stared into its sad, lonely, fearful eyes....

The burst of energy slammed into Johnny, too. He sat up with a large gasp, eyes wide-open. They glowed an ethereal blue. He looked at all of us, but I didn't think he saw any of us.

"Anyone hear a dog yelping?" he asked. Then fell back into Gabrielle's lap.

But this time he kept breathing. In my ethereal sight his flame was a bright purplish blue glow, burning strong in his chest. I frowned. The purple to me was of the undead, of vampires like Gabrielle.

The blue tint was new, though.

Johnny's heart beat out a steady rhythm. Blood flowed everywhere inside his body, stitching tears together, healing what it could. He would make it.

I took a breath. Leaned back. Nodded.

Gabrielle saw, let out a sob, and pulled Johnny to her.

Nick and Sarah just looked at me. Both of their mouths slightly open. I touched each of them with my hand, letting the last of the ethereal energy flow into both of them. Sarah's eyes immediately cleared up. Nick took a breath and felt around his body, both his hands touching places his clothes had been cut.

Then he looked at me. "Man, you have to bottle that shit up," he said. Then grinned.

I let out a shaky breath. My friends were okay. I had kept that promise.

It was time to work on another.

CHAPTER FORTY-SIX

A jumbo jet roared overhead, screaming, one of the planes still circling, lower and lower, waiting for permission to land. The floor around us was littered with dust, bullet holes, and dead bodies. It was past midnight, and the early morning brought with it a cold darkness. There was the little thing of a quarter of the parking garage collapsing on itself, and it was maybe late enough that a lot of people weren't flying in. Still, there was a conspicuous lack of people around.

"Where is everyone?" Nick asked.

I told him what I had seen, out there. That the police and the government were outside, waiting a mile out on the terminal road. The letters on the side of the trucks and vans. Nick disappeared into the shadows and came back a few seconds later.

"SRF," he said. "They look like feds."

SRF. Some government agency I had never heard of. I wondered if they had always existed, or had just been created after New Orleans. Either way, I guessed it didn't matter much now.

"We need a ride," I said. "Something that will off-road."

"Got it," Nick said. And blurred away. I liked that about Nick. In times where action was needed, he was a man of few questions.

"You okay?" I asked Sarah.

"Yeah," she answered, and grimaced. "Maybe one too many blows to the head. How did you get here so fast?"

"I flew in," I said.

Sarah glanced at the terminal.

"I mean literally," I said. I shook my head. "I should never have left you guys, in New Orleans."

"We understood," Sarah said, putting her hand on my shoulder.

"I don't get me, sometimes," I said. "But I think I'm figuring it out."

"I think we're all just glad you're here, and everyone's safe," Sarah said. Then she looked at the Key. Her eyebrows pinched a little. "Everyone *is* okay, right?"

"So far," I said, my hand lightly touching the Key. My eyes went to Johnny. "Though just barely."

"Don't put too much on yourself," Sarah said, following my gaze.

Gabrielle had been watching us. Tiny red lines forked through her eyes. I hadn't known vampires could shed tears. But they could definitely be angry.

"My father would have done this anyway," she said. "You were the excuse."

I might have let it go there, a few days ago. Maybe Victor was going to come after Johnny anyway. It didn't mean I shouldn't have been here to stop it. I had given my word.

"Believe me," Gabrielle said. "My father never liked Johnny. Never liked his bloodlines. Never liked his manners. Never liked that he did not want to be part of the family. At least, not in the way I wanted him to …"

Her voice trailed off. Gabrielle still held Johnny in her lap, his back against her thigh, his head cradled in the crook of her arm. His chest rose and lowered gently, in a slow rhythmic motion.

"Well," I said, "he's part of the family now."

Even as I said the words, I wondered if they were true. He was definitely a vampire now. But also something else. The purple and blue flicker in his chest. I wondered what I had done when I healed him.

Or if it had been me. The bond between Jen and me seemed to go both ways.

Gabrielle acknowledged what I said, but her eyes looked a little lost. Like she was staring back in time. "I hope he does not hold it against me."

Somewhere in the garage an engine fired up. It choked a couple of times before turning over with a roar. The motor settled into something powerful and rumbling. Nick had found us a ride.

Sarah knelt next to Gabrielle. She put her hand on the vampire's shoulder, letting Gabrielle come back to the present.

"It won't matter," Sarah said. "He'll come around. If there's one thing I've learned, with us, is that we work through these things. We're going to get each other's backs. And that's something you're a part of now."

Sarah's words struck me as true. And full of purpose, like a prophecy. They resonated in my mind like a prophecy fulfilled.

We now had another member to our group. To the Wolverines. What we had called ourselves as kids, we had grown into as adults. A small group of people standing against what was wrong in the world. Against an overwhelming force, threatening to take over the world.

But really, against evil.

"Who else is fighting these demons?" my mother had asked me. *"What other force remains, stands against them, here on this earth?"*

A chill ran down my back. My friends were few. A couple of witches. A shadow-walker. Myself, and whatever Johnny was now.

"Start small. Then lengthen your reach."

Now there was Gabrielle. I shook my head, not really believing what my mother had told me. My friends and I, we were just a group of kids who had found each other at a young age, when not a lot of people wanted us around. Four of us had been orphans, or outcasts. We weren't some Justice League, out to oppose evil wherever it appeared.

Whatever we had been, though… we were one greater now.

Even if we had recently lost one. I had never read comics, growing up. Maybe I should have. Maybe I should have read something to give me some kind of belief, that I could hit the crazy goal I aimed for.

It was hard for me to really come to grips that we were it, that we were what the world had. Especially when I couldn't even protect the person I cared about most. All I did was talk to her spirit, a ghost that couldn't reply, and watch the stone prison holding her crumble more each day.

The Key thrummed on my chest. Something like worry, tempered with support.

"I know," I said quietly. And promised myself not to give in to the despair.

Sarah looked over when I spoke, her eyebrow raised. As if she was wondering what I had said. Or who I had said it to.

A four-door Jeep rolled down the rubble from the floor above, large tires working up and down in the wheel wells as the vehicle clambered across large blocks of pavement. It was a dark gray Rubicon, with a hard top and an American flag grille insert right in front of the radiator.

Nick pulled the Jeep to a stop next to us. He had rolled down the windows, and raised his eyebrows, as if asking, *Will this do?* Or maybe, *You guys ready?*

The answer was yes. To both questions. The Rubicon would absolutely do. And it was definitely time to leave.

We got in. The tires were the tall off-roading kind, the floorboards were about the same height as my hip, and we all had to pull ourselves into the Jeep. Sarah took the seat next to Nick, clicking her seat belt. I helped Gabrielle carry Johnny in, and we positioned him between us in the backseat. She was careful to keep his head in her lap. The whole time Johnny breathed evenly, the deep sleep of someone who was exhausted.

Sleep was something I could use, too.

"We need to head west," I told Nick. I hadn't decided on what I wanted to do yet. It wasn't really a plan, it was more of an action. The idea was rolling around in my head and taking shape, and while it did I wanted to give us some time.

He pulled out and headed down the ramps to the first floor of the garage. The motor of the Rubicon chugged along. It was the thoughtful grumble of an untapped power that most off-roading vehicles had, rather than the roaring energy of sports cars. A blast of cold air whipped in through Nick's window. He hit a button and had it roll up.

We took the ramp down to the first floor. It was clean of rubble and undisturbed by the broken slabs of concrete that had fallen near the edges of the building. Nick got us to the exit and turned against the normal direction on the terminal road. Instead of heading out, he drove us toward the front of the airport, where people were normally dropped off and picked up.

It was there we finally saw people. Groups of them, hundreds if not thousands, all huddled behind the plate-glass windows and sliding doors, faces pressed against the glass, watching the garage. They all stared at us as we drove by, expressions scared or astonished. A few worried, quite a lot confused. Most of them on their phones, with some trying to get out the doors. A number of people manned each exit, dressed in the dark coplike uniforms of airport security personnel, and those guards worked at keeping everyone in.

Once we left the terminal, Nick took us off the highway, the Jeep lurching as we drove off the shoulder and into the fields. The grass was thick and the ground was hard under the tires, and the Rubicon bounced up and down in little motions as Nick kept us at a good speed. He was careful to keep the garage between us and where we had seen the perimeter being set.

He looked tired, and hunched a little over the wheel. Sarah, too, was leaned back against the seat and held on to the seat belt with both hands, as if it was the only thing holding her up. Gabrielle sat next to me, quiet, focused on Johnny, her clothes ripped and shredded and cuts crisscrossed around her wrists. As if she'd had to break out of cuffs, or chains.

The bond between Jen and me was silent. The connection still felt like a rope, pulled somewhat snug between us, but nothing vibrated along it. Like the other hand was holding its end a bit loosely. I wondered if she was okay. Did spirits sleep, or did they have other ways to recuperate?

Nick had the stereo off, so there was just the whine of the engine in the cabin and the thudding of the tires over the earth. The ground was fairly flat, but still the Jeep bounced up and down, enough that we all steadied ourselves by holding on to something, a seat, the dash, a door. In that way we made our way from the airport, leaving the collapsed building, the fight with my father, all the dead vampires and soldiers, all the death and destruction behind.

I shivered at a sense of déjà-vu. Just a few weeks ago I had come back to Grafton. At first, to help Jen. Then to save my friends. As a kid I had been their protector, the person who stood up to their bullies, and I found myself in the same role again. Together, we stood against Raphael and his vampire army, winning and barely escaping with our lives. After it all, we had fled the town, leaving nothing behind but bodies amid a smoking, gutted ruin.

I had wanted to save my friends in Grafton, but a lot of people I cared about had still been killed. Mrs. Tammie, shot and left to burn alive in her diner. Parker, too. Father Benjamin and Greg. Andy, a guy I barely knew, in the wrong place at the wrong time. And my last memory of Jen's mother wouldn't be her cooking us pancakes on a Saturday morning, but her as a leech, trying to bite me, nothing left in her mind but a terrible thirst for blood.

Danny had been left there, too, though he had died long before the battle. His ghost had remained to help me, though, when I gave it all up, gave everything I had. Danny had always been the brightest light in our group. The memory of him remained among us all, colored every decision we made. He might have been the glue keeping us all together, even now, a subliminal bond tying each of us to the others. Danny seemed to always help us remember who we were when we needed it the most.

After Grafton we had headed to New Orleans, trying to save Sarah from a time bomb of a spell that had been scrawled across her skin using a blend of science, demon magic, and a vampire's curse. During that trip our group had fallen into the roles we'd had as kids, with a little nervous energy here and there between us. Unsure of where each of us stood with the others, of what each of us could do, what each of us had learned, what each of us had become.

It had been us against the world. Trying to save Sarah had been a race against time, and the closer we got to New Orleans, the more our enemies had fought us. At the time I was afraid, afraid of failing my friends, afraid of being the reason they would die.

The protector mantle always weighed heavy on me. I had run from everything for so long, being responsible for them again scared me. Danny's death, it weighed on me. And I didn't know how much more weight I could take.

I didn't know if I was strong enough to protect my friends, from everything and everyone who could come after them. After losing Danny. And especially after losing Jen.

Still, I had promised Jen to protect our friends, no matter what. No matter who died. Even if it was her, at the moment we had freed Sarah from her curse, and Azazel had turned New Orleans into his own personal hellish kingdom.

Like in Grafton, there had been casualties. Hundreds of thousands of people in New Orleans had died when the Dead Zone first appeared, and maybe hundreds of thousands more as people fled the city. The bishop had died, burned in the ritual that had saved Sarah. That same ritual had also desecrated the St. Louis Cathedral and given Azazel the power to build his Dead Zones. He had freed his fellow demons from the Key and given each of them a place to live. Cities of hell on earth.

The worst thing for me had been Jen's death. I had given up, until Nick gave me hope. That hope had driven everything I had done since, until tonight.

Destroyed buildings. Corpses. An enemy, if not victorious, then confident they would have another shot at me, my friends. That seemed to be what I left behind.

So the déjà-vu made a morbid kind of sense, as we left the airport terminal here in Denver, the crumbling garage, the dead bodies scattered across the floors. Every place I had stayed, a motel, the Welcome Center, a town or a city, all and everything laid to waste because I had been there. Leaving death and destruction had become the norm for me and my friends.

And each time something like this happened, the lives of my friends hung in the balance. Or the balance tipped over, and they were killed. I could count on one hand the people who were left, out of the people I had known, who had once loved me or taken care of me.

It had been Johnny's turn, in Denver. He had been with us the whole time. He had actually stayed in Grafton, even after I left. Even though he had no special power to speak of.

I admired his courage. Or maybe it was just the desire to stay and do the right thing. To protect what he loved. Even after Grafton, when we all left, he had chosen to come with us. Maybe it had been because of some reason between Gabrielle and Victor, or maybe not, but he still had come. For Sarah. For his friends. For the Wolverines.

I was tired. And angry. Nick was exhausted, covered in ichor and his clothes cut and soaked. Sarah's hair was clumped with caked blood. Johnny was covered with it. We were fleeing this airport, with no idea what tomorrow might bring. Or the day after.

Victor Dumont had taken the opportunity, with me and the geas, to rid himself of Johnny. Maybe to put his daughter in line. It wasn't something any of us had been ready for, or could have prepared for. The vampire had seen a weakness, and he exploited it.

My friends might never be safe. This world seemed to be made in a way that encouraged that danger. If we lived through these days, who else in the future might see my friends as a way to get to me? Would Azazel, or Belial, or Raphael try to exploit what they perceived as a weakness in me? Or would some unknown monster in the days ahead, someone like Victor, would they wait in the wings to take out my friends, as soon as I dropped my guard?

How could I not fail my friends, with what seemed like the entire world after us?

I thought – like I had leaving Grafton ten years ago – that leaving my friends behind would keep them safe. I had thought working with Raphael would be risky enough, without leading them into a trap. And I had thought I had been doing the right thing. The *safe* thing.

I had been wrong.

Maybe it could be argued that I should've known better. But I was hardheaded. I've been accused of needing to learn things a few times before the lesson took. So this time I promised myself to learn the lesson well. Because how many chances did I really have, to protect those I cared about? Who knew what would come after us next? Come after *them* next?

Words mattered. I knew that now. I was constantly learning there was a wide gulf between the knowing and the understanding. Even though my experience was changing me, changing the inside of me, the core of who I was. Every act narrowed that gulf, I knew more, I understood deeper. So if I kept learning from my mistakes, I *would* become better. Greater. More.

Maybe if I lived long enough, the knowing would become the understanding. Right now, though, even if my head knew something, my heart wouldn't realize that same understanding, not until it experienced it. I needed to feel it in my core. Success or failure, only by experiencing both of those concepts could I grow. And become something better.

Maybe that was ultimately why I could summon the sword now, and even fly.

Not because I was an angel, and those things were the powers of an angel. But because I was transforming into someone I had always wanted to be. A hidden truth I had long been scared of. A truth I had run from as a kid, because taking responsibility for those around me had been too much.

I could see it now, though.

I had always been someone who stood up for those who needed it. When I did that, when I followed through on the promise I had made to myself, I *was* a different person. A better person. Because words did matter. *Promises mattered.* And not just in some contract. They mattered most of all to *me*.

To who I was, and who I was meant to be.

If I said something, I needed to follow through with it. And if there was more evil in the world to threaten my friends, then I needed to do something greater. Something large enough to threaten them all back. I was tired of reacting. Of running from things. Of hoping, *this time*, that we would all come out of this alive.

I didn't know if I was capable of anything, of *more*, as my mother had told me. But she was right about one thing. I needed to be at the Conclave tomorrow.

I could be more than someone who came after the fact. Someone who righted the wrongs done to those he cared about. I could be more than a creature of vengeance. I could be something much more powerful. I could be something to be *feared*.

CHAPTER FORTY-SEVEN

Nick angled the Jeep across the fields until we found a road, circling from north to south. It was some kind of bypass looping around Denver. The city lights shone in the night to the southwest of us, a bright domelike glow on the horizon, set against the backdrop of black night.

Emergency lights flashed south of us, heading east. That made our decision of where to go easier. Nick took the parkway north and west, circling around Denver. At one point we passed the Humvees and large camouflage trucks of the National Guard, all lined up in a single file, driving opposite us. The column of vehicles struck me as something with purpose.

We followed the parkway for a few miles. The glow of Denver worked its way behind us, opposite the movement of the waning moon overhead. Each of us remained quiet, lost in thoughts, worry, exhaustion: three things that always seemed to stay around long after a fight was over.

Nick swung around a car in front of us. Its taillights weaved back and forth, like the person driving had drunk one too many. Nick goosed the accelerator and the Rubicon shot forward, leaving the wandering car in the rearview.

"Have a plan?" Nick asked.

"Yeah," I said. "Sleep."

"Okay," he said. "After that?"

"Tomorrow, we get serious," I said.

There must have been something in my voice. Nick caught my eyes in the mirror, briefly. Sarah turned her head around a little, her torso twisted just enough to see me, her eyebrows raised. She still hung on to the top of the seat belt, and her chin rested between the back of one of her hands and her shoulder. Gabrielle even looked up, curious.

"I'm going to the Conclave tomorrow night," I said. Then amended my statement. "We're going to the Conclave tomorrow night."

Gabrielle actually smiled, something dark and evil. Like it was something she wanted. Which, after seeing her tonight with Johnny, I supposed she did.

The cabin of the Jeep reverberated with a quiet stillness, a pulsing vibration of the tires rolling along the road. Sarah took a deep breath and held it. Nick's head motioned a little left and right, like he was thinking about what I had said.

Surprisingly it was Johnny who spoke first. "Aren't those the guys that just tried to kill us?"

He still lay in Gabrielle's lap, but his eyes were open and staring at me. His face looked harder, somehow. Leaner. But he still gave his trademark eyebrow waggle. "Or were they just trying to kill me?"

Gabrielle pulled Johnny up and enveloped him in a hug. She was quiet, her face pressed against the side of him. Johnny held her in return, his arms in a somewhat awkward position because of how he had been lying. The moment between them became a little intimate, and we all looked away.

Maybe a few seconds of quiet passed, with some little sounds and murmurs. Until Nick broke the silence.

"Johnny and Gabrielle, sitting in a tree," he sang, intentionally horribly, smiling in the rearview mirror. "K-I-S-S-I—"

He couldn't finish it. We all laughed, and somewhere in the laughter Johnny had found a way to sit up between me and Gabrielle.

"I take it, it was close," he said.

"Close," Sarah said, holding her thumb and forefinger together. "Razor thin."

"Yeah," Johnny said, checking himself out. His hands patted his chest, and he pulled the neckline of his T-shirt out and stuck his face into it. Like he wanted to see the scar. His voice came out muffled. "I feel different."

"That's because you are," Sarah said. She exchanged glances with Gabrielle.

"Oh," Johnny said. Then a moment later, his head still in the shirt: "Damn."

Gabrielle's face looked hurt. Scared. Worried.

Johnny's head turned a little, as if he was looking through the shirt at her. "I wasn't sure this was something I wanted."

"You were going to die," Gabrielle answered, voice breaking.

"I know," Johnny breathed out. "I know."

The tires rumbled over the road. The engine's rumbling reverberated in the cabin, a dull throaty growl that grew louder in the silence. Gabrielle's expression flickered from worry to anger, back to worry, as if she couldn't decide what emotion she should be feeling. Or maybe she wasn't making a decision, she was just unsure. Of how she felt. Of how Johnny felt. Maybe it was the great unknown of not knowing how the person you loved really felt.

I lowered my head, placing my mouth outside where his ear would be, and spoke low. "It is what it is," I said. "You can sit there and complain about it. Or you can look forward to an immortal life with someone you care about, and who cares about you."

It hurt a little to say those words. Back in Grafton, I had asked Gabrielle what kind of life Jen and I could even hope to have. I laughed at the idea of white picket fences and kids. Now I just wanted her back.

I hoped Johnny understood what I was saying. I hoped he got it. He had an opportunity, if he wanted it, to be with someone who loved him.

I didn't even want an immortal life with Jen. I just wanted a life with her. At that moment, I really wanted to feel something from the Key. Anger, sorrow, whatever. I would take anything from the bond between us. But it remained quiet.

Johnny's head moved in his shirt, like he had snorted. His voice cracked. "Man, I don't know if I can … I don't know if drinking someone's blood is something I can do."

Gabrielle winced. He had said it thoughtlessly, but his words came across like a slap. Like what Gabrielle did to survive was something Johnny abhorred.

I understood where Johnny came from. In order to do the things I had to do, I lived the lives of murderers, rapists, thieves. When I drew too much, I lived their blackest memories, some of the ugliest things a person could think to do to another. I had vomited more than once, after some of the worst.

Maybe some people, when given the choice between power and death, would happily choose my powers. To heal anything, be fast and strong. But living those memories would change them. I feared the memories would change me, but it was the way I could protect my friends, and so it was worth it.

If I was given the choice to do what I do, or something else, I don't know that I would choose anything different than what I'd done. I now understood there was a reason behind my powers. But I would definitely pause, before making the choice.

Johnny and I maybe weren't facing the same thing. But our problems swam in the same ocean. He would have to come to grips with the thing that allowed him to survive. That might even give him a larger purpose. Maybe he couldn't face it, but it was up to his friends to get him back on that track. To keep him going, when he didn't know if he could.

It was what we did.

"So you're okay with letting the people who did this to us get away with it?" I asked him. "You've hung around Grafton for ten years, fighting this fight. You went to New Orleans with us. And you came here, for me. This is where you tap out?"

Johnny stayed silent, stuck inside his shirt.

"None of us can control what happens to us," I said. "But we can control how we respond." I lowered my voice. "You know that's something I learned from you guys."

A long moment passed. When Johnny spoke, he sounded a little more like the fun-loving friend we all knew. "You're making me sound like an ass."

"If it was me," I said, "I'd probably feel like I deserved it."

He finally pulled his head out of his shirt. His smile was back, if a little sheepish. And his eyes still looked worried, unsure. Like a fawn, finding itself alone in the forest, without its parents, for the first time.

Gabrielle had the same look, to the side of him. As if she didn't know what Johnny was going to do or not. I couldn't tell if she was happy Johnny was going to try to come to grips with who he was now, or if she was upset that he couldn't become the thing *she* was.

Neither one of them looked like they knew if they were going to be the same, or not.

Johnny lifted his shoulders a little as if to ask me, *Now what?* I motioned to Gabrielle with my eyes, trying to tell him he was still being an ass. His eyes widened, like the thought hit him, and he turned toward her. Her hands wrapped around his back, and they held each other close.

But the embrace still looked awkward. As if neither could quite commit.

It was a much different world now than what I had believed as a kid. Growing up, we had all watched superhero cartoons and run around pretending to be them. Our group had grown into teenagers, banded together at Partisan Rock, and become the Wolverines. Some of us had fallen in love, others had dreamed about a different life, but I never would have thought one of us would fall in love with a vampire, and then become one himself.

They just don't ask you those kinds of questions when you go to school. No one responds they want to be a vampire, when they're asked what they want to grow up to be. Or a witch. A shadow-walker. Or a bastard kid of an angel.

I caught Gabrielle's eyes. "Do you know where the Conclave is being held?"

Her head was nestled next to Johnny's, her face lying against the back of his neck. She made a negative motion, slightly moving her chin left and right.

"We're definitely going there?" Nick asked.

"We definitely are," I said. I was tired of running. Tired of worrying about my friends. Tired of worrying about the geas, what Dominic or Victor might do, what Azazel might do. It was time to stop running, and start fighting. It was time to make others start to worry about what might happen to them. And lucky me, there was a place nearby where I could instruct others on their bad choices. And also a person to get me there. "Borrow your phone a minute, Nick?"

"Sure, man." He patted his vest with one hand, then his pants, and finally tugged his phone out of his front pocket.

It had dried blood across its face. I wiped it off and dialed the number for my phone. It answered after a couple of rings.

"Yo, Nicky," Raphael's voice came, the thrumming of my Camaro in the background, "How's Sarah? You tapping that yet?"

I was glad I hadn't put the call on speaker. My voice was flat. "Raph."

"Grimm." Raphael's voice sounded excited. "So you made it, my man."

"I did," I said. "You should be more careful in how you talk to my friends."

"Come on, Grimm," Raphael said. "What's a little joke between us?"

"Let's not find out," I said. "There's enough going on around here."

"Ha," he said. I sensed his smile across the phone. "We got a real Cain and Abel thing going, don't we?"

Cain and Abel. I wondered who he thought I was.

"You called me," Raphael said. "What's up?"

"I need to get to the Conclave," I said. "You happen to be the person who knows where it's held."

"The Conclave?" Raphael said. "*You* want to walk in there?"

"Yeah," I said.

"You know what'll happen to you, right?" He didn't have to mention the geas.

I hoped I was enough to handle it. I hoped I was *more*. "Look, I don't have time to go over every detail. Are you in or out?"

"Oh, I'm in," he said. "I didn't drive all this way in the middle of the night for bad coffee and a scintillating phone conversation with you."

"Belle with you?" I asked.

"You hear her, right?"

I didn't, but I got what Raphael was saying. She didn't talk much.

"Hold on," I said. I asked Nick where we were. There was an exit coming up, with all the signs telling us about all the places to stay, eat, and gas up. I relayed that information through the phone, and told Raphael we'd be at the first inn or motel we came upon.

"Got it?" I asked.

"Sure," Raphael said. "We're coming up on Denver now. Probably be where you're at in thirty or so."

"See you then." I hung up.

"Raphael?" Nick asked.

"Yeah," I said. "Before we all get upset, he's got a part to play here."

"That part's going to get us killed," Nick said. His hands wrapped tight around the steering wheel, and I wasn't sure if it was what he was saying or the large curved clover-leaf exit we had just taken. The Jeep slowed into the curve, and the turn was tight enough that the Jeep's transmission downshifted into a high-pitched whine.

Centrifugal force pushed us all to the outer wall of the Jeep. I braced myself against Sarah's seat in front of me. As we finished the turn we saw the hotel, something tan with a red roof, bright white sign high in the air. A coffee shop sat next to it, and a fast-food place lay across the highway from them both.

The trifecta. Three for three. Like I had always said, back when I was on the run from Azazel, from everything and everyone. Back when a night in a motel was a luxury. Having a meal and a place to sleep was what I looked for. The coffee was a luxury, most of the time. You learned to give up a lot of things, running.

Parker came to mind then, a few of the things he used to teach me.

"You used to be a fighter."

Johnny waking up interrupted my train of thought. And it had been an important train. Something I had needed to put together for myself. Something that had been running around in the back of my brain since Grafton.

"Grimm," Sarah said. Her face was worried, and her eyes flicked between Nick, Johnny, and me. "Can't we just run?"

I shook my head. "I'm tired of running."

"Run or fight," Nick said. "It's the same to me."

My friends were all tired. Johnny was still covered in his own blood, matting his shirt and hair. He looked unsure, at best. Sarah looked exhausted, and worried. Nick looked like Nick, quiet and ready to be deadly, or ready to keep driving. Gabrielle, out of our group, looked like the only person ready to do what I needed them to do.

"Look, I'm not saying we aren't all going to die, if we walk in there," I said. "But run or die, we're ending something tonight."

The Jeep slowed to a stop in the parking lot. There were a few tall streetlights, but their light didn't make it to the motel. Nick pulled around to the far side, into the dark, where the end of the motel met a few trees.

He shut the Jeep off. The cabin was as quiet as the night around us. Not many cars traveled the highway, as if everyone had heard about the airport and had decided to stay in tonight.

"I'm in," Nick said. He saw Sarah's worried glance. "Whatever it takes."

I was in, even though all of us looked exhausted. We all needed sleep. My friends were tired, covered in blood and dust and grime. Surprisingly I was the guy who didn't look like he had been in a recent firefight, with holes in his shirt. "I'll grab some rooms."

The icy cold air of Denver flooded in when I opened the door, and I shivered as I got out, rubbing my hands up and down my arms. It didn't take long to go pay for four rooms and hand out the keys to the group, with the suggestion we sleep in and get some breakfast when we woke up.

Nick and Sarah stayed for a moment. Jen's younger sister looked at me, both eyebrows raised, silently asking me the question. I placed a hand on the Key, or what was left of it, and shook my head. The stone was still quiet.

She patted my shoulder for a moment, her eyes sad. Then she turned to Nick, and they both headed to a room. Their door closed with a quiet *snick*.

I stopped feeling the cold. The night air was dark and empty above me. I walked away from the motel and to the stand of trees to the side. Tall spruces, spaced feet apart here and there, leaving a quiet cushion of needles to walk among.

My mother's last conversation rolled around in my mind. Her words mixed with Parker's. He had told me I used to be a fighter. My mother had asked me who else was fighting the demons. Who remained to stand against them, here on this earth.

There had been others. Good people always fought. I had seen some of them die. Humans, priests, Templars. Who knows how many, across the earth? I didn't know. More than just me.

But I was the one still around. I had been knocked down, but I also kept getting back up. Every time. Not always on my own; sometimes I had needed a hand, when getting up seemed impossible to do on my own. So my friends had been there when I needed them. Danny. Nick. Johnny. Jen. Even Sarah.

Maybe I understood a little about what my mother had said about the group of us. What we could accomplish together. Starting small, and growing larger. We weren't the only group out here, fighting Azazel, vampires, the Dead Zones, but we might be the best chance of turning the tide.

I snorted to myself. Look who was getting a big head.

The branches of the spruces lay between where I stood and the night sky. For a moment I was alone, among the trees, the world quiet around me, the scent of pine faint but unmistakable.

And then I was no longer alone.

Jen stood across from me, her form blue and ethereal. She looked a little like a princess, lost in the woods, waiting for her Prince Charming to come save her.

If I hadn't already snorted, I would have again.

We faced each other.

"Hey," I said.

Hey, she mouthed back.

"Can you hear me?" I said, slowly.

Jen shook her head. Then stopped. Her mouth formed the word *sometimes*.

"Yeah," I said. "Me, too."

I was still learning the rules between us. Maybe our relationship was something the world didn't have a definition for. Something different from anything Plato or Darwin or Einstein could dream of.

"Are you okay?" I asked her.

She nodded, and pretended to yawn. But there was something else there, too. Something she was hiding.

Jen knew I knew it, too, that I understood she was hiding something. And after another moment, she looked away.

The wind cut through the trees, shivering and rattling the branches. The limbs creaked, and the air made a shushing sound through the spruce needles. All of a sudden it felt much colder than it really was. I took a big breath and let it all out.

"We need to talk," I said.

Jen agreed, and then wiped the corner of an eye with the palm of her hand. Ghostly tears shimmered in her blue irises.

Jen was so close, and yet so far away. Her ethereal form shimmered blue and white against the darkness around us, lighting the spruce trees around us so that it felt like the two of us were tucked away in a small grove, in the middle of nowhere. It was intimate, and for the time we were here, it was just us.

It was always just us.

We sat down next to each other, backs against one of the trees. The branches hung heavy above us. I laid a hand on her leg, and it fell through and landed on dry, pinchy needles.

She was so close, yet so far away. I closed my eyes, took a few deep breaths, then let them all out. When I opened them again, Jen was looking at me, waiting. Face worried.

"I'm afraid," I said.

Me, too, Jen said.

"I figured out how to keep my promise." I spoke slowly, making sure to exaggerate each word. I didn't know how much Jen would actually get. "I know what I have to do now. But I think by keeping my promise, there's a chance I'm going to lose you."

Jen tried to smile. The ethereal light really lit up her eyes. They were iridescently wet and blue and beautiful. Her lips moved in the same exaggerated motion as mine. *It's what I had you promise.*

"I think it's more than that," I said. "I think it's who I am. Maybe who I should have always been."

Her smile was real, this time. *I'm glad you finally see it.*

I laughed at that, a low and quiet sound, shaking my head. I had never believed in myself as much as Jen had. I think a lot of what had happened, in the years I was away from Grafton, would never had happened if she had been around. She was the foundation of everything I was, the reason I was here now, and still, I wondered how much I could lean on her, with the Key crumbling by the day.

"You know, I've spent this whole time trying to rescue you, to bring you back," I said. Nervous about where I was taking this. "But … can I ask you something?"

Jen looked puzzled. *Of course.*

I waited to say it, not wanting to say the words. My jaw tightened, my fists clenched, and the question stuck in the back of my throat. Until I forced it out.

"I never asked you if you *wanted* to come back," I said, not looking at her. And with the dam broken, the rest of the words rushed out. "Maybe I didn't know what I was doing, putting you in the Key. And maybe I don't know what I'm doing now, but I remember Danny, and how happy he was when I saw his ghost, and I wonder sometimes, if I'm keeping you from that place, from *him*...."

Jen's face was frustrated, her brows lowered. Like she had only gotten part of what I had said, and was puzzling out the rest. So I closed my eyes and asked the real question. "Jen, all I've been doing is trying to keep you here, *with me*, and I guess I'm asking, should I let you go? Am I holding you back from something greater?"

I was learning more about this world. There were places outside this earth that existed. Hell seemed to be real, if I trusted what Azazel and Raphael and Belial had told me. So it stood to reason there might be a heaven somewhere.

I was just guessing, though. Jen would know more, maybe. She was more on that side of the fence than I.

Perhaps that's why ghosts could never speak. Maybe to keep us from really knowing. Maybe Belle was right, and knowing something like that was a form of cheating. People *should* be good for their own reward. I was beginning to understand a few things, but there was a canyon-sized gulf between the understanding and the knowing.

And there was an even larger gulf between wanting something and needing it. I didn't just want Jen, I needed her. And I was so afraid, asking her if she wanted to go on to whatever place might wait for her, that she would say yes. I shut my eyes and kept them shut. Until the need to know became greater than the fear.

Then I took a hesitant peek, pausing for a moment, like a kid hiding under a blanket, slowly peeling back the blanket to see what waited outside.

Jen had moved in front of me, kneeling so that she straddled my legs. Her face was soft, kind, and as soon as I opened my eyes she reached out and hugged me, her arms around my back, her face nestled on my shoulder.

I could almost feel her.

After a long moment she pulled back. Jen tried to grab the sides of my face with her hands and tried not to look frustrated when she couldn't. Still, her thumbs made little motions at the corners of my eyes, until I wiped them myself. My palms came away damp, and I looked away.

She waited, though, until I turned back and caught her stare. Beautiful blue eyes, shiny, stared back at me. I was reminded of the nights I used to look up at the stars and think of her, knowing that she was doing the same thing, wherever we both were.

You and me, she said. *Forever.*

My breath shuddered as it came out. "Forever," I repeated.

Jen nodded.

"Okay," I said.

I had needed to hear those words. I had *needed* her to say them. One of the things I had realized was how much I had thought only of myself, the past few days. I had been going after my mother not to free her, but to ask for her help. To try to bring Jen back from where I had put her, to try to bring her back to life when I didn't even know if she wanted to be saved. It had all been about me. Leaving my friends. The contract with Raphael. Rescuing Jen. All the way up until now, when I had left my personal crusade to help my friends.

That was the Grimm I wanted to be. I didn't want to be the guy who kept running when things got tough. Or left those he cared about behind because he was scared he couldn't protect them. Who chose doing something because of a fear.

The Grimm I wanted to be was the guy who did the right thing, because that's what his friends needed. I wanted to be the guy who kept doing the right thing. I hadn't always been that guy, and I wanted the good to wash away the wrong.

I thought, that way, I could become better. Even Greater. Doing good, to balance out the wrong I had done. Balancing my scale.

However, it was one thing to try to bring Jen back because it was what I wanted. Because I wanted to balance the wrong. Because *I* needed *her*.

It was a much more powerful thing to do it because it was what she wanted. What Jen needed. Doing something for someone you loved, not for yourself, but wholly and unconditionally for them.

"Good," I said, then said it again. "Good." Feeling a strength radiate outward from my chest, a warmth that fought the chill cover of the night as the heat spread across my arms, my legs, the back of my neck.

Jen placed a ghostly kiss on my forehead, and this time I did feel her lips. At least, a tingle of a sensation upon my skin.

"I'm going to the Conclave tomorrow," I said.

She nodded again.

"I'm going to keep my promise to you," I told her. "I'm tired of these people coming after us, after our friends. I'm going to set them straight."

She smiled, the Jen smile that always made me feel taller. Stronger. A smile that made her feel more *here*, more in this world. Then her lips formed two words. *About time.*

"It's going to be as dangerous a thing as I've ever done," I said. And it was. Between my mother and father, the geas, Dominic and Victor, and who knew how many vampires, it was the lion's den of all lion's dens. Not to mention, I was bringing Raphael and Belle with me. Two people I trusted the least.

"I'm worried, if we use too much of your power, you will disappear," I said.

Jen shrugged. *Let me worry about that.*

"How much is too much?" I asked. It was all a guessing game with ethereal energy. "I know you pull from it. I want you to be careful, too."

They are our friends, Jen said. *We'll protect them. Whatever it takes, it takes.*

I sighed. She was hardheaded. And so was I. Still, I would have to trust her. At least in this. "Promise me you'll be careful."

Jen arched an eyebrow at me. I couldn't look at her, still. She waited until I finally did.

Gus, she said, mouthing the words slowly, her face serious, *I am stronger than you know.*

"I hear you," I said. "But it's hard to stop it. The worry."

Worry is good, she said. *Worry means you care. Just don't let it overwhelm you. Or control you.*

I trust you. So trust me back.

"Okay," I finally said. *Maybe ...* "Okay."

She winked.

And then a sound broke our peace, working its way through the trees. The familiar rumble of the Camaro, chugging as it pulled into the parking lot.

Raphael had arrived.

"I've got to go," I said.

Jen leaned forward, and we kissed. As much as a guy and a ghost could. Both of us were disappointed when we pulled away from each other. Her eyes were misty. So were mine.

I went to say, *Be careful* again, but caught the look on her face right when I opened my mouth. So I promptly shut it.

Her smile was real. She understood.

"You and me," I said, aloud. Our stares locked into each other.

Until she winked at me. *Forever,* she said. Then faded away. With her left the light, and I was left with the quiet darkness of the woods, hidden shadows, and the creaks and cracks of limbs shifting above me.

"Whatever it takes," I promised myself out loud, the words a thin barrier against the cold night.

CHAPTER FORTY-EIGHT

I walked out of the woods. The Camaro was parked close to the Rubicon, and Raphael and Belle were getting out of the car. She stalked away, then realized she didn't know where she was going, and then stood there, undecided about where to go or what to do about it. Raphael had one hand on the door of the Camaro, one on the hood, and stood there, watching, until she turned back.

Interesting.

Raphael looked over as I neared. He frowned a bit, noticing where I had come from. "Grimm! You know there's a motel right here, if you're looking for a place to sleep."

"Funny," I said.

"So, what are you doing in the woods?" Raphael asked.

"I'd say it's none of your business, but …" I let the words hang.

"Ah." Raphael grinned. He seemed happy about something. "Secret Grimm stuff."

"Whatever." I held out my hand, and waited until he handed me the keys. It was nice to have the Camaro back, and it seemed none the worse for wear when I looked it over.

Raphael stood to the side, amused, while I checked out the car. "So, what's the plan?"

"I'm planning on killing a lot of vampires," I said.

"That's the plan?" Raphael asked, arching an eyebrow.

"That's the part of it you should know," I said. There wasn't much to plan for, actually. And I wanted to keep what plans I had to myself, for as long as possible. The longer people knew what I was doing, the more it gave them a chance to wreck it. Especially these two. "You can get me there, right?"

I meant the Conclave, and Raphael knew it. "Whatever you need, boss."

Whatever had happened between Raphael and Belial had put him in a playful mood. And I needed some sleep. "Good," I said, handing him the card to their room. "See you all then."

"I am not sleeping with him," Belle said, suddenly. And frowned as soon as she had said the words, then corrected herself. "Not in the same room."

"That's up to you," I said. "You have better digs down below?"

Belle paused, looking between the two of us. She looked angry. Raphael laughed and walked to his room, pausing at the door and turning back to us. "We getting breakfast in the morning? A little group get-together?"

I shook my head. I wanted to keep Raphael and Nick separate, for as long as I could. Nick could handle it, but Raphael would likely needle him the whole day, and I wanted everyone sharp for tomorrow night. "Get up and get what you want, whatever. Just get ready for a fight."

"Fine by me," Raphael said. "You got my number, you need anything."

Then he winked at Belle, backed into the room, and slowly shut the door.

Weird. I started toward my own room.

"That man is trouble," Belle said, quietly.

I stopped. "I don't want to hear it."

"You trust him?" she asked.

"I just don't care," I said. I didn't want to listen to her complaints. She would have been perfectly happy if I had killed Dominic before freeing my mother. She had tried to steer events that way so that I would die, my parents, too, with the blowback of the geas. I didn't trust Raphael, but I trusted her even less. "I expect him to keep his word. And I expect you to *enforce the agreement*. It's what you're here for, right?"

"You don't understand," she said. "There is nothing like him down there. He is learning that. He is learning he is unique, among the creatures of hell."

"You are so different, so … more." My mother had hinted at the same thing, with me. That I was different than anything she had known. That I was more than she could have hoped.

Maybe Raphael and I were opposite sides of the same coin. Maybe we were like Cain and Abel, and the things we did now would have repercussions throughout time, after we both were dead and gone. Though, whatever we were, it was going to have to wait one more day.

"He'll have his chance," I said. "He knows it. I know it."

"If you wait too long, he will destroy you," she said. "He will destroy us all."

I wanted to keep walking, but there was something in her voice. A conviction. Something I recognized. A kernel of truth, believed, whether it was real or fiction. Whatever was going on between the two of them, it had nothing to do with sleeping together. She had seen or witnessed or been a part of something with Raphael that had her scared.

And she worked for the big man in hell. What could have her scared more than that? More than what Azazel had already done?

I didn't know, and I didn't want to. There was nothing I could do about it now. I wasn't going to try to sneak into Raphael's room and kill him. I wasn't an assassin. I was more of a face-to-face guy.

Besides, I needed him tomorrow. And Raphael and I had signed a contract. A contract that — yet again — Belle was trying to have me break. For a person who had been so worried about Azazel, and what she had said about words mattering, that seemed odd.

"I'm not buying it," I said. "I don't know why you keep trying, but I'm telling you this. I'm not going to be the person here whose word doesn't matter."

She shook her head, her lips pressed thinly together. "I would you had not signed that thing. If we had known —"

"Known what?" I interrupted. "You want to clue me in to whatever it is you and Lucifer are worried about?"

"I told you," she said, spitting the words. "He is *different*. He is *more* than what he should be. There is nothing like him in hell, and he is starting to realize that."

Different. More. Attributes Raphael and I appeared to have in common.

For thousands of years angels had been trapped by the geas. For thousands of years evil had had its influence unchecked across the earth. And for those thousands of years, my mother believed the good side had been gathering its strength, for a counterstroke. That she believed I was the swing of that sword.

If I was that sword, if I was the swing of the side of good, was Raphael evil's parry? Was he that side's answer to me? Or was he something much worse?

The battle tomorrow would be huge. If I made it out tomorrow at all, I would be exhausted. It would be the perfect time for Raphael to be the killing stroke, for evil to end everything that good had been building, for thousands of years. Since the first angel had been put under the geas.

It was a distraction to think about. And events were in motion. My course was set. I was going to the Conclave. To free my parents, but also to let people know what would happen to them if they fucked with my friends.

Right now that was what I had to focus on.

"Whatever Raphael is doing, or whatever he is, that seems like it's more in your court than mine," I said.

"Like Grafton?" she asked. "You leave that man unchecked now and run around for another decade. Then see what you come back to. He's *learning* from you. I promise, it'll be much worse than some drug vampires get hooked on."

My hand clenched. Belle was wrong. I was already living my worst-case scenario. Grafton had led to New Orleans. Had led to me losing Jen. Had led to this moment, right here. With Belle laying the responsibility for Raphael on my shoulders.

"Why is this my problem?" I said, quietly. "Because I killed him? Or because he's somehow still alive?"

She was quiet a moment, as if unsure of how much to say. Then her head tilted down, then up. As if she had made her decision. "Neither. I tell you it is your problem, because you might be the only person who *can* stop him."

Another burden put on my shoulders, for something I had to take care of, because I was the only person who could. This time a demon, hinting at some unknown power I was supposed to have. It was laughable, and frustrating. My hand opened and closed into a fist, over and over, as it underwent uncontrollable spasms.

Grafton, the Dead Zones, Jen, those problems were all mine, and those were enough for anyone to carry. I didn't know what Belle's ultimate game was, but I wasn't going to play it. "I signed a contract. Raphael is safe, until I kill Azazel."

"Do you think *he* is going to play by the same rules?" she said.

I wasn't sure. But I was surprised to find that part of it didn't matter to me. I wasn't any more responsible for Raphael's actions than I was for some gas station attendant, four states away. It wasn't up to me to hold everyone accountable for what they did in life. It was just up to me to hold them accountable in death.

I was staying the course. There was a power in me, a power that only came out when I walked the walk. To become the person I wanted to be, the person I had promised Jen I would be, I needed to walk that path to its final destination.

I wasn't taking detours, or shortcuts, and throwing all of that away because Belle was worried about something Raphael had going on. I needed to do the things to protect my friends because no one else would. Nothing now would keep me from that.

No matter what Belle was worried about. I was tired of this game. Tired of her lies. Tired of her attitude, and definitely tired of her trying to force me to take care of whatever problem she dreamed she had.

The curtain in Raphael's room shifted a little. Like the heater in the room had kicked on, or as if he had been holding it open, slightly, and then let it fall. The whole game they had going on between them bothered me, and Belle trying to play me into it was maddening. Tomorrow night was going to be dangerous enough, without this.

I turned to Belle, struggling to keep my hand from clenching again. "I don't care what rules he's playing by," I said. "I only care about what I say. What I do."

"Then whatever happens from here," she said, her lips thin, "it'll be on your head."

I snapped. Whether it was her tone, or the dismissive look on her face, it didn't matter. It only mattered that it tipped me over. I was exhausted, sad after speaking with Jen, and frustrated before. Now I was boiling angry.

"Whatever the hell that means," I spat. I mocked her then, getting more and more angry as I repeated her words. "It'll be on my *head*. On *my* head. *On my head!*"

I shouted the words at the end. Belle stepped back a bit. I took a deep breath and let it out. I stepped close and leaned into her space, making sure she saw how serious I was. Making sure she heard every word.

"You be careful what you put on me," I said. "Because if you want me to take care of it, I will. And you may not like how I go about it."

Her gaze flickered to the room Raphael was in and back. She looked afraid, for the moment, to say anything. Like a rabbit, caught between two wolves. I held her stare, though, until Belle agreed. Whatever her problem with Raphael was, it could wait. I couldn't even be sure she was being honest.

Though her fear seemed real enough.

After Belle signaled she understood me, I pulled back. Just a little. She held up a finger, like a student, tentatively wanting to ask a question. The finger shook, a little.

"I want to tell you something," she said.

Maybe it was the shakiness of that one digit that held me there.

"If you let this go now," she said, "later will be too late. No one else will be able to oppose him."

That seemed a bit thick. I thought of the creature, deep in the lake at New Orleans. There must be more monsters like that in hell, creatures that had been around since our universe began as a primordial soup. Surely Raphael wasn't that big a problem.

I wondered what he could be. If I was one side of the pendulum, if I was the good side's response to an evil that was thousands of years in the making, what could Raphael possibly be? I mean, he had just shown up again. Could evil's response be that quick, to balance out something that good had taken thousands of years to craft?

Belle was blowing smoke. And distracting me from what was really important. I took a few breaths, before I spoke. Until the words sounded civil.

"Seems to me the best thing for you would be to make sure I survive tomorrow," I said. "You know, enforce the agreement."

Her brows lowered in the middle, as if *she* was the one frustrated. Her eyes were even a little wet, as if she was holding back some emotion. She went to say something. I cocked my head. I set my jaw. Then I waited.

She kept her mouth shut. A compressor kicked on outside, to one of the heat pumps of the motel. The sound rattled and hummed around us. Then Belle finally nodded.

I echoed the motion, and left her there, going to my room. I slammed the door harder than I needed to, and stared at the same single bed, the same dark dresser with the mirror above it that had been in every other motel I'd stayed at. The room was dark, the air compressor was still loud outside, and whatever room it was trying to heat wasn't this one.

It had been cold outside. It was still cold in the room. I sat on the bed and looked at myself in the mirror. All I seemed to be able to see were my eyes, liquid and cold and focused in the darkness around me.

The next day was going to be hard enough, even with a normal amount of worry about what Raphael might do. Now some unknown fear of Belle's had entered the equation. I wondered if Raphael was playing me, if he was just waiting for the moment to get near his father so he could kill him, and rid the world of me and the last of the angels.

I didn't know. I couldn't know. But I did think that Raphael wanted me, *needed* me to take care of Azazel for him. It was why we both were here now. Why we had signed the contract. Still, after Belle's speech a minute ago, I was worried now that Raphael had learned he might be able to kill Azazel himself.

I still was happy, though. I had stuck to my word, talking to Belle. That felt important. There was a Grimm, not too long ago, that would have lost sight of the bigger picture for this smaller one. He would have lost himself in the worry and the fear, and not done the thing he said he was going to do.

Words were important. Words mattered. I would walk what I talked.

I *was* changing. Into something greater? I didn't know. But I understood, a little, what my mother was trying to get across to me. I was becoming something more. I didn't know who that final person would be. But the path was before me.

Raphael was changing, too. I didn't know what had happened after I killed him, back in Grafton. How he had come back. His explanation had made a kind of sense, but that didn't tell me what he was becoming. Only that the vampire part of him was gone.

Belle was worried about Raphael, though. She had seen something that scared her. So he was changing, and I was changing. I guessed, when the time came, I would put what I was changing into up against what he was becoming, and we'd settle it, once and for all.

But that day was going to be in the future. For now, there was tomorrow. And the Conclave. My parents deserved to be free. The world needed more angels around. There seemed to be more demons crawling out of the woodwork.

And people needed to know what happened when they came after me. I couldn't be around them, all the time. I had to do something that instilled a great enough fear in vampires and monsters and demons that they all would think twice before coming after us again. I needed to make sure they all understood that the cost would not be worth the effort.

Tomorrow I would begin that. I would show them all, so there would be nothing left uncertain of what would happen. There would be no more hit men sent after us in airport terminals. A lot of times vengeance was a frigid thing, planned years after the offending action. A cold blade of retribution.

But vengeance could also be searing, furious, angry. Immediate and unrelenting. Molten metal, carving out its repayment in hot blood.

I was planning on being the latter.

So I sat on the edge of the bed, holding the Key in one hand, staring at myself in the mirror. My face was shadowed in the dark room, and the Key was cold, cradled in my palm. My eyes, though, my eyes shimmered with fury.

I spoke the promise aloud. "I will protect my friends tomorrow. I will free my parents. I will be strong enough to fight the geas. I will make them all pay, all of them, for what they've done."

I squeezed the Key, a little. "I will keep Jen safe, through it all."

It was a long night. And a sleepless one. I made those promises, over and over, like a mantra, until it was early morning. The darkness behind the curtains lightened into a gray. Sunrise wasn't far off. Still, I kept saying the words, over and over, binding myself to the path I wanted to follow. If I could've written the words across the walls, I would have, creating a room, a prison, a contract to myself. Something unbreakable.

The Key was quiet in my hand, the bond silent between Jen and me. Still, I hoped she heard me, that she knew she was part of this. That I would be strong enough for my friends, my parents, and her. I kept saying them, over and over, as I leaned back on the softness of the mattress, letting it swallow me. Saying the words, until I finally fell asleep.

My words mattered.

My actions mattered.

And, as my enemies would find soon enough, I mattered.

CHAPTER FORTY-NINE

I woke suddenly, to the same grayish color from the windows I had fallen asleep to. For a moment I thought I had only been asleep a few minutes. I was in the same position, feet on the floor, knees bent, lying flat on the bed, head tilted to one side.

A chill pool of drool against my cheek told me I had been out much longer. I had gone deep. My brain was sluggish, in a deep fog, like I had come out of a vivid dream. I remembered a bight whiteness, like I was in the middle of a cloud, with the sun behind it, casting a dark shadow behind me.

Jen was there. She was climbing up a white fluffy set of stairs, up into the sun. The whole time she was waving at me. I wasn't sure if she was waving me to come on, or waving me away. Was it a warning? I thought I could hear her voice, but whatever she was saying, the words ran together, indistinct.

I kept shouting at her, asking her what she was doing, what was going on, where she was going. Each time I opened my mouth, little pieces of cloud got in my mouth and muffled my words. She motioned to her ear, like she couldn't hear me, and kept climbing higher and higher, no matter how loud I tried to yell.

Then a shadowed darkness rose with her, following her up the stairs, slowly coating each step in an inky blackness.

And that, of course, was when I jerked awake. Heart racing. Chest pounding.

Dreams. I hadn't had one in a while. Not like this one. And I didn't like the feel of it. It was like my subconscious was trying to tell me something.

I groaned and pulled myself off the bed, leaving a Grimm-shaped indentation on the thick quilt. My knees ached from being locked in the same position for who knows how long. Little pops and clicks came from them as I stood. I wiped off my cheek with the back of my shirt.

Then I realized what had woken me. Shouts from outside the room. I staggered over to the door, still a bit groggy, and threw it open.

Raphael. Which I had figured. And oddly enough, Gabrielle. They stood a step away from each other. Raphael wearing his cocky grin, and Gabrielle furious. Though she was shorter, she was chest to chest with him, right in his face.

"I tell you one last time," Gabrielle said. Her words curt and cold. "Stay away from him."

Johnny stood beside the front fender of the Jeep, a little behind Gabrielle. He kept reaching out to her and pulling his arm back, in little motions. As if he had tried to pull her away once, and was afraid to try again.

"What's the harm?" Raphael said. "Aren't you curious?"

Gabrielle just stood there, staring back at him. As if she had said her piece. She held both of her arms straight by her sides, as if she was holding herself back. Her right hand was balled in a fist, and trembled.

Nick and Sarah were on the far side of the Jeep, standing by the front fender. Nick had a white plastic bag in his hand, like they had come back from somewhere and then been caught in this sudden storm between Raphael and Gabrielle.

"Hey," I interrupted, from the door.

"Grimm!" Raphael's smile grew broader. "Can you tell Gabs here that I'm on your side?"

I was tired. The sleep hadn't refreshed me at all. And the dream had me worried; my heart still beat fast in my chest. The back part of my brain had put something together that the front part of my brain hadn't registered yet. I needed to figure that out. I didn't need any of this now. And I definitely didn't need it tonight.

I summoned the sword, holding it down and away from me. It crackled into appearance, the translucent blade hard to see in the early-evening light, transparent like a tinted windshield, except for slight traces of electric blue running across its surface.

I raised both of my eyebrows at Raphael. "Do I have to intervene here?"

His smile grew thinner. His eyes focused on the sword. "Not at all," Raphael said, his voice carrying an edge.

Gabrielle looked at me as if angry that I had interrupted them. That I had stopped some important business between her and Raphael. I gave her the same stare I had given him. People needed to be focused. We all needed to cool down a bit.

Even me. My nerves writhed under the surface of my skin. My muscles wanted to twitch, to jump, to do anything. It was everything I could do to hold the sword steady at the moment. The blade had a heft to it, but not a weight. Like I only felt how heavy it was when I was swinging it. When I held it still, the sword felt light as air.

And I wanted to swing it. I fought to remain still. I looked around at my friends, and my enemies. Nick and Sarah, quiet off to the side. Johnny, worried. Gabrielle, angry. Raphael, mocking. Belle, composed. Giving nothing away.

This was the group I was taking into battle. Some of my friends hurt, some of them healing. My enemies apparently poking and prodding fresh wounds. They were fractured, at best. I was counting on all of them, and we couldn't even get along just enough for us to get to the Conclave.

Much less come out of there alive. It seemed like the more I tried to hold true to myself and the person I wanted to be, the more distractions popped up. Jen, with the dream. The crumbling Key. Belle, with her grand speech on Raphael. Raphael, an enemy I should never trust. And now Gabrielle, picking a fight with Raphael.

A deep fear flushed over me. My breath caught, and my heart felt like it was going to pound itself out of my chest. I was worried. Worried that I wasn't going to be enough. Worried that tonight some of my friends would die. Maybe my parents would die. Jen. Even me. I closed my eyes, tight, and clutched the sword so hard the hilt cut into my fingers.

Breathe ... The word came from the bond, softly, yet at the same time hard and loud. Like Jen was standing next to me, speaking into my ear.

"Jen?" I whispered. I opened my eyes again. They felt wet. The woods were empty behind Nick and Sarah, just spruce branches waving in a night breeze. After the dream, I wanted to see Jen again. I hoped the past night wouldn't be the last time I would ever see her.

Raphael's head was cocked, like he was studying me. I took a breath, then another, and felt Jen along the bond, supporting me. Reminding me to breathe, over and over, with a whisper of comfort that was more sensed than heard.

Nick was looking at me, face carefully composed. Almost relaxed. The look had worry behind it. He tilted his head, then turned back to Raphael. Measuring. Patient. It seemed like of all the people I had been worried about around Raphael, he was doing the best he could, by me.

Johnny had finally pulled Gabrielle back a bit. Her face was blank, as if she had seen something in me and didn't know what it was. I wasn't sure if she was confused or worried, or maybe afraid.

I swallowed, my throat working hard to push the knot of worry down. Then I let the sword disappear. It went without a sound, leaving a faint scent of ozone behind it.

"You guys okay?" I asked Gabrielle and Johnny.

Gabrielle stood there, furious. It was Johnny that motioned things were okay.

"Grimm, all I did was ask a question," Raphael began to say.

I held up my hand. For a wonder he stopped.

"Belle tells me you're going to betray me," I said.

"That's not what I said," Belle said.

I stared at her. "You need to stay quiet, right now."

I was still on the edge of something. And it showed in my face. Even though her face was frustrated, she shut up.

I turned back to Raphael. "So, you betraying me or not?"

His eyes were cold. So was his smile. "I told you what I was going to do," he said. "You can believe what you want."

For a moment he seemed larger. Like the rest of the world had disappeared, and there was just the two of us, facing each other across a large distance, in a gray world. There were only shadows, his and mine, and his seemed so much larger. I was sure it was my imagination, but still …

Whatever he was becoming, he and I had agreed, we would deal with it then. After all this. "Good enough," I said.

"You are trusting him?" Gabrielle said.

"I'm doing what I have to," I said. "Are you going to be a problem?"

"Grimm," Johnny said, shaking his head.

"*He* is going to be the problem," Gabrielle said.

"And I'm telling you that he's *my* problem. You're going to have to trust that I can handle him," I said. The words came out fast, and loud, so I tried to lower my voice. "I need to know if I can count on you tonight."

Her jaw flexed. Johnny spoke softly into her ear. I caught the word *Wolverines*. His arm snaked around her middle, and he pulled her back into him, and when he was done speaking, Gabrielle appeared to listen. She didn't look the least bit happy, though.

"We good, Grimm?" Raphael asked.

I didn't know. I glanced between Raphael and Belle. Her eyes narrowed, and her chin jutted out. Raphael's lips curved in a sardonic grin, one eye lightly arched. As if he was wondering if we were going to go at it, right here.

He looked ready for it.

"We're good," I said. Trying to do what Jen had told me. Trying to find a moment to breathe. To relax. To be ready for tonight. "Why don't you two go find something to do for a bit?"

Raphael's smile grew larger. "Sure thing, man." He raised his eyebrows at Belle. "Coming?"

She looked at me. Then back to Raphael, her shoulders lowered. The two of them walked toward the highway. Across the street was a gas station, with a fast-food place as a part of it. Something with a bucket and a chicken. They headed that way.

"All righty, then," I said, looking at the sky. It was early evening, and I wanted to show up at the Conclave after true night fell. We had a little time. "You guys do what you have to do. We'll leave in an hour or so."

"I'm guessing we have no real plan," Nick said.

"We do," I said. "It's the usual."

"The Grimm special?" Nick grinned. Maybe he remembered the same thing I did, back in Grafton. "You sure?"

"Sure enough," I said. I wasn't one for subterfuge, or plots upon plots. I preferred doing things straight up. Dominic and Victor would find that out about me. And hopefully more.

"Good," he said. Nick liked simple. The rest of my friends looked worried. Or maybe anxious. I assumed the Conclave would be a massive thing, and though we had fought an army of vampires in Grafton, this time we didn't have the benefits of C-4, or a water tower, or a priest, or anything else. Just us.

I wanted to reassure them, but I also wanted a moment alone. The dream still stuck with me. *I* was still anxious, worried, stressed. And for me to calm down, I needed that moment. I hoped to have it with Jen.

"I'll be back," I said. I walked past them, heading into the woods. It took a minute, but I found the grove I had seen Jen in the night before, and sat with my back against the same tree. Waiting.

Jen wasn't here. Or at least, not here as a ghost. The bond reached out to me, though. The feeling of it was hard to describe, but it was like the two of us were holding hands, with our grip centered in my chest.

I waited in the quiet, trying to relax, trying to breathe like they tell you in all the meditation commercials. The ones that tell you to count your breaths going in, and out. It seemed to me the only thing I did was count faster, but over a period of time my breaths became deeper, longer, slower.

The grove was dark, hidden away from lights surrounding the motel, the tall poles lining the street. Spruce branches hung low over me, almost forming a cup around me, holding a tiny piece of the world isolated from everything. Only illumination from above found its way down to my circle, from a moon rising above the world, and even that light was shadowed and flickered as tree limbs shifted above me.

I let out a deep sigh. The bond tightened and grew hard in my chest, around my chest, like the two of us were holding on to each other as tight as we could.

"I wish you were here," I said aloud. She would be, if it was up to her.

Another squeeze of the invisible hand in my chest, the feeling coming from the bond. An increase and decrease in the tightness of it. Like she had hugged me, one hard time.

"It's okay," I said. "I understand." Even though I didn't.

It would have to be enough, for me, this time I had now with Jen, whatever we had together. These last few minutes, before I went to the Conclave and attempted the impossible. Before, maybe, the Key broke and I lost Jen forever.

"You know I'm going to do this thing," I said. "These people are going to learn what happens if they come after our friends. Our family."

The hug and release from the bond again.

My hand touched the Key. Parts of it flaked off, like dry crumbs off stale bread.

"I'm going to save my parents," I said. "And we're going to figure this out. The Key. You. Bringing you back."

A third squeeze.

"You know I promised you I'd protect our friends," I said. "And I will."

No squeeze this time. As if Jen knew where I was going.

"But long before that, I promised to protect you. And now I find out I can't. The Key is breaking, you leave and I don't know where you go, and when you're here, I *know* you're using your power. I *know* you're trying to help me," I said. "So I need you to promise me you'll be careful. You'll keep yourself safe. *Alive*. There's going to be so much happening, I need you to be careful for me. Please."

I waited, and waited, until the faintest squeeze came from along the bond. Something so light I might have imagined it.

It was what I expected. Jen would do anything to protect those she loved. I would, too. And something in that thought reminded me of my dream, of her ascending those stairs into the bright sun. The shadow climbing each step just a bit faster, after Jen. Enveloping everything.

The time we had with each other was always fleeting. With Jen, it had come and gone before I realized it had left for good.

"You know, the whole time I was running from Azazel, the only thing that kept me going with thinking of you," I said. "There were a lot of times I wanted to come back. To you. But I was afraid that what I brought with me would hurt you."

A long breath. "So I never did. Until you called."

The bond hugged me then, slow, like we were on the couch together and I was lying back in her arms. "And then you called. And I came back. And what I brought with me *did* hurt you.

"So it's all my fault," I said. "It's my fault you're here. I brought Azazel. I brought us to New Orleans. I'm the reason you're dead…. And you know what, all I can think of is how unfair it is, that I only got to spend a couple of days with you."

It was a selfish thought. It was okay to admit it. I did want to be the person who stood up for his friends, who did everything he could for those he cared about, but there was a part of me, maybe the same part that was in everyone, that only thought about how the world affected himself.

And if Jen were here, she'd probably tell me I was wrong to take all of this on myself. She would tell me Azazel was already in Grafton, working Raphael, and that I had been just a piece of that puzzle. Not the whole thing. She would tell me to stop holding all this in, to stop putting everything on myself, and share some of the blame. To lean on my friends, to count on them, to know I didn't have to be everything.

But she wasn't here. So part of me felt about these things the way I always thought about them. Not believing I was enough. Wanting to be stronger, to stop these things from happening to my friends. To protect them. Wondering how I could fix it all.

"Hey." The word was spoken lightly, from across the grove. For a moment I thought Jen was here, that it was her staring at me from the edge of the copse. But instead it was Sarah. She looked enough like her sister that for a moment I did mistake her for Jen. And I was sure that showed in my face.

Sarah noticed. She stepped in, carrying the white plastic bag. Nick followed her. She waved a little wave at me, and smiled a sad little smile. "We brought you something to eat."

I took the bag from her and opened it. Cinnamon pastries, covered in icing and wrapped in cheap plastic. I swallowed, hard, remembering the trip to New Orleans and all the little conversations I had had with Jen about these things. How they were too sweet for her, and just right for me. A tear, warm against my skin, left the corner of my eye and rolled down the side of my nose, until I wiped it away.

"Thanks," I said.

They both sat opposite me. "We wanted to talk with you," Sarah said.

"I'm okay," I said.

"You're as okay as you'll let yourself be," Sarah said. Nick tried a smile, as if he knew where I was, and understood.

"I'll be okay," I said, again.

"Hey, man," Nick said. "We figure we might know a little of what's going on. What you're going to do. And maybe what it might cost you."

"Yeah?" I said.

"So we wanted to come to you," he said. "And tell you it's okay if we run. We're all okay with it. Us." Nick nodded at Sarah. "Johnny and Gabrielle, too. It's something we want to do. Maybe give you some more time, you know, to figure things out."

He meant figure out how to save Jen before the Key broke.

"They'll keep coming after us," I said. Azazel. Victor. Dominic. And who knew who else now? The world was changing too fast to keep up.

"We know," Sarah said. Her voice, always so light, seemed ethereal in the grove. Like an angel's. "We'll figure it out."

I snorted, softly. That's something I always said. But I hadn't done such a great job at it. The figuring-out part. My parents. Victor and Dominic. Azazel, the demons, and the Dead Zones. Raphael and Belle.

I had kept acting, and kept saying that I would figure the rest out. That somehow I would be enough. Yet here they were, all my friends, in danger because of all the above, and because of me. I was in the middle of a big messy pile of trash, and the only way out was picking up one piece of trash at a time, until the mess was all cleaned up.

I pulled out a bun from the bag. The plastic around the pastry crinkled under my touch, and the crinkling got louder as I unwrapped it and took a bite of sticky bread. The cinnamon was strong, the icing sweet, and the memory of Jen and me eating one together, well, it was just good.

"Thanks," I finally said.

"So you'll do it?" Sarah said, her voice hopeful.

I shook my head. I had run for a long time, before coming back to my friends. Running was just putting things off. I knew firsthand what that resulted in. Problems just built up, if you ignored them. They built up until they became something monstrous, and killed the people you loved.

I had made a promise, long ago. I had been a different person then. A person I was trying to come back to. A fighter, Parker would have said. A defender, Jen might have told me. If I left now, even if my friends wanted me to, I would give all that up and just be a runner. Maybe for the rest of my life.

Nick grinned. One of his hands lay on top of Sarah's on her thigh. They seemed more comfortable together now. "We still wanted you to know."

He wanted me to know that my friends put me and Jen first. Before their own safety. Before anything else. They cared for me that much. Not just me, but Jen. Us.

I didn't wipe the tears this time. I just let them trickle down, one after the next, and I had to turn away from Nick and Sarah.

"Thanks," I said. My voice hoarse.

"It's all good, man," Nick said. "You know it's likely to be a shit show tonight."

"It will," I said. There wasn't anything else, though, but to do it. To make those who hurt my friends pay. To make them fear. To make sure nothing like this ever happened again.

"We'll get through it," he said. "You know we've got you."

"I'm counting on it," I said. And I was. I had set a tall task for myself. But I had done so knowing I had great friends. Tonight was something we were going to do together.

I took another bite of the pastry, letting memories of Jen and me wash over me. She and I as teenagers, up on the water tower in Grafton, looking down at the city in the night, the people walking here and there, the tiny glow of headlamps from a car as it pulled out of the town. An image of her in the hospital bed in the factory, when I first had found her again. And then one of her and me, back to back in the cemetery in New Orleans, getting ready to go face Azazel for the last time.

At first, lost in the memories, I didn't notice the feeling. The pull. The call. It was subtle, and only grew as I ignored it. But it grew nonetheless.

Come, come. Come, come...

Dominic, in some control of himself, using the geas to try to pull me to him. So he knew I was here. Which meant, likely enough, that Victor did as well. The geas would get stronger, and my ability to resist it would weaken. The sooner we got going, the better.

Part of me was relieved. Nick and Sarah's offer was more tempting than they knew. It was easy to run, to feel like we were safe, hiding from the world and all the evil it could bring to bear. It was easy, so easy to live in fear.

It was a lot harder to be brave against overwhelming odds. Especially when, by running away, I could put off that moment. I had done that for years. And I had shaken that person off, at least for the most part. Some part of him always remained, and he came back from time to time, checking to see if my resolve to become a better person had weakened.

I had felt that old me a moment earlier, pushing me to run, to accept Nick and Sarah's offer. It was that relief I felt when the geas began working me. The relief that I was doing the right thing, ignoring the old me. The guy who always ran.

Tonight would come down to a fight, whether I ran, or stayed. The geas would make sure of that. Make sure that there was always going to be a battle. Hundreds or thousands of vampires. Heads of the families, the strongest of the undead. My parents, assassins without peer. Raphael and Belle, maybe on my side tonight, maybe not.

With all that waiting for us, calling me with the geas was something I had hoped would happen. It would make me getting into the Conclave much easier. It would set the stage for my friends. I just had to be able to overturn the curse when the time came.

It was light enough of a call that I could resist it now. Much easier than back in Grafton. I wasn't sure if that was because of something Dominic was doing, or wasn't able to do, or because I was much stronger now than I had been then.

Nick and Sarah stayed silent. Nick had his head back against the tree, eyes closed. Hand in Sarah's. Enjoying the quiet evening. Sarah's head was tilted, as if she was studying me.

"It's time," I said.

Sarah understood, though her expression was still a little sad. Nick opened his eyes. His face was grim, but ready. He knew as well.

"Thanks again," I said. They were good friends. The best.

"It's what we are, right?" Nick said.

"Yeah," I said. "What we should always have been."

The two of them got up and got ready to leave the grove. Nick patted my shoulder, something awkward between us, yet still familiar. Sarah gave me a quick hug. She didn't smell like Jen, not like honeysuckle and rain, but something earthier. Like a forest, after a storm, maybe.

Then they were gone. I stood there, feeling the call in my chest, the low pounding of the geas in the same rhythm as my heart. It was peaceful here. Quiet. It wouldn't be that way later tonight.

I sighed and stepped to the edge of the grove. The spruce branches had carved out a tiny kingdom here, something isolated from the world. It was as good a place as any to have seen Jen again. Even if it might have been for the last time.

The bond pulsed, something quick and hard. Like a playful punch.

A corner of my lip turned up. Jen was right. I beat up myself enough. It was time to take my anger and frustrations and fears out on others.

I couldn't stop worrying about Jen, but I could also hope. I was as stubborn a bastard as ever lived. And I had set my mind to saving Jen. I had set it to protecting my friends. To freeing my parents from the geas. I had promised myself all of that. And whatever the cost, I would make sure it wouldn't cost me Jen.

I would see to that. Or I would die trying.

"You be careful," I said one last time. Knowing Jen would press her limits, like I pressed mine. That she would put herself between us and all the evil out there tonight, just like me.

With us, that was always going to be the question. Which of us stood last, at the end. Protecting the other. It was what I feared the most. If I was strong enough, I could protect her, and keep Jen from burning too much of herself up. I *had* to be strong enough.

If I wasn't, if the geas and my parents and Victor and Dominic and Raphael and all the other undead tonight overwhelmed me, if Jen put herself between all of them and us, she would burn herself away, keeping me as safe as she could, until she was gone.

That was going to be my toughest job tonight. Keeping my friends alive. Freeing my parents. Timing it all just right so that Dominic would be killed, and fulfilling that part of the contract. And doing all of that while keeping Jen from using herself up, to protect me.

The bond passed along a last hug. As if Jen knew what I was thinking. And that was how I left the peaceful grove, the moonlit branches of spruce, the tiny circle of peace tucked inside a world full of demons and monsters and Dead Zones, and headed into the darkening night.

CHAPTER FIFTY

The beating of the geas grew a little louder, and it began to shake along my nerves. Instead of the sharp bass note pounding in my body, echoing the rhythm of my heart, it felt something more like a snare drum. Each call rattled inside me. Like the person on the other end of it wasn't fully in control, didn't have a hard grasp on the curse.

I pushed that thought away, along with the weird feel of the geas. No sense in worrying about things I couldn't control. Or, hopefully, things that couldn't control me.

I let out a breath and pulled the Camaro out on the highway. My foot jerked on the pedal, and the car leaped onto the road with a short squeal of the rear tires. Raphael sat in the passenger seat, Belle in the back. The three of us lurched back and forth as the Camaro bounced from the edge of the motel lot onto the street.

Raphael's eyebrow crept upward. "Feeling okay, Grimm?"

"Fine," I muttered, and made a quick correction with the wheel until the car lined up on the road. Heading toward the interstate. "Where to?"

He grinned and thumbed the direction behind us. "That way."

I cursed under my breath. He could have told me before I turned towards the interstate. I swung a U-turn at the next light and headed south. Lucky there wasn't a lot of traffic, I kept overcorrecting and the

Camaro swerved a few times across the dotted yellow lines in the middle of the lanes. Fucking geas.

The others followed in the Jeep. Nick drove, and the Rubicon hung a bit back, still close enough though that its headlights flashed across my rearview mirror. I tilted it down some. My phone in my pocked buzzed once, twice, and I ignored it, focusing on holding the wheel steady.

"How far?" I asked.

"You think I drive this a lot?" Raphael snorted. "An hour? Give or take?"

The Camaro felt a little jumpy in my hands. The car bucked and twitched at the slightest press of the gas pedal, and was more squirrely in the turns. At least, it felt that way. I wanted the Camaro to be mad at me, for letting Raphael drive it. I didn't want all these tiny corrections on the wheel, the quick, hard brakes, and the jerking takeoffs to be the geas.

I didn't want to be affected by the curse. Not this far away. I wanted to *know* I could beat it. Especially as erratic as it felt. And right now I was worried.

Finally Raphael looked over at me from the passenger seat, one eyebrow arched, as if to ask what was up.

I didn't have a response. The darkness of early night hid the road from the Camaro's headlights. Sharp turns were revealed too quickly ahead of us. I had to keep tapping the brakes, and at some point I wondered if it was the geas, the car, or just me.

Come, come. Come, come…

Fucking thing. I *would* beat it. I grabbed the steering wheel hard with both hands, told myself we were heading toward the holder of the geas. Trying to minimize how much the curse affected me.

"So, how do you do it?" Raphael asked.

"What do you mean?"

"Summon the sword?" he said. "With the lightning and all?"

That wasn't a trick I wanted him to know about. If he put two and two together, with Jen in the Key and the lightning on the sword, he might guess at more. Right now he had a broad idea of why I wanted to talk to my mother. He knew Jen was dead, but he didn't know she was with me, right now.

I changed the subject. "Where is the Conclave?"

"What?" Raphael said. "Is the sword more of the secret Grimm stuff?"

I sighed. "Raphael. The Conclave?"

The ex-vampire, current demon was grinning. As if he was having a ball. Belle had raised her eyebrows in the backseat, as if to say, *See what I mean?*

"You don't trust me to guide you there?" Raphael said, feigning injury. "I'm hurt, Grimm."

"You know," I said, my voice flat. Both hands holding the wheel. Feeling the rattling of the geas up and down my arms. "All this isn't helping me to trust you tonight."

"When has there ever been trust between us?" Raphael asked.

"Dammit, Raph," I said. "You know what I mean."

"I do." Like the Cheshire Cat, where the rest of the cat's body disappeared, and only the teeth remained, his smile seemed to grow more real. "And I'm enjoying it."

I shook my head and concentrated on driving. The best thing to do would be to stay silent. He was in some kind of mood, and it wasn't lining up with mine. And it wasn't something helping me feel better about the geas.

Raphael kept talking, though. "Tonight's going to be something, Grimm. I keep wondering if it's going to be the end, or the beginning of something new. Something *different*."

"Raph, I just want to know where the fucking Conclave is," I said. "Tell me, or direct me, but otherwise shut the hell up."

"Hear me out," he said. "You and me, we've always been enemies. I hated you from the moment we met. You with your ragged blue jeans standing on the edge of the playground. As if you were too good to hang with the rest of us."

I didn't remember that at all. I had always thought he had hated me because I had stood up to him. Turns out, he had started not liking me way earlier. Because I was okay as a loner. Because I was comfortable on my own.

"These things keep going full circle, between us," he said. "Each time, the consequences are greater. I'm beginning to believe whatever's happening, it's going to be settled one way or the other, with you or me."

"Whatever," I said. I didn't need to think about him right now. I didn't need to think about him last night, with Belle. He was the least of my worries.

"Whatever." Raphael laughed, though the sound of it was dark, and low. "You told me once, you were where all this ends." His eyebrow rose. "You still believe that?"

I had said that to him, right before punching a broken bat through his skull. That he remembered it told me how much he had thought about it, because I hadn't thought about it since I did it.

Maybe Belle was right, and I should be more worried about Raphael. Thing was, I had Jen first. My friends. My parents. Azazel, and his demon posse. Where the hell could I fit Raphael into all of that?

"So we got into fights, as kids. The fights grew bigger as we grew older," Raphael said. "They grew bigger. I killed Danny. You killed me. Grafton gets wiped off the earth. Now this Azazel demon and all his Dead Zones, but you and I, we still keep going. There's still something unfinished between us."

"None of this speech is helping me trust you tonight," I said.

"I've told you what I'm going to do," Raphael said. "Trust me, or don't. I'm tired of trying to convince you."

A sharp turn came up. There must have not been a sign, because I corrected hard and the Camaro fishtailed around the bend. I shook my head and focused on driving.

"Thing is, Grimm," Raphael said, "I hate you, but I admire you, too. I've even learned something from you. And I *trust* you. I *trust* the fact that you hate me."

His voice grew dark. Guttural. "But in the end, you fucking killed me, Grimm. So why the fuck would I make any of this easy for you?"

The lanes evened out, and opened up into the night. The Camaro sped faster down the road. "You want to learn more about the sword, Raph," I said. "You're about to get a close-up look at it."

He laughed some more, calling my bluff. "Sure, Grimm, sure." He was grinning. So confident of himself, in this moment. So sure of where we were going, and what was going to happen. A surety I lacked.

The road we were on led away from Denver. The streetlights spaced farther and farther apart. Occasional office buildings and stores became homes, and became trees, until we were driving a road headed up into the hills. Green signs, brightly lit by the Camaro's headlights, proclaimed we were close to Mount Morrison Park. It wasn't long before they started reading Red Rocks Park and Amphitheatre.

The first time the amphitheater showed up on a sign, Raphael turned to look at me.

"Here?" I asked.

"Here," he said. Smiling.

I turned off at the next exit, struggling to make the turn nice and steady. The Camaro wasn't sinking into the turns and accelerating out, like I was used to. I had to make it keep going, by working the pedals.

From there Raphael directed me. We turned off the road onto something called Red Rocks Park Road, and headed higher and higher into the hills. I drove slower and slower. Past the Colorado Music Hall of Fame, which looked more like a redbrick Alamo than a hall of fame.

We drove slower, leaving Red Rocks Park Road and coasting over a gravel road, where the car spun and slid if I tried to go too fast. Still, the geas urged me to push the pedal down. Go faster. Get there sooner. Soon enough, we came upon a dead-end sign.

"It's not a dead end," Raphael explained. "There's a trail ahead."

"Where's that go?"

Raphael raised his eyebrow at me. "Secret Raphael stuff."

"Dammit, Raph." I hit the brakes and threw the car into park. The three of us rocked against our seat belts. I turned and faced the demon. Vampire. Whatever the fuck he was.

The geas was tugging on me. My friends were counting on me. My parents needed me. And Jen, Jen's life depended on me. And I was having to play games with *this* guy.

"You need to stop this bullshit," I told him. "Now."

He just smiled.

"I need you to be on board with this," I said. "Or the two of us are going to have it out right here." I almost summoned the sword, and fought to control myself.

Belle leaned forward, eyes lit.

Raphael's eyes narrowed. He actually took a deep breath, and let it out. Then another. When he spoke, his voice was low, but more normal. "You're right."

We were about to have it out. Him admitting I was right surprised me, though. Enough that I leaned back from him a bit. "I am?"

He chuckled, once, rocking his head back and forth in a slight motion. "Yeah."

This was a side of Raphael I didn't see often. Or ever. "So?"

"It's hard, isn't it?" he asked. "Being so close to something you've wanted all your life. It creates these urges … they are hard to fight."

He was talking about his father. He had wanted to kill him for a long time. I had seen it in him, back at the baseball field in Grafton. The desire to kill the man who had created him.

Not birthed him. Created.

But I understood what he meant, about being close to something you desperately wanted. For me it was Jen. Most of what I had done in life, running, coming back, taking care of my friends … those moments began and ended with her.

I was so close to bringing her back, sometimes I was overwhelmed with that feeling. The feeling of being with her. Even with the geas pulsing in me.

The bond squeezed me, a little. The power there echoed between Jen and me, and I realized it was just us there. In the bond. Not the frustration with Raphael. Just Jen and me.

"Are we doing this, then?" I asked. Not sure if I meant the fight between him and me, or going on to the Conclave.

He let out another breath. "Yeah."

There was a knock on my window, a light tapping of metal on glass. I jumped, startled, so focused on Raphael.

Nick stood outside the window, shotgun in hand. Pointed past me at Raphael. The Rubicon sat parked far behind us.

I turned off the Camaro. Nick backed up as I got out, shotgun pointed at the passenger seat.

Raphael got out, closing his door with a light *snick*. The grin was back on his face, though it looked fake now.

"What's up?" Nick asked.

"Just a discussion," I said. My heart had settled back down, though it still beat in the odd rhythm of the geas.

Nick motioned down the road. "This is a dead end."

"There's apparently a trail," I said.

"Not apparently," Raphael said.

"It lead to the Conclave?" Nick asked.

"You're a bright boy, Nicky." Raphael was getting some of his swagger back. "Nailed it in one."

Nick rolled his eyes.

"The amphitheater is set up like an old coliseum," Raphael said. "It's all under the open air, except for the stage. There's a tunnel leading from here to the back of the stage."

"An escape route?" I asked.

"Back then it was," Raphael said. "I'm not sure anyone has ever used it. It should take us up right behind where my father is. Where the heads of the families will be."

The Rubicon shut off. The rest of my friends got out, and walked up toward us. Nick looked at me, his eyebrows raised. Asking about the plan.

Back at a gas station Raphael and I had come up with one. To pretend I was under the geas, with Raphael controlling me. To walk up to his father's fortress in Colorado Springs and take a shot at him.

I wanted to go into the Conclave alone. I wanted to walk up and lure everyone else into my trap. Let my friends sneak up from behind.

I didn't trust Raphael with them. I wanted him with me. If I was lucky, it would distract Dominic even further. Maybe he would lose his grip on the geas, and that would help me try to free my parents.

"Hey, guys," Johnny said, as they walked up. He looked tired. Wan. And maybe hungry. I wondered if eating was enough for him now.

The rest of the group didn't look my better. Gabrielle said nothing, but stood between Johnny and Raphael. Sarah had her sad smile on, and leaned on Nick's shoulder.

Belle got out of the Camaro as well. Her gaze was studious, imperious, and perhaps a little resigned.

"I guess it's time," I said, and looked at Raphael. "Is that tunnel going to be guarded?"

He shrugged. "I would guard it."

"Is it easy to get to?"

"Easy enough," he said. "You want me to show them?"

"No," I said. I gathered them all around. It was cold out. Clouds had moved in, so the night sky was a black blanket above us. A tiny spot of yellow among the wisps of dark gray revealed where the moon hid, tucked in above the world for the evening.

The geas pulsed harder, unhappy I was resisting it. Pulling me toward the Conclave.

"You guys know the deal," I said, eyeing Nick.

He nodded once. "The Grimm Special."

"The Grimm Special," I echoed. "You guys are going to go through the tunnel. You should end up behind Victor and Dominic. I'm going to go in the front, and I'm going to wreck that house."

"Be a distraction," Johnny said.

"I am going to be a distraction," I said. "But that's not why I'm going in. I'm going in to show them what happens when they fuck with us. I'm going in to kill everyone there. Everything and everyone, alive or dead."

"Look at you, Grimm." Raphael grinned. "Getting all biblical."

His Cain and Abel reference went through my mind, and I frowned at him. I didn't need *our* thing to get in the way of *this* thing. Tonight didn't have to be about us. It needed to be about setting an example.

In order to do that, my four friends had to keep Victor and Dominic from controlling me, or my parents, with the geas. I needed them held, by four people I could count on. "Thing is, there's a timing component involved," I said. "We can't kill Victor or Dominic until my parents are free."

"Are you certain you can free them?" Belle said. She looked surprised, head tilted a bit, eyebrows raised. "What happened to them isn't something that can be broken easily. Azazel would make sure of that."

She had been around and watched Azazel for thousands of years. The demon took everything into account when he did a thing. His plans had plans, and everything was outlined to the finest detail. But there was something Azazel couldn't have planned. He couldn't have known about me, thousands of years ago. Or Jen. *Us*.

The tendril connecting my parents to their vampire keepers, that tendril could be cut like any other. Especially with my sword, its translucent edge sharp, lightning tracing up and down the blade. It cut through things effortlessly. Weightlessly.

"Yeah," I finally answered.

Belle took a step back, at that. Her face lost all expression, one of her hands kept grasping at air, and she looked high up into the cloudy skies as if she could look past them, and into the universe. As if the ground underneath her was shaky.

I couldn't worry about that now.

"So there's a timing component to this," I said. "Dominic is going to try to control me. Victor might, too. I need you all to get to them and stop them – without killing them – until I can free my parents."

"That will be tough, for me," Gabrielle said. "For us. Not only because of me. Or Johnny. But these are master vampires."

Her eyes radiated anger. Her father had tried to kill Johnny, *had* killed Johnny, and that kind of pain was impossible to really control. She would always carry a burning vengeance now. Until it was satisfied. It would be hard for her not to kill her father, should the opportunity offer itself.

"I get it," I said. "Hold out as long as you can."

The plan was chancy at best. Victor and Dominic were vampire lords, the highest of their undead food chains. Asking my friends to kill them would be a herculean task, but asking them to not kill them, to hold them hostage, with all the other vampires and whatever was left of Victor's hit squad …

That was going to be close to impossible.

But we had done impossible before. We could do it again. We were used to going up against insurmountable odds. We were the Wolverines. It was how we were made. And, as I was beginning to believe, who we were supposed to be.

"I don't know any other way to go about it," I said. If we could free my parents, then the three of us could turn on Victor and Dominic. It wasn't like we could sneak in. Not with the geas able to sense and control me, as I got closer.

"You need it, we'll do it," Nick said, simply.

I was glad Nick and I thought along the same wavelengths. It was Gabrielle that worried me, with her dark, focused eyes and thin, angry lips. Johnny, who looked strung out and tired. "Just give me what you can. Every second you can."

I connected with all of them, locking their eyes with mine, one by one.

"But stay alive," I said. "That's what this is about. If you have to make a choice between killing one of them and your life, choose your life."

I let that sink in.

"Okay," I said. Feeling the geas grow more urgent, feeling the call pull me toward the Conclave. My foot began to jerk, as if it was going to step that way on its own. "I have no idea how guarded that tunnel is. Or how long it might take you to get there. But I can give you thirty minutes, maybe."

Nick raised his eyebrows. "That's it?"

I held my legs straight, feeling them want to flex, to draw me toward the Conclave. I shook my head. "At best."

"I can go with them," Raphael volunteered. "Show them the way. Maybe some of my father's guards will recognize me. Make it faster."

"No," I said again to that idea. I would not let Raphael out of my sight, until the night was over. "You had an idea, back in Colorado Springs."

"You want to try that?" Raphael said. "Now?"

"Yeah," I said. It was as good as any idea I'd had. I wasn't putting either Raphael or Belle with my friends. If they were going to betray anyone, it was going to be me. And if that happened, to hell with our contract. "You and Belle will be with me."

Raphael grimaced. Or smiled. It was hard to tell. "Your funeral," he said. "Or maybe theirs."

It was quiet then. Johnny was more noncommittal than anything else. As if afraid to cast a vote.

Gabrielle was angry at Raphael, maybe even furious. She was still covered with healing cuts from the night before. I wondered if she had drunk some from Johnny, or if she had found someplace else to heal. Or someone. Johnny looked thin, tired but wired, as if he had gone nights without sleep and had just drunk four or five energy drinks in order to keep going.

Sarah's face carried a sadness. Her eyes were full of it, and her hair hung loose around her shoulders. Her gaze kept flicking to me and then to the Key, on my chest. Nick was the lone one of the four who just looked ready. Capable. There were some small scars on the backs of his arms, his face, still healing, but he wore his flak jacket and had restocked his vest of knives.

These four would have to handle whatever the hidden tunnel threw at them. They would have to do it quickly, and make it to Dominic and

Victor in time to keep them from using the geas on me. And then they would have to distract the two vampire lords without killing them, or hold the two hostage if they could, while I freed my parents. While I took out as many of the vampires there as I could.

It was a tall order.

"We can still leave," Sarah said. Johnny and Nick paused, waiting. Gabrielle's eyes narrowed. Then the vampire looked away.

Leaving wasn't going to be an option. Not with the me I was trying to become. But it was still nice to hear, from people whom I loved. Sarah was worried about Jen, but it felt good to know that I had real friends, people that cared about me.

I shook my head. "We'll make it. And by the end of tonight, people will think twice about messing with the Wolverines."

Raphael snorted, and rolled his eyes.

Nick just smiled, and kept his eyes on Raphael. "Simple enough."

"Then let's do it," I said.

Raphael gave them directions. The three of us watched my friends leave. We didn't get together in a group hug, or put our hands in a circle with a shout of *1-2-3, Wolverines*. None of us wanted to make this feel like a good-bye.

And in a way, it wasn't. It was just another fight, for us.

I gave my friends as much time as I could, holding my legs and arms tight to my sides, locking everything in place. Feeling the geas beat hard inside me, my feet and hands shaking, feeling the rattling control of a vampire on the edge of madness. Knowing what waited us all, ahead. Vampires. Thralls. Vampire lords. Whatever was left of the airport hit squad.

I couldn't hold out long. It felt like just a minute or two. It might have been more. When it became too great to stand still, I looked at Raphael. Who had been watching me quietly the whole time. Studiously. That frightened me, for some reason.

Still, he looked ready.

"Let's go to a concert," I said.

Raphael grinned. "About time."

CHAPTER FIFTY-ONE

The layer of clouds thickened overhead. As if a quiet storm was brewing, in the dark of the night. It was too cold to rain, but the air carried a wet chill to it, like a heavy snow lurked beneath the wind, ready to fall upon all of us. For all that we were about to do, the air smelled clean. Fresh.

Raphael and Belle and I had gotten back in the Camaro. I had a little trouble turning it around, until I convinced the geas I was headed toward the Conclave. I had started with a three-point turn that became a seven-point turn, before I got the car worked around.

"This is interesting to watch," Raphael commented, during the last turn.

I put the shifter in drive for the final time and pulled out, not answering. The tires spun a little on the gravel, and I drove slow until we got back onto blacktop. From there I circled around back the way we had come in. I had seen signs for parking lots.

Over the trees and to the west were a few lights, just enough to outline large cliffs jutting out above the slopes. I rolled down the window and heard music, faintly. Something with strings and woodwinds, a thumping percussion beat. Some kind of orchestra piece.

I had been overconfident with the geas. I had convinced myself I was different. That I was stronger than the curse. Yet here it was, dragging me toward the Conclave, with it taking everything in me to not jerk the wheel and try to drive the Camaro straight up the hill, through the brush and trees, toward the vampire calling me.

It had been a few weeks since I was subjected to it. Maybe that was enough for me to forget the incredible power it had over me. Maybe – because I had found out I was part angel – I thought that would be enough. My mother had told me I was *more*.

And here I was, struggling against the geas. I didn't know what waited for us. This evening would fall apart, if I couldn't fight the curse, whether it was just Dominic and Victor there or the entire Conclave. And my friends, my parents, they would all die.

Nothing to do about it now. I had to find a way around the geas, over it, or through it. People were counting on me. Lives were counting on me. And I had promised.

My chest warmed, a feeling spreading through it like drinking a cup of hot chocolate on a snowy night. Jen, trying to reassure me. The moment felt so real I almost remembered it, like we were kids. The two of us on her couch, a thick quilt lumped on top of us, Jen and me drinking a cup of hot chocolate with a big melted marshmallow in it. I think I remembered her laughing, when I took a drink and came back with marshmallows on my nose.

Maybe Jen was reassuring me. Or maybe she was trying to make me not think about the geas so much. I wasn't sure it worked, but I drove a little better afterward.

Like always, I checked around for ghosts. There were a few close by, some in the hills around the large rocks I had seen. Others spread out, over a distance, into the rising mountains around us. And a large number back toward Denver, clumping together near the city.

The last time I had faced Dominic, there weren't many ghosts. What there were, I had to make. This time, I would have plenty of spirits to tap into. I wouldn't lack for ethereal energy, which I was thankful for. Jen somehow had been able to tap her own energy and use it, the last few times we fought.

I hoped she would be careful, though I didn't think Jen would. Using her power might be why the Key was crumbling. It just wasn't built to hold Jen, and what she could do.

There was too much I didn't understand.

I was hoping – this time – Jen would be cautious. With the number of ghosts around, I hoped we could avoid using her power. I would, but Jen always had her own mind about things.

She was with me, as much as I could tell. The bond between us felt warm against the cool, wet evening air. Almost like a never-ending hug.

I followed the signs to the Upper North Lot. I don't know if I was surprised or not that it was full. Sports cars, limos, the stretch Hummers with thick doors and windows so black they reflected everything around them.

And then there were the guards. Men and women, mostly. Thralls armed with tactical gear and assault rifles. Dozens of them patrolled the parking lot, a pair of them sat at the edge of the road that led into the lot, and one of those waved us over with a bright white fluorescent marshaling wand.

I slowed to a stop and rolled down my window.

"Fergus Grimm?" the first of the pair asked, a tall man with dark stubble and blond surfer's hair, an assault rifle slung over his shoulder. His partner was much shorter, with her vest too tight between her waist and bosom.

"That's me," I said.

"We were told to expect only you," the man said. "Who's with you?"

I motioned to the man to take a look.

He peeked in and did a double take.

Raphael grinned. "Hey, Harry."

"Holy shit," the man said. "Aren't you dead?"

"I don't know," Raphael said. "Am I?"

The man frowned. His partner said something into a microphone on her shoulder.

"What are you doing here?" Harry said.

"What's it look like, Harry?" Raphael said, his voice sharp. "Bringing dear ol' Dad his favorite toy."

Harry hadn't waited for an answer. He had immediately pulled his rifle up instead.

"Come, now, Harry," Raphael said. "Is that any way to treat me?"

"You know it's Harold," the man said.

"Whatever," Raphael said. "You going to send us along, and let my dad know I'm coming? *Harold*?"

The man's partner whispered something in Harold's ear. Her eyes flicked at us, and they had too much makeup.

Harry, or Harold, whichever, set his jaw. Then motioned forward with his gun.

"You go on ahead," he said. "They'll be waiting for you."

"I'm counting on it," Raphael said. The demon looked eager in the low light of the parking lot.

I pulled the Camaro forward. It started with a jerk, and bounced back and forth as I forced my foot to hold steady on the pedal.

"You know the deal," I said. "Your father waits until my parents are free."

"Oh, I'm aware," Raphael said. Looking at me with an expression I couldn't read. "We started this thing because of you. It'll end that way."

I glanced in the rearview mirror, eyeing Belle. "You, too."

"I don't fight," Belle said. "I am here just to enforce the agreement."

"I hear you," I said, steering the car where another set of guards waved me. Around a red Lamborghini Diablo, which just seemed like a stereotype tonight. "Just don't do any enforcing around Dominic and Victor."

Her eyes still had some of the weirdness she had exhibited outside the car. They flicked all around, as if looking everywhere.

"Can you really free your parents?" she asked, again.

I had better be able to. Tonight kind of rested on it. "What's it mean to you, if I can?"

She didn't comment. I flicked on my ethereal vision, curious. Masses of tendrils, hard to see even in the spirit world, hooked into Belle. They left her and looked strung out over the world. Near the trunk of her body lay one thick and heavy. Bulbous and undulating next to her.

Were all those some kind of geas or curse, chaining Belle to her actions? Or were they just contracts she was supposed to enforce? And what was the largest one? Lucifer? Something worse?

"Grimm," Raphael said. *"Grimm."*

I slammed my foot down on the brake. The car jerked to a stop, right before we crashed into the broadside of a stretch Hummer. A guard had jumped aside, twisting away from the Camaro's bumper. The limo was dark in my ghostly sight, with faint blue handprints where the guard had been leaning on it.

My door opened, and two assault rifles pointed at us. Two different guards than Harold and his partner, but the same attitude. "Funny man. Turn off the car and get out."

I blinked back to normal vision. Unbuckled my seat belt, slowly put the Camaro in park, and switched it off. The car felt nervous to me, and shuddered quietly before going still. Then I pushed the emergency brake in as far as it would go, feeling the clicking of it in my foot, the ratcheting *tat-tat-tat*.

One of the guards tugged me out by my shirt. I kept my hands up, carefully watching the other guard hold his assault rifle on me. I shivered as the first blast of wind hit me, blowing across the parking lot and fluttering the bottom of my shirt. The air carried more chill up on the top of the hillside, out in the open.

The guard turned me around and pushed me against the side of the Camaro. He patted me down. I wasn't carrying; the .38 still rested in the side of the car door. My shotgun was in the trunk. I was going to miss that tonight. The Benelli was a security blanket, something I counted on.

Tonight it was just going to be me.

I held still and endured the search. I caught the guard staring at me in the reflection of the window. Just a few short weeks past I had been in the same position. Facing the side of my car, in a parking lot outside a motel, a vampire behind me. That was the night I had first gotten the call from Jen. Before Grafton and New Orleans and all of this.

It seemed like forever ago.

The geas kept moving me during the search, and the guard kept jerking me back, until the second guard placed the barrel of his assault rifle in the middle of my back. That got me focused on holding my feet steady, my arms out.

Raphael was next. He had a couple of knives inside his jacket, and a nine-millimeter tucked into the waistband of his pants. I wondered where he got them.

"You need a gun?" I asked him, over the roof of the car.

"Felt appropriate," he said, then rolled his eyes as the guard dug back into his search.

Could I trust him? Raphael had given me no reason not to, this trip. At the same time, we were enemies. Had always been enemies, even though he wanted it to be just me and him, after all this was said and done.

Was that what was next? Were we headed to the end? Was Raphael going to kill his father, and in turn kill me, my mother, my father, and the rest of the vampires he had been birthed from?

I didn't know. But I hoped not. It was all I had, hope and depending on Raphael's ego. His desire to beat me, man to man.

Belle got patted down next. She had nothing, and took the search mindlessly. Like her thoughts were elsewhere.

She was the person I couldn't trust. She had tried to get me to kill Raphael. And maybe she had asked the same of him. There was a real fear there from her concerning Raphael.

We were escorted up a small hill. The music I had heard earlier grew louder. Violins and woodwind instruments, with some heavy percussion thumping along. Heard over the music was the heavy mumble of people talking, like all crowds do, the murmur of hundreds or thousands of vampires all talking among themselves.

"So, what's the deal, between you and me?" Raphael asked.

"I thought you had already given me your deal," I said. Looking straight, focusing on my steps. The geas pulling me up the hill. Wondering how I was going to beat it.

"I know what I told you. I know what I'm going to do," Raphael said. "But it'd be nice if we were on the same page. Maybe come out of this alive."

"You worried about death now?" I said.

There was a pause from the man. I slowed, until one of the guards prodded me with his rifle. Like I needed something else pushing me to the Conclave.

"I don't know," Raphael said. "But I don't like being tied to things."

I hadn't, either. For a decade I had fought being tied to anything. I had just run. Being tied to things just got those people hurt, or got me in trouble. I hadn't realized living in fear was a chain of its own.

I had grown since then. Learned. There were good ties and bad ties. The warm feeling I got from Jen, along the bond, was my best example. But I had more. The connections to all my friends. Nick. Sarah. Johnny. All those were ties I was lucky to have. Likely Gabrielle, too. My parents, I had hopes for.

Then there was my link to Azazel. Though that one was more obligation. Something personal, between just him and me.

There was the geas, pulling at me even now, the cursed tether between the vampire lords and what was left of the angels. Raphael, and the contract I had with him. The circle between Raphael and me, ending with his promise that – in the end – it would just be the two of us.

"You and I are tied together," I pointed out. "The contract."

And more. Evil versus good. One response tied to the other.

"I agree," Raphael said. "But what happens if you get killed? Or I do?"

I hadn't given that much thought. Maybe I should have. Behind us, Belle smiled a little. "The contract will still be enforced."

It clicked. All the little strings attached to Belle. Thousands, maybe millions of contracts tied to her, from those who had wanted something out of their lives. Not knowing what might happen after they had made their promise, should they not fulfill their side of the agreement.

Raphael didn't want to be beholden to Belle. And Belle had wanted me to kill Raphael. Upon which I would have been in forfeit, and perhaps under her control. Was that her end game?

It felt like Belle thought she could handle me. But she was in fear of Raphael. I wondered what made her think either of those thoughts. Or if it was the person she was bound to that carried the real fear.

I was headed into a battle I needed to win. Against insurmountable odds. With one arm tied behind my back, with the geas. And with way too many questions unanswered.

I could reduce the questions by one, though. In for a penny, in for a pound. So I gave Raphael the answer I knew. "I'm going to do what I said I'd do."

He nodded and took a deep breath. Jogged his shoulders up and down, once or twice. Loosening up. Getting ready for a fight. "Good enough."

We got to the top of the hill and crested it. Red Rock Amphitheatre lay underneath us, majestic in the lighting around the rocks. The hill sloped down and away until it hit the stage, the stage just slightly higher than the bottom of the slope, and sitting between huge juts of stone.

Down the hill also lay row after row of stone benches, spreading upward from the stage, toward us, flat rock seats stretching in wider semi-circles. Red Rock looked like all the pictures of a Roman amphitheater, the kind the Greeks and Romans favored, where people gathered to listen to Plato, or Aristotle, or maybe watch some play, some tragedy unfold.

Lights were thrown up on the clifflike rocks surrounding the amphitheater. Large faces of stone, colored like the Key, sandstone, with horizontal lines of red running through the rock like veins. Tall speakers sat under the stones, playing music over the murmuring of the crowd, violins, some flutes, the heavy beat of percussion that pulsed in a geas-like rhythm.

The entire place was packed. The stone benches circled around the stage, higher and higher, all the way up the hill to where we stood. I stopped at the size of the crowd. Every row was full. I wasn't up against hundreds of vampires tonight. Or even thousands. I was up against much, much more.

The Benelli wouldn't have made a dent in this.

"How many people can fit in here?" I asked, my voice low.

"Something like ten thousand," Raphael said. "Getting cold feet?"

Ten thousand. There were at least that many vampires here. Probably more. The seats were full, vampires sitting shoulder to shoulder, but others walked around, stopping to greet someone. Many stood on the stairs, talking in large groups. Hundreds more circled the tents at the top of the amphitheater, grabbing drinks and cocktails there. Laughing among themselves.

Like any other concert. Just filled with undead.

The murmuring slowed to a stop. The music, soft enough, died away to a last cry of a violin, the last beat of percussion. And one by one all the vampires turned to look at us. Or me.

CHAPTER FIFTY-TWO

It was amazing how quiet a large crowd could get. Especially when they were all together in a concert hall, celebrating and drinking and laughing, with violins behind every conversation. Right then, after the last note had played out, with everyone on every bench turning around to face me, waiting to see what was next, all I heard was the heavy thudding of my heart, pounding against my chest.

The air was full with a silence, one of expectation, where the audience knows something is about to go down and they are trying to figure out exactly what that will be.

I wanted to figure it out as well. I knew what I wanted to accomplish, I just didn't exactly know how to go about it. I would have to play things tonight as they were laid down. As they happened. I had no other choice, with ten thousand vampires and thralls staring at me, and whatever waited on the stage below.

The fluttering wind tugged at my hair, my shirt. I wondered when I would be able to keep a jacket around more than a day or two. The one I had recently bought was likely still in my room in Colorado Springs. And I seemed to always need one. You'd think I'd have backups to my backups by now.

Come, come. Come, come…

I was stalling. The geas fixed that for me. The curse pulled me down the stairway, tugging me down the middle of the large crowd of undead. All of whom watched me and whispered among themselves.

Talk all your talk now, I thought. *I'll make sure it stops here in a minute.*

I stumbled on a stair. The geas kept tugging at me. I needed to pay more attention. So I did, focusing on how I placed my feet each and every step. Gravity worked with the curse, and the center of the stage felt like a black hole pulling me toward where large black tables were set. Like obsidian desks, or tables. Maybe altars. The blocks lay in a semicircle, with the middle block closest to me.

Seven vampires sat at each obsidian table. I guessed all of these were the heads of their families, and I didn't recognize any but Dominic. He sat immediately to my right of the center block, and looked nothing like the man I had seen in Grafton. Then he had radiated menace, he had carried a dark power with him. He had been a large dark cloud of death. This man was so thin he looked emaciated, his skin stretched tight over his face, lips a pencil-like blue line.

His eyes, though. They still carried anger. At me, sure. But as Dominic looked past me, to his son, his pale lips smiled, as if he had just tasted something sweet and delicious.

My mother stood behind Dominic, in her usual stance. Parade rest, hands behind her back, feet slightly apart. Frowning slightly, as if concentrating. She gave no sign of seeing me, that I was even there. Her eyes constantly scanned the crowd, Raphael, and the man a few paces to her left.

My father. He was behind another man, and stood with his arms folded. The hilt of his large sword poked over his shoulder. Like my mother's, his eyes scanned the crowd, but they did pause briefly upon me. He gave a wink so slight I might have misunderstood the gesture.

The vampire in front my father must be Victor. Gabrielle's father. I didn't see much of her in the man. Gabrielle was slight, with straight black hair and a fine bone structure. Olive skin with slight freckles, a sharp nose, nice cheekbones, and full lips. As Italian as someone could look.

Victor was shorter than his daughter, and much wider. Stout, though not fat. He was thick, with a lumberjack-type brawn. He didn't have the look of the head of the most powerful vampire family here. He looked like he had just come from plowing a field. The expensive tailored black suit he wore still didn't fit him quite right. The jacket still looked rumpled.

I wanted to grin, and held it back. Dominic, in his state, looked more like a head of a large vampire clan. Even emaciated, the vampire carried a menacing air. Even his coat looked evil, every crease a knife edge of elegant cloth.

Victor gave the appearance of someone pretending to be a lord. His hair was so blond it was almost white, with a few strands of black running through it. His skin looked like he used a tanning machine, a tan so dark it was almost brown. His face was wide, without the elegant cheekbones of his daughter, and somewhat ruddy with a bulbous nose.

Victor looked at me with a curious face, as if he recognized me from somewhere. His eyes narrowed. Like who I really was circled around in his brain, escaping conscious effort to retrieve it.

If he turned around, he would likely get it.

He didn't know I was the son of the man standing behind him. And Dominic didn't seem to see it, either. His attention was turned to Raphael with a focused, burning hate. A slight tic throbbed underneath Dominic's eye, and his hand closed tight on the obsidian block in front of him. Knuckles pushed against the stone.

I was glad for the distraction. The likeness was hard to miss between my father and me. It seemed obvious to me. We were almost clones, though I wasn't his size. My father seemed a giant.

"Stop," Dominic said. His voice was nearly a whisper, but carrying across the stage and up into the crowd.

I stopped. The command froze me like a statue. I hadn't been paying attention. Or holding myself still. The geas had kept me walking forward. Now it felt like iron bands encircled me, holding me in place.

"It's nice of you to come to us, Fergus Grimm," the vampire lord said, his voice wavering a little, but still carrying some of the dark strength I had heard from him, back in Grafton. "It saves us the trouble of finding you."

"You know the saying," I said. "Be careful what you wish for."

Dominic snorted. "I'm curious as to why my son is here," he said. "Or, to phrase it differently, how he came to be here."

"I came here with him." Raphael pointed a thumb at me. Which, I guessed, was technically true, since this whole thing had started with me trying to find my mother. "And apparently I'm glad for the warm welcome."

"I asked you *how*. I *know* you were killed." Dominic inclined his head toward me. "By him."

"You know, Father, death is a funny thing," Raphael answered. "I'll give you a hint. You created me from your blood and the blood of a demon. Guess which one remained, after I was killed?"

"I cannot sense his heartbeat," Victor said, aloud. His accent Italian, and each word precise. Exactly like his daughter spoke.

"It's a neat thing, isn't it?" Raphael said next to me, grinning.

I found a ghost, a young woman's spirit on the side of one of the taller hills around us. I pulled a little ethereal energy and tested it against the geas. The bands grew tighter around me, my chest constricted, and I found it hard to breathe.

It hadn't been thirty minutes. My friends weren't here yet, but I was running out of time. The energy of the entire Conclave was building, some kind of swarm of hate and desire to hurt. Thousands and thousands of vampires, waiting for the word to kill.

I flicked on my ethereal energy and looked around for a tendril, binding me to my mother. Nothing bound me, even though I clearly saw the tether from my mother to Dominic, my father to Victor. The thick black appendages waved slightly in the air, as if swaying in a breeze.

Why couldn't I see those same ropes connect to me? Could we all not see the things that trapped us and bound us? Was it so easy, to see the chains around others, and yet not be able to see the same cage around myself?

The tendrils had to be there. I could feel the geas, ordering me. Why couldn't I see what I could feel? I fought it harder, and the geas clamped down, until I could barely breathe.

Dominic's lips curved in a gigantic smile, as if he could feel my struggle. A pale white canine tooth revealed itself, and his tongue flicked out over the sharp tip of it. "My son is one thing, but one wonders why you came back, Fergus Grimm."

I stood firm, my feet planted underneath me. As if the curse weren't binding me in place. Every minute I bought was a minute my friends could use to get here. "I wanted to right some wrongs."

Dominic frowned. As if wrong was an inconceivable concept. "Wrongs?"

"One big one," I said, setting my sights on Victor. "This guy tried to kill some friends of mine. I'm here to show him why that was a bad idea."

My mother looked at me then. Still frowning. Her jaw clenched. There was a slight narrowing of her eyes, and she carefully shook her head. Once.

I frowned back. She had asked me to be here. I'd assumed to help her and my father get free of the geas. After all that talk, about me being more, and the geas coming to an end. About facing the evils in the world.

What else did she need from me? Why did she want me to be here, if it wasn't to help her and my father be free?

I couldn't help them if I couldn't break free of the geas. That seemed unlikely now. The curse held me like a vise. The more I pushed against it, the tighter it gripped.

It occurred to me that I might die tonight. In the next minute or two. I had foolishly thought I was something special. Something greater. Something more.

And I might have led my friends to their deaths as well. They might be dying now, and there was nothing I could do about it. I pulled from the ghost and pushed energy against the geas, harder, until the curse's chains wrapped me so tight I couldn't breathe. The chain was thick and heavy. The geas weighed on me like an anchor, dragging me to a helpless, dark doom.

I couldn't fight it. Not enough to matter to do anything. And both of the vampire lords knew that. I wondered if my mother had known, too.

My words had stirred something in Victor. Furrows appeared in his wide forehead, and his eyebrows came down in anger. His voice was edged with something dark, hoarse. "Those born under the geas don't get to *warn* anyone. Especially *me*."

"Whatever you thought was going to happen," Dominic added, "you only came for your death."

I tried to move and couldn't. I tried to pull more ethereal energy, but shots rang out, steady *rat-tat-tats* that echoed through the amphitheater. Assault rifles at close range, behind me.

I wasn't ready for gunfire. I hadn't really thought about it, and it was going to cost me. I had thought this was going to be a fight. Something medieval. Swords. Fists. Knives. Killing people from close up.

I had made a mistake. And I was going to die from it. I took enough energy from the woman that she disappeared, hardened my skin, felt the bullets dig into it in that slow-motion-time sense I got in the middle of a fight.

I reached for another ghost, hoping to tap it and grab more energy and keep my skin hard enough to bounce all the bullets.

The next ghost had a tether, though.

And the next one.

My mother and father both stood like statues, but behind the stillness they were watching each spirit I raced to try to tap, and one of them was getting to that ghost first. They had fought battles against people like them many times before.

I hadn't. A fear washed over me. I was going to die. I really *was* going to die. And not sometime tonight. Not in some battle of revenge. Right here and now.

A burst of lightning flickered out from my chest. Several bursts, over and over and over, accompanied by a sizzling sound, like hot meat hitting a frying pan. Ozone and the smell of molten metal washed over me. The bullets that had been slowly digging into my skin exploded outward in a bright wave that had everyone close their eyes.

The entire Conclave drew in their breath.

"Who *are* you?" Raphael said, from my side. Looking at something behind me and shaking his head.

I glanced. Warm bits of metal, red-hot, dotted the stage in a circle around me. Like molten lava had splattered everywhere, little drops of fiery rain.

That wasn't something I did. Or could do.

A warmth swelled in the center of my chest. From a different kind of bond. Someone I was tied to, in the kind of way only two people can be. In the type of way that, once you find that person, nothing else matters. Who could breathe the same air as you, live the same moment, laugh at the same jokes. Who wanted, like I did, to keep our friends safe. But who also wanted, just like me, to show someone what a bad idea was. Who wanted *vengeance*.

Jen.

The link between us drifted over me, like I had been tucked inside a large, warm blanket. I took a deep breath – well, I tried, and then Jen took a deep breath for me. My hand flexed, just a little, like it wanted the hilt of the sword in its palm.

Jen, I thought along our bond. *What are you doing?*

Her words came back, loud and clear. Not from along the bond we shared, but inside me. Inside my head. *What you can't, Gus.*

Our conversation was like she was me, and I was her. Like we shared a brain. Or were in the same space. I checked, and what was left of the Key swirled in my ethereal sight. Lightning blues, brilliant starlike whites, and yellows and oranges and greens spun together and disappeared into the stone. Some of the colors washed over me. And as I watched, the Key aged, turning white, like the cold ash left on a log after the fire had burned out.

The curse controlled me, but it had no call over Jen. Together, we were something more. Something different.

Something the world had never seen.

Can you pull a ghost for me? Jen asked. *Is that what you call it?*

She was tapped into her own ethereal energy now. We could do the impossible tonight. I just had to make sure Jen stayed in the Key, that the Key stayed in one piece, and that I always had ghost on hand, to keep Jen from using herself up.

I reached out to a ghost. My mother was waiting, though, and quickly tethered herself to the same spirit, before I could. Her gaze remained unchanged, staring at me.

So I found another. This time my father got there first. The corner of his lip lifted, in a *What are you gonna do?* type of grin. I tried a couple more spirits, those close to us, and the two of them worked in concert to keep me from the source of power we all used.

Gus? Jen asked.

"I'm on it," I said, aloud. I tried another ghost. As soon as I sensed my mother reaching out to the same spirit, I reversed and feinted to another. Feinting to a second ghost, and feeling my father begin to tether himself to it. After faking twice, I reversed my senses and stretched them far away. Some ghost on the road back to Denver. The farthest I could tap into one.

I locked in on the spirit. Some plumber with a Peeping Tom habit.

Quickly I bound him to me and pulled ethereal energy to me. I had never reached so far, and it took a moment for the energy to fly back into me.

My mother's eyebrow arched, delicately. The corner of my father's lip turned into a full grin. He even winked.

Now that I had something, I pulled more. Jen focused and poured that energy into my hand. We tested out summoning the sword.

For a flicker of a second the blade flickered into existence, and then I let it go.

Game on, Jen said.

"Game on," I echoed aloud.

Raphael was staring at me, taking it all in. Not surprised that I was somehow overcoming the geas, just taking it in.

His father stood. Dominic's eyes narrowed, and his emaciated jawline stood out, as if he grinded his teeth together. Maybe he couldn't believe that I was defying his command. Beating the geas. And when he spoke, his voice was edged with malevolence. "I told you to *stop.*"

I winked at the vampire lord. "You guys are in a world of hurt now."

"Stop!" Dominic said again, his voice almost guttural with the command.

I shook my head. "It's *just* a little too late for that."

I stepped forward, toward their little semicircle of blocks. Actually I tried to step forward. I had to wait until Jen moved my leg for me.

I moved one step. Then another. The whole motion felt a little stiff, and I probably looked like a sheriff, walking down a street in the Old West, spurs jangling with the hard placement of each foot.

I hoped they took it as a person walking the walk. Because the talk was on its way. Right after Jen and I worked all of this out. This team-work thing was going to take a little coordination, and a little time.

I wanted to make sure we weren't caught off guard again, so I worked some of the ethereal energy into my skin, hardening it. Jen saw what I was doing, and pushed some as well. Learning how I did things and mimicking me.

I caught Victor's eyes. I made sure he saw the anger. I made sure he understood tonight he was going to meet his maker. If that maker was around. I wasn't sure where vampires went, after they were killed. And frankly I didn't care.

I wanted the vampire lord to feel how angry I was, *see* it in me. After all, tonight was about showing the world what would happen if they fucked with me or my friends. It was about setting a precedent.

I raised my voice, allowing the acoustics of the amphitheater to carry what I said up into the crowd. "It was too late for you when you decided to come after my friends. When you thought you were above retribution. You're going to find out, tonight, what that costs."

Victor's face turned red. The vampire must not be used to getting spoken to like that. A vein throbbed on his temple, a motion I always found curious with vampires and the undead. When Victor spoke, his voice was measured. Controlled. "You have no idea what you face."

"I could say the same." I held his eyes, and made sure my anger washed over him. My words were loud, firm, and clipped. "Only one of us is going to be right."

Victor didn't look away. Maybe he thought he was up for this. I was going to prove him wrong.

"I've had enough of fools." He spoke low, almost a whisper, as if to himself. The vampire faced the crowd, holding both hands up in the air. He didn't shout, but raised his voice loud enough that the acoustics of the stage carried his words over the crowd, and up into the surrounding hills. "A seat at the table, for whoever brings me the heads of these two!"

Two?

I glanced around, quickly. Belle had disappeared. Just like back at the motel. I wasn't sure how she expected to enforce any agreements without getting a little dirty. The only friend I had here, using that word loosely, was Raphael. And we were against some long odds, ten thousand to two.

The chatter of assault rifles filled the air, until the night was full of thundering automatic fire. Bullets slammed into Raphael, the amount and force of which picked him and threw him far across the ground.

Then I was picked up and tossed as well, feeling bites and stings of bullets hitting me, hundreds of them pinging me and flattening into disks. I tried to push more energy into my skin, but Jen was already working on it.

We had always worked well together.

Then a wave of bodies flowed over me. Vampires, from the crowd. Maybe ten, maybe twenty, maybe more. I was surrounded by them, like I was on a football field, at the bottom of a scrum, with hundreds of players jumping on top of me.

With no more time to think, I got into a fight for my life.

CHAPTER FIFTY-THREE

Powerful grunts. Raging screams. The fetid, decaying smell of expelled breath from mouths that feasted on flesh. Vampires pressed on me from all sides. They picked me up and tried to pull me apart, they tried to bite me and tear my arms and legs off; occasionally one even yanked on my hair, trying to snap my neck off.

I guessed bringing Victor my head was going to be a literal thing.

Basic human survival became my only thought. I rolled and punched. I lost sight of Raphael. Belle was gone. And my friends hadn't arrived yet. There seemed to be a few kinks in my plan, and if I was going to be honest with myself, plans not coming together was something I should have expected.

I just hoped my friends were okay. That their delay didn't mean they were dead. Not that I could help them, at the moment. Not with Bethany bloodsucker and Vincent vampire each trying to pull an arm off me.

Balling up into the fetal position wasn't an option. Not just because of the vampires on me, but because the geas still held me. All I could do was keep pouring energy into my skin, my muscles, my ligaments and bones. Keep everything as hard as I could, as locked in, as strong as possible.

But that wasn't going to be strong enough. Not to overcome hundreds or thousands of vampires. More hands grabbed my limbs, pulling me straight. A vampire lay on me, chest to chest, his face buried in my neck, his fangs scratching at the hollow there.

I kept taking more energy, keeping my skin hard, but the plumber's ghost wasn't going to last forever. Even now his spirit dwindled away, with memories of the fat man placing little wireless cameras in the homes he entered. At the edges of my ethereal sense, I felt my mother and father waiting to see what ghost I went to next.

All in all, one of the more uncomfortable positions I'd ever been in.

Time to do something about it.

Jen, I thought. *Need a hand here*.

On it, she said. *Large hand or small hand?*

Massive, I said.

Get ready, she said. *Going to need more energy soon*.

A tingling came over me, the kind of tingle you get when a piece of clothing comes out of the dryer and hits your skin, where all the hairs on your arms lift up and stick to the shirt. The kind of tingle where you hear the little pops and cracks of electrical charge as you pull the shirt off your skin.

The tingling was the same, but greater. More. Like a hundred-foot shirt came out of a house-sized dryer. The tingling grew larger and larger, the buildup greater and greater, until even the vampires touching me felt it.

Most of them even stopped pulling on me, confused. Wondering what was happening.

Then the plumber's ghost gave out with a sick image of the overweight man pumping himself in front of a laptop. And a thunderous boom blasted the stage.

It was the deafening sound of a battleship firing all its guns. My vision went bright blue-white, then just white. Everything around me disappeared in muted screams I barely heard over a high-pitched whine.

I was on my hands and knees, but couldn't see. Jen pushed a little ethereal energy into my eyes – *why had I never thought of that?* – and a cooling sensation came over them. I blinked once or twice, then took in the carnage around me.

The explosion Jen had unleashed blew back the obsidian blocks, the vampire lords seated behind them, *and* my mother and father. Everyone and everything was blasted away from me in a rolling wave of lightning that stitched the ground, like thunderous cannons.

Jen had to heal my ears, next. I had gone deaf.

Little bits of vampires plopped down around me, dropping in from the sky. It was raining vampire. Charred arms and legs and an occasional head bounced off the stage. Knives and swords lay around the stage, some of them bent, as if a vampire had tried to jab the blade into me and found out the metal wasn't strong enough.

My mother struggled up from behind one of the blocks.

I almost missed my chance. It was a near thing, but I latched on to the closest ghost before my mother or father could see what I was doing.

I had never tried it before, but I passed that bond to Jen, and tried to grab another. Getting two for one. Both of the spirits fought, hard, and Jen helped.

… Fucking Rand, thinking he can keep sleeping around while I'm at work …

… Who's that bitch think she is? Working all the time and leaving me with the house, the kid. Coming home all the time tired, too. Like she's fucking somebody …

We were able to tap both. It was hard to focus on them. It was hard to focus on anything for a moment, with Jen and me talking inside my head, and two more memories I was living through. Some couple who had offed each other.

Ethereal energy coursed through me. I got up. All around the stage, the bottom floor of the amphitheater, and the first few rows of benches, was clear of vampires. Thousands lay tumbled together in the stands, as if a wave had blasted them upward and pushed them over each other. A few of those groaned, some screamed, but all of them moved slowly.

Raphael lay off to the side. There were a number of daggers in him, and one katana, plunged down through his chest and coming out somewhere out his back. That one seemed to have him stuck in the rock.

"Was that you?" he asked.

I nodded.

"Thanks for the breather," he said. He pulled out the katana. It stuck for a second before coming out with a sucking sound. Then he got up, pulling out the daggers one by one and dropping them next to him. The blades clattered on the stone, and the cuts and wounds left behind, as he pulled each one out, healed quickly and with a tinge of red mist in my ethereal sight.

Raphael pulled the last one out and shook the blood off the blade. He looked over the stage. My mother was helping his father pull himself up, the vampire leaning heavily on one of the blocks. Their gazes caught.

Raphael grinned. Dominic hissed, his fangs came out, and the vampire lord jumped onto his son. My mother quickly followed. Blade flashing in the night air.

For a moment I almost jumped in as well. If Raphael was going to betray me, now was the time. He could end his father, my mother, all the vampires around us, with one quick twist of his father's neck.

Instead, Raphael grabbed his father and threw him into the crowd, then turned to take on my mother. Her sword. His dagger.

I was surprised, and I wasn't. Like me, he really didn't want to be indebted to Belle.

I turned back to where Victor had been. My father was tossing one of the blocks aside. He reached down and yanked Victor off the ground. The vampire lord had a flap of skin hanging down from his cheek, and his rumpled jacket was torn across the back. Victor's mouth opened as he saw me, his incisors curved and sharp, as if he were challenging me. Some kind of vampire thing, like how mountain goats butted horns.

"I told you, only one of us," I said, grinning. I made a show of dusting myself off. "That all you got?"

The vampire lord's neck spasmed, a thick vein throbbing large in the side of his neck. Like it pumped blood. He was furious, but he still smiled back at me. "Fool."

"Me?" I said. "I'm winning here."

Victor shook his head, slightly. The smile more of a smirk. The flap of skin hanging loosely from his cheek. "You came here to extract vengeance on me. For attacking your friends. So where are they, *right now*?"

He knew. They both knew. And I wondered why. Raphael had led me to believe his father's passage was a secret. A safe escape.

The bond shook inside me. Jen, angry. Fearful. Angry again.

Just then the ground rumbled, shaking under my feet, like an earthquake. South and west of me, back in the direction where we had left Nick and my friends, a quick brilliant burst of light lit the night sky. Like an explosion.

"Dominic told you?" I said, fear crawling over my skin, goose bumps popping up over my arms.

"Faced with possible death, *real death*, why wouldn't he?" Victor said. "You think you are the only person to vow vengeance against me? To threaten me? There's a long list of those, and you're the only one left standing."

Victor Dumont had been around a thousand years, give or take a few hundred. It was tough to think in those terms, that the person you were facing was someone who had seen it all. I should have guessed that he would have all the angles covered.

"We even knew when they were coming," Victor said. "One of your friends had something that called vampires to them."

"No," I said. I remembered the dead vampire Nick had shown me, outside the barn. When we had been headed to New Orleans. Sarah's curse had been at its greatest power then. Calling to all vampires around to come take a bite.

The bishop had exorcised that from her, though. "We cured her of that. That's gone."

"It's gone for most." Victor smiled, dark black blood running from his face, onto his teeth. "But not one."

Dominic. He had been injected with so much of the drug that controlled the vampires. The cursed blood of the witches. Of course he could still feel Sarah; the drug in his blood was the counterpart to Sarah's.

"Now you understand," Victor said. The smirk opening into a predator's grin, incisors pointed, laughing.

The bond screamed inside me. Jen, wanting vengeance. *I* didn't have to worry about Raphael killing his father too soon. I had to worry about Jen and me killing Victor before the right moment.

The explosion seemed like overkill. Were our friends alive? Had they been killed, or were they just trapped?

Jen, we need to find that entrance, I said.

How? she answered. *Where?*

I don't know, I said. *But we got to figure it out.*

When we had a moment. Which seemed unfortunately like never.

"Kill him," Victor ordered my father. Cronan unsheathed his large sword and winked at me.

Quickly, I added.

CHAPTER FIFTY-FOUR

Furious grunts came from my left. The whisper of a blade cutting the air, the slip of a sword, too fast to see. Clanging rings, from metal on metal. It sounded like my mother was bringing everything she had against Raphael.

My father leaped down in front of me. He landed in a solid thump on the ground, something that echoed along the stone and along the soles of my feet.

"The fight is a little unfair," he said, his accent heavy on the i's.

I brought the sword out. It flickered into being, with a constant electrical pulse running across its surface. My father's eyes went to the blade, and he tilted his head a little. Studying. Cautious.

Now was the time I could change the battle in our favor.

I reached out to Jen. *I need a distraction.*

A streak of lightning left the blade and hit Victor in the chest. The bolt threw him into the back of the stage, among the other obsidian blocks and the rest of the vampire council.

I grinned. *That'll work.* And felt Jen's grin in return.

My father was caught between me and the curse that controlled him. I sensed the geas as a conflict inside him. He was torn between protecting Victor and the vampire's command to kill me, fighting as much as he could. But as strong as he appeared, he wasn't strong enough. No one really could be.

I blinked into my ethereal sight and struck. My father brought his sword up quick, too fast to see for such a large blade, ready to parry the killing blow he thought was aimed at his chest.

I had a different target in mind, though. His parry was way off. While my father watched, I took an overhand swipe past him, at the tether binding him to Victor.

The blade sliced clean through.

There was no snapping sound. No gushing of energy from either end of the tendril. Both sides lay there, black, cleanly cut. The ends wriggled a bit, like a worm, cut in two.

All of a sudden I was lighter. Like I had been dragging a cinder block behind me, and the rope that had tied that block to me was cut. Free.

I wondered how that freedom would feel to my father. He had already moved from his parry position, cutting his huge blade horizontally in the air, toward me. Then he stumbled, jerking the blade to the side, stumbling to one knee.

A scream of rage and pain came from the mass of vampires and people, where Victor had fallen.

My father looked at me, incredulously. In my ethereal sight he was a large, dark shadow, with a flickering white light inside his chest. Tinged with a dirty gold.

"You're welcome," I said.

"Free," he whispered, the word almost a question. He looked over at where my mother was fighting Raphael. "Oh, *Ariel* ..."

Was that my mother's name? Like my father, she was a dark shadow. White flicker in her chest. The gold color even dirtier. Like it was smudged with smoke.

"I didn't think it was possible," my father said, his eyes still following the blur of a katana through the air.

"You going to argue about it, or help?" I asked.

"You need to know something," my father said.

"Tell me later," I said. "We need to find my friends, and then free Mother."

My father winced. His jaw tightened. Behind him, I saw the ends of the geas, where I had cut, stretching themselves thinner. Reattaching themselves.

I could feel it as well, from far off. A tiny pulsing. Like a dark cloud, low and heavy on the horizon, bringing a promise of a thundering storm.

I swung my blade again. And again. Chopping up the tether. The more I did so, the more the tendrils tried to avoid the blade. As if the geas was learning, and adapting. It felt like a game of whack-a-mole; the more I chopped up the tendril, the more pieces of it tried to pull themselves back together.

"Stop," my father said, reaching his arm out to me, midswing.

"What?" I jerked my arm away, furious. They could be free. Both of my parents could be free. All I had to do was keep cutting.

"Son, you can't break it," my father said. Though his grin was back, it felt forced, and his eyes were sad.

"I'm breaking it *right now*," I said.

"You're just pissing it off," he said. "Look at it, and tell me different."

I hated him for saying it, but he was right. I had cut up the tether so much that the ground below me looked like a plate of wriggling worms. All dividing up, over and over, reaching out to themselves.

"I was so *sure*," I said. I was supposed to be *more*. I was supposed to be *greater*.

The wriggling parts of the tendrils sucked up inside each another, like drops of water did as they slipped next to each other.

My father took a deep breath and let it out.

"You've got fight, son," he said. "Spirit. I wish I could have known you more. But I'm proud, nevertheless."

The tendril was pulling itself back together, absorbing itself in an accelerated motion, as I watched.

"Where are my friends?" I asked. Knowing that even if I could not free my father, I had to rescue them.

My father shook his head. Beads of sweat showed on his forehead. "Keep fighting, son. And know your mother and I, we're proud."

"Stop saying that!" I shouted. *"Where are they?"*

My father screamed then, and balled up both fists. He pounded the ground with them, over and over. The tendril was now whole behind him, and where I had cut it now swelled with a pulsing, tumorous growth.

And behind my father was Victor. Who stood at the very edge of the stage, just a few feet from my father and me. Looking at both of us.

And getting it.

Victor glanced quickly at my mother, fighting Raphael. She was in the middle of a quick slice, ducking under his swing and planting her katana through an armpit. The tip of the blade came out of his other side, gouging his arm.

Raphael grunted, and stepped back. Wisps of crimson circled Raphael in my sight, already binding and tying wounds together. My mother raced up to where Dominic had landed.

"Traitors," Victor said, looking back at my father.

"How can a slave be a traitor?" my father spat back.

I lost it. I couldn't free my parents, and my friends. I hadn't protected them. I screamed and jumped over my father, bringing my ethereal blade high above my head. Jen already was charging it, electricity crackling above me.

"Stop," Victor said, simply.

One geas the two of us were fighting. Then the second geas woke up in me. Pain ripped through me, as each of the geas fought for control over me. I couldn't think, I couldn't move, and I couldn't help Jen.

I froze in midair and landed poorly, face-first. The sword disappeared from my hand. I bounced off the ground and came to a stop in front of Victor.

I couldn't see him. There was just Raphael, tugging on the katana in his side. The angle and the placement of the blade made it hard for him to yank it out.

Big heaving breaths burst from my chest. Each of the geas felt like it was blending my insides together. I think I screamed, wasn't sure.

Jen was in me, trying to heal me. What she healed, the geas tore quickly apart. Frustrated, she started moving me. My arm. My legs. Getting me to one knee. Turning my head toward Victor. Trying to summon the sword.

Gus, help....

I tried. I really did. But the pain was too great. It was hard to keep my eyes open, and when I did images flashed too quickly around me. It became a struggle to stay conscious. Then the ghost I was tethered to popped, and was gone.

We were in trouble.

Jen was trying to move me. My body was getting up, slowly. Like on old man, struggling with his balance, getting out of a chair. Victor watched me, curious. His head tilted a little.

"Fascinating," the vampire said.

Raphael was at the edge of my vision. He was spitting blood, his face furious. He had grabbed the katana's hilt and he was trying to pull it out, by working it forward out of his chest.

All this I got in glimpses. In the middle of the pain. Jen burned through her ethereal energy, the ghost she was tapped to, pushing me to stand. My hand twitched, like it was calling for the sword.

"Take care of him," Victor said. The vampire's feet appeared, right in front of me.

My father walked over, moving like an automaton. He kicked Raphael down. Planted his large sword through the middle of Raphael's chest, driving the blade deep into the stone, until the hilt rested against skin.

Raphael kicked once, twice. He reached up for the sword. My father put one fist into his face. Then struck Raphael a few more times, until a wet, squishy sound came at each blow. Then my father stood, shaking his hand, spattering blood across the stage.

His expression was blank.

Victor was still watching me. "How do you do that?" he asked.

Gus, Jen pleaded.

I pushed past the pain, tried to summon the sword. Tried to grab what energy I held, what was left of the second ghost, and still the blade just wouldn't come. I didn't think I had enough energy, and I wasn't pulling any more from Jen.

Victor's eyes grew more focused. As if he had thought about me long enough. The vampire lord reached out and pushed at the center of my chest. Like someone might tip a cow.

I toppled over to the ground.

The ruddy farmer's face of Victor appeared over me, with its flap of skin hanging from it. Gruesome, but Victor looked pleased. "Which one of us do you think understands correctly *now*?"

I didn't answer. Jen moved my arms and legs, but the limbs moved like a baby's. Without any real control.

The only thing I could do was stare at Victor with every ounce of hate I had in my body.

"That's a look I've seen many times, in those I've beaten," Victor said. And smiled, leaning closer. His voice softened, although each word was still spoken precisely. "You see, there really is nothing I haven't seen before. Nothing I haven't tried. Nothing I haven't … prepared for."

We had lost. We were trapped and awaiting the end. My friends ambushed and possibly dead. My parents still under the geas. I had come here to show real vengeance, and I had failed again….

"Son, there is a power to words, you said." My mother had just told me that, back at the airport, her hand latched tightly on to mine. *"So promise me. Do anything but despair…."*

She had known that was something I couldn't promise. She saw I was flawed in that way. That I took too much onto myself, and if I couldn't protect those I loved, to me it meant I was weak. That I wasn't strong enough.

If I was all that the good side had been able to put together over the past couple of thousand years, all that was here to stand against evil, then our side had made a mistake.

I just wasn't good enough. Powerful enough. Great enough.

The bond whipped inside me, angry.

Gus, Jen said. *You keep fighting.*

It's what I've been doing, Jen, I said. *I've been fighting everything, and look where it's gotten me. Look at you. Now our friends. Look at* us.

It was my choice, Jen said. *Stop taking that from me. Stop taking it from us.*

Whatever, Jen, I said. The word that would be placed on my tombstone. *Whatever.*

You promised.

I didn't answer. That promise would be just another broken one, in a long string of them. Seemed about right. One more half-ass thing I had tried, and failed.

Jen grew angrier. *Dammit, Gus. You don't get to give up. It's not you. It's* not you*!*

What am I really, Jen? I tried to shrug. Neither of my shoulders moved. One more thing I couldn't do. *I'm no angel. I'm not something great. I thought I could at least fight, and one fucking word keeps me paralyzed. I'm going to lose it all, just like I lost you, Jen, and it's all so fucking bullshit. It's* bullshit *and I hate all of it.*

I stopped trying. And as soon as I did, the pain from the geas fighting eased. Both of the curses, the one from Dominic and the one from Victor, still fought each other for control of me. But it was like the geas understood it didn't have to work as hard now.

It was like everything was telling me to quit and let go. That it was easier just to let things happen as they would. A thought burst out of nowhere.

I think I've had enough.

"Speaking of being defeated," Victor said. "Dominic? You still alive, *old friend?"*

The older vampire was being half carried down through the crowd by my mother. Spittle dripping from his lips. His eyes, half-mad.

"Why didn't you tell me that this man here"—Victor kicked my face —"is the son of your assassin and mine?"

My mother paused, in midstep. She looked over at my father, whose expression was blank. The edges of his face hard, like his teeth were pressed tightly together. As if he knew what was coming, and was resolved to see it through.

I had no idea why I felt that from him. From my mother. But I did. I wondered if the two of them knew something I didn't. Something neither had shared with me.

Dominic frowned. He pushed away from my mother and wiped his mouth with the back of an arm. He stumbled down to look at me, then looked at my father. Dominic's eyes cleared a little, and then narrowed with anger.

My mother stood rock-still. A statue. Precise.

"Explain," Dominic demanded.

My mother answered with a lift of her shoulder. "We had sex," she said, as if talking about the weather. "It's something people do."

"Was this some kind of plan of yours, to get back at me?" Victor interrupted. "Because of your exile from Europe?"

"I had nothing to do with this," Dominic answered. He was taller than Victor, and maybe even angrier, but stick-thin next to Victor's thick build. The drug had taken a large toll.

Once he had been among the most evil things I could imagine. Back when I had first seen him, at Parker's. Now he was just one evil thing among many.

Dominic stepped close to Victor, chest to chest, lowering his voice. Sharply edged coat next to rumpled, torn suit. "And my revenge for my exile was complete the moment you banned me."

Victor's face immediately paled. "My sons …"

The edge of Dominic's lips curved up in a quick motion. "You were so proud of them. Of *having* them, when I had none."

For a moment the vampire lords stood toe-to-toe, a breath from erupting into violence. Each of my parents took a stance behind the person who held their geas, ready to fight. My mother's eyes open and shimmering. My father with what I'd come to think of as his half grin.

"This will be settled," Victor finally said.

"By all means," Dominic answered.

The chitter-chatter of assault rifles being loaded rolled across the stage. More thralls now surrounded the concert hall. I wasn't sure which ones belonged to the Antonados and which ones belonged to the Dumonts. They all looked the same, from flat on the ground.

A lot of the vampire crowd was back as well. There were quite a few bodies still in the stands, but the number of dead was a drop in the bucket compared to the rest of them. The crowd had formed two semicircles around us. One behind Dominic, one behind Victor. Everyone on the edge of violence.

Somewhere behind Dominic one of Raphael's feet twitched. I laughed. Or tried to laugh. More of a choking sound came from my throat. Almost hollow.

Both vampires looked down at me.

"You lied to me, Victor," I said. "Or didn't you just tell me about the long line of enemies you've killed?"

Dominic's smile grew wider.

"It feels good to be one of your failures," I said. "Feels like good company to keep."

Victor kicked my face. It spun me around, laying me on my back, the Key jostling on my chest. It caught his eye, and he knelt next to me.

Gus –

I tried to move. As soon as I did the geas responded. Both of them did. They fought each other for control of me, and I tried to fight it back. To more pain.

"What is that thing?" Victor snarled. He placed his hand on the Key.

Gus, don't let him take —

Victor ripped the Key off me.

Jen —

I screamed then. All that came out of my frozen throat was a warbling moan. As soon as Victor had taken the Key, I was shut off from Jen. The bond felt thin. Almost gone.

"Something important to you?" Victor grinned. He hefted the Key like he was weighing it, and then cocked his head. "Or … someone?"

I battered myself against the geas, and maybe a finger moved. Maybe. I forced the energy I had left down our bond, toward Jen, trying to break through the wall between us.

It was like running headfirst into the side of a building.

"Is this how you overcome the geas?" Victor asked.

"What is it?" Dominic asked.

I ran into the wall again. And again. Trying to reach Jen. And still I felt nothing from the other side of the bond. Only that the wall was there.

Both vampires faced each other. Dominic's eyes flicked to the Key.

"We need to take care of this first," Victor said. "Then we'll deal with what's between us."

They both looked to me. Dominic's nod, when it came, was slow. "So – are we saying the peace of the council lasts?"

"For now," Victor said.

"The moment he's dead, the peace is broken," Dominic said.

Both of the vampires smiled. As if a long, burning, mutual hate was going to end, at last.

"Just so," Victor said. Then the vampire turned to my father. "Stay," he told him, like someone would tell a dog. Victor waved the crowd back with one hand, and he kept looking at the other hand. Where he held the Key. The vampire moved slowly backward, toward the stage.

Jen, I thought. As hard as I could. With no answer. No *feel.*

Dominic followed him, then took a seat on one of the blocks. The vampire's legs shook a bit, but his bearing once he sat was imperial. Like an emperor, surveying the crowd. His coat lying behind him like a cloak.

My mother and father remained. Facing each other, six or seven feet apart.

"I thought we had a better understanding," Dominic said, staring at my mother. "You've put all of us into a dangerous situation."

"Sometimes you all are more trouble than you are worth," Victor added, staring at Cronan. "With this damn contract."

My father's lips twitched, humorlessly. Though, since he was facing away from the stage, only my mother and I saw it.

"Stand," Victor told me.

I screamed then, for real. One of the geas was telling me to stop, the other to stand. The two curses fought each other. My body felt like it was being ripped apart. As if every muscle fiber was being pulled in two different directions.

Victor looked over at Dominic. "Say the word."

Dominic rolled his eyes. "Stand."

The pain stopped, immediately, leaving sharp tearing pricks up and down my arms and legs. In my chest, every time I tried to breathe.

Slowly I got to my feet, panting shallow breaths. Trying to avoid any large motion. The pain felt like someone was stapling me, thousands of times, over and over. Just putting the stapler against my skin and clicking and clicking and clicking.

Both geas still fought each other, inside me, as if one wanted dominance over the other. Like each of their masters. The darkness swarmed inside me, tendril fighting tendril. My stomach roiled, bile rose in my throat. I swallowed hard to keep from throwing up.

"What are you doing?" Dominic asked. He wasn't facing me, though.

I focused on Victor. He had the Key before him again, in his fist. Tiny wisps of sparks emanated from the crumbling stone. As if Jen was trying to break out.

Don't, Jen.... That last thing she had felt from me was despair. It was dark, and real, and I knew that hopeless feeling from me would have Jen give up everything she had to save me. She would use whatever ethereal energy her own ghost had until she disappeared into whatever afterlife awaited her.

Just to give me a chance.

Victor shook his head, like he woke from a dream. The flap of skin waggling out and back, from his face. "I think we should have the people who created this problem be the ones who remove it."

Dominic looked again at my mother. "Fair enough."

My father's eyes shut, once. He mouthed the word Aerial. My mother, facing the stage, did nothing. Though her eyes were locked on my father's. She was smaller than him, thinner, elegant and precise. My father was large, mountainous, brutal and overpowering.

Surrounding us, the stage, were all the vampires that were left. Each body and face blending into the next until the crowd was a mass of the same person. The same bloodless face next to bloodless face. The same angry eyes, the excited expressions, the pale tongues flicking out from hungry mouths.

They crowded all of us, leaving just a circle around me and my parents, and Raphael, who lay at the edge. A vampire stepped on the body, then kicked it once or twice. Raphael's knee bent, and he reached weakly to the hilt of the sword in his chest. The vampire kicked the hand away, spat, and then froze. Then stepped away, quickly.

Others gave Raphael's body a wide berth.

Guns and knives and swords lay all around us. Weapons of the dead. High above us all, on the rim of the stands, hundreds of thralls. Armed with automatic rifles, here and there a rocket launcher. All pointed to the floor of the amphitheater. At the three of us, my father, my mother, and me.

There was Jen, in the stone, in Victor's hand. I wondered what would happen to her if I died. Would she be trapped in the Key, or was Victor sensing her now? Sensing the bond. Was that something he could use as well? Were the sparks around his fingers Jen breaking out, or could Victor use her power, just by holding the Key?

I thought I had been special. Unique. I thought Jen and I were something different. That we were *more*, *together*. But my mother was wrong. I wasn't anything special. I was just a guy a step slow, a minute late, always in the wrong place at the wrong time. Never strong enough to protect or save his friends. Just strong enough to keep living, after they died.

The universe had a funny way of always showing me the new lows it would descend to.

"Stand between your mother and father," Victor told me.

Dominic muttered the same words with a sneer.

I took mechanical steps until I stood precisely between my mother and father. I faced my father, with my mother behind me. My father tilted his head to the side a little, studying me.

"*Son*," my mother whispered, "you *are* greater. Remember that."

Maybe she wasn't clued in on the situation. Victor had Jen. And my friends were trapped or dead. And she was about to be ordered to kill me. I was about to be greater than dead.

Maybe, dead, I could let all this go.

Victor smiled, on the stage. The vampire was clearly outlined above my father's shoulder. He had the Key held tightly in a closed fist, and electric arcs were running over and between his fingers.

"He's given up, Ariel," my father said. His half smile gone. His eyes not sad, but … disappointed.

"Fuck you, Dad," I said.

"Son," my mother whispered, from behind me.

"I thought you were a fighter." My father shook his head. "Maybe you only fight the easy battles."

"What the fuck do you know?" I asked him.

"Son," my mother whispered again, urgently.

"*What the fuck do I know?*" Cronan roared, so loud that everyone took a step back. So loud my ears rang. Then he leaned into me. "You fucking pussy."

Dominic stood, and took a couple of steps closer to the edge of the stage. His eyes watching everything carefully, but especially my mother.

My father turned back to Victor. "Let me kill him now. This is no son of mine."

"Son," my mother pleaded, one last time. Her voice so low I didn't know how I actually heard it, after my father's roaring scream. "Be strong. It'll be over soon."

I was *so* tired of being told to be strong. "Fuck you, too, Mother."

"*Son*," she said. Sounding surprised. The word carrying disappointment, hurt, and maybe regret. Maybe my mother and father had endured a lot of evil. Suffered a lot. But it wasn't anything I related to. I didn't really know them. And they shouldn't pretend to know me.

Dominic had seen something he didn't like, between my mother and me. Or maybe he was just tired of the wait. Or wanted to be first. "Go on, then," the head of the Antonados ordered my mother. "Kill him."

At the same time, the lord of the Dumonts motioned my father to me.

The next moment happened quickly. My father picked up a blade, one of those scattered on the ground. The sword looked small in his hands. "This world is hard, son. You need to buck up."

"You shouldn't tolerate failure," my mother said, from behind me. "Especially in yourself."

I could only stare my father square in the face, but my words were for both of them. I had come here hoping to rescue them. Instead I had lost it all. Them. My friends. Jen. "I've heard enough talk."

The corner of his lips lifted. He stepped to a very precise place, in front of me. Close. Too close. Then he plunged his sword through my chest. Right in the middle of my heart.

At the same time another blade entered my back, sliding alongside my father's just in the opposite direction.

The pain was tremendous. But I had just experienced a greater agony, with the geas tearing me apart. So, while having my heart cut in half was painful, it was far below that pain of the Richter scale of agony. Which meant that although it was torturous, the pain wasn't overwhelming. It was just something I was used to, by comparison.

So I put the pain aside. I didn't try reaching out for any ghosts. I wanted death, and I welcomed it.

"Finally," I said. Letting out my last breath. Relieved.

"Finally," my father spat. His brows lowered. "Son, the shit for you is just beginning."

He said the curse with an *I* sound, like *shite*. Odd that I would notice that then.

I realized then my father had spat out a glob of blood. It hung from the side of his mouth like a blob of crimson saliva. He had stepped close to me when he delivered the blow. And the blade my mother had punched through me had also gone through my father. Right through his heart.

I felt then my mother's chest tight to my back. Elegantly and precisely placed. And I knew, I *knew*, that my father's sword had pierced her heart as well.

My parents were both dying.

As their hearts slowed and stopped, each of their geas grew larger in me. Each curse swelled out of my parents' bodies and poured into me. More monstrous. Angry. Both of them fighting each other for control of me. Swallowing each other whole, as they circled around inside me.

My body jerked. The blades cut deeper into my chest. My muscles spasmed until my father and mother both reached around me and held me tight. Blood coating us all.

Come … to … Conclave.

Trust. Me.

This had been their plan, all along.

"Mother?" I whispered.

"Son," she said softly, simply, her lips next to my ear.

Whatever plan my father and mother had, they would never have been able to talk about it. I don't know how they had communicated it to each other, over the years, without anyone else finding out. How they had formed the plan, and gotten it to this point.

The point where the geas would finally end.

Still, the curses poured into me. Flying out of my parents. Each geas fought and tangled and grew larger and larger in me, one trying to best the other.

And yet at the same time they were wasting away. Stealing chunks from each other, like two snakes swallowing each other's tail. Growing smaller. Canceling each other out.

My parents had figured out how to beat the geas. Not for them. But for me.

Ethereal energy wrapped me. From both my mother and father. As they died, as the geas left them, they had that much left to give. A cool healing washed over me, knitting my heart back together. Snapping the metal of the blades off at the wounds, pushing the pieces out. Keeping some of the pain of the geas from tearing into me.

The bodies of my parents shielded everything from Victor and Dominic. They hugged me in that quiet moment, in the timeless bubble using ethereal energy seemed to provide.

"You *are* going to have to finish this," my father said, through teeth clenched together. Healing me despite being told to kill me. "So don't be a pussy about it."

Then he winced. Tried to turn the wince into his half grin. As if taking the edge off the words. Maybe I couldn't know what he had done through his life, what he had endured, but I understood what he was giving me now.

What both my parents were giving me. Freedom. Somehow they had planned all this, had decided a long time ago they would give their lives for mine. Even though I had failed them both, they were not failing me.

I shut my eyes hard at a sudden, sharp pain. The curses yanking through me, whipping around, but growing smaller and smaller as both snakes ate more of themselves. Tears pushed from under my eyelids and streamed down my cheek.

My father's face bobbed closer to me, like his head was loose on his neck. His arms hugged me tightly, then let go. I tried to hold him up, but I couldn't move, could only watch as my father's head lolled back, as if nothing held it up.

My mother gasped in my ear. The side of my neck was wet. She was crying, too. My insides spasmed, and I would have doubled over, had my mother not held me up.

"Mother?" I said.

"Son." Her voice was weak. Less than a whisper. Low enough I might have imagined it. Except for the words. "You should have a better name. Something not so dark, maybe —"

And then she shuddered, too, like my father. Her arms loosened, and I felt coolness as her warm form left my back. The sound she made, falling away, was something between a sigh and a moan.

Both of my parents had a sword in their chest, exactly in the middle of their heart, the blade broken off after it left their skin. Blood smeared each of their fronts. I was covered in it as well.

The whole thing had only taken a moment. The ethereal time sense had made it seem like much, much longer. As time sped back up, as my father slipped to the ground in front of me, as my mother dropped away behind me, both Dominic's and Victor's eyes opened, slowly, wide.

My parents hit the ground.

The curse grew smaller in me, but the pain grew larger. As if the geas – the closer it came to dying out – fought harder to survive. I fell to one knee, my fist tightly pressed to the ground, as if it was all that held me up.

What did I know about sacrifice? My parents had given their lives for this. For *me*.

Jen had done the same, in New Orleans. She had gone into battle willingly, without reservation, and had given the ultimate sacrifice.

Danny had done it, too. He had stood bravely and taken a hit that should have been for me. I had fled Grafton, minutes later, never to return.

I couldn't handle my friends dying. I had built myself into this guy who could protect them no matter what, but the truth was that I was too brittle a person to handle them dying. That me promising aloud over and over to keep them safe was just a promise from a guy who couldn't handle his friends dying. Because I should be strong enough to keep them alive.

Life just didn't work that way. It was unfair. Danny, Jen, my parents. Nick, Sarah, Johnny, Gabrielle. I could blame all their deaths on me. But the truth was, life sucked sometimes. Even if I felt like I could do more, *be more*, sometimes people died.

I needed to accept those sacrifices. I needed to use them as fuel. And then I needed to extract vengeance.

I should be taking as many of these motherfuckers down as I could.

Dominic screamed a command for my mother to live. Her eyes rolled up in the back of her head, her legs jerked up and down, her arms flailed. Like she was a marionette at the hands of a drunk puppeteer.

The curse took large chunks out of the inside of me. I tried to reach out for a ghost, but the geas still held me from doing anything. I screamed over and over, until my voice grew hoarse, and held my stomach with one arm. Trying to hold myself together.

Dominic leaped down off the stage and swatted at me. I sprawled across the ground. He stood above me, fangs out, hands out like claws.

"I should have left you dead in Grafton," the vampire lord said.

A sword burst out of his stomach. My father's sword. Raphael suddenly was behind Dominic, one arm around his father's throat, the huge blade jutting out of his father's belly. Raphael's face was a mess, all crushed cartilage and broken bones. One eye looked like a squashed grape, hanging on his cheek.

He looked like a zombie from a movie, but his sneer was all Raphael. "No one is killing Grimm but me, *Dad*," Raphael said.

Dominic screamed. His eyes turned solidly black, his face twitched with fury. The vampire tried to throw his son off, and my father's sword jerked up and down in Dominic's belly. Black liquid spurted everywhere. Raphael took a step back, the two twisted around, and then the crowd of vampires closed around them, taking them from my view.

My mother's legs still drummed on the ground. My father hadn't moved. I extended my senses to my mother, the ethereal sense I had, and saw nothing. Felt nothing. No beat of the heart, no pumping of the lungs. Nothing but the twitching of the geas, fleeing my mother's body and entering mine.

I closed my eyes and screamed. From the pain of the geas inside me, or my mother's dead body twitching beside me, I didn't know. Probably both.

Bodies jumped on me. Vampires, getting revenge. They bit me over and over again, tearing chunks from my skin. Ripping through my shirt, my jeans.

I could do nothing. The two curses kept twisting and whipping inside me. Smaller now, but their struggle also seemed sharper. Their combat had a deadly edge, and as much as I tried to flail against it, both of the geas forced me still. If I could just tap into one ghost …

"Hey," came a precise voice, by my ear. Victor, squatting next to me. He was so close the flap of skin brushed my ear, something cold and dead, like a cool piece of rubber. The other vampires backed away a bit from the vampire lord. "I felt like thanking you, before you died. As much as Cronan did for my family, for *me*, I never did like having that noose around my neck."

I wanted to answer, but words failed me. I didn't know what to say that I hadn't already said. There was just this wave of anger in me, pounding the shore over and over. But anger could only bring me so far.

"And I have this new toy now." Victor kept talking, holding up his hand. The sparks playing around his fist had grown stronger, thicker, brighter. As if Jen was trying to break out. "I appreciate you giving me a demonstration."

Jen.

The wave of anger pounded the beach. I roared and fought the geas with everything I had. The curse stretched around me, until the geas felt like the thin skin of a balloon, inflated so big that at any second it would pop. Every muscle in my body tensed up until they began spasming, and still I pushed more energy into me.

Just ... another ... second ...

Victor smiled. Patted my head, like a good dog. Then whispered a command. "Die."

Like Dominic, back in Grafton. I had done this before. I knew what the pain would be like. I knew what would happen.

And still I couldn't stop it. The curse from Victor stopped my heart. The other geas held me rock-still. All the while, both curses circling and twisting and eating each other inside me, smaller and smaller. So small now, almost nothing could be left of them.

I tried screaming again, and couldn't. My chest hurt terribly, my heart screaming to pump one more time. My lungs burned, trying to draw a breath. Spots flecked over my sight, thick black spots that darkened the world around me. My vision grew dark, then red, then began to fade.

If I could just tap one ghost. Just one. Just to get something to keep me alive a moment longer. Just until the geas died out. Then I would show this motherfucker vengeance. And I wouldn't be a pussy about it.

Victor's hand lit up, a ball of lightning, so many blue arcs crackling over his fist his fingers were no longer visible. His arm hidden by the storm.

Jen must be experiencing what I was. Feeling my body's pain, feeling my heart stop and my lungs try to breathe. I didn't know how she felt it. Our bond was the faintest of connections, and I felt nothing from her.

But she obviously felt something from me. Maybe my pain was too great. I screamed at her to stop, to not use herself up. Not for me. *Oh, please, God, not for me ...*

Jen, no ...

Our bond came alive, burning with energy, bursting with it. Lightning poured out of my eyes, my open mouth, my fingers. Bolts shot everywhere, in a continuous stream of electric power, blasting everything and everyone else away ...

And then I was me. Not him *me, but* me *me. I was on top of the water tower, back in Grafton, legs loose and dangling off the platform. My arms crossed over one of the bars of the railing. It was a bright summer day, the sky clear and blue above me, the breeze bringing the fresh scent of honeysuckle so prevalent this time of year.*

A lunch sat behind me, some sandwiches of peanut butter and jelly, with enough jelly to soak the bread, like I liked it. A couple of thin sand-

wich bags, full of potato chips. Salt and vinegar, which I didn't like too much, but Jen did. A big thermos of Kool-Aid, grape. Cold and delicious, with a little extra sugar in it.

Jen sat next to me. Her hip tight to mine, her legs loose and free, her arms crossed over the same railing, both of us looking in the same direction.

Toward Main Street. Toward the place where Danny had died, the alley behind the liquor store.

Oh God, I wasn't living a memory....

Jen's hand came up behind me, rubbing my back. Her palm warm and soft and yet still firm. Strong. Her head leaned onto my shoulder, and her hair brushed my cheek, like silk.

"I think I understand now," she said.

I didn't talk. Was afraid to talk. Anything I said might be the wrong thing. And for some reason I wanted this moment to last forever. Because I was afraid of what the next moment might bring.

"Danny showed it to us," she said. "His sacrifice."

I tried to break my arms free of the rail, to wrap my arms around Jen, to hold her. But they stayed locked over the rail. The sky above us seemed to get brighter and brighter, as if the sun was coming closer and closer, and the brightness began to wash everything else out.

"It's what we do for each other," Jen said. "If we love each other that much, we should be willing, right? To give our lives for those we love? When they need it most?"

"Jen," I finally said, my throat tight, my voice thick and hoarse.

"We can't ever decide the time, Gus," she said. "I think we just have to accept it, when it comes."

"Jen," I said again. "Don't. Please don't."

The light grew brighter around us, bright like we were inside a star. A shooting star, blazing across the heavens. And taking Jen from me.

"I love you, Gus," she said. "Be strong."

The light grew so bright I pressed my eyes together. The memory of peanut butter and jelly, of grape Kool-Aid, of the scent of honeysuckle and fresh rain, it all washed away in that last moment. I felt, more than saw, Jen get up next to me. Her hand lingering in mine. Her face westward, and turned up slightly, as if facing the sun ...

I closed my eyes and screamed.

I broke free of the dream, of the memory, of whatever. Jen's energy flooded into me. All the bites, the ragged tears in my skin, the cuts, instantly healed. My fists swung around and connected with bodies around me, things that were soft, plump sacks of skin that burst under each swing. Vampires flew away at the slightest touch. Lightning shot out of me, out of my mouth, my nose, eyes, my fingers. Bolts crackled and sizzled across the stage, tossing vampires aside, burning them to piles of ash.

I lost track of where I was, who I was, and what I was doing. I just kept screaming. I just kept swinging.

And then I was standing, whole, in the middle of the amphitheater. A storm of lightning swirled around me, flew over my skin, the sheer voltage of it snapping and crackling. Ozone was in every breath I took, and thick bolts of electricity forking across the stage, up the stairs, and through the crowd, burning every vampire they touched to quick flashes of cinder.

The stadium lights blew, one at a time, around us all. After that the only light in the place was the bright blue flickering of electric arcs, strobing out of me at every beat of my heart. Victor appeared among the blue flashes, still somehow standing next to me, his hand open, his eyes wide with terror.

I took the Key from his hand.

The stone was completely white, and crumbling. Chunks fell off, until all that was left was a tiny pebble. Small, like an acorn.

And the bond between the Key and me, between Jen and me, slammed back into me.

There was a lightness about me I had never felt before. Like I had been carrying around a hundred-pound pack, and it had just vanished.

I was free of the geas. It was gone. My mother and father had given their lives, and for that I was free. To do whatever I wanted.

And I knew exactly what that was. I would be damned if Jen had to give her life, as well as my parents. I didn't care about Victor, about Raphael and Dominic, or Belle. Or whatever was left of the vampires and the thralls around me. Nothing of the fight between vampire and vampire.

Danny had given his life for me. Not just once, but twice. The first time, I had run away. I had let his sacrifice go to waste. He had given his life for me, and I had run in fear.

The second time, I had taken his gift and done something with it. I had become something more. Something greater.

After Jen had died, I tried to run away. I tried to give up. I didn't want to live in that world. And my friends wouldn't let me. They gave me hope.

They gave me the path that ended right here. Where I was now. Right now. With vampires dying all around us, where Jen was trying to be like Danny, and give herself up again. Make me greater, so that I could live on without her.

I didn't want to be that great. Not alone. I dove back along our bond, pushing everything I had into the Key, and Jen....

I was back on the water tower, back on the platform. Still sitting, legs dangling below. And not just me, but me and Jen. Her fingers still latched on to mine. Her face still looking up. Looking west.

"Hey," I said.

She looked back, surprised. Tears coated her cheeks, but there was also a resolution in her eyes. An acceptance.

I waited.

"Hey," she finally said, with a sad smile.

I tugged her back down, to sit next to me. Like we were kids, with everything below us. The white light was everywhere, but I could see through it, like a cloud. Bits and pieces of the town revealed themselves, underneath.

"Gus ...," Jen whispered, her glance west, toward where her house in Grafton would be. A tear on her cheek. "You know I have to go."

"Maybe," I said. Then asked, "Where?"

She sighed. "Something pulls at me. Has always pulled at me, since ... since this." She fluttered her hand around.

Since she had died.

"Jen," I said, "can you answer one question for me? Again?"

She shook her head, as if she had given everything she could give. "Gus —"

"Hush." I turned her head to mine, my hand soft against her cheek. Her eyes wouldn't connect with mine, she kept turning away, but I held her there. Patient.

Finally her ocean-blue eyes stared straight into mine.

"Just tell me one thing," I said then. "Do you want to go?"

Jen's eyebrows lowered. "I've told you that answer, Gus."

She was angry, but I was grinning.

"What are you smiling at?" she asked. Then punched my shoulder.

I had asked her the same question, the night before, and she had answered. She had given me her word, that she wanted to stay with me.

You and me forever.

Words have power.

But I didn't explain all that to her. I just kissed her forehead, and held her close for a long, long moment. Until all I felt was her. The beat of her heart, with mine. Until all I could smell was honeysuckle and the fresh scent of a summer rain.

Then I pushed her away, gently. Each of my hands on each of her shoulders. I kept our gazes locked, and I felt everything in me that I had felt the moment I first saw Jen. She was someone who made me stand a little taller. Braver. Someone who did what they said they would do. No matter what.

I winked.

She tilted her head a little. Worried? Curious? I didn't know.

But I knew what I should do next.

"Jen, you've given enough," I said. "Let someone else take a turn."

Then I got up and jumped off the water tower. Falling through the air, west. Jen's hand tried to grab me, then slipped out. She cried out as I fell, shouting, but I lost the words.

Then wings caught me midair, the ethereal wings I had back in the real world. Here they were big, feathered angelic wings. My momentum and the cool breeze carried me west. The light grew brighter around me, and I began to soar. Higher and higher, through the bright clouds and into a light so blindingly white that Jen, the water tower, the world below just faded away.

Still, I rose higher. Faster. The puffy clouds around me streamed by as if I were a spaceship, leaving earth. Always up. Always west.

At one point I heard sounds ahead. Voices. Maybe what had called Jen. The voices became the murmuring of a crowd. Maybe the sounds I would hear at a ball game, outside on a beautiful blue sky sunny day …

Everything I heard and saw I also felt, and it all felt good. Truly good. Whether or not I was really feeling everything, or it was a figment of my imagination, it all felt like home. I felt home.

Ahead. Onward and upward. A crack of the bat split the air. The crowd roared.

Did you see it? *The same words I had heard in another place, another time. A small park. When it was just me and the rest of the gang, playing around on a beautiful sunny summer day.*

Another crack of the bat. Another roar of the crowd. In it voices, voices I knew, voices once lost to me. Maybe I imagined them. But I smiled anyway, because even imagined, they felt good to me. Right.

It went forever…

I gave in to it all. Maybe it didn't matter what I heard, or said, or even did, here. I reached out with an arm, as if giving someone a hug.

It sure did, bud.

Another crack of a bat. Another roar of the crowd. This time, the roar grew so loud it consumed me.

CHAPTER FIFTY-FIVE

I woke. Maybe that was the wrong word. Waking didn't seem to fit, somehow. But I couldn't describe it another way. The air was cold around me. Fresh against my face. Like I was standing on top of Mount Everest, a bracing chill of air blowing across me. Thin. Cold. Brisk.

My eyes were closed, with real darkness behind the lids. A loud rushing sound echoed in my ears, a fluttering and flapping of strong winds, like the roaring of a jet plane. Currents of air battered me, and I wondered where I was.

I couldn't feel any ground underneath my feet.

I thought I was flying.

Finally I opened my eyes.

It wasn't dark at all. The world around me was brilliantly lit, with a bright white light. So bright everything was white around me. Where everything was new again. A blank slate, beyond the glass. A canvas, something unpainted and untouched …

An ethereal end, maybe. But also, a beginning.

In many ways I felt like a newborn, opening his eyes to the world for the first time. I moved my head where I thought was up, then left and right, and still all I found was the bright whiteness. The blank canvas. A fresh world.

Finally I tried down. Where my feet should be standing. Where they had been standing, on solid ground.

I was flying. The whiteness thinned out below me, stretched out in long white tails, and became narrow pale wisps threading through a blue-black night sky.

I was high up in the air. So high the world was small underneath me. So high that clouds brushed across me. Maybe the whiteness was a cloud right now, lit by the face of the moon and the gathering stars, the cloud moving away, leaving the earth behind, leaving little white puffy arms pointing me below. Pointing me to the world below, which grew larger and larger underneath me.

I was high up in the air.

But I was also falling.

I descended through the air, gathering speed, feeling the wind whip past me. The bright white light I had woken to stayed with me. It lit the underneath of the clouds above. It took me a moment to realize the whiteness of the cloud wasn't because it was lit from the moon.

It was me. I was glowing. Not just glowing, but glowing *brilliantly*.

The white light was me, my skin illuminated, light bursting from each pore. My wings were back, ethereal and blazing white. So white that as the wind whipped past, the currents pulled little trails of light behind me. Like a comet's tail drifted in my wake. Or maybe stardust.

My sword was back, too. Not transparent, but shining with a starlike opalescence. Pure.

I dropped through the air like a comet. Until the earth became a map of the United States. Until the United States became the entire Rocky Mountain Range, winding north and south, tall ice-covered peaks pointed high up in the horizon. Until the Rocky Mountains became Colorado, then Denver.

The rushing of the air around me gathered into a roar. I found a ghost. The spirit never fought me. Just bowed and accepted the connection. As if waiting for judgment. I burned a little ethereal energy, enough to slow time down as I descended.

There was a fight still, around the amphitheater. Thousands of vampires left. Hundreds of thralls. The parking lot a mess, as some cars tried to leave, until car smashed into limo, limo into truck, until multiple wrecks logjammed the road out.

Some of the vehicles then tried off-roading.

West of the theater was a set of small hills and cliffs. A smoking hole rested on the sharp slope of one of the hills. Rubble had been strewn down the hillside, as if some explosion had blown everything outward.

My friends hadn't been trapped. They had, instead, found a way out. I focused and saw no flickering lights in bodies, no Nick or Sarah or Johnny or Gabrielle strewn about the rubble. Or in the entrance to the hole

I found them around the battle instead.

Nick twitched in and out of my sight with a pair of knives. His light appeared quickly, in flashes, only when he paused to stab a vampire with a silver blade. Then it was gone again.

Only to reappear in another place. Another stab. And gone.

Johnny and Gabrielle were back-to-back. Fighting mostly barehanded. Johnny had a shotgun in his hand, and was using it like a bat. Gabrielle was tearing out throats and ripping off arms with bare hands.

The three of them were working toward the center of the stage, at the bottom. Where the crowd was the largest. Victor there, in a crowd. Raphael and Dominic, still fighting.

Then I saw Sarah. Or what I thought was her. I heard the faintest of screams from the western rim of the stands. Something thick and black-blotted whipped around there, with long, large octopus-like arms flailing out from its center. White flickered at its center, the white swirling with colored sparks.

Each thrall an octopus arm touched, even the lightest of taps, fell over. Dead. Leaving nothing, not even a ghost behind. Other thralls fired into the darkness that was Sarah. Assault rifles and the whooshing sounds of missiles leaving rocket launchers. One of the missiles exploded into the black cloud, bright yellow and orange flames bursting out into the air like fireworks, the red and orange flames undulating underneath me.

None of it stopped Sarah. She, too, was working her way down. Maybe they were just killing everyone. Nick had that kind of vengeance to him. Maybe they were looking for me.

I guessed I needed to make an appearance, and find out.

I folded my wings and dove. The light around me grew brighter, if that was possible. My sword blazed like a thousand suns. The entire sky over Red Rock lit up, as if it were the middle of the day. It was so bright everyone stopped fighting and just looked up as winds tossed white sparks off behind me, leaving a cometlike trail.

I landed right in front of the stage. Right in the center of the pit. At a hundred miles an hour or so. Rock and stone shattered outward around me. The earth shook and tossed vampires left and right.

I stood, slowly. The white light illuminated everything in a stark film noir way. Bodies lay around me, some moving, some not. I surveyed it all, then calmly reversed my grip on the sword, grabbing the hilt in both hands, then plunging the blade into the rock before me. The earth swallowed the sword, greedily, and the light went with it, disappearing until the blade was all the way in.

There was a moment of darkness then. The darkness of a deep cave, a room with no windows or doors, the pitch-black of space without no stars or suns.

Moaning, breathing, sobbing was all around me.

Then light burst out of the ground, a whiteness so pure it rivaled the brightest stars. The cleanest of snows. Every vampire it touched just ... disappeared. Thralls stumbled and fell to the ground, bodies twitching. A wild ringing accompanied the light, like the tone of a perfectly cast bell, struck over and over in a heartbeatlike rhythm. Pounding with joy.

I covered my ears. The ringing grew louder, pulsed harder, until even I closed my eyes.

Then there was silence.

I opened my eyes again. I stood alone in the pit, all the vampires that had lain around me just ... gone. Farther away some scattered here and there, fleeing. I was glad. Not many had survived, but enough. Word would spread from here, those vampires and thralls left would describe it all, and when they told the story it would end with a warning.

Don't fuck with me or my friends.

Most of the bodies were gone, from around me. My mother and father remained. Some other thralls or vampires lay in the stands. Raphael was among them, my mother's sword still stuck through his side. He held his father in a choke hold, and dragged him down the theater to stand a few feet away from me. Raphael's eyes captured everything, the sword in the ground, me. Like he was analyzing it for further study.

"Thought you were dead," he said.

"Yeah," I said. "I guess I thought so, too."

I had no idea what had happened, after I jumped off the water tower. I remember the sounds and feel of a ball game. The crack of a bat. Maybe, *maybe*, a conversation.

"We good?" he asked, holding his father out to me. As if he was showing him off. Dominic struggled weakly in Raphael's arms, knotted tightly around his father's throat. His eyes pressed tightly together, his mouth open, but nothing, no sound coming out. The older vampire looked thin, emaciated, and beaten.

My parents' eyes were open. They lay a few feet apart from each other. My father with his half grin. My mother, face composed. Precise, even in death.

Their bodies glimmered with the residue of the white light, like a shimmering wetness covered them. The iridescence moved across their clothes and skin, faintly, as if a candle's flame traveled over their bodies, its flickering light reflected back at me. As the light worked up and down, they seemed to become transparent. A little more, with each wave of light.

Until they disappeared.

They had freed me. And in doing so, they had shown me the way forward. To becoming *more*. There was still a lot ahead of me. Azazel. The Dead Zones. Raphael. I promised my dad I would try not to be a pussy about any of it. And then I promised my mother …

What could I promise someone like her? The person who had brought me into the world? Who loved me so much, she had given her life for me? Had watched me, in the past few days, and seen my highs and lows. And still had believed in me. Had planned her sacrifice, all along, even after I failed. Maybe, especially then.

There had been a center inside her, a core untouched, that no one had known about. Not even Dominic, with the geas. My mother had kept a part hidden, had kept *me* hidden, and had only let out how she felt in an occasional trembling touch, like when she had wanted to brush a lock of my hair.

"You find a little part of yourself…. You tuck it away, where nothing can get to it. You hope the smaller part is greater than the evil."

All I had promised my mother was to try not to despair. To try to do my best. And to try to be greater than the evil.

I hoped that would be enough.

I finally nodded at Raphael. "We're good."

Raphael grinned, then casually ripped his father's head off.

Dominic began to scream, something high-pitched and girly. It ended quick, after a ripping of skin that turned the scream into a gargle. A moan. And a gasp.

Then that cry was gone. There was just the sound of Dominic's head bouncing across the rocky ground. Tiny thumps against stone.

Raphael looked at me, and I looked at him. Taking each other's measure.

"You've changed," he said.

I grinned then. Something dark, and full of power. Something that said, *Don't fuck with me*.

Raphael understood. "Something for me to look forward to, then," he said.

I wondered if he meant our battle. Or if he thought he would change as well. In the world we lived in, where one side rose up to fight the other, it made a perverse kind of sense. I had less doubt now, that he was my opposite on this coin. Evil's response to *me*.

The world seemed to work that way.

"Maybe," I said.

"Then it's Azazel's turn," Raphael said. "Six hundred and sixty-four days or so, right?"

"You have my word," I said. And I meant it.

A form flickered down the stands. Stopping quickly at anything moving. Stabbing and moving on. As soon as I noticed the form, it was gone.

Then it became Nick, standing between us.

"Man." I grinned. "I'm glad you guys made it."

"It was a close thing," Nick said, waving a hand at Raphael. "His little demon girlfriend helped us."

Belle? Both Raphael and I must have looked surprised. And then the demon herself appeared, the fourth point of our little group's compass. Each of us equidistant from the other.

"You saved them?" I asked.

"I did," she said. Tiredly.

"Ensuring the agreement?" I asked.

Belle's eyes focused on the sword, planted in the ground before me. It was no longer opalescent, no longer transparent, but something in between. "Maybe. Maybe a little side bet as well. A hedge."

I saw her again, all the tendrils that led out from Belle, contracts binding others, contracts binding her, and wondered what hedge she was making. Demons and their secrets.

Sarah appeared, heading down the stairs. Johnny and Gabrielle, from around the stage. All of us looked tired. All of us looked like we could use a long rest. But—I smiled—all of us looked *alive*.

I don't think any of us really thought that would be the case.

"What's that?" Nick asked, looking at the sword. I realized something was stuck in the middle of the hilt. I grabbed the blade with my hand and willed the sword to disappear.

Something dropped off in my hand. Small, like a pebble, but smooth. And heavy for its size.

I opened my hand.

It was a piece of stone. Polished quartzite. What sandstone turned into, under a lot of pressure and heat. A hardened teardrop of rock, colored pink and sandy with thin lines of blue. Curved at the tail, just a little.

The tiny electric lines moved over the surface of the stone. They played over it, like a subdued version of one of those plasma lightning orbs. A tiny show of lightning.

Jen. The bond rested tightly between us, like always. She was still with me. Still here.

We had all made it, then. Not in the way I wanted to, maybe. Not in the way I hoped, definitely. But *here*, nonetheless.

I could work with that.

CHAPTER FIFTY-SIX

There was a lot of standing around, after the battle. Not knowing what to do next. There was a lot of cleanup needed at the Red Rock Amphitheatre, but we were going to leave that for the next owner.

Sarah and Nick stayed by me, for a bit. Sarah hugged me, after finding out Jen was still here. Nick just standing, steady. There if he was needed. Not intruding if he wasn't.

He seemed to get it.

Johnny and Gabrielle went through what vampires were left. She wanted to see Victor's body, and I couldn't blame her. I told them about the light, and how the vampires touched by the light had just disappeared, but she wanted his dead corpse at her feet.

Johnny was along for that ride. He looked tired. Hungry. Worried. Well, I think we all looked each of those.

In the movies people celebrated after a win. They danced and screamed, music blared out, some victory song. They hugged and kissed and pumped their fists.

In real life it was different. We were exhausted. We had won something here, but we weren't sure what that would lead to. What was next. There was no overarching plan for us to follow.

And really, we just needed rest. So, at some point, long after Gabrielle had kicked over the last vampire, we decided to head back to the motel we had stayed at last night. We still had the rooms, and there was a place to eat by it. A coffee place, too.

The trifecta.

Not all of us headed back, though. Raphael and Belle left us, after Red Rock. Belle in her usual method. Raphael in something much more normal. There were a thousand cars needing new owners in the parking lot to the amphitheater. He walked through until finding one he liked. A Lamborghini Diablo.

That car purred when he pulled up to me and the Camaro.

"You know you're driving a cliché?" I said.

"One thing I've learned, Grimm," Raphael said, "is to be who you are."

I wondered what he thought he had gotten from the few days with me. The whole time Raphael had been with me, he was coming to grips with his new life. His new goals. He had pushed me with questions. He had observed the things I performed, like he was memorizing them to try later. He seemed to take it all in. Learning the ropes. Becoming *more*.

At some point, he and I were going to have to settle things. Once and for all. I was afraid of what I might find when that day came.

If he was the response of evil, to me and my friends, what would he finally become?

"When are you going after Azazel?" Raphael asked.

"I hadn't quite thought that out," I said. "I wasn't sure I'd survive this."

"You got some time," he said. "But it comes up, eventually."

"I know," I said. My voice a little clipped.

Raphael laughed. "Relax, Grimm. There's no rush from me. I got some catching up to do anyway."

He pulled away, the Lamborghini gliding down the lot, the engine going from a low purr to a full-throated roar.

I didn't think I could relax. If there was one thing Belle was right about, it was that Raphael would be something to worry about. The more time I gave him, the stronger he would get.

I might not be able to afford giving him ten years, this time.

Nick found an H2 in the lot with its keys, and fired it up in a chugging rumble. Sarah and Johnny and Gabrielle went with him.

"No offense, Grimm," Sarah said. "But riding in the back of the Camaro is a little … cramped."

So Sarah and Gabrielle got in the H2. Johnny walked over and talked to Gabrielle for a moment, then came back to ride with me.

For a while we just drove. The clouds had left the night sky, and we rolled under the fading light of the moon, the thousands of stars. I followed Nick back. The Camaro was quiet. Steady. Smooth into and out of turns. Flying down the straightaways. The baseball still hanging from the rearview, bobbing on its string.

"Hey, man," Johnny said, "I think I can see ghosts."

"Really?" I said.

"Yeah," he said. "Like little bluish-white things. See-through. I can feel them, too."

"I guess that's … interesting," I said.

"Yeah," he said again. "Sometimes I can hear what they are thinking. At least, I think that's what is happening. I've been seeing them, more and more, lately."

Johnny looked at me. "You know, with the hunger."

"I see," I said. He didn't want to bite people, to drain them of blood, just to live. And the thirst was likely growing in him. From what I had learned about vampires, it would continue to grow, until he gave in.

Johnny had died, back in the parking garage. And I had healed him in a rush. Maybe, like the rest of us, he was becoming different. More.

"I don't know what I can do, man," I said. "But you need something …"

"I know," he said. And that was all we said about it. He knew I would be there, if he needed me. Johnny would figure it out, if he could. If not, his friends were here. We were Wolverines, after all.

The motel was quiet when we pulled in. The lights were out, except for the tall one by the lobby. The streetlights only illuminated part of the lot. We parked, and all of us got out slowly. Like old people do.

The gas station and food place still had their lights on, across the street. A few cars parked outside the restaurant.

"Hungry?" Nick asked, shutting the large Hummer door with a heavy thunk.

I was and I wasn't. There was something I wanted to do, before I did anything else. The bond called to me, and I glanced over at the woods next to the motel. "I'm good."

"You sure?" Nick tilted his head. Knowing what had happened at the amphitheater. Knowing the old me would have blamed myself for not being enough. For not being able to save my parents, for Jen, still trapped in the stone.

I wasn't the easiest person to get to share his feelings with. I was working on that. Nick wasn't a sharer, either. But he had started this journey for me, for all of us, with his idea. That I could bring Jen back to us. To me.

Nick knew how much it hurt now, not to have her. There was an ache inside me that wouldn't let go. Sharp and poignant claws digging into my stomach, a bitter taste in the back of my throat. But maybe some sweetness, a little happiness, as well.

Because I hadn't failed. Jen was still here. With us.

Nick and I both smiled at each other, and each of us clapped the other on the shoulder. Understanding a lot, in that moment. Growing closer.

All of us, all of my friends, were more than when we began this journey.

Maybe my mother had been right. Maybe we were growing, evolving, together. I couldn't imagine what we would be, at the end.

I kept my grin up. "I'm sure, brother. Go get some food."

My friends left. Slowly. Leaning on each other, shoulders hunched. Steps slow, and short. Exhausted.

I wandered over to the woods. I pushed the branches left and right, tiny pricks of needles jabbing my palms, taking deep breaths of the thick pine scent that lay around the spruce trees. I kept working my way in. The branches closed behind me as I passed, and the light of the street faded away in bits and pieces until the darkness of the woods swallowed me whole.

I headed to the spot. The little circle of trees, open to the sky, enough branches overhead to create an isolated world. For a moment it was just me breathing; then a breeze fluttered past, branches rustled in the night air, and some bird warbled in the treetops above. The bird was up long past its bedtime.

Or maybe it was just up before the worm. It was that time of night. Or morning.

I found the grove, the hidden magic circle I had been in the night before with Jen. I leaned back against the same tree, feeling the hard trunk against the middle of my spine, and let out a deep breath.

And waited, holding the Key, the little teardrop shape, in my hand. The small stone vibrated in my palm, and was an odd mix of both cold and warm to the touch. Cool, like the feeling of swallowing peppermint. Warm with passion, like the beating of a heart.

I looked with my ethereal sight.

The stone almost blinded me. It was a bright white, the brightest of whites. Like the sword had been, earlier, high above the earth. And yet lines of blue swirled in the Key, as if a storm of lightning circled inside it, from a place deep inside the stone.

The storm hypnotized me, and I watched it for a long time. Turning it in my hand, looking at it from different angles, wondering what I had created. And how I had done it. Maybe how Jen and I had done it, together.

Curious.

Time passed, with me entranced, studying the Key. The storm inside. The whiteness. An ethereal feeling to the stone, like what I felt when I pulled from a ghost. It felt like the stone held an energy, a mix of ethereal energy and a lightning storm, and maybe the sheer power of everything inside was what had turned the sandstone into quartzite.

A power greater, together. Something different, but also something *more*.

The blue and white of the stone colored the world around me. I blinked away my ethereal sight. The world stayed blue around me, and I realized it wasn't the stone anymore, but Jen.

She was here, kneeling in front of me. Beautifully, ethereally, here. Shimmering with a translucent blue light. With that smile that made me feel like I could do anything.

Goose bumps rippled up and down my arms. The sweet ache inside slipped away, and became a happiness of being with the person you were supposed to always be with. I took a big breath of cool air, the fresh pine. And smiled back.

"Hey," I said.

Hey, she mouthed back. And smiled.

"I'm glad you're here," I said, using the same slow mouthing of the words.

I didn't mean here, as in the grove. I meant here, with me. Still in this world, and not in the next. Whatever that was, whatever I had done after jumping off the water tower and flying into that bright white light, it had kept us together.

Me, too, she said. Her eyes wet, with a shimmering, ethereal moisture.

She slid around to sit next to me, lying down on the earth, pretending to lay her head on my lap. I had no idea how she could do that, but in the same spirit, I laid my arm over her midsection, trying to balance my wrist on my knee, so it looked right. Felt right. Like we were two kids again, on her mom's couch, tucked under a blanket, watching something on television together.

At first the pose felt silly. A little uncomfortable. After a bit, though, it became something we got used to.

The night lay heavy over us. The branches withdrew into dark shadows. The early bird above us warbled on overhead, then grew quiet, leaving just the tiny chirping of crickets, until even that died away into a heavy silence.

Our magical world became just the two of us.

Jen shifted a bit, like she was getting more comfortable. Her blue eyes gazed at me under heavy lids, and the stare took me again back to when we were kids. When our eyes would connect, and it was she and I, and nothing else existed but us.

I started speaking, aloud.

"I think I've figured something out, Jen," I said, wanting to run my hand over her stomach, in small, slow circles, like we had done while watching TV as teenagers. "Something you helped me to learn, actually."

I kept going.

"Maybe you already knew it," I said. "I think you did. I think you tried to tell me, back in Grafton. You wanted me to lean more on you. To count on my friends. To know they would be here for me. Not to fear what might happen, and keep running."

Jen was quiet, though her lips curved a bit. Encouraging me to keep talking. Watching my mouth, to make sure she understood what I was telling her.

"Then we went to New Orleans, and you had me promise to keep going," I said. "To stay around, and protect those I cared about. I think now you were trying to tell me that there was only one way through this, but I had become scared of that weight. After Danny, I had always feared I couldn't protect anyone. That I wasn't *enough*."

"You understood that," I said. "That being enough wasn't a matter of strength. It wasn't a matter of what powers I had, or what I could do. That being enough was simply just *being there*."

I laughed, and the laugh was a little dark. A little bitter. What I was processing, it was hard to face. But it was also important. So I had to get it out, because I knew saying it aloud was important. The *words* were important.

"Funny, isn't it, that I feel like everything that's happened has steered me in this direction?" I said. "To help me become this person that I am right now. I had run, after Danny's death, because I thought I was protecting you all by leaving. But it wasn't me protecting you all. It was because I was scared of never being enough. Of not being worth Danny's sacrifice, not being worth someone else's *life*."

I was nervous, and scared, but that feeling also told me I was onto something. We all fear the hardest truths. "Danny even showed me again, when I came back to Grafton. And I thought I understood then what he was telling me. To become greater, and be someone who was worth that kind of sacrifice."

My heart thudded in my chest. I took a few long breaths to try to settle it down, but it kept racing harder. Like a train heading down a steep slope, rolling along and building up speed, no matter how the engineer tried to slow it.

Jen's head lay in my lap, her face turned up to me, her hair spilling out over my leg, like my thigh was a pillow. Blue light shimmered all around her, and I saw she had a Key, too, shaped like a teardrop, the stone nestled between her breasts. Like it was one of a pair, like we were a pair, like stone versions of a yin and yang.

"So we went to New Orleans," I said. "And you tried to get me to be strong. To always keep swinging. To be there for you, for my friends, no matter what happened. I thought that was the whole point. To make myself so strong that I could protect you all. That I could always keep you safe."

Jen tried to grab for my hand, the one I had been using to rub her stomach. She got frustrated, as both of her hands circled mine, until I picked that hand up. She opened her fingers and waited for me to open mine, and then she worked her fingers through mine. Entwining them, like we used to.

Giving me support, and understanding. Like she always did.

I made a pretext of laying my other hand on her forehead. I moved it slowly, like I was running my hand over her hair. My fingers trailing through the ethereal strands. The moment almost felt real.

My heart still beat hard against my chest. The long inhale and exhale in my lungs felt like it was holding something back. The horrifying fear of what came next.

"I wasn't strong enough," I tried to say, calmly. Feeling all kinds of emotion coming out, in my words. "I understand now I can *never* be strong enough to protect everyone. That there was a different kind of strength, something I lacked. The strength just to *be there*, to stand with your friends, your family, no matter what. No matter the loss, to keep going."

Jen leaned her cheek against my stomach. I kept smoothing her ethereal hair. Somehow our entwined hands stayed connected together. I closed my eyes for a moment, wanting this moment to be real. In the worst possible way.

In the quiet of the grove, in this little secret world, it almost felt real. And I would take what I could get. For however long I could get it.

My cheek felt wet. I hadn't realized when I had started crying. I wiped the tears away, quickly, and took another breath. I was coming to the hardest part of the truth.

Jen's eyes gazed at me, open and guileless. She was simply there, like she always was, accepting me for who I had been. Who I was becoming. Always in my corner. Always seeing the best of me. Even when I couldn't.

That kind of love, that kind of trust, didn't exist just anywhere.

"Then I lost you," I finally said, hoarsely, my voice choking on the words. My hand tightened in hers, and her ghostly fingers wrapped around mine. "And I found out I wasn't strong at all."

That was all I said, for a moment. All I could say. I couldn't breathe. There wasn't enough air in the grove. The pine scent too strong, the branches too close.

I tried again to slow my heart down. I took long breaths, and let them out. Counting them. Once. Twice. Once more. And again. Over and over, until I could talk again.

These words were important.

"So I fled again," I said. "Like with Danny, just this time because of you. And I almost missed it, I almost missed the point, through this whole trip. Even after you had me promise.

"All these people showed me," I said, shaking my head. "Danny. You. My mother and father. You again. Nick and Sarah and Johnny, coming after me. All of you, willing to give up your lives for me. A word kept rolling around this whole time. *Sacrifice.*"

Jen smiled, holding my hand still. Letting me get this out. All the words and the fears. Once I had started, they wouldn't stop. Thoughts of the whole trip flowed through me, of Raphael and Belle, the stupid contract. How words mattered. My promise to Jen. My friends, risking their lives to help me. My parents, giving their lives to save me.

And then Jen, in her dream. Us together, at the end.

"And it clicked, at the end," I said. "With you and me, at the water tower. I understood then what a promise really meant, the kind of strength I would really need. I understood that my words mattered, if I wanted to be the person my friends really needed. But most of all, I understood that words were just sounds if I didn't back them up with action."

I almost felt a squeeze of her hand, Jen's support. Always there.

I had been running a long time. But not because my friends might die if I had stayed. Because I feared I couldn't be strong enough to keep handling the losses.

But there was a cost to living. To this world. That cost was loss. People would die, no matter how much evil I could beat. No matter how much revenge I took. No matter how strong I could become.

"I still almost missed it, *again*," I said. "Except for you, and us, on that water tower. Do you remember what you said?"

Jen arched an eyebrow, and shook her head. I moved a lock of hair off her face, and kept smoothing the strands.

This whole time, I hadn't felt worthy of any of my friends' sacrifices. Not from Danny. Not from Danny's gift, as a ghost. Not from my parents. And definitely not from Jen, at the end. When it had been she and I, in her dream, up on top of the water tower.

I *was* hardheaded. It might be my most defining characteristic. Still, Jen had said something, up on the tower, that had made it all *click*.

"I think I understand now…. If we love each other, we should be willing, right? To give our lives for those we love. When they need it most?"

There was the answer.

There was the strength I had been looking for.

Honeysuckle drifted up to me then. A cool rain. And I said the words I knew to be true, because the lesson had been the hardest to learn. My voice clear and firm.

"The words are the deed."

I took a deep breath of her hair. The honeysuckle scent always lured me to another world, like it was just she and I, in a special place outside time.

It was a different kind of strength. I didn't know if others just had it in them, or they had to learn it, too. I think Danny had been born with it. Maybe Jen, too.

The only way to be strong enough, to be able to lose those you love, is to be strong enough to give your life for them. Only then, only by unreservedly sacrificing your life for theirs, would you really know, really *know*, you had that kind of strength.

Our eyes caught, her blue eyes misty and ethereal, locking with mine. Jen's hair spread out behind her, my hand smoothing the silky strands, over and over. The two of us, together. Her, the pillar that kept me standing. Even now. Her gaze so intense, I looked away.

"I had never felt I was worthy, not of any of you," I said, staring anywhere but at Jen. "I thought my value to the group was that I could fight. That I could protect you all by being the biggest badass around."

I had thought that was how I could be worthy of my friends. That by fighting, and protecting them, I could deserve their friendship. Their sacrifices.

But anyone can fight, for anyone, or anything.

Not everyone can give their lives for another.

It was something no one knew about themselves, no matter what they said. Until the moment came. I hadn't known, with all my talk, until I was there on the water tower, with Jen, staring out into all the whiteness, and believing she deserved more.

"The word is the deed," I said, softly. And again, my voice trailing off: "The word is the deed."

Those words echoed in my head, connected to something inside me, resonated in my bones. A promise wasn't a promise unless an action backed it up. It was easy to talk the talk. Much harder to walk the walk.

And the walking was what mattered. It was part of the contract, when a person said something they meant. What a person said, they had to then go *do it*, for their words to mean anything.

The word was the deed.

It was funny to me. If I hadn't met Belle, if she hadn't given me the talks about how words mattered, I might never be here now. Jen might never be here, or my friends. We would have been overrun by Dominic and Victor, killed. Maybe enslaved.

I had done the things I had said I was going to do. I was stronger for it. A certain confidence radiated in me, because I had committed myself to a course of action, and followed through. I believed now I could be capable of more.

That realization had come not from my ability to fight. But by giving. *Sacrifice.* There was a bond now, forged between me and my friends. From them to me. Something that made me greater. Made us greater.

More.

Jen lay underneath me. Smiling. Her hand gripping mine. I felt her grip and her strength and wondered how I could have done any of this without her. I wondered what more I could be capable of with her.

I closed my eyes. My voice came out in a whisper. I thought I'd have trouble with the words, but they were easy to say. "I wouldn't be this me without you, Jen."

Her fingers tightened around mine. She was a pillar for me, the strongest pillar, the person who kept me standing.

Actions mattered, but those actions started with words. The contract. The deed. A promise, between me and my friends, me and the world, or, like now, just me and Jen.

"I love you, Jen," I said.

I didn't know if I had ever told her that. Or if she had said those same words to me. What we felt, it was always something we each understood about the other. We didn't have to express it to *know* it. But in a time when words mattered, I wanted her to hear those. To hear everything.

"You'll always make me greater than I could ever be on my own," I continued. "I want you to know, I understand it all now. What you were trying to tell me. What you and Danny and our friends were trying to show me."

What even my parents had shown. I think I even finally got what my mother was telling me. That I could be more. That my friends and I, we could be more together. And handle whatever it was that came next.

"I will always be there," I said. "For you. For Nick and Sarah and Johnny. For whatever I can do for this world. Whatever it takes."

I knew now that I could trust myself. That I could hang in and stay. That some people were worth everything to me.

Only that one act can really show you that about yourself. Can show others what they mean to you. Until then, whatever you believed about yourself was just words.

Words mattered. All of them, big and small. Those words became greater when we acted in accordance with the words.

The deed was the thing. And one deed reveals who you are, what others mean to you, more than any other. A deed that holds a certain power unto itself.

Sacrifice.

I opened my eyes. Jen was smiling up at me. It was the smile I would run through walls for. Her eyes shimmered, too. A tear rolled down her cheek and then slipped down the side of her neck. I let go of her hand, cradled the side of her head, and went to wipe the next tear away with my thumb, her skin warm under my palm. The tears wet against my skin.

Her skin warm under my palm.

The tears wet.

I froze. My heart thundered inside my chest. I didn't take a breath, *couldn't* take a breath.

A weight rested on my lap. The comforting weight of someone lying against you. A person nestled against you, each of your bodies warming the other. As if both of us lay under a blanket, together against whatever lay outside, in the cold, dark night.

No ethereal glow illuminated the grove. Jen was lit with small slivers of moonlight, tiny beams that broke through the branches of the trees. The tiny pendent still on her chest, which matched mine. A little teardrop of a stone, lit by the moon, maybe just radiating a touch of ethereal blue.

I stroked her hair, one more time. The strands real between my fingers. Thick, but light, like silk. I watched each strand fall from my hand. The air flowed with honeysuckle. A hint of rain, cool on a hot summer day.

The scents surrounded me, and I took a long, shuddering breath. Tears rolled freely down my cheeks now. I couldn't stop them. I didn't want this moment to end. But still, I had to know for sure.

"Hey." I tried the word out, aloud. It came out rough.

Jen's arm slipped around me in a tight hug. Her face leaned hard against my chest. Against my heart, thudding loudly in my chest. Then she glanced up, at me. Our eyes locking.

"Hey," she said back, her voice a little hoarse as well.

With us, that had always been enough.

EPILOGUE

It was a week later, and early in the morning. Hints of the sun rose in the east. The sky itself was a dark bluish gray that always led to a deep winter afternoon blue.

Wisps of clouds streamed above us, flying in from the Atlantic, from a stiff breeze that came from the ocean outside Charleston and blew inward, scrubbing away the night smells and leaving a thick, salty scent in the air.

It was the time in the morning that newspapers were being placed in bins. That baristas were opening stores, making their first cups of coffee. The time that alarms were being snoozed, all across town. The time, I used to think, that the best donuts were made. The first batch of the day. The donuts soft and warm and fresh, with sticky icing and sweet strawberry fillings.

When I used to struggle out of a hotel bed and find a sugar fix.

Charleston was an interesting town. Full of old and new. Historical streets hundreds of years old mixed with high-rises being built along the water. Tech industries kept coming in, and with them jobs. Even if people slept in now, the town would be bustling later.

Another burst of the breeze, another whiff of salt from the ocean. The wind whipped past us and stirred the edges of my coat, a dark gray peacoat Jen had found for me. She liked how it cut across my shoulders. I seemed to be more fashionable, this past week.

I lifted the Keydrop from its chain on my chest. It's what I was calling it now. *Testing, testing, one … two … three.*

"You know I'm right here," Jen said, next to me. Her peacoat was more of a blue, with a darker belt wrapped around her midsection. The coat was trimmed to her figure, revealing just the right amount of curves, and she walked with an athletic grace.

I rolled my eyes. "I know," I said. "Just checking."

Good enough? Jen's voice, in my head.

Our bond still existed between us. I wasn't sure how, or why. Maybe we had changed the Key, maybe the Key had changed us. Or maybe the two of us had become greater, together.

More.

"So you call all this the trifecta?" Jen asked.

We walked away from the place we had stayed in. Not a hotel, but a nice bed-and-breakfast, close to the water. Something Jen reserved online, through an app.

A coffee place was in the parking lot next door. Cars had already filled the lot, and a line of them circled around the building. People who hadn't hit snooze, and who needed that jolt of energy to get going on their morning, to whatever job waited for them.

A bed-and-breakfast wasn't a hotel and a diner. It was nicer. Warm. Inviting. And the coffee place next door was a fancy one.

Sleep. Food. Caffeine.

"Not the typical one," I said, "but yeah."

The three things I had needed, on the run. The bare necessities, places I had stumbled in, exhausted. Trying to get through one more day.

All that was just a few weeks ago, for me. And a lifetime ago as well. Six long years, after finding the Key, finally coming to an end.

Jen smiled. "It explains a lot."

"What?"

"Oh, I don't know," she said. "Probably your twitchiness, while you sleep, for starters."

I frowned. "I am not twitchy."

"Running away, fighting, then running away again," Jen continued, as if I hadn't spoken. "All that flip-flopping."

"Hey," I said. "I worked all that out."

"And the grouchiness," she added. Making a stern face. "Definitely the grouchiness."

I was quiet for a minute, before grinning. "That one's probably fair."

After all, my name was Grimm. It wasn't like I was born to be a comedian. There were other things I was slated for.

Jen kissed me, lightly on the lips. The kiss was soft and warm and all kinds of electric. "You want your usual?" she asked.

"Definitely not," I said. I had moved on from black coffee, with its bitterness. I was for treating myself now, when I could. "We're celebrating."

"I'll surprise you then," she said.

The two of us got to the door of the coffee place. There we paused for a moment. Knowing that all kinds of things were about to matter.

You ready? Jen asked, through the Key.

I nodded. "I haven't been more ready about something in a long, long time."

We walked in. A bell jangled on the door. The thick smell of espresso flooded our senses at the same time as the sound of a murmuring crowd. Even this early in the morning there were a number of people sitting at tables, standing in line, waiting for their five-dollar coffee before running off to work.

Find us the table? Jen asked.

Sure, I answered. *It feels weird for you to be getting me coffee, though.*

Men, Jen said.

I worked my way through the crowd. The tables were mostly full, some people sitting at a table for four, holding the chairs. It made it hard to find our table, even in the small coffee shop. People sat everywhere. I navigated through the maze of the crowd, seeing most of them were on their phones, but a few had laptops out and were typing away.

I finally found what I was looking for. A table with a pair of empty chairs. One person sat there, a large newspaper held open in front of him. His face tucked behind the paper flaps. A large latte cup to the side, perfectly square to the edge of the table.

I waited a moment before making a coughing sound. The paper stayed up. The front page, as always now, held a lot of headlines.

Dragon Undefeated Verses French Air Force …

Templar Army Lost Inside Italy's Dead Zone …

President Meeting with Presumed Person in Charge of New Orleans …

It was an interesting world now.

Armies of people had gathered, both in and out of the Dead Zones. Not armies like the one I had joined, but more like militias. People who weren't there to fight the demons and the other creatures from hell, but instead wanted to join them. People who wanted to make the Dead Zones real countries, add them to the Geneva Convention, include them in trade agreements.

I had a feeling I'd be seeing a lot of those people as ghosts.

Evil was like that, though. Instead of fighting it, people embraced it. It was always easier to take than provide. Easier to tear down than build. Easier to accommodate it than make a stand.

They never understood. Evil was something that just *got along*. It swallowed everything before it. There could be no compromise there.

The edge of the paper flicked down, as if the person there finally realized he had company. Then the paper moved down a bit farther. The man sitting there, in a nice pin-striped white suit, checked his watch. He looked at me, then the door, then me again. Maybe confused.

"Grimm," Azazel said. "I wasn't expecting you."

"I know," I said. "This meeting was kind of arranged on the sly, as the kids say."

His mouth pressed tightly together. "Belial."

I nodded. "Just so."

Azazel shook his head. He went through his pretending-to-be-human motions, folding the paper up, resting it on the table. Just so.

The demon drank out of his coffee, grimacing at the taste. "Think they put the fake sweetener in this," he said, complaining. "A guy asks for skim milk in his latte, and they take that to mean I don't want the real sugar, too."

"I'm sure that's put a wrench in your day," I said.

"Why can't they just take the order?" he said. "Whatever the order is, it is, right?"

"What you say matters," I said.

"Exactly," Azazel said. "You get it."

"Maybe I didn't before," I said. "But I do now."

His fingers went out and touched the newspaper. Adjusted it a micro-centimeter to the left. Though it looked square to the edge of the table to me.

There was a moment of silence between us. Where Azazel watched me, maybe wondering what I was doing here. For a man who had planned out the past couple thousands of years, who had plans for his plans, and backup plans to those, I was definitely a wrench in his day.

I planned on being more.

"See you're meeting the president soon," I said, commenting on the article.

"You read that?" Azazel smiled. "It's a new world, Grimm. A man should celebrate."

"My thoughts exactly." I motioned to one of the empty chairs. "Mind if I sit?"

The demon kept his smile on, but it never made it to his eyes. Instead, activity circled there, as his mind raced to figure out my game. His hand touched the paper again, and he looked at the newspaper with a frown.

"By all means," he finally said.

I took the chair, leaning a little toward the demon, holding both hands clasped on the table in front of me. Just two friends, meeting for coffee, to all appearances.

The two of us were much more, though.

"You remember asking me once, if I ever lay awake and wondered who I really was?" I asked Azazel. "If I ever wondered why I can do what I can do?"

Azazel's lips straightened a bit. His brow lowered as he searched for the memory. The demon grunted, and rocked back a little, when he found it.

"The motel," he said. "The hamburger."

Then, "What of it?"

I smiled. It was a smile full of fury and anger. Of six years of running from Azazel. Of all the people he had hurt. Of *Jen*.

"Just wanted to let you know, I figured it out," I said, staring right at the demon.

And flexed.

It was early morning. The sun was not quite yet out. And there were enough ghosts around for my purpose.

Wings, ethereally, translucently white, spread out from behind me. The sword appeared, point down, in my clasped hands. A crackling sound of lightning accompanied it, forks of electricity played over the blade, and, like always with Jen, a slow rumble of thunder came from far away, in the distance.

Show-off, Jen said through the Key. Though her voice carried a smile.

I like new toys, I answered back along our bond.

I smiled. This smile was more one of power. Of a righteous anger, and a promised vengeance. The smile of a hunter, after he had found his prey, hunted him down, and had him dead to rights.

The whole scene had come and gone in a blink. Fast enough most people in the store hadn't seen any of it, or if they did, it had been a flicker in the corner of their eyes. Some of those people looked at our table curiously, or glanced outside to the clouds, checking the weather from their phones.

One of the laptop people swore, folded his laptop up with a snapping sound, and ran out to his car.

For the demon's part, Azazel remained sitting. Though both of us knew I could kill him. He had a chance, he could always disappear, he had that gift.

But he stayed. Maybe to find out where this all was going.

"Well, let me find my gold star," the demon said. "For the prize pupil."

Got the order, Jen said. *Paying now.*

"I'm sure you're wondering why you're still alive," I said.

The side of Azazel's mouth curved, slightly. He made a *go on* motion.

"If it was up to me, you'd be dead already," I said. "I've given my word on that. But apparently, I've got some time. And someone suggested something I could do with it.

"You'd appreciate the plan." I smiled.

"Who is this person?" Azazel said. "I need to thank them for the warning. For giving me a little time, to plan something in return."

"That person is me," Jen said, her voice cutting through our conversation. She stared at the demon a long second before placing a tall coffee cup in front of me. A to-go cup, because we weren't staying long.

I sipped the coffee, the paper warm in my hand. It was heavy on the cream and caramel. And I thought something smoky, maybe a little spicy, maybe … "Is that cardamom?"

Jen smiled at me, a little in surprise. "It is."

A week or two ago, I hadn't even known what cardamom was. Now I was getting it in my coffee. It was a brave new world.

"I like it," I pronounced.

"I thought you might," she said, taking the chair next to me. "Have you gotten to the appreciate part yet?"

"I just said it," I said. Though she knew I had; she had been listening in, I was sure.

"I know you said he likes that word," Jen said. Her eyes were so blue they felt like they glowed. "The appreciation of the scope of a thing."

"He does," I said. "He's funny that way." Thinking back to the motel room, to the jail cell. The coffee shops. Including me when he was planning something, or when a plan had worked, because Azazel had told me no one else could really admire them.

I thought it was more because the demon had alienated everyone who could have, but that was just my guess.

"Hey," Azazel said, waving his hand nonchalantly. "I'm right over here."

He stopped waving when Jen turned back to look at him. I had no idea what he saw in her face, but Azazel paled under his white pin-striped jacket. He knew he had killed Jen. He thought he had finished me.

But now he knew he hadn't. That I was here. And Jen was here. And that Jen was pissed.

Azazel looked away. Drank his coffee for a few long moments. No grimace this time, just his throat bobbing with each hard gulp. Then he set the coffee back down, a little *tink* sound ringing from when the demon settled the cup on the platter.

"So," Azazel said. His face a little more composed. "What's this about, then?"

"Well, like I said," I said, "I could have already killed you."

"But we know how much you like your plans." Jen took over for me, the two of us knowing what we had come here to say. "We thought you might get a kick out of ours."

"We're going to go around and tear all your houses down," I said. "All your pretty little homes, here on earth."

Azazel's head rocked, just a little. The demon tried to covered the motion up with a snort, and when he spoke, his voice carried a depth and a weight to it. A gravity, as if he was working through everything we told him, and found all of it indignant. Insufferable. "Who do you think you are, Grimm?"

You were right, Jen said along our bond. *This appreciation of a thing is fun.*

All this was your idea, I thought back. *I just added the part where we told him first.*

Yeah, well, she said, *killing him wasn't ever going to be enough.*

Jen patted my hand, on the table. I flipped that hand over, and our hands clasped. Both of our grips tight. Then I turned back to the demon, leaning forward. I noted that Azazel moved back a little when I did, and I enjoyed it. My voice, when I spoke, was low. "I'm where things end, Az," I told him.

For once, Azazel was speechless. His jaw worked up and down, as if he had something ready to say, and now couldn't remember what those words were going to be.

"You've spent thousands of years building all this," Jen said. "So we're going to take a year or two and tear it all back down. Whatever friends you have left, we're going to kill them. Whatever world you thought you were building here, we're going to take it away."

"And then the part I like," I said. "Coming back to kill you."

The demon's eyes narrowed. Azazel was angry, but there was a fear there, too. A fear of something he had spent forever building, something all his, being taken away. Right when he had achieved his dream.

"You do this," he said, "and I'll take it out on the people of your world. I'll start a war like you've never seen."

"Let's be honest," I said, adding a shrug. "You were going to do that anyway. It's not in you to share."

He tried the next obvious thing. "I'll kill your friends," the demon said.

"You've tried that," I said. "It doesn't take like you think it would."

"Hell, Grimm," Azazel said, staring directly at me. Pretending a nonchalant smile. The thumb of one hand rubbing his forefinger. His voice picking up in its intensity. "I've killed angels before. I was a part of the fall. I *was* the fall."

"Sure," I said. "That was what, thousands of years ago? Since then, all I've seen you do is pick on people who can't fight back."

Until you, Jen said.

Until us, I said back.

I grinned at Azazel. "Me, I've killed two heavyweight demons and a couple thousand vampires, just in the past week or so."

A slow rumble again rolled out from the clouds, and over the shop. I hadn't noticed, but enough people had left the shop now that there was an empty circle around our table. People trying to beat the sudden storm.

I took another sip of the cardamom-cream-caramel coffee. And wondered if I could say that three times really fast. And smiled at the thought.

"This is really good," I said, smiling at Jen. "A little smoky, maybe a little spicy, but still sweet."

"It is," she said, and did a Johnny waggle of her eyebrows, which had me laugh.

I set my coffee down. The two of us got serious, turning back to Azazel. The demon's expression had gone blank. His thumb had stopped its rubbing motion. His head rocked a little. As if a thought kept going back and forth in his mind, over and over, pounding one way, then the other.

"You once gave me a choice, Az," I said. "So here's yours. You got something to protect now. You can try to protect it, or you can watch it crumble as we tear it all down around you. You can try to go back to hell, see if Lucifer will unbar that gate to you, and hide from me."

When he spoke, his voice was low, and a little guttural. And, if I had to put a feeling to it, pleased. "A new game, then."

"Sure," I said.

Azazel loved his games. He couldn't help himself. I thought maybe he liked to break things, just because it meant there were more pieces on the board to play with.

Grafton had been a long time ago. The thing with Danny, Jen, my friends, that was all before. Azazel had happened after. What the demon had started between him and me, it had happened overseas. With a different group of friends, and the Key.

Raphael was the real beginning for me. So it felt fitting that he should be my ultimate ending. That I should close these chapters with Azazel first, before I turned the page to whatever Raphael was.

Azazel had found me a long time ago. He had murdered my team, people I had cared about, just so I could pick up the Key. Our first fight had been an awakening for me, the very beginning of the person I now had become.

I still remember the birds chirping in the Hindu Kush. The sun, cresting the hills. The promise of a new day, as the rays bathed the broken rubble and scattered bones of the people I used to call friends.

It had taken me some time to get up. To get moving. Even to get to where I was today. Some great truths. Some hard conversations. A lot of focused steps, placing one foot after the next, a long journey from then until now.

I got up, flashed a grin at Azazel. It was a smile that did not reach my eyes. It was also a promise I meant to fulfill.

"Or the beginning of the end," I said. "Call it what you will."

Enjoy *An Ethereal End* and looking for more of the Grimm Saga?

Then today is your lucky day, because *Crown of Bones* is ready for you now at your favorite book seller.

I love these stories, *Crown of Bones* is a part of the Grimm series that I'm calling (in the back of my mind) The Demon Wars, as Grimm and his friends take on Azazel and his demons.

Also - take a moment and visit chrisjcranford.com, be a part of the Grimm Universe. Discover all the other worlds I'm building. Or just reach out and say hello.

ABOUT THE AUTHOR

When Chris isn't trying to figure out how to write a bio, he spends time contemplating the fate of the universe. Probably while walking into a door jamb. He's accepted that the two go hand-in-hand.

He currently resides in Florida, though he has some Magellan in him, and loves to wander.

It is his dream to write stories that – through their telling – influence others to live a little better. Stand a little taller. Smile a little wider. Hold someone a little longer. Fiction should be the dream real life aspires to be.

Dogs are his buddies. Football is his hobby. Books are his passion.

Find out more about Chris here:

www.chrisjcranford.com

 facebook.com/chrisjcranford

 x.com/chrisjcranford

 instagram.com/chrisjcranford